Naked G

Richard Glyn Jones trained and worked as an experimental psychologist before embarking on a career in publishing. In the late 1960s he was an editor of the innovative sf magazine *New Worlds*. He also worked as an illustrator, and drew a comic strip for the underground newspaper *IT*. He went on to found his own small press, *Xanadu*, where for ten years he published an eclectic range of books. He currently works as a writer, editor and critic, and has compiled some thirty anthologies to date. He lives in London.

NAKED GRAFFITI

Edited by

Richard Glyn Jones

INDIGO

First published in Great Britain 1996
as an Indigo paperback original

Indigo is an imprint of the Cassell Group
Wellington House, 125 Strand, London WC2R 0BB

This collection and introduction © Richard Glyn Jones 1996

The right of Richard Glyn Jones and the contributors to be identified as authors of
this work has been asserted by them in accordance with the Copyright, Designs and
Patents Act, 1988.

A catalogue record for this book is available from the British Library.

ISBN 0 575 40005 6

Typeset by Textype Typesetters, Cambridge
Printed and bound in Great Britain by Guernsey Press Co. Ltd,
Guernsey, Channel Isles

96 97 98 99   10 9 8 7 6 5 4 3 2 1

Contents

Introduction

'Erotica is all the rage in publishing at the moment,' remarks one of Linda Jaivin's heroines in 'Fireworks', and she's right: the bookshops are full of the stuff.

This vogue for erotica is both welcome and worrying. Welcome because for most of the past two hundred years it has been impossible to write freely and openly about sex – an area of human experience of keen interest to most of us; and worrying because given this sudden and fabulous freedom to write about things as they really are, much of what is actually being written and published as erotica is sheer fantasy, and badly written fantasy at that.

Dip into almost any novel published under the 'erotica' banner and you are liable to find yourself plunged into a strange world where every cock is enormous, every erection instantly rock-hard and infinitely sustainable, where every woman is nubile, moist and endlessly willing, and where every desire is something to be instantly gratified – and usually is. Little or no mention is ever made of such matters as impotence, menstruation, wet patches, venereal disease, pregnancy, babies, the family or any of the other things that make real life so, er, interesting. In this fantasy world AIDS doesn't exist at all. Its inhabitants do not even use condoms since pausing to fit one would interrupt the (literary) flow, though I notice that some publishers have started putting notices at the front of such books saying that of course the characters do use condoms *really*, and so should we. Which is like saying that the murderer really used a cardboard knife.

Not that there is anything wrong with fantasy *per se*, provided we understand that it *is* fantasy, but it is troubling when most of the fiction that concerns itself with sex is written in this highly unrealistic manner; at best it's misleading and at worst it's downright dishonest, and it is to try to redress this balance that the stories in this book have been collected. Martin Amis's hero, for instance, is deeply worried about his level of sexual performance, whilst AIDS is very much a part of the lives described by John McVicar and Adam Mars-Jones. Fay Weldon's heroine has a gynaecological history which we learn in some detail, prostitution is realistically depicted by Althea Prince and by Evelyn Lau, who writes from personal experience, whilst child abuse figures in Pete Townshend's fascinating glimpse into the life of a rock star (called Pete).

If this begins to sound grim, I should quickly add that other stories are wildly funny, as real-life sex often is. At Emily Prager's college reunion the women get stoned and wear carved wooden phalluses while they compare notes, and on the other side of the world Linda Jaivin depicts three more young women relating some very different escapades. Tama Janowitz's fairy tale of New York high society gives a drastically different view of modern life from that in Kathy Acker's gritty story of street level existence, or from James Kelman's . . .

No one book can encompass everything, of course, but in *Naked Graffiti* I have tried to offer a composite and fairly representative picture of love and sex as they actually are in the run-up to the end of the twentieth century, and I believe that the picture is a pretty truthful one. I hope the quality of the writing, by some of the best authors around, will speak for itself; the writing on this wall is by some distinguished hands, and I'm grateful to all those who have allowed me to include their work.

Oh, and do use a condom.

Richard Glyn Jones

SUSAN MINOT

Lust

Leo was from a long time ago, the first one I ever saw nude. In the spring before the Hellmans filled their pool, we'd go down there in the deep end, with baby oil, and like that. I met him the first month away at boarding school. He had a halo from the campus light behind him. I flipped.

Roger was fast. In his illegal car, we drove to the reservoir, the radio blaring, talking fast, fast, fast. He was always going for my zipper. He got kicked out sophomore year.

By the time the band got around to playing 'Wild Horses', I had tasted Bruce's tongue. We were clicking in the shadows on the other side of the amplifier, out of Mrs Donovan's line of vision. It tasted like salt, with my neck bent back, because we had been dancing so hard before.

Tim's line: 'I'd like to see you in a bathing suit.' I knew it was his line when he said the exact same thing to Annie Hines.

You'd go on walks to get off campus. It was raining like hell, my sweater as sopped as a wet sheep. Tim pinned me to a tree, the woods light brown and dark brown, a white house half hidden with the lights already on. The water was as loud as a crowd hissing. He made certain comments about my forehead, about my cheeks.

We started off sitting at one end of the couch and then our feet were squished against the armrest and then he went over to turn off the TV and came back after he had taken off his shirt and then we slid onto the floor and he got up again to close the door, then came back to me, a body waiting on the rug.

You'd try to wipe off the table or to do the dishes and Willie would untuck your shirt and get his hands up under in front, standing behind you, making puffy noises in your ear.

He likes it when I wash my hair. He covers his face with it and if I start to say something, he goes, 'Shush.'

For a long time, I had Philip on the brain. The less they noticed you, the more you got them on the brain.

My parents had no idea. Parents never really know what's going on, especially when you're away at school most of the time. If she met them, my mother might say, 'Oliver seems nice' or 'I like that one' without much of an opinion. If she didn't like them, 'He's a funny fellow, isn't he?' or 'Johnny's perfectly nice but a drink of water.' My father was too shy to talk to them at all unless they played sports and he'd ask them about that.

The sand was almost cold underneath because the sun was long gone. Eben piled a mound over my feet, patting around my ankles, the ghostly surf rumbling behind him in the dark. He was the first person I ever knew who died, later that summer, in a car crash. I thought about it for a long time.

'Come here,' he says on the porch.

I go over to the hammock and he takes my wrist with two fingers.

'What?'

He kisses my palm then directs my hand to his fly.

Songs went with whichever boy it was. 'Sugar Magnolia' was Tim, with the line 'Rolling in the rushes/down by the riverside.' With 'Darkness Darkness', I'd picture Philip with his long hair. Hearing 'Under My Thumb' there'd be the smell of Jamie's suede jacket.

We hid in the listening rooms during study hall. With a record cover over the door's window, the teacher on duty couldn't look in. I came out flushed and heady and back at the dorm was surprised how red my lips were in the mirror.

One weekend at Simon's brother's, we stayed inside all day with the shades down, in bed, then went out to Store 24 to get some ice cream. He stood at the magazine rack and read through *MAD* while I got butterscotch sauce, craving something sweet.

I could do some things well. Some things I was good at, like math or painting or even sports, but the second a boy put his arm around me, I forgot about wanting to do anything else, which felt like a relief at first until it became like sinking into a muck.

It was different for a girl.

When we were little, the brothers next door tied up our ankles. They held the door of the goat house and wouldn't let us out till we showed them our underpants. Then they'd forget about being after us and when we played whiffle ball, I'd be just as good as they were.

Then it got to be different. Just because you have on a short skirt, they yell from the cars, slowing down for a while, and if you don't look, they screech off and call you a bitch.

'What's the matter with me?' they say, point-blank.

Or else, 'Why won't you go out with me? I'm not asking you to get married,' about to get mad.

Or it'd be, trying to be reasonable, in a regular voice, 'Listen, I just want to have a good time.'

So I'd go because I couldn't think of something to say back that wouldn't be obvious, and if you go out with them, you sort of have to do something.

I sat between Mack and Eddie in the front seat of the pickup. They were having a fight about something. I've a feeling about me.

Certain nights you'd feel a certain surrender, maybe if you'd had wine. The surrender would be forgetting yourself and you'd put your nose to his neck and feel like a squirrel, safe, at rest, in a restful dream. But then you'd start to slip from that and the dark would come in and there'd be a cave. You make out the dim shape of the windows and feel yourself become a cave, filled absolutely with air, or with a sadness that wouldn't stop.

Teenage years. You know just what you're doing and don't see the things that start to get in the way.

Lots of boys, but never two at the same time. One was plenty to keep you in a state. You'd start to see a boy and something would rush over you like a fast storm cloud and you couldn't possibly think of anyone else. Boys took it differently. Their eyes perked up at any little number that walked by. You'd act like you weren't noticing.

The joke was that the school doctor gave out the pill like aspirin. He didn't ask you anything. I was fifteen. We had a picture of him in assembly, holding up an IUD shaped like a T. Most girls were on the pill, if anything, because they couldn't handle a diaphragm. I kept the dial in my top drawer like my mother and thought of her each time I tipped out the yellow tablets in the morning before chapel.

If they were too shy, I'd be more so. Andrew was nervous. We stayed up with his family album, sharing a pack of Old Golds. Before it got light, we turned on the TV. A man was explaining how to plant seedlings. His mouth jerked to the side in a tic. Andrew thought it was a riot and kept imitating him. I laughed to be polite. When we finally dozed off, he dared to put his arm around me, but that was it.

You wait till they come to you. With half fright, half swagger, they stand one step down. They dare to touch the button on your coat then lose their nerve and quickly drop their hand so you – you'd do anything for them. You touch their cheek.

The girls sit around in the common room and talk about boys, smoking their heads off.

'What are you complaining about?' says Jill to me when we talk about problems.

'Yeah,' says Giddy. 'You always have a boyfriend.'

I look at them and think, As if.

I thought the worst thing anyone could call you was a cock-teaser. So, if you flirted, you had to be prepared to go through with it. Sleeping with someone was perfectly normal once you had done it. You didn't really worry about it. But there were other problems. The problems had to do with something else entirely.

Mack was during the hottest summer ever recorded. We were renting a house on an island with all sorts of other people. No one slept during the heat wave, walking around the house with nothing on which we were used to because of the nude beach. In the living room, Eddie lay on top of a coffee table to cool off. Mack and I, with the bedroom door open for air, sweated and sweated all night.

'I can't take this,' he said at three a.m. 'I'm going for a swim.' He and some guys down the hall went to the beach. The heat put me on edge. I sat on a cracked chest by the open window and smoked and smoked till I felt even worse, waiting for something – I guess for him to get back.

One was on a camping trip in Colorado. We zipped our sleeping bags together, the coyotes' hysterical chatter far away. Other couples murmured in other tents. Paul was up before sunrise, starting a fire for breakfast. He wasn't much of a talker in the daytime. At night, his hand leafed about in the hair at my neck.

There'd be times when you overdid it. You'd get carried away. All the next day, you'd be in a total fog, delirious, absent-minded, crossing the street and nearly getting run over.

The more girls a boy has, the better. He has a bright look, having reaped fruits, blooming. He stalks around, sure-shouldered, and you have the feeling he's got more in him, a fatter heart, more stories to tell. For a girl, with each boy it's as though a petal gets plucked each time.

Then you start to get tired. You begin to feel diluted, like watered-down stew.

Oliver came skiing with us. We lolled by the fire after everyone had gone to bed. Each creak you'd think was someone coming downstairs. The silver loop bracelet he gave me had been a present from his girlfriend before.

On vacations, we went skiing, or you'd go south if someone invited you. Some people had apartments in New York that their families hardly ever used. Or summer houses, or older sisters. We always managed to find someplace to go.

We made the plan at coffee hour. Simon snuck out and met me at Main Gate after lights-out. We crept to the chapel and spent the night in the balcony. He tasted like onions from a submarine sandwich.

The boys are one of two ways: either they can't sit still or they don't move. In front of the TV, they won't budge. On weekends they play touch football while we sit on the sidelines, picking blades of grass to chew on, and watch. We're always watching them run around. We shiver in the stands, knocking our boots together to keep our toes warm, and they whizz across the ice, chopping their sticks around the puck. When they're in the rink, they refuse to look at you, only eyeing each other beneath low helmets. You cheer for them but they don't look up, even if it's a face-off when nothing's happening, even if they're doing drills before any game has started at all.

Dancing under the pink tent, he bent down and whispered in my ear. We slipped away to the lawn on the other side of the hedge. Much later, as he was leaving the buffet with two plates of eggs and sausage, I saw the grass stains on the knees of his white pants.

Tim's was shaped like a banana, with a graceful curve to it. They're all different. Willie's like a bunch of walnuts when nothing was happening, another's as thin as a thin hot dog. But it's like faces; you're never really surprised.

Still, you're not sure what to expect.

I look into his face and he looks back. I look into his eyes and they look back at mine. Then they look down at my mouth so I look at his mouth, then back to his eyes then, backing up, at his whole face. I think, Who? Who are you? His head tilts to one side.

I say, 'Who are you?'

'What do you mean?'

'Nothing.'

I look at his eyes again, deeper. Can't tell who he is, what he thinks.

'What?' he says. I look at his mouth.

'I'm just wondering,' I say and go wandering across his face. Study the chin line. It's shaped like a persimmon.

'Who are you? What are you thinking?'

He says, 'What the hell are you talking about?'

Then they get mad after, when you say enough is enough. After, when it's easier to explain that you don't want to. You wouldn't dream of saying that maybe you weren't really ready to in the first place.

Gentle Eddie. We waded into the sea, the waves round and plowing in, buffalo-headed, slapping our thighs. I put my arms around his freckled shoulders and he held me up, buoyed by the water, and rocked me like a sea shell.

I had no idea whose party it was, the apartment jam-packed, stepping over people in the hallway. The room with the music was practically empty, the bare floor, me in red shoes. This fellow slides onto one knee and takes me around the waist and we rock to jazzy tunes, with my toes pointing heavenward, and waltz and spin and dip to 'Smoke Gets in Your Eyes' or 'I'll Love You Just for Now'. He puts his head to my chest, runs a sweeping hand down my inside thigh and we go loose-limbed and sultry and as smooth as silk and I stamp my red heels and he takes me into a swoon. I never saw him again after that but I thought, I could have loved that one.

You wonder how long you can keep it up. You begin to feel as if you're showing through, like a bathroom window that only lets in grey light, the kind you can't see out of.

They keep coming round. Johnny drives up at Easter vacation from Baltimore and I let him in the kitchen with everyone sound asleep. He has friends waiting in the car.

'What are you, crazy? It's pouring out there,' I say.

'It's okay,' he says. 'They understand.'

So he gets some long kisses from me, against the refrigerator, before he goes because I hate those girls who push away a boy's face as if she were made out of Ivory soap, as if she's that much greater than he is.

The note on my cubby told me to see the headmaster. I had no idea for what. He had received complaints about my amorous displays on the town green. It was Willie that spring. The headmaster told me he didn't care what I did but that Casey Academy had a reputation to uphold in the town. He lowered his glasses on his nose. 'We've got twenty acres of woods on this campus,' he said. 'If you want to smooch with your boyfriend, there are twenty acres for you to do it out of the public eye. You read me?'

Everybody'd get weekend permissions for different places, then we'd all go to someone's house whose parents were away. Usually there'd be more boys than girls. We raided the liquor closet and smoked pot at the kitchen table and you'd never know who would end up where, or with whom. There were always disasters. Ceci got bombed and cracked her head open on the banister and needed stitches. Then there was the time Wendel Blair walked through the picture window at the Lowes' and got slashed to ribbons.

He scared me. In bed, I didn't dare look at him. I lay back with my eyes closed, luxuriating because he knew all sorts of expert angles, his hands never fumbling, going over my whole body, pressing the hair up and off the back of my head, giving an extra hip shove, as if to say *There*. I parted my eyes slightly, keeping the screen of my lashes low because it was too much to look at him, his mouth loose and pink and parted, his eyes looking through my forehead, or kneeling up, looking through my throat. I was ashamed but couldn't look him in the eye.

You wonder about things feeling a little off-kilter. You begin to feel like a piece of pounded veal.

At boarding school, everyone gets depressed. We go in and see the housemother, Mrs Gunther. She got married when she was eighteen. Mr Gunther was her high school sweetheart, the only boyfriend she ever had.

'And you knew you wanted to marry him right off?' we ask her.

She smiles and says, 'Yes.'

'They always want something from you,' says Jill, complaining about her boyfriend.

'Yeah,' says Giddy. 'You always feel like you have to deliver something.'

'You do,' says Mrs Gunther. 'Babies.'

After sex, you curl up like a shrimp, something deep inside you ruined, slammed in a place that sickens at slamming, and slowly you fill up with an overwhelming sadness, an elusive gaping worry. You don't try to explain it, filled with the knowledge that it's nothing after all, everything filling up finally and absolutely with death. After the briskness of loving, loving stops. And you roll over with death stretched out alongside you like a feather boa, or a snake, light as air, and you . . . you don't even ask for anything or try to say something to him because it's obviously your own damn fault. You haven't been able to – to what? To open your heart. You open your legs but can't, or don't dare anymore, to open your heart.

It starts this way:

You stare into their eyes. They flash like all the stars are out. They look at you seriously, their eyes at a low burn and their hands no matter what starting off shy and with such a gentle touch that the only thing you can do is take that tenderness and let yourself be swept away. When, with one attentive finger they tuck the hair behind your ear, you —

You do everything they want.

Then comes after. After when they don't look at you. They scratch their balls, stare at the ceiling. Or if they do turn, their gaze is altogether changed. They are surprised. They turn casually to look at you, distracted, and get a mild distracted surprise. You're gone. Their blank look tells you that the girl they were fucking is not there anymore. You seem to have disappeared.

MARTIN AMIS
Let Me Count the Times

Vernon made love to his wife three and a half times a week, and this was all right.

For some reason, making love always averaged out that way. Normally – though by no means invariably – they made love every second night. On the other hand Vernon had been known to make love to his wife seven nights running; for the next seven nights they would not make love – or perhaps they would once, in which case they would make love the following week only twice but four times the week after that – or perhaps only three times, in which case they would make love four times the next week but only twice the week after that – or perhaps only once. And so on. Vernon didn't know why, but making love always averaged out that way; it seemed invariable. Occasionally – and was it any wonder? – Vernon found himself wishing that the week contained only six days, or as many as eight, to render these calculations (which were always blandly corroborative in spirit) easier to deal with.

It was, without exception, Vernon himself who initiated their conjugal acts. His wife responded every time with the same bashful alacrity. Oral foreplay was by no means unknown between them. On average – and again it always averaged out like this, and again Vernon was always the unsmiling ring master – fellatio was performed by Vernon's wife every third coupling, or 60.8333 times a year, or 1.1698717 times a week. Vernon performed cunnilingus rather less often: every fourth coupling, on average, or 45.625 times a year, or .8774038 times a week. It would also be a mistake to think that this was the extent of their variations. Vernon sodomized his wife twice a year, for instance – on his birthday, which seemed fair enough, but also, ironically (or so *he* thought), on hers. He put it down to the expensive nights out they always had on these occasions, and more particularly to the effects of champagne. Vernon always felt desperately ashamed afterwards, and would be a limp spectre of embarrassment and remorse at breakfast the next day. Vernon's wife never said anything about it, which was something. If she ever did, Vernon would probably have stopped doing it. But she never did. The same sort of thing happened when Vernon ejaculated in his wife's mouth, which on average he did 1.2 times a year. At this point they had been married for ten years. That was convenient. What would it be like when they had been married for eleven years – or thirteen. Once, and only once, Vernon had been about to ejaculate in his wife's mouth when suddenly he had got a better idea: he ejaculated all over her face instead. She didn't say anything about that either, thank God. Why he had thought it a better idea he would never know. He didn't think it was a better idea now. It distressed him greatly to reflect that his rare acts of abandonment should expose a desire to humble and degrade the loved one. And she was the loved one. Still, he had only done it once. Vernon ejaculated all over his wife's face .001923 times a week. That wasn't very often to ejaculate all over your wife's face, now was it?

Vernon was a businessman. His office contained several electronic calculators. Vernon would often run his marital frequencies through these swift, efficient, and impeccably discreet machines. They always responded brightly with the same answer, as if to say, 'Yes, Vernon, that's how often you do it,' or 'No, Vernon, you don't do it any more often than that.' Vernon would spend whole lunch-hours crooked over the calculator. And yet he knew that all these figures were in a sense approximate. Oh, Vernon knew, Vernon knew. Then one day a powerful white computer was delivered to the accounts department. Vernon saw at once that a long-nursed dream might now take flesh: leap years. 'Ah, Alice, I don't want to be disturbed, do you hear?' he told the cleaning lady sternly when he let himself into the office that night. 'I've got some very important calculations to do in the accounts department.' Just after midnight Vernon's hot red eyes stared up wildly from the display screen, where his entire sex life lay tabulated in recurring prisms of threes and sixes, in endless series, like mirrors placed face to face.

Vernon's wife was the only woman Vernon had ever known. He loved her and he liked making love to her quite a lot; certainly he had never craved any other outlet. When Vernon made love to his wife he thought only of her pleasure and her beauty: the infrequent but highly flattering noises she made through her evenly parted teeth, the divine plasticity of her limbs, the fever, the magic, and the safety of the moment. The sense of peace that followed had only a little to do with the probability that tomorrow would be a night off. Even Vernon's dreams were monogamous: the women who strode those slipped but essentially quotidian landscapes were mere icons of the self-sufficient

female kingdom, nurses, nuns, bus-conductresses, parking war-
dens, policewomen. Only every now and then, once a week,
say, or less, or not calculably, he saw things that made him suspect that life might have room for more inside — a luminous
ribbon dappling the undercurve of a bridge, certain cloud-
scapes, intent figures hurrying through changing light.

All this, of course, was before Vernon's business trip.

It was not a particularly important business trip: Vernon's
firm was not a particularly important firm. His wife packed his
smallest suitcase and drove him to the station. On the way she
observed that they had not spent a night apart for over four
years — when she had gone to stay with her mother after that
operation of hers. Vernon nodded in surprised agreement,
making a few brisk calculations in his head. He kissed her goodbye with some passion. In the restaurant car he had a gin and
tonic. He had another gin and tonic. As the train approached
the thickening city Vernon felt a curious lightness play through
his body. He thought of himself as a young man, alone. The city
would be full of cabs, stray people, shadows, women, things
happening.

Vernon got to his hotel at eight o'clock. The receptionist
confirmed his reservation and gave him his key. Vernon rode the
elevator to his room. He washed and changed, selecting, after
some deliberation, the more sombre of the two ties his wife had
packed. He went to the bar and ordered a gin and tonic. The
cocktail waitress brought it to him at a table. The bar was scattered with city people: men, women who probably did things
with men fairly often, young couples secretively chuckling.
Directly opposite Vernon sat a formidable lady with a fur, a hat,

and a cigarette holder. She glanced at Vernon twice or perhaps three times. Vernon couldn't be sure.

He dined in the hotel restaurant. With his meal he enjoyed half a bottle of good red wine. Over coffee Vernon toyed with the idea of going back to the bar for a crème de menthe – or a champagne cocktail. He felt hot; his scalp hummed; two hysterical flies looped round his head. He rode back to his room, with a view to freshening up. Slowly, before the mirror, he removed all his clothes. His pale body was inflamed with the tranquil glow of fever. He felt deliciously raw, tingling to his touch. What's happening to me? he wondered. Then, with relief, with shame, with rapture, he keeled backwards on to the bed and did something he hadn't done for over ten years.

Vernon did it three more times that night and twice again in the morning.

Four appointments spaced out the following day. Vernon's mission was to pick the right pocket calculator for daily use by all members of his firm. Between each demonstration – the Moebius strip of figures, the repeated wink of the decimal point – Vernon took cabs back to the hotel and did it again each time. 'As fast as you can, driver,' he found himself saying. That night he had a light supper sent up to his room. He did it five more times – or was it six? He could no longer be absolutely sure. But he was sure he did it three more times the next morning, once before breakfast and twice after. He took the train back at noon, having done it an incredible 18 times in 36 hours: that was – what? – 84 times a week, or 4,368 times a year. Or perhaps he had done it 19 times! Vernon was exhausted, yet in a sense he had never felt stronger. And here was the train giving him an erection all the same, whether he liked it or not.

'How was it?' asked his wife at the station.

'Tiring. But successful,' admitted Vernon.

'Yes, you do look a bit whacked. We'd better get you home and tuck you up in bed for a while.'

Vernon's red eyes blinked. He could hardly believe his luck.

Shortly afterwards Vernon was to look back with amused dis-belief at his own faint-heartedness during those trail-blazing few days. Only in bed, for instance! Now, in his total recklessness and elation, Vernon did it everywhere. He hauled himself roughly on to the bedroom floor and did it there. He did it under the impassive gaze of the bathroom's porcelain and steel. With scandalized laughter he dragged himself out protesting to the garden tool shed and did it there. He did it lying on the kitchen table. For a while he took to doing it in the open air, in windy parks, behind hoardings in the town, on churned fields; it made his knees tremble. He did it in corridorless trains. He would rent rooms in cheap hotels for an hour, for half an hour, for ten minutes (how the receptionists stared). He thought of renting a little love-nest somewhere. Confusedly and very briefly he considered running off with himself. He started doing it at work, cautiously at first, then with nihilistic abandon, as if discovery was the very thing he secretly craved. Once, giggling coquettishly before and afterwards (the danger, the danger), he did it while dictating a long and tremulous letter to the secre-tary he shared with two other senior managers. After this he came to his senses somewhat and resolved to try only to do it at home.

'How long will you be, dear?' he would call over his shoulder as his wife opened the front door with her shopping-bags in her hands. An hour? Fine. Just a couple of minutes? Even better! He took to lingering sinuously in bed while his wife made their morning tea, deliciously sandwiched by the moist uxoriousness of the sheets. On his nights off from love-making (and these were invariable now: every other night, every other night) Vernon nearly always managed one while his wife, in the bath-room next door, calmly readied herself for sleep. She nearly caught him at it on several occasions. He found that especially exciting. At this point Vernon was still trying hectically to keep count; it was all there somewhere, gurgling away in the memory banks of the computer in the accounts department. He was averaging 3.4 times a day, or 23.8 times a week, or an insane 1,241 times a year. And his wife never suspected a thing.

Until now, Vernon's 'sessions' (as he thought of them) had always been mentally structured round his wife, the only woman he had ever known – her beauty, the flattering noises she made, the fever, the safety. There were variations, naturally. A typical 'session' would start with her undressing at night. She would lean out of her heavy brassière and submissively debark the tender checks of her panties. She would give a little gasp, half pleasure, half fear (how do you figure a woman?), as naked Vernon, obviously in sparkling form, emerged impressively from the shadows. He would mount her swiftly, perhaps even rather brutally. Her hands mimed their defencelessness as the great muscles rippled and plunged along Vernon's powerful back. 'You're too big for me,' he would have her say to him sometimes, or 'That hurts, but I like it.' Climax would usually be synchronized with his wife's howled request for the sort of thing Vernon seldom did to her in real life. But Vernon never did the things for which she yearned, oh no. He usually just ejaculated all over her face. She loved that as well of course (the bitch), to Vernon's transient disgust.

And then the strangers came.

One summer evening Vernon returned early from the office. The car was gone: as Vernon had shrewdly anticipated, his wife was out somewhere. Hurrying into the house, he made straight for the bedroom. He lay down and lowered his trousers – and then with a sensuous moan tugged them off altogether. Things started well, with a compelling preamble that had become increasingly popular in recent weeks. Naked, primed, Vernon stood behind the half-closed bedroom door. Already he could hear his wife's preparatory truffles of shy arousal. Vernon stepped forward to swing open the door, intending to stand there menacingly for a few seconds, his restless legs planted well apart. He swung open the door and stared. At what? At his wife sweatily grappling with a huge bronzed gypsy, who turned incuriously towards Vernon and then back again to the hysteria of volition splayed out on the bed before him. Vernon ejaculated immediately. His wife returned home within a few minutes. She kissed him on the forehead. He felt very strange.

The next time he tried, he swung open the door to find his wife upside down over the headboard, doing scarcely credible things to a hairy-shouldered Turk. The time after that, she had her elbows hooked round the back of her knee-caps as a 15 stone Chinaman feasted at his leisure on her imploring sobs. The time after that, two silent, glistening negroes were doing what the hell they liked with her. The two negroes, in particular, wouldn't go away; they were quite frequently joined by the

Turk, moreover. Sometimes they would even let Vernon and his wife get started before they all came thundering in on them. And did Vernon's wife mind any of this? Mind? She liked it. Like it? She *loved* it! And so did Vernon, apparently. At the office Vernon soberly searched his brain for a single neutrino of genuine desire that his wife should do these things with these people. The very idea made him shout with revulsion. Yet, one way or another, he didn't mind it really, did he? One way or another, he liked it. He loved it. But he was determined to put an end to it.

His whole approach changed. 'Right, my girl,' he muttered to himself, 'two can play at that game.' To begin with, Vernon had affairs with all his wife's friends. The longest and perhaps the most detailed was with Vera, his wife's old school chum. He sported with her bridge-partners, her co-workers in the Charity. He fooled around with all her eligible relatives — her younger sister, that nice little niece of hers. One mad morning Vernon even mounted her hated mother. 'But Vernon, what about . . . ?' they would all whisper fearfully. But Vernon just shoved them on to the bed, twisting off his belt with an imperious snap. All the women out there on the edges of his wife's world — one by one, Vernon had the lot.

Meanwhile, Vernon's erotic dealings with his wife herself had continued much as before. Perhaps they had even profited in poignancy and gentleness from the pounding rumours of Vernon's nether life. With this latest development, however, Vernon was not slow to mark a new dimension, a disfavoured presence, in their bed. Oh, they still made love all right; but now there were two vital differences. Their acts of sex were no longer hermetic; the safety and the peace had gone: no longer did Vernon attempt to apply any brake to the chariot of his thoughts. Secondly — and perhaps even more crucially — their love-making was, without a doubt, *less frequent*. Six and a half times a fortnight, three times a week, five times a fortnight . . . : they were definitely losing ground. At first Vernon's mind was a chaos of back-logs, short-falls, restructured schedules, recuperation schemes. Later he grew far more detached about the whole business. Who said he had to do it three and a half times a week? Who said that this was all right? After ten nights of chaste sleep (his record up till now) Vernon watched his wife turn sadly on her side after her diffident goodnight. He waited several minutes, propped up on an elbow, glazedly eternalized in the potent moment. Then he leaned forward and coldly kissed her neck, and smiled as he felt her body's axis turn. He went on smiling. He knew where the real action was.

For Vernon was now perfectly well aware that any woman was his for the taking, any woman at all, at a nod, at a shrug, at a single convulsive snap of his peremptory fingers. He systematically serviced every woman who caught his eye in the street, had his way with them, and tossed them aside without a second thought. All the models in his wife's fashion magazines — they all trooped through his bedroom, too, in their turn. Over the course of several months he worked his way through all the established television actresses. An equivalent period took care of the major stars of the Hollywood screen. (Vernon bought a big glossy book to help him with this project. For his money, the girls of the Golden Age were the most daring and athletic lovers: Monroe, Russell, West, Dietrich, Dors, Ekberg.

Frankly, you could keep your Welches, your Dunaways, your Fondas, your Keatons.) By now the roll-call of names was astounding. Vernon's prowess with them epic, unsurpassable. All the girls were saying that he was easily the best lover they had ever had.

One afternoon he gingerly peered into the pornographic magazines that blazed from the shelves of a remote newsagent. He made a mental note of the faces and figures, and the girls were duly accorded brief membership of Vernon's thronging harem. But he was shocked; he didn't mind admitting it: why should pretty young girls take their clothes off for money like that, like *that*? Why should men want to buy pictures of them doing it? Distressed and not a little confused, Vernon conducted the first great purge of his clamorous rumpus rooms. That night he paced through the shimmering corridors and becalmed ante-rooms dusting his palms and looking sternly this way and that. Some girls wept openly at the loss of their friends; others smiled up at him with furtive triumph. But he stalked on, slamming the heavy doors behind him.

Vernon now looked for solace in the pages of our literature. Quality, he told himself, was what he was after — quality, quality. Here was where the high-class girls hung out. Using the literature shelves in the depleted local library, Vernon got down to work. After quick flings with Emily, Griselda, and Criseyde, and a strapping weekend with the Good Wife of Bath, Vernon cruised straight on to Shakespeare and the delightfully wide-eyed starlets of the romantic comedies. He romped giggling with Viola over the Illyrian hills, slept in a glade in Arden with the willowy Rosalind, bathed nude with Miranda in a turquoise lagoon. In a single disdainful morning he splashed his way through all four of the tragic heroines: cold Cordelia (this was a bit of a frost, actually), bitter-sweet Ophelia (again rather constricted, though he quite liked her dirty talk), the snake-eyed Lady M. (Vernon had had to watch himself there) and, best of all, that sizzling sorceress Desdemona (Othello had *her* number all right. She *stank* of sex!). Following some arduous, unhygienic yet relatively brief dalliance with Restoration drama, Vernon soldiered on through the prudent matrons of the Great Tradition. As a rule, the more sedate and respectable the girls, the nastier and more complicated were the things Vernon found himself wanting to do to them (with lapsed hussies like Maria Bertram, Becky Sharp, or Lady Dedlock, Vernon was in, out, and away, darting half-dressed over the rooftops). Pamela had her points, but Clarissa was the one who turned out to be the true co-artist of the oeuvres; Sophie Western was good fun all right, but the pious Amelia yodelled for the humbling high points in Vernon's sweltering repertoire. Again he had no very serious complaints about his one-night romances with the likes of Elizabeth Bennett and Dorothea Brooke; it was adult, sanitary stuff, based on a clear understanding of his desires and his needs; they knew that such men will take what they want; they knew that they would wake the next morning and Vernon would be gone. Give him a Fanny Price, though, or better, much better, a Little Nell, and Vernon would march into the bedroom rolling up his sleeves; and Nell and Fan would soon be ruing the day they'd ever been born. Did they mind the horrible things he did to them? Mind? When he prepared to leave the next morning, solemnly buckling his belt before the tall window – how they howled!

The possibilities seemed endless. Other literatures dozed

expectantly in their dormitories. The sleeping lion of Tolstoy – Anna, Natasha, Masha, and the rest. American fiction – those girls would show even Vernon a trick or two. The sneaky Gauls – Vernon had a hunch that he and Madame Bovary, for instance, were going to get along just fine . . . One puzzled weekend, however, Vernon encountered the writings of D. H. Lawrence. Snapping *The Rainbow* shut on Sunday night, Vernon realized at once that this particular avenue of possibility – sprawling as it was, with its intricate trees and their beautiful diseases, and that distant prospect where sandy mountains loomed – had come to an abrupt and unanswerable end. He never knew women behaved like *that* . . . Vernon felt obscure relief and even a pang of theoretical desire when his wife bustled in last thing, bearing the tea-tray before her.

Vernon was now, on average, sleeping with his wife 1.15 times a week. Less than single figure love-making was obviously going to be some sort of crunch, and Vernon was making himself vigilant for whatever form the crisis might take. She hadn't, thank God, said anything about it, yet. Brooding one afternoon soon after the Lawrence débâcle, Vernon suddenly thought of something that made his heart jump. He blinked. He couldn't believe it. It was true. Not once since he had started his 'sessions' had Vernon exacted from his wife any of the sly variations with which he had used to space out the weeks, the months, the years. Not once. It had simply never occurred to him. He flipped his pocket calculator on to his lap. Stunned, he tapped out the figures. She now owed him . . . Why, if he wanted, he could have an entire week of . . . They were behind with *that* to the tune of . . . Soon it would be time again for him to . . . Vernon's wife passed through the room. She blew him a kiss. Vernon resolved to shelve these figures but also to keep them up to date. They seemed to balance things out. He knew he was denying his wife something she ought to have; yet at the same time he was withholding something he ought not to give. He began to feel better about the whole business.

For it now became clear that no mere woman could satisfy him – not Vernon. His activities moved into an entirely new sphere of intensity and abstraction. Now, when the velvet curtain shot skywards, Vernon might be astride a black stallion on a marmoreal dune, his narrow eyes fixed on the caravan of defenceless Arab women straggling along beneath him; then he dug in his spurs and thundered down on them, swords twirling in either hand. Or else Vernon climbed from a wriggling human swamp of tangled naked bodies, playfully batting away the hands that clutched at him, until he was tugged down once again into the thudding mass of membrane and heat. He visited strange planets where women were metal, were flowers, were gas. Soon he became a cumulus cloud, a tidal wave, the East Wind, the boiling Earth's core, the air itself, wheeling round a terrified globe as whole tribes, races, ecologies fled and scattered under the continent-wide shadow of his approach.

It was after about a month of this new brand of skylarking that things began to go rather seriously awry.

The first hint of disaster came with sporadic attacks of *ejaculatio praecox*. Vernon would settle down for a leisurely session, would just be casting and scripting the cosmic drama about to be unfolded before him – and would look down to find his thoughts had been messily and pleasurelessly anticipated by the

roguish weapon in his hands. It began to happen more frequently, sometimes quite out of the blue: Vernon wouldn't even
notice until he saw the boyish, tell-tale stains on his pants last
thing at night. (Amazingly, and rather hurtfully too, his wife
didn't seem to detect any real difference. But he was making
love to her only every ten or eleven days by that time.) Vernon
made a creditable attempt to laugh the whole thing off, and,
sure enough, after a while the trouble cleared itself up. What
followed, however, was far worse.

To begin with, at any rate, Vernon blamed himself. He was so
relieved, and so childishly delighted, by his newly recovered
prowess that he teased out his 'sessions' to unendurable,
unprecedented lengths. Perhaps that wasn't wise . . . What was
certain was that he overdid it. Within a week, and quite against
his will, Vernon's 'sessions' were taking between thirty and
forty-five minutes; within two weeks, up to an hour and a half.
It wrecked his schedules: all the lightning strikes, all the silky
raids, that used to punctuate his life were reduced to dour campaigns which Vernon could perforce never truly win. 'Vernon,
are you ill?' his wife would say outside the bathroom door. 'It's
nearly *tea*-time.' Vernon — slumped on the lavatory seat, panting
with exhaustion — looked up wildly, his eyes startled, shrunken.
He coughed until he found his voice. 'I'll be straight out,' he
managed to say, climbing heavily to his feet.

Nothing Vernon could summon would deliver him. Massed,
maddened, cart-wheeling women — some of molten pewter and
fifty feet tall, others indigo and no bigger than fountain-pens —
hollered at him from the four corners of the universe. No help.
He gathered all the innocents and subjected them to atrocities
of unimaginable proportions, committing a million murders

enriched with infamous tortures. He still drew a blank. Vernon, all neutronium, a supernova, a black sun, consumed the Earth and her sisters in his dead fire, bullocking through the solar system, ejaculating the Milky Way. That didn't work either. He was obliged to fake orgasms with his wife (rather skilfully, it seemed: she didn't say anything about it). His testicles developed a mighty migraine, whose slow throbs all day timed his heartbeat with mounting frequency and power, until at night Vernon's face was a sweating parcel of lard and his hands shimmered deliriously as he juggled the aspirins to his lips.

Then the ultimate catastrophe occurred. Paradoxically, it was heralded by a single, joyous, uncovenanted climax – again out of the blue, on a bus, one lunchtime. Throughout the afternoon at the office Vernon chuckled and gloated, convinced that finally all his troubles were at an end. It wasn't so. After a week of ceaseless experiment and scrutiny Vernon had to face the truth. The thing was dead. He was impotent.

'Oh my God,' he thought, 'I always knew something like this would happen to me some time.' In one sense Vernon accepted the latest reverse with grim stoicism (by now the thought of his old ways filled him with the greatest disgust); in another sense, and with terror, he felt like a man suspended between two states: one is reality, perhaps, the other an unspeakable dream. And then when day comes he awakes with a moan of relief; but reality has gone and the nightmare has replaced it: the nightmare was really there all the time. Vernon looked at the house where they had lived for so long now, the five rooms through which his calm wife moved along her calm tracks, and he saw it all slipping away from him forever, all his peace, all the fever and the safety. And for what, for what?

'Perhaps it would be better if I just told her about the whole thing and made a clean breast of it,' he thought wretchedly. 'It wouldn't be easy, God knows, but in time she might learn to trust me again. And I really *am* finished with all that other nonsense. God, when I . . .' But then he saw his wife's face – capable, straightforward, confident – and the scar of dawning realization as he stammered out his shame. No, he could never tell her, he could never do that to her, no, not to her. She was sure to find out soon enough anyway. How could a man conceal that he had lost what made him a man? He considered suicide, but – 'But I just haven't got the guts,' he told himself. He would have to wait, to wait and melt in his dread.

A month passed without his wife saying anything. This had always been a make-or-break, last ditch deadline for Vernon, and he now approached the coming confrontation as a matter of nightly crisis. All day long he rehearsed his excuses. To kick off with Vernon complained of a headache, on the next night of a stomach upset. For the following two nights he stayed up virtually until dawn – 'preparing the annual figures,' he said. On the fifth night he simulated a long coughing fit, on the sixth a powerful fever. But on the seventh night he just helplessly lay there, sadly waiting. Thirty minutes passed, side by side. Vernon prayed for her sleep and for his death.

'Vernon?' she asked.

'Mm-hm?' he managed to say – God, what a croak it was.

'Do you want to talk about this?'

Vernon didn't say anything. He lay there, melting, dying. More minutes passed. Then he felt her hand on his thigh.

Quite a long time later, and in the posture of a cowboy on the back of a bucking steer, Vernon ejaculated all over his wife's face. During the course of the preceding two and a half hours he had done to his wife everything he could possibly think of, to such an extent that he was candidly astonished that she was still alive. They subsided, mumbling soundlessly, and slept in each other's arms.

Vernon woke up before his wife did. It took him thirty-five minutes to get out of bed, so keen was he to accomplish this feat without waking her. He made breakfast in his dressing-gown, training every cell of his concentration on the small, sacramental tasks. Every time his mind veered back to the night before, he made a low growling sound, or slid his knuckles down the cheese-grater, or caught his tongue between his teeth and pressed hard. He closed his eyes and he could see his wife crammed against the headboard with that one leg sticking up in the air; he could hear the sound her breasts made as he two-handedly slapped them practically out of alignment. Vernon steadied himself against the refrigerator. He had an image of his wife coming into the kitchen – on crutches, her face black and blue. She couldn't very well not say anything about *that*, could she? He laid the table. He heard her stir. He sat down, his knees cracking, and ducked his head behind the cereal packet.

When Vernon looked up his wife was sitting opposite him. She looked utterly normal. Her blue eyes searched for his with all their light.

'Toast?' he bluffed.

'Yes please. Oh Vernon, wasn't it lovely?'

For an instant Vernon knew beyond doubt that he would now have to murder his wife and then commit suicide – or kill her and leave the country under an assumed name, start all over again somewhere, Romania, Iceland, the Far East, the New World.

'What, you mean the –?'

'Oh yes. I'm so happy. For a while I thought that we . . . I thought you were –'

'I –'

'– Don't, darling. You needn't say anything. I understand. And now everything's all right again. Ooh,' she added. 'You were naughty, you know.'

Vernon nearly panicked all over again. But he gulped it down and said, quite nonchalantly, 'Yes, I was a bit, wasn't I?'

'Very naughty. So *rude*. Oh Vernon . . .'

She reached for his hand and stood up. Vernon got to his feet too – or became upright by some new hydraulic system especially devised for the occasion. She glanced over her shoulder as she moved up the stairs.

'You mustn't do that too often, you know.'

'Oh really?' drawled Vernon. 'Who says?'

'*I* say. It would take the fun out of it. Well, not *too* often, anyway.'

Vernon knew one thing: he was going to stop keeping count. Pretty soon, he reckoned, things would be more or less back to normal. He'd had his kicks: it was only right that the loved one should now have hers. Vernon followed his wife into the bedroom and softly closed the door behind them.

KATHY ACKER

Girls Who Like To Fuck

1

Daddy was a drunk, and mom had decided to be a crip, but I didn't mind them too much. Quentin came back from Harvard with all these ridiculous *theories*. He told me Freud had said that all women are naturally masochists, though he didn't say that that simply.

I understood what Quentin meant and I got angry at him. 'They teach you stupid things in universities and universities are no good for anybody.' I was angry, though I didn't know why.

I had never known Quentin. Or anyone. It's impossible to know a person who's always fantasizing about you and about whom you're obsessing.

I saw Quentin as someone who desperately wanted to touch me but never could because he was mean.

All these men wanted me; well, maybe they did and maybe they didn't. They say 'I love you' that means nothing to me it doesn't touch me that means they want something from me.

Quentin wants something from me.

Daddy and mommy are dead and they should stay that way.

Who am I? That's not quite the question which I keep asking myself over and over. *What's my story?* That's it. Not the stories they've been and keep handing me. My story.

I fuck every man in sight. Men open me up or sex with them

opens me up, so I learn something about myself. My story has something to do with opened-out flesh.

When Quentin came back from Harvard, he was more mixed up than before he couldn't get anything straight.

Quentin was still sharing my bedroom (when he wasn't in college), though we were too old for that. There was nowhere else to go. I disappeared into my bedroom and, after I heard mommy and daddy close their bedroom door, curled up into my bed. Through all the walls, I could hear Father telling Mother in this high whining voice he used when he was trying to assert himself that he was supporting her so she should be properly grateful. Then I heard Mother really cry.

I didn't give a shit. I decided that sleeping with a lot of men doesn't go far enough, far enough into me. Because the guys who sleep with me and Quentin say, 'You've got whore blood in you. You sleep with every man because you want to be hurt because you've got whore blood in you.' Their saying this reveals that they sleep with me but they don't perceive me so their sleeping with me doesn't open me up far enough.

I've decided I'm not going to sleep with every male.

Then, from his bed, Quentin started to tell me about Harvard. 'It's a Jewish university,' he said, 'but most of the universities around there are Jewish, everyone knows Jews have the most brains. Though that might not be true now that Jews are fundamentalists too.'

'Weren't they always?' I said. Cause I wasn't listening. 'What is it about Jews?'

'Because their god is simply horror, they're outside the range of God. Not only of our fucking familial respectability, of love, but of God too.'

I remembered I was unable to be loved because I was sick or because my mother had taught me I was unable to be loved so I fucked every guy I could lay my hands on. Women have always been taught to hate themselves. That's history. And they have to deny that by not allowing themselves to fuck around. Maybe: to be whores. I wanted to tell my brother about history. 'Outside the law,' I said. 'People either do what they're told or they go outside the law, find something else, maybe themselves.'

'There were two kinds of Jews at university. The first kind had made themselves out of the past. Nazis. I learned nothing in university. I wanted to escape the compulsion of having a past, like the Jews, but I couldn't find any past, I couldn't find any past to escape. I can't find a past and a future. Father says that nothing human matters. That must be part of my past too. The past I can't find. Meaninglessness. I wanted to leave . . .'

'I fuck,' I said.

'. . . but of course I wasn't ready to leave school yet. I stopped going to classes. All the students around me, Capitol, anyway, were insane. Though Harvard has the largest psychiatric staff of any college in the country, the students who are really mad don't go anywhere near the psychiatrists cause the psychiatrists might see the razor blade marks on their bodies and have them locked up. A friend of mine who popped pills every day, he didn't care what pills, and took pot to come down, worked in one of those houses. Stately homes for rich American youth. He said, there you can't distinguish between the inmates and nurses and doctors because all of them piss on the walls and fuck around.'

'Fuck you-know-who, fuckface.'

'It was awful, Capitol. There. There was a buzzing in my

brain. Being in a dentist's chair and the dentist is drilling. The doctors, actual doctors, tried to find out what was physically wrong with me, but they couldn't find anything.

'The worst pain is when consciousness hurts because you can't get away from consciousness.'

I didn't want to hear about other people's problems.

'You're a slut, aren't you, Capitol? You do it with every boy and you don't care. Father said women are diseased and have no respect for anything living *their own flesh and blood curses them* and Father said nothing matters.'

He was sick but so, then, are most men. Because women hold the repositories of life and death or of time in them, women know that both the material and the measure of living is time. Time to humans is painful. I could spit on men because they're weak.

I got out of bed into the cold, walked over to Quentin's. I put my arms around him and told him to get to sleep. 'We're not nothing. We're our stories.'

'Mother never wanted to have me. She had me only cause she had an unknown disease and the doctor told her getting pregnant would cure this disease. You're the same way, Capitol. Don't you think it's sick to fuck, to fuck only out of fear, loneliness, and other evil emotions?'

I looked down at him. I had decided I would never fuck a man whom I loved.

It was nighttime.

'Orpheus looked back,' Quentin said, 'I stopped going to classes, failed three out of four courses, and now I've left university forever. The nearer I got to this house, when I was traveling home, the louder the buzzing in my brain grew.'

Father ate only hamburgers, steaks, and lamb chops; he said that all other kinds of meat and most vegetables were nigger-food. Father was searching for his bottle. Mother had hidden it, locked it somewhere in their closet. Father told her to get it out for him. Mother accused him of being alcoholic. Father replied that all businessmen have one or two drinks when they come home. Mother said that any drink made a man into an alcoholic. 'Shut up,' said Father. 'I've given you everything you own.' He was crying.

Quentin named the buzzing for me:

'The quarter of an hour before I was back here was when the buzzing was the worst, worse than when I had been in school and when I was finally with you. As I entered this section of town, I couldn't hear what anyone was saying to me and I couldn't see the buildings in front of me.'

It was dark in our bedroom.

'Though I didn't think I saw anything, I remember seeing: Wood boards on the empty houses. Pieces of black dog shit. A young boy cried out. Our town was brighter, in colors, than it had been in my mind in university. Light, but not neon, colors: the yellow women wore wasn't the yellow of the sun. The pinks of young girls' cheeks weren't . . .'

Now I knew some of it. I could begin to touch the buzzing.

'Some of the women have prams. You said that women have babies in their blood. Sometimes two prams. One of the babies squalls; a young woman walks over to it . . . her, him, whams the cheek, "Shut the fuck up." The buildings aren't tall until you come into the center of town. The businesses here, at the edges, are crummy, like people who know that their lives'll always resemble prisons. Sure everybody has a story, Capitol.

Eventually, if they make it to anything besides death. Isn't that what Harvard's supposed to be about? Meaning? The town has always shifted away from descriptions: not that it doesn't want to exist, it just wants to be safe. There've been no major radical political movements in America since the thirties.'

'Huh?'

The bedroom was dark.

'Harvard was another world. They knew what terrorists were there and maybe who. Maybe they even make them up, those snotty Harvard tenants, maybe they make everything, the outside world, that's how they own. In Harvard I was taught to know, Capitol, know because known, *known* as in *own*; I was taught to remember what I didn't and can't know.'

I was only half listening to this. Maybe, like, cause of the buzzing in his head he couldn't see, so I couldn't hear. Only I didn't hear or hadn't heard cause of what was going on inside or as me. Feeling. Nothing made sense but feeling. I don't mean sentimentality; I mean sensations. Either some portion of the inside surface of my skin moved, or else there was nothing. For this reason, I've never and don't need to say anything to anyone and I let them say whatever they want to me. I'm happy whenever I rub up against someone like a dog.

My brother said, 'I remembered and finally I saw some low-cut houses running along the green like rats. I was now about half a mile from here. I wondered whether, if I stepped on their tails and gouged out their eyes, like a poor kid who lives with rats, I could eat them for dinner. My daddy'd drink whiskey and my mommy'd be a low whore.'

'Blood,' I said, 'drink your own blood. I want to go to sleep.' I put my hand on a cheek which I couldn't see. 'You're the

whore because you've got the maturity of a three-year-old and
I'm not going to stick with you because no one sticks with
whores.'

'*Schwartzertown*. That's what mother used to call it . . .'

'You're as disgusting as they are.'

'. . . I was being forced to go back home by instructions in
my head. A hand in my head was clenching and unclenching
itself. The instructions decided I actually had an hour or so till
D day.

'I walked up and down, then down that long hilly road
mother used to walk every morning to get us fresh eggs, and I
came to a short stretch of white sand and then the ocean.

'A boat was effortlessly moving, as if propelled by nothing
and no one, across a sheet of water. Since there were many
kinds of time here, the hand could no longer control me.

'For instance, I looked away from the water and saw areas of
suburban life that wanted to be progressing as fast as possible
and, at the same time, wanted no time, invulnerability, wholesomeness. Isn't wholesomeness untouchability?'

I knew who I was. Now.

'The ocean was another kind of time. Time like blood.'

'Is blood untouchable?' Maybe, finally, it is, as are all things. I
thought that women are sane because they're ruled, not so
much ruled as pulled, by their menses. Little did I know.

'I knew it was time to go back to the terror (don't say it,
doom) that was ticking in my blood.'

'You don't want to fuck me, do you?' Every man or boy in
this town wants to fuck me and they know who I am. You can't
ever leave me, don't. 'Terror (doom),' I said, 'like everything
else, has to do with babies.'

A few weeks later, Mother disappeared. I shouldn't have been scared when it, that, happened because being crazy, she could do whatever she wanted. She had lied all the time. But despite all my reason, my blood knew doom. I learned about blood. The cops who didn't give a shit said that she hadn't suicided but been murdered but no one could know. And then, she who was in my blood wanted me to be dead.

I asked him, why don't you do it normally? 'Why don't you do it normally, Quentin?'

'What do you mean *normally*?'

'With another person?'

I knew Quentin knew what I was talking about, but he had already fallen asleep. I snuck outside. The moon was going somewhere and from somewhere, but nobody saw where. I had no intention of going to sleep ever again or doing what they told me to do.

2

Will you be my daddy? I wanted say. No one can tell me what to do. Sometimes I'm in ecstasy and I want to fuck every man in town and I don't care what the face is on the body I'm fucking. That's not evil it's ecstasy.

During the day, Quentin and I walked down to where the swans were. Here I felt peaceful. I hadn't seen them because, for a long time, it had been winter. I had been scared they died in the cold and I couldn't bear when living things die. It's the helplessness, but I don't know whose helplessness.

It was winter and the swans were OK. They came glided ran over to me as if they were in the right proportion to the water and air and so controlled their own existences. 'Snake-necks' I called them.

There is a myth.

Quentin stood at the side of the bank on some concrete while I put the bottoms of my legs into the water even though I knew I wasn't supposed to because the water was polluted. Hair and weeds. Rimbaud had told me, he's always instructing, that the people who tried to suicide cause of love or money or just out of stupidity in the adjoining river and were too stupid or unlucky to succeed had to have their stomachs pumped. Swans never have to have their stomachs pumped.

Quentin told me I'd better get out. I was up to my waist in mud and reeds and weeds and water and a swan was waiting about half a foot from me.

Against my wishes and better judgment I did what he said. I sat down on the bit of the concrete that sloped into the water and mud in my clothes so stiff from the wet and cold they stood out from my body and made a noise as they scraped the stone.

'Why don't you wring your dress out do you want to catch cold?'

The water was rippling or waving, against itself, here and there, as if it were remembering to whom it belonged. Maybe everything's alive. There were some baby mallards, grey ugly, and they were running through the water without any shyness to investigate our human doings. Quentin wanted to ask me, again, why I fucked with every boy in town, but he managed only to ask me if I loved every boy with whom I had sex.

I knew the real question and I placed one of his hands over my breasts. I knew what he was asking and what I could never ask. 'I don't love anyone,' I said that wasn't the correct answer. 'Look at the fucking water, Quentin.'

'Do they have some hold over you?'

'Of course.'

'Do they have some hold over you,' my brother continued as the sky grew darker, 'that you spread your legs for them? You're barely anything else but a child. Maybe you want to be hurt by them or, maybe, cause you're a woman, you want to be pregnant.'

I thought he didn't understand anything about women. No man did. I had learned to pay no attention to what all men thought, but just to take what I wanted from them.

That wasn't exactly it. Something to do with hatred. That this was my brother confused me.

'I'll kill them, Capitol. I will Father won't find out Father doesn't care about anything I know who, what he is . . .'

I know what sex is and I'm a young girl.

'Afterwards he can find out afterwards nothing'll matter cause there'll be some freedom.'

'We'll run away,' I said gleefully.

'I'll take the money Father gave me for tuition. School just teaches you how to fuck like those men fuck you. You hate those men (you fuck), don't you, Cap?'

My fucking and fucking mattered to him: he was a man. A boy-man, my brother, and a man. There's no man who isn't sexually jealous.

'You hate those men you fuck.'

I didn't hate anybody I did I did. I had to be open to him cause he was my brother. Open to what was inside him so now I put my hand there.

'You hate those men, don't you?'

'Promiscuity is basically a compulsive, illusory attempt to create object relationships, doomed to failure, for the promiscuous girl is flying from a frustrated experience with a mother who she feels didn't nurture her properly. I hate Father.' My hand was still there and there plus my hand had something to do with the ocean. It wasn't the ocean. It was a thick pole in the middle of the ocean. I could come around it he was inside.

I couldn't stop this although it was against me cause I had to be open to him vulnerable skin gets bruised don't hurt me again I got hurt before I was born. 'I hurt.'

Concrete.

With Quentin I didn't know who was taking care of whom and I don't think he knew, but knowing isn't the same as or necessary to doing: Openness and the flesh do.

I looked up at him and I could see him thinking and not thinking because he wasn't able to think. Then I could just see the skin of his face. I think we had the same breath, the flesh meeting. I saw his eyes looking down at me. I couldn't bear to see him looking down at me. I couldn't bear anything but exactly what was happening because it was all of me and I didn't know what he thought. His left hand was under me I must have been crushing the blood out of it. Blood is somewhere. 'Quentin, I hate them, that's why I do it with them. That's not why I do it with them. (Fuck.) I don't hate you I do it with you.'

(Afterwards I started to want and I'm not sure if I wanted to want.)

Then I saw it coming out. I've never again wanted to see anything else.

I've heard you can use it as skin lotion and it's good for your skin.

I don't know if Quentin knew (saw) (wanting) even though he had done it.

51

That's what it is: not *it*, but *wanting*.

Quentin was in love with suicide. I got up and draped the wet cloth around me. 'Quentin's dead,' I said. 'Oh, I didn't mean that. You know the first time I ever saw a penis?'

Quentin was looking away from the bank, toward the river. It all looked stagnant, but not as dead as a dead man's face. Or even more, someone who's about to die. Father. 'The first time I saw a penis was Father's. I was in Mother and Father's bedroom. I walked into the bathroom where Father was standing over the toilet, I hadn't known he was in there, and I saw it for the first time. It was standing away from him and looked weird. I had never seen anything like it, some part of the body and yet not part of the body, opposite to it. I immediately knew I was seeing what I wasn't supposed to see and I felt disgusted or frightened or both and I got out as fast as I could. Out of the bathroom. Freud said, you told me, girls always want their fathers, sexually. You think that's why women are sluts, don't you? That's just why I fuck everyone. I only thought that penis was weird.'

Quentin was crying.

'The first time I was ever loved was when I was fucked. Loving has to be fucking. If it isn't: there's nothing. I fucking know it isn't. Mother and Father hate us.'

Quentin said, 'You and I.'

The river looked as it always did, faintly disgusting, only faintly. The warehouses on the other side of the liquid were or looked empty and the shopping carts that always lay like dead horses in the river held the water stagnant in their manes. We walked to and reached the riverbank.

The sky was dark but not so black that you couldn't see. I had never cared about Quentin because I knew all he cared about was death. You can't care about a person who's more dead than a rat or enclosed than a living flea. Father had taught Quentin to want to die. Mother had taught me I should. That's what parents do.

Maybe cause we had done it, though both of us weren't sure if it meant anything, or maybe cause of no reason at all (no reason humans can know), Quentin started revealing facts about himself.

That he had fucked lots of girls. He said. In college. He was horrible to them, physically and, worse, mentally, cause he was so passive or uninterested that they fell in love with him and then fantasized he loved them. Quentin couldn't love anyone. Not even enough to say 'No.' 'No, I will never love you.' 'I held a knife to her throat,' he said.

The riverbank was more desolate than the pond's and the cold. I sat down on the cold. I could see little figures, across the water, standing on part of a white building, white like flesh. 'Who?'

'I've been in love with every girl. I've never cared for a girl. I was horrible.'

'Don't cry.'

'I'm not crying, Cap.'

I say every dirty word out loud cause that's who I am. *I compulsively and indiscriminately look in men for what I miss in contact with my crip mother.* (a book) I say every dirty word loudly, but I can't say aloud what he does to me sexually when he's doing it. He was touching his own cock. 'Are you going to . . . ?'

'Do you want me to touch myself, Capitol?'

'Yes.'

Then, 'Don't cry,' I said as I touched, a rubber, and then his hand took away my hand while, still crying, he watched his cock and my face which was watching upwards to the sky, under him, and I almost asked 'What?' while liquid came out onto my face. I put my hand into it and gasped and I don't remember if he was crying.

'I hated him. I don't hate him. He's too weak to hate.'

'Who?'

'Father.'

'Quentin.' I was still rubbing in the stuff. And smelling. I fuck everybody I can, Quentin. I didn't say that out loud because something else had happened. Somewhere I was open. I gathered my muscles and stood up.

We went back home.

3

'Let's go,' Quentin had said. He had turned back to his cold part. He was warm only when he was wanting to fuck me.

Fucking me (for a man fucking any woman) was destroying what I should be, a perfect enclosure, by hurting penetrating opening me up, all that he shouldn't do especially to his own sister. Virgins have to want to be virgins so only men know and can know virgins whereas we were made to carry life, be unclean. Now Quentin was a cold fuck and we were going back home . . .

. . . down a path where since the sky was now almost black, the branches sticking out could poke away one of our eyes. 'You'll know it when it happens.'

This was one of my favorite times being by the river. Cause time is material. I liked the shapes of the leafless branches of

winter that only appeared when you were right next to them
and meanwhile the tree trunks, trees blown over and cut down
by the storm last year, took on other shapes, always metamor-
phosing depending on the changing distances between them and
you. Dreams emerged as we walked. The river began to appear
the mirror it would be when there was no more light in time.

Time too can totally go away. I know we are really nothing;
that's why I like this night.

I wanted to go back to the riverbank to see whether the
swans were sleeping or were hurt by all the darkness. They
couldn't be dead cause when you or a swan dies, time dies. I
told my brother I was going to leave him.

'It's late,' Quentin replied. 'Capitol. It's time to go home.'

I kicked a stone that being material must be time. My foot
hurt. Time must be antihuman or time was human and humans
were antihuman. Fuck Quentin fuck him fuck him. Cold fuck.
All he cares about is himself. He doesn't know dog shit. He
doesn't know what it is to fuck. He doesn't have any responsibility because he has no relations to the world so he should die.

'Capitol. We're going back home now.'

'Fuck yourself.'

'Now.'

I stood as strong as I could I looked at the water cause I
belonged somewhere. I was confused. I didn't know where the
part of me who fucked every boy in town had gone to. The
other me, new, didn't hate him and hated him because he didn't
love me. (I want to kill you.)

His hand was raised somewhere. 'Are you going like I told you?'

Half of me hated him and half of me didn't. 'I didn't hear you
say anything.'

'Capitol.' His arm swung and met. I looked out, I couldn't see anything, and said, 'I'll do what you want. OK. I'll do what you want.' I looked at him though I couldn't see him, and didn't move.

'We're going back, Capitol, now.'

(I had forgotten about the high school boys. But what I hadn't learned yet was that it wasn't only my decision. The more Quentin wanted to touch me, the more he was unable to touch me, not because of guilt, but because he wanted to remain in love with death, frigid. Nothing in him, and sexual desire wasn't the strongest of these impulses, was going to make him grow up. I didn't want to be in this world where people had no protection against being hurt and I was.)

'You shut up you shut up,' Quentin quickly said to me he quickly came over to me and shook me.

I looked out of my eyes, but I couldn't see anything but my blood. 'Tell me everything,' I said again, 'tell me what you're thinking about tell me everything.'

My brother slapped me.

'You tell me everything you're not one of the bimbos I fuck, *fuck screw*, you've got to tell me everything, you are, Quentin.'

'Shut up. Shut up.'

I opened my eyes and *my* hand on *his* cheek was burning hot
In the dark
we walked past the brick wall of a deserted factory. Along the river. I remembered there had been graffiti. Quentin said, 'You're going to do whatever I say?'

I said, 'Yes.' But I didn't want to go home.

'Go up against that wall and masturbate.'

While I started to do what he said, which was easy, he

stepped away from me and then stood still. While I was doing what he told me, I said that from now on he and I would fuck our brains out with each other and we wouldn't care about anything but physical pleasure and I murmured 'Quentin Quentin' and then I explained I wanted a home Mother and Father weren't a home cause she had decided to be a crip, him a drunk, sex (with Quentin) must be a home.

When I finished masturbating, Quentin took me back home.

4

I want to be dead, I thought when I got back home. Mother and Father were in their bedroom per usual. Since I knew Mother's every movement and emotion during a day, due to her love of pills, I knew she wouldn't be asleep yet. Mother's rigid schedule, as if she were an athlete, was this: in the mornings, as soon as her beautiful green eyes opened, she was in a lousy mood, a bitch. That must be from where I got my sweetness. In the early morning no one was near Mother. Fifteen minutes to an hour after she had imbibed her first meal of dex, she was in a glorious mood, friendly, everything an American mother should be. Now gaily, now timidly, depending on their natures, her children would venture into her room and asked her for favors and for love. Gradually my mother became more frenzied until by late afternoon she was physically shaking, but she never drank. One drink would turn a man into an alcoholic. Mom was only a crip.

(In the late afternoon sometimes she would disappear. We knew she was out gambling.)

When my father returned home and began his (home) drinking, Mother, at the peak of her irritability, took her first Librium. She had scored this Librium from Father who had been prescribed it for heart attacks, though actually, being rich, she could score anything. An hour later, she was sensual and would walk around or sit in her bedroom, naked. She and Father never did anything. That's what Father had said.

This was how, though I wasn't yet grown up, my life was run by drugs.

When I had said I wanted to be dead, Quentin said to me he wanted to go back to Harvard because everything was dead there. Good and dead I said, but he couldn't get a joke up anymore.

Back in my parents' house.

Mother kept on taking drugs, but we didn't think of them as drugs cause Mother was a child, then a crip, because her Librium was legal, and because Mother had always instructed us that drugs are evil. 'One puff of pot leads to worse things.' That's what both Father and Mother told Quentin right before he went to Harvard for the first time, but they neglected to tell him what *worse things* might be. Quentin must do everything in his power to reject the evil pot-seducers who hung around those college campuses like fleas.

Father was too alcoholed up and sweet (naive) to notice Mother was a drug user. He worshipped the ground she rarely walked on. Mother and her friends were too rich for her rich friends to notice that she was increasingly unable to perceive whatever it is we call reality.

She had always been abusive to Father. I will never be like my mother because I hated her guts or, rather, she hated mine. Just after Father had had another heart attack and was now out of the isolation ward, in a private hospital room, recovering or not recovering (nobody really cared), I saw Mother standing outside his hospital door. *Mother was as popular as a young girl.* All the old people told me. One of her girlfriends was saying that Father *had been* a good husband to her.

('Choose a good husband, Capitol. Nobody's going to take care of you but you.')

Mother, in a voice as loud as the other woman's, answered, 'Oh.' She looked at her red fingernails.

'Though you've never loved him.'

'Oh.'

But whatever Father heard as he lay dying (he didn't die that time) (we all die), Mother must have loved Father, whatever *love* is, because the next time Father had a heart attack and this time came so close to death that the doctors told Mother he was, Mother's perception of reality started to decrease. Rapidly. Mother needed a man.

Quentin was going cold on me cause he was too scared to feel to trust. The only safety he knew was to fuck women in his head, in actuality to throw them over to hurt them. 'Keep your hands off me,' he said to me, 'don't you know any English besides the word *us*? Get that cigar off the mantel.'

We didn't know that Mother was crazy only that a great deal of money was disappearing. Every day new clothes, five differently colored versions of the same designer dress or coat, would appear in one of the many closets. Mother owned them all. Mother was spending more and more time in bed.

'I used to hold you like this,' Quentin said to me, 'I wasn't strong enough was I you are the one with the strength.'

'I don't want to be. I want to be loved.'

'I thought you were going to be strong enough for me

59

because I'm not strong enough.'

I could cry because humans are so stupid.

Winter is the most hateful season. Winter is death.

Whenever it had been Christmas or my birthday, Mother had given me a minimal sum of money because she had felt she had to. Now, as ice was living in the blood of the earth, she called us into her bedroom, asked all of us what we wanted as presents. We had never before been asked what we wanted: when the blood had first come down between my legs, I had been told it was carrot juice. None of us said anything. I wondered whether Mother had decided to like me because I looked exactly like her only she was beautiful. I fucked every boy in town.

Quentin disappeared totally from me. For he didn't want to die anymore and something had to die.

Quentin.

A week before Easter, Mother disappeared. She had never disappeared for more than three hours before this. I was scared for another reason. Because I knew.

For a week no one knew where Mother was.

I fucked every boy in town. One of the men I was fucking was a French professor at our local university. Because he was older and dictatorial, I turned to him when Mother disappeared.

I had told Quentin I was going to marry him in order to get back at Quentin, in order to get Quentin back again.

After Rimbaud had informed me over the pay phone that Mother had disappeared and Father was too drunk to know, I followed the French professor out of the artists' bar in which he hung out, desperate to prove his purity, in the filthiest part of the downtown area, three whores too worn out to make it to New York and a dirty mag store complete with flashing neon green . . . followed partway down the street just like the dog I want to be until he turned to me and told me to go home.

'Do you want,' the French professor inquired, 'me to be your mommy?'

'Keep your nasty old hands off of me it's all your fault.' I don't think I've ever had anyone to talk to.

Since a woman has to be perfect intact to be worshipped from afar (that's what Quentin wanted of me), a woman who needs isn't whole.

A week after she had gone, when the cops came to our apartment, Father was still so drunk he was almost dead. 'I didn't do it!' was all he managed to say. The cops told my brothers and me we would have to accompany them to the cop station to identify the body of a woman they believed to be my mother.

I asked them where had they found the body.

'Did you love them, Cap, did you love them?'

'When they touched me, I died.'

Only Quentin and I went with the cops. Though I had never seen a dead body before, I recognized Mother. I don't know what Quentin said when he saw because I was screaming. I don't remember anymore about being downstairs in the morgue. Upstairs, when I asked the cop who seemed to be in charge of her case how she had died, he looked at the case file and said, 'Pills.' A bottle of empty pills had been found on her body. Since both madness and despair are motivations for suicide, I asked him whether she had suicided. 'No.' 'Why?' 'The evidence pointed the other way.' Then she had been murdered. But to prove that, it would take three months until the cops could do an autopsy because morgues are as overbooked as jails. By that time it wouldn't matter how she had died. It's cops' job not to give a shit.

Quentin and I walked out of the cop station through some streets, hand in hand, but Quentin still didn't want to fuck me.

As soon as we got home, I cried out loud. I didn't cry, I cried out loud. I shoved his hand against my throat. Where the heart is. 'You fucking, stinking bitch. If you don't love me – I don't care. I will have ecstasy. Whatever else happens: the whole bloodied world gone to hell. My emotions *will* be free. I don't care what the pain is. I don't care what the rules are. I can't bottle up and maintain all the death you've given me. Death – to not admit my needs. Death – to not fuck. Death – to not feel every feeling there is. I will be free. I will live – you fucker, you you,' I shook Quentin. 'You Fuck.

'I'll live in all my disastrous insane emotions and I won't hide anything like the sailors whom I love live in ships, ships slipping through, hiding under the waves' dragon wings . . .'

Quentin looked at me as if he no longer saw me.

I told Quentin I fuck every boy I can get hold of because I want to fuck my brother.

'I have an illimitable courage for rhetoric and know or care for little else,' Quentin said.

'I won't be dead.'

Quentin didn't suicide because he became an artist. In order to become an artist, he made friends with those whom our general society considered evil, low-life sex industry, gamblers and beauticians. He himself became a gambler. He wasn't yet actually making any art, for he was drinking and learning to be silent.

Writing is one method of dealing with being human or wanting to suicide cause in order to write you kill yourself at the same time while remaining alive.

For the rest of his life, Quentin would drink cause drinking was a way of moving among people without having to touch or be touched. Not having to belong. Ever again past death. Who gives a shit how your mother died or if you have a real father. Only stupid Oedipal-obsessive theorists care about that sort of thing. 'Cap,' Quentin said, 'Cap.' He took a wife, but he wasn't sure who she was; any kind of sex except the kind of sex you're supposed to have in marriage drove him into fleshly hardness. I need anything, anything, that will stop me from living in the kind of death the bourgeois eat, the death called comfort. Quentin said. The ways we're supposed to touch each other and present ourselves. May all that go into silence. I have to be American. My need to be American is to get what I want, viciously, viciousness is sex, to just keep going out. There. Drunks don't need to be touched.

I self-destructed, motherfucker, years ago. Died in every way a person dies except physically, everyone around me died, that was childhood. Fuck it. Throw it away, keep on drinking, keep from sinking into that sentimentality called contact.

Quentin started drifting. It's as if he swam down the Mississippi, huge waves carried him safely to all the places he wanted to see but not live in. Touch, but never hold on. He needed to turn away from everyone and, finally, that takes unhuman stability.

Do you care now do you do you? No man has ever cared for me. I loved my brother and my brother went away. I want to be an artist, he said. Men worship work.

Me. I am my mother.

Quentin was Orpheus. He knew if he looked back, he was

going to die. Looked back at whom? He didn't remember. Maybe a woman. So a writer has to be fucking alone, he said, not to a novelist, he avoided novelists for the ambitious poseurs they are and hated their literary talk. A writer has to be alone because if he really touches anyone, which must involve looking back, he dies. But to be a great writer, you have to perceive. So: you are playing with death.

I can see Quentin in all his faglike clothes, which he couldn't afford, laughing, masses of envy bitterness greed insecurity stubbornness agree to any vice but the truth. I don't give a goddamn what you do, I say, I've learned to be in pain. I am my mother and I fuck whenever a man will have me no man tells me when to fuck and when not to fuck.

MARCO VASSI
Subway Dick

He may have seen her hundreds of times before he noticed her. Every weekday morning for over four years he had reached the Christopher Street station at a little after eight o'clock and stood with scores of others waiting for the train to take him to the world uptown where he spent half his waking hours, sitting in a cubicle, performing obscure and largely meaningless rituals with thousands of sheets of paper. Like the millions who descended daily into the tunnels to be shunted back and forth like cattle, he was usually in a foul mood. But the woman changed all that.

She had just lost a dime in a gum machine, and was standing in front of it, fuming and banging at the coin slot, when he passed by. Something about the quality of her energy at that point arrested him and he stopped to look at her. He drank in her features with a single visual gulp. But the subway car came thundering in and braked to a halt with a sickening screech of metal against metal, and he was jolted out of his stance. He did not think about her further that day.

The next morning, he saw her again, and once more swallowed her whole with his eyes. He stopped, taking a more detailed look at her, scanning her jet black hair, worn in a pony tail, her thin nose with flaring nostrils. Her body was wrapped in a thick winter coat, protection against the February cold. To his surprise, she glanced at him, her eyes oddly troubling, and then looked away.

During the next few weeks, although he made no special effort, he ran into her almost every morning. She was beginning to take on the air of an acquaintance. Once he started to greet her before he checked himself, remembering the strict New York etiquette which absolutely forbids talking to, smiling at, or in any way being friendly to other people on the street. It took him a while to realize that he was coming to relish seeing her, that it added a spark of interest to an otherwise dull and tedious beginning to his days.

By the end of March, he knew a good deal about her. The range of her wardrobe, the texture of her moods, the rhythm of her walk, had all been openly accessible to his study. It was amusing to speculate. Judging from the quality of her clothing, she probably made no more than a hundred and thirty dollars a week. She was probably a secretary. She wore no rings of any kind, and almost certainly lived alone. She used a minimum of makeup, a faint flush of lipstick and light eyeshadow. Her reading taste was random, as she might carry St Augustine's *Confessions* one day and a popular book on astrology the next.

It wasn't until the first week in April that he felt a desire to get closer. The first day on which it was warm enough to do without a coat, she appeared in a tight skirt which outlined a full high ass and rounded thighs, and in a jacket which, when unbuttoned, showed breasts that were just large enough to fit into each of his cupped hands. The thinness of her mouth, at first glance giving her a prim look, now contrasted with the electric sensuality of her body. It occurred to him that it might be possible to fuck her.

That galvanized him into action.

From the status of a charming novelty to add a touch of mystery to his mornings, she became a goal, a prize for him to win. He began to get up earlier each day, in order to shower, to choose his clothes with care, and prepare his mood. He went through the mating ritual which is common to birds and fish and beasts that share the same biosexual heritage as humans. He thrilled to his own sense of purpose, and attempted to calculate whether she might find him attractive. Without describing it as such, he began to court her.

Hers was the stop before his. As the weather grew warmer and her clothing grew lighter, he arranged it so he stood closer to her in the tightly packed car. He was finally able to smell her perfume, mingled with the crisp aroma of her firm flesh. He was able to perceive the delicate whorls of her ears, the slight tensions in her throat as she swallowed. He wondered what her name was. He even became aware of her imperfections, and could judge from her complexion on which days she had her period. He also thought he could detect, from a general looseness and jauntiness in her manner, when she had fucked the night before. One Wednesday, he actually touched her, feeling the rough tweed of her skirt against the tops of his knuckles. His knees sagged and he had to grab the hanging support strap to keep from falling to one side.

That evening he pondered talking to her. It maddened him that, while on one level he knew her intimately, in terms of social intercourse they were total strangers. He had watched her walk across the platform and knew the way her buttocks jiggled as she moved, and yet he had not yet heard her voice. He considered that were he to speak to her, he might find her terribly ignorant. Too often in the past he had desired a woman's body and had his lust shrivel upon coming in contact with her mind.

'What if she is shallow?' he said to himself. And in the end decided not to make any overture just yet.

Wondering whether it was cowardice or wisdom that chose his course of inaction, he worked toward more physical contact without any formal introduction or exchange. The following morning he moved with the force and agility of a star halfback in arranging it so that he stood behind her without having drawn undue attention to himself. Sliding and jostling with consummate skill and experience, he followed her through the densely packed crowd until she stopped at one of the vertical support bars in the center of the car. He eased in close.

It had been subwaymanship of the first water, and no knight jousting for a lady's favor could have performed better. As the train pulled away from the station with its customary lurch and everyone in the car swayed with it, he looked down the length of his body. Her buttocks were less than an inch away from his cock.

'So near and yet so far,' he thought. He dared not move.

The train gathered speed as it clanged toward fourteenth street. It hit a curve and once again the mass of humanity within its iron confines, like fluid in a container, rolled to one side. Unbelievably, and to his stinging joy, the twin mounds of her ass cheeks swung pendulously back and nestled for a brief tingling second in the hollow of his crotch. Fire alarm bells went off in his groin, and he was almost instantaneously erect, the bulging cock straining the fabric of his pants.

She did not touch him for the rest of the ride, and when he got to his office he went directly to the john where he sat, massaging his cock with quiet frenzy until the autonomous ejaculation relieved him of the almost unbearable pressure. The fleeting contact was enough to serve as fuel for the most outrageous fantasies. He imagined that her cunt was endowed with a special heat-generating faculty, that merely to be near it would be enough to trigger orgasm in an army of men. He went through the rest of his day in a stupor, relegating the tasks to be done to his instinctive center, and saving his intellectual ability to enrich the pictures in his mind.

The next day was a Saturday and he was too overwrought to spend the weekend alone. He knew he was at the edge of some mammoth foolishness, but he could not help himself. 'I only rubbed against a woman on the subway,' he repeated to himself, 'I mustn't let it get blown all out of proportion.' But the woman had been transmogrified into an *idee fixe*, and he was succumbing to its magnetic power. To ease his tension, he called an old girl friend and fucked her five times in the sixty hours he had to wait before he would see the lady of the subways again.

And when he did, he knew he was lost. She wore a skirt so tight, with material so thin, that both the outline and color of her panties could be seen. Her blouse was diaphanous, and he could make out the pale gold of her skin beneath it on both sides of the brassiere which cupped her breasts in its white plastic grip. Despite the debauch of the weekend, desire boiled in his blood.

The train moved smoothly, and he cursed the efficiency of the engineer. But just before thirty-third street, it stopped altogether, and the lights dimmed. There was a two-minute wait before the conductor's voice rasped over the loudspeaker, 'There's a train stuck ahead of us, and we'll have a short delay.' It was a crashing stroke of good luck.

His strategy was to try the *mano morte*, the dead-hand technique used by the Italians. The fingers are allowed to rest against the body of the target woman in such a way that there is no suggestion of attack. If she seems not to notice, the pressure can be gradually increased. If she fidgets, he can take refuge in the fact of the extreme crowding to silently plead innocence of wanting to have touched the delicious skin in front of him.

The middle knuckle of his middle finger came to rest exactly in the center between her buttocks, where the skirt pulled tautly over the valley. For a number of seconds he dared not even allow himself to feel the sensation, so delicate was his approach. Then, she shifted her weight, going from one leg to the other, and her cheeks moved, suddenly, grandly, sweeping across the width of his hand. A burbling moan of pleasure chugged to his lips, but he suppressed it sharply. He waited a short while, and then put his hand against her once more. Again she shifted, and again the treasured ass slid beneath his touch.

Now he was in a quandary. Was she unconscious of what was happening and moving randomly, or aware of his touch and showing her annoyance, or aware of his touch and cooperating in the encounter? It seemed as though his entire manhood was on the line. He had waited a very long time, and now was the moment to test their relationship. Boldly, he pulled back his hand and with a sense of historical finality, shuffled forward two tiny inches, just enough to ease the front of his body against her back.

Sheet lightning played over his sensorium. He was as alert and balanced as a man on a tightrope. She might whirl around and say something ugly, something terribly ugly, and inflict a wound on him that would take a long time to heal. Or she might respond to his overture. He waited, tortured by the suspense.

And upon that, quite easily, simply, and gently, she relaxed into her heels, throwing her weight back, and let her body rest with utter passivity against his. She had accepted the touch.

The train leapt forward just as his erection began to poke into the space between her legs. They rode that way until reaching her stop, his cock sizzling with the secret contact in the packed subway car, while his face remained calm, his eyes darting about to see if anyone saw, and finding nothing but the stunned gazes of the city's wage slaves being transported to another day of empty drudgery. When they came to her station she stepped away from him quite deliberately and before getting off looked once over her shoulder and into his eyes. He could not tell what her expression meant.

It escalated rapidly after that. He was soon pressing into her very tightly, pushing his pelvis with tiny surreptitious strokes as she squeezed her buttocks and released them. On some days she wore no panties and he gave up his boxer shorts altogether. He almost screamed the day she reached behind her and caressed his cock with her hand.

They took to meeting at the back of the subway car so she could lean into the corner while he covered her. If he kept his raincoat on he could slip his cock out of his fly with no one seeing. One morning she wore slacks and he put his erection between her legs, coming in her woolly crotch as the train slugged its way uptown. They suffered a near fatal accident one morning when a young schoolboy, recklessly making his way from car to car, opened the connecting door and they almost pitched forward into the narrow platform. He had a wild impression of gleaming tracks before he recovered his balance and pulled himself back in, grabbing her waist to keep her from falling. The boy caught a glimpse of his cock and blinked in disbelief before a slow smile spread over his face and he whispered, 'Sorry to crash in on your party, mister.'

Still, he was loathe to speak to her. 'What can I possibly say at this point?' he thought. 'We've already progressed beyond conversation.' And then, 'Why spoil a good thing? If we start dating, instead of being the most extraordinary experience of my life, she'll show up as just another woman.'

He was amazed that the affair had progressed from discovery to infatuation to consummation to cynicism so effortlessly, and all within the parameters of an eight-minute subway ride.

Yet, what could be accomplished in the crowded car was painfully limited, and he was bursting for a more total encounter. Then one morning, as he waited for the train, he saw her standing next to the women's toilet. She nodded, and he edged toward her. She backed up, put a nickel in the slot, and opened the door, beckoning him to follow. Like one in a trance he moved past her into the tile room. She slammed the door behind them and jammed the lock with a piece of metal.

They were alone in the white gleaming cubicle.

'This is insane,' he hissed, the first words he had ever spoken to her.

By way of reply she peeled off her clothes. He watched mesmerized as the long-desired body appeared before him. When she was naked she abruptly threw herself at his feet, begging him to fuck her. She tugged at his pants and licked his shoes, rolling across the filthy floor. The woman of his dreams lay before him, a panting slut, fingering herself shamelessly.

Propelled from the mundane to the baroque with such rapidity that the pulse in his temples began pounding painfully, he tried to put the event in some context. But it was all exploding too quickly, too forcefully. The girl groaned with desperate want and he could do nothing but succumb to the moment.

The many months of slow building broke in the instant, and for the following five minutes they did practically everything possible for a man and woman to do together, playing out Krafft-Ebbing and the Kama Sutra at high speed. At one point she lay bent over the porcelain pissoir, her face in the water, as he whipped her with his leather strap. Some instinct told him he would never have another chance with her and that he had to get it in all at once. And it was not until he found himself foolishly ejaculating in her right ear that he came to his senses, aghast at the situation he found himself in.

He stepped back and leaned against the wall; he was slightly delirious. The woman dressed. When she was ready, he fumbled for something to say before they left the john. But his eyes grew wide as she reached into her purse and pulled out a police badge and a .357 Magnum revolver.

'You're under arrest,' she said. And added, 'I've had my eye on you for some time now.'

The case, when it finally appeared, was thrown out of court. The city, due to the uproar being raised by Gay Activists' Alliance, was enjoying a spell of liberalism in what were technically considered sex crimes. The judge ruled that the man was a victim of vice squad entrapment, and, as such, his arrest was unconstitutional.

He was so shaken by the entire course of events that he moved to San Francisco. He was just recovering from his ordeal when he learned they were planning to build a subway there. He then jumped off the Golden Gate Bridge.

The woman began another long lonely vigil, seeking sex offenders in the tunnels beneath the city, riding the rails until some man touched her, and then rubbed his cock against her, letting him have his way until he was fucking her and stomping her and pissing on her and doing god-awful things to each of her orifices, at which point she would arrest him. She felt that sex was holy, and had chosen her job to keep it that way.

LINDA JAIVIN
Fireworks

'So, Julia, tell us all about it.' Helen was helping Chantal set the table. 'Every detail.'

Chantal, glancing every so often at a copy of *Vogue Entertaining* she'd left open on the sideboard, shadowed Helen, rearranging, fiddling, calibrating spaces between silverware and plates.

'No worries,' replied Julia. 'But I want to hear what you've all been up to as well.' Chantal noticed Philippa flinch. Odd, that. What had Philippa been doing anyway?

Julia handed round summer cocktails of raspberry puree, lemon juice, Cointreau and sparkling white wine. 'Happy Australia Day, by the way.'

'Ta. Happy Australia Day,' Helen responded. 'May it soon be changed to a more ideologically acceptable date than January 26, the anniversary of white settlement.'

'Cheers.' Philippa took her drink and plonked herself down in the zebra chair.

Helen returned to her task of setting the table. As she placed the final few pieces of cutlery on the table, she watched out of the corner of her eye as Chantal discreetly repositioned them. Helen was not resentful; she was looking for tips. She had resolved to become more stylish in every aspect of her life. Last

Saturday, Chantal had given her an afternoon of retail therapy, helping her alleviate her wardrobe stress by picking out some new clothes and shoes. In the end, of course, it turned out to be more of an update than a makeover. Helen still baulked at short skirts and didn't care that stiletto heels were coming back in a big way – there were some principles on which she would not compromise. And she thought that the thumb ring Chantal had urged her to buy made her chubby fingers look even pudgier. (Well, she thought she had chubby fingers. Chantal had just laughed and shook her head. Then again, Chantal, who was an elongated whippet of a thing, could laugh.) Helen had, how-ever, taken Chantal's suggestion about applying a touch of makeup, even if mascara always made her feel like a drag queen and sometimes left greasy stripes on her glasses.

For her part, Chantal had purchased the colourful new plates in the shape of hearts and diamonds that Helen was putting on the table. Reviewing the place settings with satisfaction, Chantal sipped at her cocktail. 'This is yummy, Jules,' she said, her gimlet eye on Philippa.

Philippa rose suddenly from her perch, as though sensing that she had come under scrutiny. 'I'd better get started on my soup.'

'Want a hand?' Helen volunteered.

'Uh, maybe,' said Philippa. 'I do need some grapes peeled.'

'I thought you got stunning young men to do that for you.'

'How many times do I have to tell you girls that I write erotic stories, I don't live them.'

'Right, Phippa, anything you say,' Helen chuckled, following her into the kitchen. She hadn't forgotten that lipstick smudge on Philippa's neck the day they'd met at the post office.

The phone rang. Chantal patted her sleek brown hair — she'd become a brunette two days earlier — and waited for three rings to pass. 'Never pays to let people think you're sitting by the phone,' she explained, picking it up on the fourth. 'Hello? Uh, yes, yes, she is. Hold on a tic.' Chantal called out, 'For you, Phips.'

'That's funny.' Philippa emerged from the kitchen, frowning. 'I didn't tell anyone I was going to be here. Hello? How did you . . . look, can we talk about this later? It's really not conven . . . what do you mean, gold medal in the Olympic kissing marathon . . .' Philippa took the phone and, with an apologetic grimace, carried it into the hallway. Helen joined the other two in the lounge; they exchanged glances. If they concentrated, they could just hear Philippa's voice above the Portishead CD on the player. 'What were you doing at Nielsen Park? Who says it was me? Lots of girls wear black jeans and studded leather belts. How would I know whose boot fell in the sea . . . Really . . . can I talk to you later . . . don't . . . don't be like that, please . . .'

'A boy?' Julia queried Chantal in a whisper.

'A girl,' Chantal answered under her breath.

'I thought so,' nodded Helen, smugly.

'What? Do tell,' Julia demanded, tugging on Helen's sleeve. Her silver bracelets jangled.

Chantal shushed them both with an impatient gesture. 'Darlings, I'm trying to eavesdrop.'

'I'll talk to you later. I'll call you tomorrow . . . Yeah, I promise . . . Tomorrow . . . I dunno, ten-ish? . . . C'mon, don't worry, OK? . . . I'll talk to you then . . . yeah . . . yeah . . . really . . . me too. Bye.'

They heard the click as Philippa hung up. Julia dipped into the kitchen to whip up some more cocktails. Philippa emerged a minute or two later, looking flushed and bothered, but she walked the gauntlet of their frankly curious stares without explanation. 'I'd better get back to that soup,' she murmured before anyone had a chance to ask any questions.

'Darling, it sounds like you've got more than soup on the boil,' observed Chantal.

'Actually, the soup's not on the boil; it's served cold.'

'C'mon, Phips, fill us in.'

'On what?' Philippa asked innocently.

'What's this about kissing marathons?' Julia smirked, following her to the doorway of the kitchen with her blender of cocktails. 'Don't tell me that was the Olympic Committee proposing a new event for the Sydney 2000.'

'No,' replied Philippa, deadpan. 'That was, uh, Richard actually. Oh, ta. Just half a glass this time . . . that's not half. Oh, okay. But if you think you can make me talk by getting me pissed, forget it. Besides, there's nothing to tell.' Julia returned to the lounge and shrugged in the direction of the others. An incredible banging sound emanated from the kitchen. Everyone jumped. Philippa poked her head out. 'Sorry. Have to crush the almonds.'

'Almonds? In soup? But wait a minute. Did you say *Richard*? I'm sure that was a girl's voice.' Chantal cocked her head incredulously.

'Oh, right, of course. That's just his latest guise. He's writing women's erotica.'

Helen and Julia exchanged significant looks. Helen reconsidered her previous assumption that the lipstick came from a woman. Maybe, she thought, it came from a cross-dressing man. In which case Philippa's sex life was even more interesting than she imagined, and she'd always imagined it was pretty interesting. But *women's erotica*? Was there nothing belonging to women that men were not capable of taking over? Helen recalled the controversy over the politician who opened an envelope marked for Koori women's eyes only. The Kooris feared that the sighting of its contents by a man would bring a curse on their women, causing them to fall ill and possibly even die. Helen wondered why the curse shouldn't have been directed to the man who opened the envelope.

Chantal arched one perfectly formed, pencil enhanced eyebrow and expressed their common incredulity. 'He's writing women's erotica? That's a bit off, isn't it? Besides, isn't that elbowing into your territory?'

'Erotica is all the rage in publishing at the moment. And cross-dressing is all the rage in everything.'

'That's true,' Julia concurred. 'It's a kind of fin-de-siecle, end-of-millennium sort of thing. Did I tell you girls, by the way, that just before I went to China I got a commission from *Image* to do a photo-essay on drag queens? One of my big coups on the China trip was getting a Beijing drag queen to pose for me.'

'A Beijing drag queen?' Chantal was immediately fascinated.

'Look, I wouldn't have believed it either, but there you go. Besides, Chinese men tend to have a lot less body hair, and more slender builds than Westerners. They make excellent drag queens. Really beautiful. This guy was stunning.'

'For some reason, I never even thought there would be gays in China,' Helen admitted. 'But I suppose that's silly. Why wouldn't there be? Do you have the pictures here?'

'I'm still developing them. But I'll show you as soon as they're ready. Together with other photos from the trip.'

'Come to think of it,' said Chantal, 'I've always associated China with a kind of gay aesthetic. I remember finding this book with photographs of those, what did they call them, revolutionary operas or something? There were all these really gorgey blokes done up with rouge and lipstick and eyeliner and leaping about in stylised army uniforms. I thought, how utterly, absolutely *camp*. I showed the book to Alexi and he loved it. In fact, he kept it.' Chantal held her glass out to Julia for a refill.

Philippa breathed a secret sigh of relief. This change of topic was most welcome. 'So tell us more, Jules,' she enthused from the kitchen. 'Tell us everything. And speak loudly enough for me to hear in here.' Julia happily obliged, saving Mengzhong for last. They were suitably impressed.

'A snake-charmer!' cried Chantal. 'How perfectly exotic.'

Helen remembered promising Philippa a hand and joined her in the kitchen. Julia followed with an empty blender.

'That's where the blender is!' Philippa exclaimed. 'I'm going to need that in a sec.'

'Maybe it's time to open up a bottle of wine,' Julia said, rinsing it out and handing it to her. 'What are you making?' she asked.

'Ajo blanco, an Andalusian white soup, made with garlic and almonds and grapes.'

'Garlic and almonds and grapes? Wild.'

After Julia had taken a bottle of white from the fridge, Philippa shooed her and Helen out of the kitchen. She decided she didn't need help with the grapes after all. Just as they were exiting the room, however, she thought of something. 'Hey,

Helen, whatever happened with that letter you were trying to get back? Did you ever find it?'

'What's this, Helen?' Julia demanded.

Helen launched into the story of the lost letter. 'It's so weird,' she concluded. 'Everyone replied to my letters except Bronwyn, a colleague in Melbourne. I was pretty sure then that she'd got the hot one. Very very embarrassing, but better, I suppose, than my parents or that academic journal. Just to be safe, I sent her an innocent little note asking whether she'd received my letter and if she'd be sending me her paper soon. When Bronwyn wrote back, it was to say she had meant to mail me her paper right after getting my first letter. She apologised for not responding sooner. So it's still a mystery. Sometimes I wonder if I wrote that letter at all or if I just imagined it.'

You wrote it all right, Philippa thought.

Philippa preferred to be alone when she cooked. To make the soup, she first took the crushed almonds and poured them into the blender. Then she picked up the bread she had soaking in milk and pinched it between her fingers, letting the milk run over her hands as, mashing the soft pulp, she squeezed out the last drops of liquid. She dropped the bread pulp onto the almonds. Extracting four large cloves of garlic from the head, she lay them on the cutting board and crushed them under the flat end of a large carving knife. They gave in under the pressure with a tiny 'phht'. Separating the lacerated and juicy flesh from the skin, she dropped them on top of the bread pulp and almonds. She put her fingertips to her nose. Inhaling, she drew in the strong garlic odour of her fingertips and then licked them, savouring the sharpness. She turned on the blender until all the ingredients turned to paste. She added the olive oil, a few drops at a time, then in a flow. Finally, she added water that she'd been cooling with ice, a touch of salt and white vinegar, and poured the creamy thick mixture into bright green bowls. She tore the skin off several fat and juicy green grapes, cut them in half, scooped out the seeds and floated them in the white liquid.

It was the first time she'd been able to face grapes since that morning with Jake. After he'd left, she'd suddenly remembered how he'd counted aloud as he'd sucked the grapes out of her. One. Two. Three. It only occurred to her later that there had been four altogether. What had happened to the fourth? She pulled down her pants, bent down and prodded with a finger. Unbelievable. The thing had lodged just out of reach in the cavity just beyond her cervix. She was able to touch it and roll it around with her finger, but no matter how she tried, she couldn't pry it out. Two days later, it was still there. Red-faced, Philippa fronted up at the Sydney Hospital's Sexual Health Clinic. A nurse, assuring her she'd had to remove far stranger objects from both women and men, managed to extract it with a speculum and a probe. Philippa decided then and there that some things were better left to the realm of fiction. Eat me, indeed.

When at last she emerged with the soup, the girls oohed and aahed and eagerly took their places. Julia poured white wine into each of their glasses as they collectively marvelled at Philippa's creation.

'You know,' giggled Helen, 'maybe I'm just a bit silly from all those cocktails, but this looks suspiciously like semen to me.'

'Oh, *nice*,' Chantal spluttered. 'Thanks for sharing that with us, Helen.'

'What's wrong, Chantie,' Julia teased. 'Don't you swallow?'

'Darling,' Chantal replied, dabbing at her lips with a napkin, 'I don't even taste. But seriously, it's delicious, Phippa.'

'It is,' Julia concurred. 'Absolutely yummy. Speaking of swallowing, did you hear the one about the boy who had to break up with his vegan girlfriend?'

Now it was Philippa's turn to choke. Helen patted her on the back. 'Lethal soup, Philippa,' she commented. 'If things continue in this vein, we'll never make it to dessert.'

Philippa, stifling coughs, signalled that she was all right.

'You sure you're okay, Phippa?' Julia looked concerned.

'So what was the story?' Chantal prompted. 'About the vegan?'

'Oh right,' said Julia. 'Well, it seems she wouldn't have oral sex – didn't believe in swallowing animal proteins.'

Helen and Chantal chortled. Philippa's voice, on the other hand, disappeared altogether, having apparently followed the ajo blanco down the wrong tube. 'Who told you that one?' she finally managed to croak.

'Oh, that boy I'd been seeing, you know, the young one. Jake.'

'Jake?' Her voice fled even further down her oesophagus, and the name came out like a tiny squeak. The others burst out laughing.

'It's not that funny a name,' Julia protested.

'So, what's the latest news on that front?' Chantal asked.

'Oh, I don't know. It's off, it's over, kaput, end of story. I think.'

'Why? And what do you mean, you *think*?' Chantal sucked a peeled grape into her mouth and toyed with it on her tongue, popping it out again between her full lips and then sucking it in again.

'God, stop that, Chantal,' Julia laughed. 'You're making me free-associate. As for Jake, he sort of did the nineties thing before I left, you know, saying he didn't really think he wanted a relationship. All I said to prompt this was, I'll write. It spun him out. I mean, he looked so panicked, you wouldn't believe it. Tell me, is it too much to ask for a little commitment? Like, say, a promise that he'd open and read one or two pieces of mail? Is that really asking too much?'

'But I thought,' Helen interrupted, 'that the casual nature of it really appealed to you. That you didn't actually want a "boyfriend" as such. That's what you said when you told me about it, anyway. Did you change your mind?'

'Who knows,' Julia sighed. 'Does anyone know what they really want? I mean, casual's fine, and it lasted longer than I expected in the first place. So, like, it's cool. On the other hand, everything seemed to be going so well. And when it's going that well, I really wouldn't mind, to be honest, if they'd just stick around for a year or two. Like till they turned twenty-four or something. Is that really asking for too much? This new generation really is beyond me. Without a second thought, they can make lifetime fashion commitments, to tattoos, to having earring holes all over their faces, but they can't cope with a relationship that lasts more than a few weeks.'

'Does Jake have piercings and tats?' Chantal asked.

One eyebrow, one nipple, thought Philippa. And a tattoo of a scorpion on his right shoulder.

'One eyebrow, one nipple,' replied Julia. 'And a tattoo of a scorpion on his right shoulder.' She sighed. 'Never mind.

The sex was great. Atomic. While it lasted.'

Helen frowned, more in perplexity than annoyance. 'Sex, sex, sex. Do you think we talk about sex too much?'

'I don't know. I mean, it's not like we're just bimbettes with nothing else on our minds,' Julia countered. 'We all work pretty hard and spend most of our time pondering serious things like, oh, you know, social issues, and aesthetics, and f-stops and there's all your academic work, Helen, and . . .'

'Fashion,' Chantal contributed. 'My mind is deeply engaged with the style issues of the day.'

'I suppose,' Helen nodded. She was well aware that she thought about sex even more than she spoke about it. 'And, after all, we're all planning to go to that Green rally next Sunday.'

'Besides,' said Julia, 'sex is the eternal mystery. It is our most private experience, yet, unless you're talking about wanking, it's always shared with someone else. Sometimes a stranger. As far as careers and other aspects of our lives, well, they respond pretty well to logical analysis. But sex rarely does. So we're always trying to figure out what it is, what it means.'

'Relationships are pretty mysterious too, of course,' Helen added. 'And they seem to be getting more so, for some strange reason.'

'Exactly,' Julia enthused. 'I don't think that either relation-ships or sex were less mysterious, say, in our mothers' time. But at least they didn't have to work out the form of things from scratch, and every time at that.'

'Quite,' Chantal agreed. 'It used to be, a boy brings you roses or sings under your balcony, you date, you establish a relation-ship, then, after a ceremony in which you get to wear the most excellent frock of your life, you have sex. Now it's all, well, arse-about. We jump straight into the sex, and then – if we feel like it – we start worrying about the relationship. And frocks don't come into it at all, really.'

Philippa had finally regained her voice. 'I get to think about sex all the time because I'm writing about it.'

'Sounds like a good excuse to me,' Julia chortled.

'I don't know about that,' commented Chantal. 'You've chosen to write about sex. If you were a responsible, socially aware writer, you'd do, I don't know, environmental thrillers or childcare mysteries or something. Then again, we probably wouldn't be so keen to read them. How's it coming along, anyway?'

'Seven chapters down. Five to go.'

'You pleased with it so far?'

'Keeps me amused and off the streets.'

'Is it all going to be based on real life?' Julia demanded.

Philippa hesitated. She thought guiltily of Jake, and had a vision of red velvet. 'What's real life?' she countered. No one had an answer.

Surveying the table, she observed, 'Well, it looks like everyone's decided to swallow here,' and began stacking the bowls. Julia refreshed the wine glasses.

'I suppose I should go and get the main course ready.' Chantal rose from her chair, took the bowls and plates, and disappeared into the kitchen.

When she emerged, each plate boasted a tangly pile of black squid-ink pasta topped with a generous spoonful of pesto, dramatically garnished with cherry tomatoes, yellow pear tomatoes and a leaf of basil. She served up a large mesclun salad in an emerald green bowl with a sprinkling of miniature vegetables and brightly coloured flowers. A matching bowl contained the rest of the pasta.

'This is beautiful, Chantal!' For about the twentieth time that evening, Helen wanted simply to *be* Chantal. Helen had no trouble turning out nourishing, tasty dishes but, for some reason, they always turned an unappetising and uniform brown-grey (curries) or brick red (pasta sauces). She imagined herself preparing the squid-ink pasta dish for her colleague, Sam. After they'd finished, she would clear the table, still basking in the warmth of his compliments. He would follow her into the kitchen and stand behind her as she put on the kettle and poured the milk into a jug for the coffees. He would fold his arms around her waist and apply his lips to the back of her neck. She'd relax against his body and he'd press himself against her. His hands would move up to her breasts, and free them from her new, daringly low-cut blouse. He'd take the creamer of milk from her hand, and spill the cool white liquid slowly down her chest, rubbing it into her breasts and then turning her around to lick it off her skin. Her eyes would be closed and her neck stretched back. Removing her milk-soaked shirt, he would work his way down to her skirt, pull it down and pour more of the milk over her stomach. He'd lick her tummy and then, rubbing her underwear with his milky hands, start to eat her through her panties, and then those would come off as well. She would open her eyes to gaze out the window of her kitchen, and her unfocused gaze would just register with her handsome neighbour standing at his window, eyes clamped upon her. He'd slowly unzip his fly and take out a dick that looked enormous even at a distance and would spank it until he came all over the window pane. Ajo blanco. She'd reach down now, wanting to pull hard at Sam's thick, salt and pepper hair. Her fingers found his head and curled round the clumps of his lime green pigtails. Lime green pigtails? Sam didn't . . . how did Marc get into her fantasy? Goodness. This was a bit off. She tried hard to reinstate Sam back into the picture, but the image dissolved as the dinner conversation forced its way back into her consciousness.

'For someone who is always claiming not to be much of a cook, Chantal, you've done spectacularly,' admired Julia, wiping a spot of pesto off her chin.

'It's all in the shopping, darling,' Chantal replied. 'I bought the fresh pasta, purchased the pesto. All I did was boil water. And throw two bags of salad ingredients together. I did give the woman at the DJ food hall a bit of a shock though. I wanted to ask for baby vegetables, but my mind was still on a photo shoot we'd done in the afternoon with some local rock stars, and what actually came out of my mouth was, 'a bag of baby animals, please'. You should have seen her face. I think she was about to call the RSPCA. But the dinner was a cinch. Credit card cuisine.'

'Too bad relationships aren't that easy,' Julia sighed. She hoovered up the last strands of pasta on her plate and took a second helping. 'DJ's could have a love and sex hall and you could just rock up with your plastic and say, hmm, could you let me have a look at that twenty-eight-year-old with the baby blues and the three earrings on his left ear who comes with the twelve-month good sex, high amusement and steady affection value guarantee with an optional yearly renewal (for just $124 a year)? Or, let's see, maybe I'll just take the twenty-two-year-old superspunk special with the cute tattoos and use-by-date of next week. They'd pick them off the shelf, slide their bums over the bar-code reader and off you'd go.' Julia giggled at the thought of what her shopping trolley might look like.

'You know,' Chantal began, a little tipsily, 'there are places like that. Escort agencies.'

'Have you ever?' Philippa's eyes lit up.

Chantal smiled mysteriously and sucked up some of the squid-ink pasta through still shockingly red lips. Helen wondered how Chantal's lipstick always managed to stay on. Whenever Helen wore lipstick, it always seemed either to feather up into the skin around her lips, or she'd have eaten it off within the hour. Sometimes, she'd look in the mirror after several hours at a party and discover, to her horror, that, as they say in academe, both possibilities had eventuated: while nothing remained on her lips, a bright red aura glowed around the edges of her mouth. But wait, what was Chantal saying?

'Well,' – Chantal toyed with a miniature zucchini, plucking as its flower with her fingernails – 'sort of.'

'Sort of?' Julia leaned forward on the table. 'Sort of?'

'Well, yes.'

Sharp intakes of breath.

'I was feeling, I suppose, a bit *needy*. I considered my options. I could have called an old lover. But then, that gets so complicated, and you have to do so much talking, and there's no guarantee of sex. I could have gone to a pub or a club and picked someone up. Too dangerous. When I say a bit needy, I mean, really, I was seething. Is this too shocking?'

'I think we all know that feeling,' Philippa replied. 'Do go on.'

'I was flipping through a copy of *Women's Forum* when I

noticed the advertisements at the end where they list male escort services, "sensuous" masseurs and so on. I chose an ad and picked up the phone. No harm in asking, I thought, but honestly I never imagined that it would go further than that. Well, this man answered the phone, "Spunkfest, may I help you?"

'Trying to suppress the nervous quiver in my voice, I asked him to explain how it all worked. He told me the prices and stuff, which differed depending on whether you wanted the "full service" or just escort or whatever, and then asked what exactly I was looking for.

'This was all getting very concrete.' Chantal sipped at her wine and examined a perfectly formed, one-inch-long carrot before popping it into her mouth and chewing thoughtfully.

'C'mon, Chantal, you can't stop there,' said Philippa impatiently.

Chantal smiled. 'I wasn't planning on stopping.'

'I have to go to the loo. Then I'm getting us another bottle of wine. Don't say another word till I get back,' said Julia.

The other three sat silently savouring the pungent aroma of the slimy black pasta, letting the pesto sauce create garlicky trails down their throats and exploding the little tomatoes in their mouths while waiting impatiently for Julia to return. 'Could you love a man who didn't love food?' Helen broke the silence. 'You know, who just ate white-bread sandwiches and refused to go to African restaurants?' A collective shudder went through the table. Most definitely not, they concurred. To revel in food and enjoy eating, they agreed, was to take joy in life itself.

Julia returned with a fresh bottle. She freshened their glasses and sat down. 'OK. Tell us.'

'So,' Chantal resumed, 'I decided to let my fantasies take over. It was just a phone conversation after all. He'd asked what I wanted. Black, I said, thinking fast. Black American. Sailor type. Gorgeous face. Big muscles. Uncircumcised. As large as they come. Into oral, not averse to tongue kissing or a bit of light S&M. With me on top.

'There was a brief silence on the other end of the line. I thought maybe you were only supposed to say something like, "light body hair, big dick". I thought maybe I should add, "or as close to that as possible, you know, a reedy brunette who wouldn't mind being tied up would do". Well, I then suddenly realised that in the background there was the faint clacking of a keyboard. This was followed by a few electronic beeps and some whirring. "Hmmm, I believe that Eddie's your man. He's a black American, six foot three, muscled, ten inches when erect, uncut. Would you like to book an appointment?"

'"Uh, sure," I said. It all felt very unreal. "How soon would he be available?" The guy said he'd call me back. I began to get the jitters. I decided that I'd say I'd changed my mind. Ten minutes later the phone rang and the sound went through me like an electric shock. I composed myself and answered, my rehearsed response on the tip of my tongue.

'"An hour from now?" I swallowed hard.'

'See, Chantal does swallow,' Julia chirped, prompting a round of giggles.

'"Yes, that will be fine," I said. I gave my address and hung up. I went into a blind panic. I tore into my bedroom and straightened it up, jumped in the shower, jumped out again because I suddenly remembered that I'd asked Alexi to stop over after work. I called him to cancel, refusing to tell him why though he definitely suspected something was up, jumped back into the shower, dried and powdered myself with scented talc, and got into my best black bra, suspender belt and stockings. Dabbed the patches of white powder off the black bra with a damp towel.'

'I hate it when that happens. Especially when you don't notice, and there you are, thinking you're all elegant in black, and there are snail trails of Johnson & Johnson down the side of your pits.'

'Shush, Julia, she's just getting to the good part.' Philippa had her elbows on the table, her face in her hands and her full attention on Chantal.

'I realised I was taking ages choosing between the stockings with the lace tops and the ones with the lace-up tops, and I had forgotten to brush my teeth. I flossed and brushed, and then buffed my patent leather stilettos. I brushed my hair and threw on a kimono. I put on some lippy. I sat down and looked at the clock. I got up and changed to a different kimono. There was still twenty minutes to go. I decided to call and cancel – I would pay the guy for showing up, but forget it, I couldn't actually go through with this.'

'It's very hard, you know, imagining you so flustered,' Helen marvelled.

'Oh, darling, I really was. I don't know how those final minutes ticked by. As you've probably guessed, I didn't cancel after all. I poured myself a drink, took two sips and brushed my teeth again. Finally, after an absolute eternity, the doorbell rang.

'I opened the door to see my fantasy come to life. The most extraordinary thing was, he was even dressed in a sailor's uniform.'

'Must be a popular request.'

'Yes, I hadn't quite realised how predictable it was. It's a bit of a worry. Next time I'm asking for an astronaut. Or a parking inspector – surely, they can't be popular. Or ET. Anyway, there he stood, grinning at me. "Howdy," he drawled, looking me up and down. "My name's Eddie and I am most pleased to be making your acquaintance."

'"Uh, g'day," I greeted him, cliche to cliche. "I'm Ramona. C'mon in, big boy."'

'Ramona?'

'I just didn't want to give him my real name. I thought I'd feel, well, freer that way. Names do tie you down. They come with so much emotional Louis Vuitton that sometimes you can barely stand up under the weight. Much less *tango*. Anyway, I doubt he was really Eddie. He was Eddie my fantasy. As Ramona, I was my fantasy too, don't you see? I offered him a drink. My hands were shaking. Perceiving how nervous I was, he put one hand over mine, looked me in the eyes and said, "Ramona, honey-pie, don't be nervous. We ain't gonna do nothing you don't want to be doing. You're the boss lady. And," he winked, "I'm made to understand you like it that way." I blushed. "You are," he added, "one bodacious lady."

'At this point, he eased his own rather bodacious bod down into the zebra chair. You know how we all sort of disappear in that chair? He actually filled it up. He looked down at his groin and stretched the cloth of his trousers over what was looking, even through his pants, like the most incredible hard-on I'd ever seen in my life. "And willya look at that," he said, shaking his big beautiful head, "the little fella thinks so too."

'"Not so little fella," I replied. I thought to myself, well,

Chantie, isn't this what you wanted? I gathered my courage, opened my arms, let my kimono fall open and then crumple onto the floor and my nervousness somehow miraculously dropped away with the rustling silk. I sashayed over to him, and, well, I must say, I did get my money's worth. With interest.'

'Oh, come on, Chantie! You can't just leave us with that. We want *details*,' cried Julia.

'Details!' echoed Philippa.

'Details!' Helen joined the chorus.

'Oh, you know.' Chantal lit a cigarette. 'You know what happens next. Kiss kiss, rub rub, lick lick. In and out here, in and out there.'

'Don't believe it,' Philippa shook her head. 'What about the S&M part?'

'It'd be a lot easier, you know, if you girls weren't such attentive listeners.'

'C'mon!'

'All right, all right. "Well," I said, "as a matter of fact, I do like being the boss. So you, sailor, will call me mistress from now on. Out of that chair, now, and on your hands and knees at my feet."'

'Wait a minute,' Helen suddenly twigged. 'Are you saying you made a *slave* out of a black American man? Jeez, Chantal, isn't that just a bit sus? I mean, when you think of the historical resonances and ideological implications . . . I don't think I could do something like that.'

'Helen, remember, we're talking about enacting a fantasy. With his consent. Not real life, darling. As much as I sometimes think an entourage of scantily-clad male and female slaves of all stripes and colours would suit me, I would probably die of embarrassment if anyone actually threw themselves at my feet begging for the opportunity to serve. So do you want me to go on, or not?'

'But . . .'

'Oh, Helen, let's save that for later,' Julia cooed, refilling Helen's glass and putting a friendly hand on her arm. 'Do let her go on. It's getting *most* exciting.'

'He dropped to his feet, and put his lips on my shoes. "May I worship your ankles, mistress?" he pleaded.

'"Have you been a good boy?" I asked.'

'Where'd you pick up this dialogue, Chantal?' Philippa interrupted. 'You sound like a natural.'

'Of course I'm a natural, darling. So he hung his head and said, "No, mistress, I've been a bad boy. I don't deserve to worship your pulchritudinous pivots, not until I've been properly punished, anyway." I strode over to the closet and took out a suede lash.'

'What were you doing with a suede lash in your closet?' Julia chuckled.

'Oh, right, it was, uh, for a costume party, yes, a bit of a dress-up thing, you know.' Chantal hurriedly resumed her narrative. 'Anyway, I walked over to behind where he was kneeling. I noticed that he'd lowered his head down onto his arms and stuck his arse into the air. I hooked a finger under the waistband of his pants, and tugged them down, exposing his dark cheeks. He was, of course, wearing no underwear. I couldn't resist running my hand over his bum. He pushed it up into my palm, and I stroked the firm, muscular globes. I ran my hand lightly down the crack, past his anus and over his balls. I heard him expel his breath with a little sigh of pleasure, at which point I drew myself up and let the lash crack down upon that beautiful flesh. He winced, and the buttocks contracted in the most aesthetic manner, all sinews and definition, rippling waves of melted chocolate. I brought it down again, and again, until a roseate glow began to blush through the brown skin, and when I felt it with my hand, it felt hot to the touch.

'"Sit up, sailor," I ordered him, and he obeyed, rocking back on his heels. "Does that hurt?"

'"It hurts good, mistress. It hurts real good."

'"Take off that top, sailor," I commanded. He took it off very slowly, raising his arms and swaying from side to side as he went, showing off the extraordinary lineaments of his arms and back. I knelt down beside him for a moment, on the carpet, right there, in fact,' – Chantal pointed to the patch of white carpet between the zebra chair and the dining-room table. Their gazes followed her finger – 'and kissed his neck and back. I trailed my fingers after my lips, digging in harder and harder with my nails until I could see the scratches on his skin and he was beginning to writhe under the pain. I stood up then and whipped his back, and his bum too, perched so pertly, as it was, upon his heels. I had put a Cowboy Junkies CD on the player, and I was just sort of swaying back and forth to the music as I lashed him. It was quite hypnotic, really, and exciting, in a rather mad sort of way. To have this incredibly large and male and muscular creature writhing in pleasure-pain on your own lounge-room floor, totally at your command, I mean, what more could a girl want?

'I ordered him to stand up, to turn and face me, and take off his boots and bellbottoms. Before he did this, he dug into the pocket of his trousers and pulled out a handful of condoms, which he tossed onto the carpet. I thought, wow, and counted, one two three four five six seven eight nine. He's certainly come prepared for some action. His ginormous meat whistle, however, had decided to take a bit of a rest. Time for a wake-up call. I flicked it lightly with my lash. Immediately, it perked up and waved at me.'

'I love it when men do that,' Julia squealed. 'It always cracks me up.'

'Then what happened?' Philippa demanded impatiently.

'I took his purple-helmeted warrior of love between my fingers and, very, very slowly, lowered my mouth down towards it. As I approached it, I could see that tiny nub of pre-cum pushing its way up to form a perfect pearl on the tip, a dollop of cream on dark plum-pudding. I licked it off, and he shuddered.

'"Now, sailor darling," I said, rising, and twisting one of his nipples, hard, as I went, "I am going to give you your instructions for the rest of the evening. You are going to tear my lingerie off me with your white and pearlies. You are going to worship my cunt as if it were the first you've ever seen, and the last you'll ever see again. You are going to lay me down and ravish me, fucking me good and hard and long as only big strong Yankee sailor boys can. You are going to fuck me so that I feel it all the way up to my eyeballs."' Chantal lit a cigarette, and blew smoke rings into the air. She seemed lost in thought.

'And?' Philippa, unable to bear the silence, interjected.

'And he did.' Chantal smiled. 'Two hundred dollars and I had the best rumpy-pumpy of my life. Fireworks! Let's go outside.'

'Oh, they really have started.' Julia was the first to realise that Chantal was being literal. Grabbing their glasses, they hurried onto Chantal's balcony, which overlooked Woolloomooloo. It was a clear summer's night, and from the balcony they had a good view of the bridge and the top sails of the Opera House. Glittering bursts filled the air over the harbour. The city centre, with its narrow ridge of tall buildings, shimmered like a giant cruise ship about to pull out of its moorings.

A spectacular red flare soared high into the air with a great whizzing sound. No sooner had it taken off than it exploded, its sparkling ejaculate dissipating almost as soon as it hit the sky.

'Boy firecracker,' observed Julia, 'of the worst sort. Gets your attention in a big way, then once it shoots its load, it's gone.'

Three soft whistles and now three twinkling jellyfish in gold, violet and green danced in the air, one after the other, waving their phosphorescent tentacles as they leisurely faded back into a pulsating sky.

'That was beautiful,' Philippa commented.

'Girl,' Julia nodded. 'No doubt about it.'

When the fireworks crescendoed with a great, multiply orgasmic explosion that filled the sky with glitter, Julia sighed with appreciation.

Helen was the first to speak. 'You know, I still find it a wee bit disturbing, Chantal, this thing about you enacting a mistress-slave fantasy with a black man. I realise that it was consensual, and that he obviously enjoyed it and made money out of it, and that no sexual practice should be considered unduly transgressive if it is mutually agreeable and, oh, I don't know. Do you think I'm overly analytical? Should I get the dessert going?'

Chantal grimaced like a naughty girl caught with her hand in the biscuit tin. 'It was a bit over the top, wasn't it?' They all sat in silence for a minute or two.

'I'd better put on the kettle.' With that, she stood up and strode into the kitchen.

Helen looked guiltily at the others. 'Do you think I upset her?' she whispered.

Julia laughed. 'Don't worry about it. I'm actually quite sure she made the whole thing up.'

'What?' Helen looked surprised.

'You see,' said Julia. 'I once did a photo essay on sex workers who specialise in bondage and discipline and sado-masochism and they told me they will never act as the bottom for a client. It's simply too dangerous. They sometimes may accede to a request if they know the client very well, but a first time – never. I don't think her sailor boy would have allowed her to do that sort of thing. If there was ever a sailor boy at all, that is.'

'Helen darling,' Chantal called from inside. 'What's happening with that dessert?'

In Beijing, on the same night, Mr Fu's wife, Yuemei, put her hands on her hips and studied her husband with a coolness that bordered on contempt. Her trousers and underpants were pulled down to just above her knees. They were standing beside the bed in their tiny bedroom.

He gestured for her, for the third or fourth time, to turn around and bend over.

'*Zhe daodi shi weishenme?*' she asked, crossly, finally acceding, her palms on the floor. 'What the hell is all this about?'

'*Bie shuo hua, haobuhao?*' he answered, unbuttoning his own pants and pulling out his erect cock. 'Can you keep quiet for a minute?'

She grunted as he entered her from behind. He came rather quickly, and, withdrawing from her, went to the other room to get them some tissues. Not much fun for her but she was relieved to be released from the uncomfortable and humiliating position. He'd behaved so oddly since that last job. If she didn't know him so well, she'd suspect him of having had an affair with that, what was she – Austrian? – photographer he'd had to escort around.

'*Qi tama guai*,' she commented under her breath when he returned, shaking her head and grabbing a tissue from him. 'Fucking weirdo.'

JAMES KELMAN
Jim Dandy

So grateful to awaken to morning, even seeing the state of the dump. Very early as usual after a drink the night before. Such an erection, the immediate need to urinate. Nothing at all in the house bar a scrimp of cheese whose wrapping paper alone turns me off. And black coffee it has to be. Huddled in front of the electric fire, the uncomfortable heat, my trouser cuffs hanging then burning my skin when I sit back. On the second smoke with the same coffee I feel better though it is possible she will die in childbirth and I to rear the kid by myself.

The newsagent has me stay for tea which we sip munching chocolate biscuits, she wanting to find out the latest information. But how will I manage to earn a living. How is it to be done. The child being taken away from me. Or me having to give it away.

Back upstairs with the morning paper and for some reason I brush my teeth and follow with a smooth shave – the Visiting. And I dress like that, then later have a bath in the public wash-house. And consider a haircut.

She is so pleased to see me: Looking so spruce. Proud of me in front of the other women. They see me as a man against their own. Maybe they dont. I nod to certain among them I recognise and also to the man three beds along who wants a boy definitely, if possible. Being told about the state of the dump cheers her up. She really wants to come home, I want that so much I dont speak. Neither of us thinks of returning a trio. On the bus home I think of that. And later I wander round to her mother's with the news and borrow two quid and my dinner. And a couple of pints with my father-in-law. She's a good lassie, he says to me, a bit like her maw in some ways but no too bad son. Always had her eye on you you know, even when yous were weans together. Aye, and me going to be a granpa as well.

Me a father.

Aye. Jesus Christ. Hey Bertie, stick us a couple of Castellas eh. Aye and listen son, dont let her maw upset you. She likes you well enough.

I know that.

Aye. Aye, well. All the best son, cheers . . . And he gives me a fiver when we split, pushing it into the top pocket of my jacket, embarrassed. Claps me on the shoulder. He likes me okay and I like him and the mother-in-law is alright. He knows that because me and his daughter share the same bed sex has to happen. Maybe he regrets all the dirty jokes with his workmates or something.

Back at the hospital nothing is doing. The feeling that they were all enjoying the female banter before us crowd showed up. The looks from the staff. I am too sensitive. They arent really men haters. If you see what they have to see and so on. My aggression just. I shake her hand to leave but she gets me awake by demanding a kiss, it brings us together. Her smell. She hates to see me walking out of the place and when I get to the door I glimpse her, small there, watching me go. Fuck it. The protective male. Is what sickens the nurses maybe. Apart from me. It is just a fact. I cannot change, all that much.

In the local hangout a cloistered male group backs onto me with the stupid jokes and the new office girls and their quick glances at the door each time it bangs open. And the girl in the mirror ordering 2 shandies. Hell of a crush, I gasp to her. She half smiles as a reply. My stupid face in the mirror. I have to get out of this bar and Subway to the Cross. Quite a while since last I was down here but the crowd are glad to see me and I explain the situation and drinks are going to get shoved in front of me I'm well aware. Soon drunk and the bouts of gabbing followed by blank silences.

On the road to somebody's home I let my legs wobble, confide to him supporting me that it's like this man, though I know it comes to everybody all the time I cant fucking help . . . The bastards in their spikinspan clothes. The shit in the back close. The yellow shades of newspaper hanging out the dustbin. The smelly black stuff puddling between the midden and the back close with bits of I dont know what floating about and the dog gangs following the bitch in their maze. The wean. And

But later I feel better – even to bawling, Dont worry about me, jim dandy, just what the doctor etceterad . . . When I overheard someone saying they should not have brought me.

The wives and the girlfriends. I slump in a chair glad to be breathing, to begin a conversation now and then. I am more acceptable, now known as married and expecting our first at that very minute. Yes. Everything's fine. So so. Cant complain and musnt bla. Course I want a dance. Feet still as fast as fuck – sorry. The girl dancing to me asks how I am doing and how it feels to be a daddy shortly and I wink. I wink. Jesus Christ. But she is there to make me enjoy being. Understands all. I see it. The Mother Earth. Someone's wife. Frank's wife. The old mate Frank. I spot him seated and chatting to a young thing – I followed my partner's eyes. And I cant be bothered at all. Everybody on the floor jumping up and down but me now, and some other girl, half hoping by the looks of things. I'm useless but, useless. I just want to be in this comfy chair wallowing and possibly getting to the stupor.

Somebody at my elbow poking me, to join in, Annie the wife of old mate Frank once again, tugging me by the arm: Come on – we're expecting a song from you in a minute.

Jesus. I hear big John singing the Green Grass of Home and everybody silent. The old hometown looks the same. Aye John. Give it laldy. The big John fellow giving it the big licks. Aye John, go on my son. And I am onto my feet and into the chorus with him. And when we finish a big round of applause when I jump to my feet once more but; Just a minute, I tell them, Back in a flash, desperately needing a jack dash.

I close the door. Out and along the road, up the Kelvin Way through into the park, crunching along the low gravel path by the river. At the first tree everything erupts. Retching for ages almost dozing on my feet there vomit I know caking the shoes and trouser cuffs, staggering along. On the hill 3 wineys, 2 males and a female share a bottle, talking; their voices carry in the night still. And asked for a smoke, by a single man on a bench and I give him one which I have to light, his hands dirt lined, warm to the touch. He inhaled deeply: Stick with me big yin, I'll get us a few bob tomorrow.

Black coffee. The television late movie. Aware of the surroundings here I am very aware, myself here. Jesus; the sheets kicked down over my feet in the smelly bed. Yet not the reeling brain thanks to vomit. Good old vomit clears heads. Is my momma and poppa. Too late to go downstairs and find out from the neighbours if I am a daddy. A note would have been pushed through the letterbox anyway. The feet freezing. Lumpen balls. I am stretching beneath this sheet now pushing my legs down my shoulders back as far as they all can go.

I shall be awake all night.

Once dressed I dipped my head into a basin of the cold water. And again. Opening the eyelids under water pulling the skin back on the sockets so the water can enter my brain. And down and out the front close sprinting along the street watching for a taxi as I go and in luck. Yes. Minutes later knocking the door and explaining about the lack of cigarette machines in the immediate vicinity so my apologies but I'll be begging smokes for the rest of the night. Apparently I am very pale. I tell Frank in a whisper I've been spending the past while spewing the ring and that. Thought so, he says, but they'll still be wanting a song off you. He poured me some beer and went to sit by his wife. I remember Annie. All around now people just sitting in couples with the music controlled. Soon as I leave the singing and the dancing stops: I shouts: What's the story at all!

Aw jesus look who's back, laughs big John. He is either Annie's cousin or Frank's cousin. I used to know which I think. Somebody takes records off and puts others on, and slips off her shoes. And a couple of girls get up, dragging their men behind. The dancing resumes. Later on I sit beside the girl I have been dancing with mainly. Sue. I vaguely know her from somewhere. The dancing halts. The bottle is spinning for another song, everybody glass in hand enjoying it all. When my turn comes Sue rises and leaves the room. She stays away even after I have finished.

The old house is still standing. At intervals I start awake and refill my glass if necessary. Snuggling close in on the floor a couple barely moving just rocking back and forth as if dancing in slowmotion. Nobody sings. Frank and Annie, big John and his wife, have been chatting to me about life in general and why me and the wife arent appearing these days. Relieved when I decide to go home. In the bathroom more cold water, and Sue steps in front of me as I come out. I have to go ben see her things or something more records maybe, well okay. I think I might have dozed off on the lavatory seat. I have a drink in my hand. And beside her on the bed thumbing through a big pile of elpees and fortyfives showing I am interested in who they all are and what they are singing, also some photographs. Big John is in the room saying hullo hullo hullo. Yes John how's tricks. Fine and that and you Sue. Hullo John. Back out he goes. The lassie's cousin big John. I never knew that. And her big sister Annie and brother-in-law Frank my old mate into the bargain and this wee sister is browned off as well I know with all the play of the front room and that with men and their wives and the back and forth repartee and the rest of it wishing she wasnt whatever age she is and married or engaged or even winching steady or. And she is leading me on not knowing what she is doing probably or maybe she does if she is at least eighteen or nineteen or seventeen or fifteen for fuck sake no but she cant be or big John would have spoken out which he might still do if I go ben fill up my glass. Good looking lassie Sue. Not bad yourself. Bit young but. Not so young as you think. Aye, easier to kiss through in the front room with all of them there like she says I did but here, and she's wondering what's up when the door opens and in comes Frank after a pause as Sue breaks off to play another record. O says the embarrassed big brother-in-law and mate Frank, I thought you were away home man. At the same time backing out the door to my smile and Sue's laugh as it clicks shut on us. Under orders from Annie maybe. I say to Sue they're probably thinking we're going to the naughty games ben here. Aye, a smile. Well. How's it going Sue. The married man I am shoves the hand up her skirt and upwards without thought forgetting I dont know her intimate at all between the thighs where her warmth begins and all she does is smile a bit Jesus Christ Sue and I am to take her now screw her I am supposed to with no lock on the door and everybody in the front room knowing what's what and Annie most likely egging on her man to come through throw me out etcetera Sue lying back and so making those thighs spread a little for me Christ Sue while she is humming with the song her skirt up fankled and wait I have to bar the door surely. I have to. I have to bar it. She waiting there look, not moved an inch nor said a word but the smile still with closed eyelids and me the pretend the chair will hold the door yet does it open in or out the way for Christ sake back by her side and the realisation but hot too hot and the shakes nervous hands and knees twitching I with effort make contact lips to lips touching no other part of her body I see rising to meet me but I dont but kiss deep and stroking her hair at the nape taking my weight on the left elbow from habit maybe or making up for the first direct thing I did too early on I think yet maybe it was fine if meant to be seducing though Jesus it must have been habit only, and now this kissing on its own even too much increasing the twitching me the randiness uncontrolled and the knowledge of in the front room and all me of before tomorrow and the wife and the rest of it the thought now gone Sue and not a movement and Christ sake if she moved I could do but no I am to act on my own the bad bastard I will be less sense or I can see any

Who's there, says Sue and sitting up placing her hand on my thigh. Me, calls her big sister Annie. We're just listening to the records, says Sue and moving her hand along where the warmth. Alright but will I bring the sandwiches through or what. Are you making them. Yes, what kind d'you want. What kind're you doing, and as speaking this last Sue's hand smoothing onto my balls outlining my hardon there between thumb and indexfinger. And cheese gammon. Gammon for me. What about. And Annie hesitating not saying my name. Gammon says Sue. Gammon's fine. Okay then from Annie. And are you making tea or coffee asks Sue slowly as she is unzipping the fly enjoying her sister and me when Annie answers the young sister has the hand inside the pants pulling out my cock and setting it alight all the time staring at the door question on question so her sister will stay there and I have to put my hand over hers for reasons, and Annie goes for supper. Stretching fully back on the bed Sue laughing to herself and not to me exactly as I realise it is she lying not doing and me in the know means I have difficulties in carrying on where I left off earlier which has to be the case I know. Hand to her breast which she likes but hard to say. Aye Sue I tell her, I know you. Nobody'll come in though. You cant know that for sure. But she says nothing. You cant know it for a certainty. She shrugs, it's okay. But I have lost it and considering a smoke and fresh drink right now she sits up and changes the record jumping the needle slightly, saying she likes this next one coming on and leaning her head on my arm at the shoulder her hand on my chest like the pictures and even tickles my ear so okay, okay, my fly is zipped now I spread her down on the bed again the way she was and. Just close your eyes Sue. I take her tights down so far and the same with the pants in a maybe professional slow way to get her going and that again though she maybe hasnt left off at all just me taking that for granted because it is so with me and the blouse out from the skirtband and unbuttoned just lifting the bra over her breasts and catching the nipple between teeth and tongue and my fingers inside her stroking down and down using my mouth when Annie comes back along with the food perhaps and knocks the door with young sister Sue arms downwards hands holding my head there and so nothing unable to move less I take myself from her and I have to do that Sue sitting up and chatting to big sister and now nude and getting the trousers down and playing with my hard thing all the time asking the questions and as Annie is answering this one she has moved her mouth forwards clinging along the tip with me there back lying out the game on the bed there and no not able to move at all knowing that door can open right now with Annie bursting straight in on wee sister Sue there doing me and me not moving but one muscle if the whole front room wife wean and in-laws all jump in together no I'll still be lying here out the game with Sue and me and her mouth and all of it Christ I'm finished Sue because of you and me.

ALTHEA PRINCE
Ladies of the Night

Miss Peggy had been whoring ever since she could remember and she felt no shame about it. 'It takes one to know one,' she said whenever anybody called her a whore.

She was not certain, but she had a feeling that she did her first whoring when she was maybe less than twelve years old. Her mother, Miss Olive, always pretended she could not remember how old her daughter had been when she lost her cherry. Eventually Miss Peggy got tired of asking Miss Olive about it. She got tired because her mother's only answer would be, 'Me doan member dose tings.' Then she would suck her teeth, going 'choopse' in disgust at being asked such a question.

Miss Peggy knew her mother was lying, knew she just did not want to admit anything. Maybe it was the way Miss Olive darted her eyes whenever her daughter asked her that question that made the lies so obvious. Deciding that it was best to leave the topic alone, Miss Peggy could see her mother's embarrassment behind the shifting eyes and angry voice. Embarrassment was not a feeling Miss Olive showed often to her daughter, but Miss Peggy knew her mother so well that there was nothing she could hide from her.

Miss Olive could have admitted the truth because it would

have made no difference to Miss Peggy who enjoyed whoring and felt a certain pride at how early she began to have power over men. She remembered her mother calling out to her as she played with some stones in the yard, 'Peggy, come child, come go wid dis man. He have money to give you.' Peggy had thrown away her stones and had gone inside their little house with the man.

She had not realised what was expected of her until the weight of the man was on her thin body and she found herself pressed into the sagging bed. She had screamed as he entered her and he had put a big hand over her mouth. When the man had put his pants back on and left the house, Peggy had got up. Feeling ragged inside herself, she had crept outside to her mother. The man was nowhere in sight and she had run to her mother, tears streaming down her face, a five-dollar bill clutched in her hand.

'Is no big ting, chile. You have to do it sometime, so take it easy. I going wash you off.'

Then she had looked at the money that her daughter still clutched in her hand. 'How much money he give you?' she had asked. Peggy had extended her hand and opened her fist to reveal the five-dollar bill. Miss Olive had smiled. 'Five dollars! And is you first time. Well, well!'

Peggy had felt a little better at having made her mother smile at her. She did not really understand how she had managed to secure so much money, but she was happy she had pleased her mother. Pleasing her mother was her major task in life at the time. Mostly she failed at it and waited for the shower of blows that always came with Miss Olive's disapproval. Little Peggy had watched as her mother added the five-dollar bill to a twenty-dollar bill in her purse but did not know that her mother had also been rewarded by the man.

Now Peggy was grown up and was called 'Miss' just like her mother. She felt stronger than Miss Olive for she knew that she was better at getting money from men than her mother had ever been. She only dealt with men of High Society, men who were from the upper classes and who were mostly light-skinned. She also serviced calypsonians from Trinidad when they came to Antigua to put on shows at Carnival time.

Her customers and the goods Miss Peggy bought with her body made her the envy of the neighbourhood. Her neighbours were not prepared, however, to pay what she paid, and they would insult Miss Peggy when they saw her and call out at her as she walked down the street, 'Whoring Miss Peggy!' That was when she would retort, 'It takes one to know one!'

Now that Miss Olive was old and could no longer ply her trade Miss Peggy looked after her. She set her up with a tray and Miss Olive sat outside of their little house on a chair with the tray on a box and sold snacks to people as they passed down the street. The tray held sweets, cigarettes and chocolates. Sometimes when Miss Peggy was in the mood she would even parch peanuts in hot sand in a doving pot and package them in little brown paper bags for the tray. Or she would make 'suck-a-bubbies' — sweetened, flavoured milk squares — in the freezer of her refrigerator.

Miss Olive felt proud of Miss Peggy but would curse her at the slightest provocation and there was never a day that went by when she did not find reason to be provoked. The surrounding area would ring with her harsh voice and sometimes people would stop and listen on their way to the market or to town, but they would soon become bored and move on because Miss Olive always cursed her daughter about the same topics: Miss Peggy's love of men and her love of money. Everyone in the neighbourhood found it strange that Miss Peggy, the biggest curser in the area, never ever answered her mother.

One day everything changed.

It started off like any other day. Everything went as usual until the early part of the afternoon. Miss Olive was sitting outside at the front of the house, minding her tray and brushing flies with a whisk brush. As the flies circled the tray she would switch the whisk from one hand to the other, the tail of the whisk making a massaging sound as she kept the flies on the move.

Miss Peggy was inside the house with a regular, twice-a-week customer . . . the only customer that Miss Peggy ever fed. He was eating goat-water and the smell of the stewed goat meat filled the street. He was the same man who had paid her five dollars to have sex when she was a little girl.

Miss Peggy went outside and asked Miss Olive for a cigarette from the open package on the tray. Miss Olive's answer was sharp and immediate: 'You not tired feed dat man and give him me cigarette? Why he don't go home to his wife and ask she for cigarette and food?' Then she sucked her teeth with a resounding choopse, still brushing at the flies throughout.

Miss Peggy stood in front of the tray, watching her mother for a full minute. Then she asked again for a cigarette and Miss Olive went 'choopse' again, ignoring her. She switched her whisk brush from one hand to the other, indicating she was busy and was not going to give Miss Peggy the cigarette. The nonchalant swoosh, swoosh of the whisk meant Miss Peggy was dismissed.

Miss Peggy charged into Miss Olive and her tray. She bit her and punched her and slapped her. The man ran out of the house and tried to hold Miss Peggy, but there was no stopping her. She picked up a stone and used it to beat Miss Olive's back. A neighbour left his tailor shop and ran, his tape measure swinging around his neck, to call the police. Nobody could stop Miss Peggy and everybody knew it. Neighbours came and tried and gave up, standing by helplessly while Miss Peggy beat her mother to the ground.

Some people were laughing and passing comments as the beating continued: 'Lord me God, is what happen to dis woman?' 'But dis is a crazy woman!'

One woman said to Miss Peggy, 'Miss Peggy, you is a advantage-taker. You is a young woman to you mother. How you beat she so?' She said it over and over as if the repetition would make Miss Peggy stop. It was no use. Miss Peggy continued to beat away at Miss Olive as if she were tenderizing conchs. Then she sat on Miss Olive's legs and ripped off her clothes. As the old woman lay naked on the ground Miss Peggy scratched at her and slapped her. Miss Olive moaned loudly while she tried to cover her nakedness and protect her face from her daughter's nails.

The neighbours found it doubly strange that Miss Olive, known for her fighting skills, did so little to defend herself from Miss Peggy's blows. She could not have done much anyway, but she did not even try; she just moaned or grunted at each blow and tried to dodge them. And Miss Peggy, known for her talk, did not say anything at all while she was beating her mother. She grunted like a wild pig and just kept on hitting her, sometimes holding onto Miss Olive and digging her teeth into her arm or her shoulder. She drew blood, spat it out and dug her teeth into another part of her mother's body. It was the worst beating the neighbourhood had ever seen. It was also the first time they had seen a woman bite someone. It was unusual for a daughter to beat her mother, let alone bite her.

As the beating continued Miss Peggy began to tire. She then switched to using only her head on her mother. She butted her in the stomach and Miss Olive made a sound like a live lobster in a pot of boiling water. Then she fainted.

Still Miss Peggy beat her mother, only now she cried as she beat her. When the police came it took three burly policemen and four of the men standing in the street to pull Miss Peggy off her now unconscious mother. Miss Olive was taken to the hospital in shock and Miss Peggy was locked up for the night in the police station. The next day, when the police took Miss Olive home from the hospital, they asked her if she wanted to lay a charge against her daughter. Miss Olive refused and Miss Peggy was charged only with causing a disturbance.

After the fight Miss Peggy and Miss Olive stopped speaking to each other, but they continued to live together. Miss Olive started to cook Miss Peggy's favourite foods on Sundays. And during the week, Miss Peggy did all the cooking so Miss Olive could mind her tray. Before the fight, Miss Peggy would insist that Miss Olive could cook and mind the tray at the same time. She claimed that she did not have time to cook as she was busy with her clients. She brought in most of the money and could not be expected to interrupt her work to cook.

Now Miss Peggy cooked willingly every morning before she began to work, and if Miss Olive tried to make a meal, Miss Peggy would firmly take the pot from her without a word and do the cooking herself. Miss Olive would look pleased but would say nothing as she went about setting out her tray on the ground outside.

After the fight Miss Olive began to do all the ironing. Before the beating she used to insist that Miss Peggy had to look after her own clothes. Miss Olive even washed all the clothes on some days although the soap powder gave her a rash on her hands. Without a murmur of complaint she would rub her hands with Vaseline after she did the washing. One day Miss Peggy brought home a bottle of sweet-smelling hand cream and wordlessly handed it to her mother. Miss Olive's face softened as she took the gift, but she said nothing. It was, said the neighbours, some kind of peace.

Two or three months after the fight Miss Peggy and Miss Olive began to go to church and take Communion every Sunday. They did this with no discussion between them. People in the neighbourhood knew that although they were going to church together they were still not speaking to each other. The first Sunday they left the house at the same time, each dressed to kill. Neighbours came to their windows to watch Miss Peggy and Miss Olive walk up the street. As the two women passed the little Sunday market on the corner, all heads turned and people stopped haggling over prices to watch.

'Is what church coming to?' Miss Tiny said loudly as Miss Peggy and Miss Olive walked passed her tray of mangoes, 'Lord have mercy!'

Everyone laughed at Miss Tiny's comment and Miss Olive and Miss Peggy edged closer to each other as they heard the laughter, but still they did not speak to each other. Their arrival at the church caused as much stir as the walk through the neighbourhood had done. The minister was very disturbed by the presence of the two best known whores in Antigua at his Communion rail and had several long talks with God in private during the service. But neither the minister nor God seemed to be able to do anything about Miss Olive and Miss Peggy being in church that Sunday morning or any other Sunday morning. Worse yet, neither could do anything about them walking up to the Communion rail, heads held high.

Miss Olive and Miss Peggy continued to present themselves at the eight o'clock service every Sunday. Piously they would walk up the aisle for the body and blood of the Lord, opening their mouths wide as the minister concluded, 'which was given for you.' After they took their sip of wine the minister would surreptitiously wipe the chalice most carefully and then spin it to a fresh spot before presenting it to his more respectable communicants.

Things went on like this for many years. Then Miss Olive died. One morning Miss Peggy noticed her mother had not got up at her usual time and she went over to her bed and shook her. Miss Peggy screamed and started crying and when a neighbour came running to see what was wrong, she sobbed, 'Me mother dead. Lord me belly, me belly. Me mother dead an ah never tell her ah sorry.'

After her mother's death Miss Peggy would struggle to find her speech, then sigh and drop her shoulders and say nothing. She did not even speak to the men she serviced regularly. With Miss Peggy the men felt as if they were taking advantage of her. Eventually they left her and moved on to the new houses where the new whores from the Dominican Republic lived. At least they spoke to their clients, even though it was in Spanish. They laughed too, and sang along with the music on the juke box.

Only one man continued to come to see Miss Peggy and he gave her money every week though he no longer touched her. He was the man she cooked for at least twice a week, the five-dollar man at the centre of the fight between Miss Peggy and Miss Olive. Over the years he came to see Miss Peggy every day. When he got old and could hardly walk he still visited her, leaning heavily on a cane as he shuffled down the street to Miss Peggy's house. He no longer went inside when he visited but would sit outside on the little bench where Miss Olive used to sit and mind her tray.

Miss Peggy now relied on selling from the tray to earn her livelihood. While she tended her tray her friend would sit on the bench and watch people passing by. Miss Peggy would sit on the steps silently, happy in his company. The man seemed very comfortable sitting there with Miss Peggy. He did not seem to need to speak.

Miss Peggy would look happier when the man came to visit her and she would fuss over him and cook for him and go to the shop and hold up two fingers to indicate to the shopkeeper that she wanted two cigarettes. After the man had eaten she would offer him the cigarettes and while he smoked she sipped her cup of chocolate tea. It was an easy, comfortable friendship between the old man and Miss Peggy, still a young woman in her thirties.

Several years later the man died. Miss Peggy found out about it when his death was announced on the radio. All his children and grandchildren were listed in the death announcement and Miss Peggy wondered how it was that a man who had so much family used to be so lonely that he would come and spend every evening with her. She cried sadly when she heard the radio announcement and could not even bring herself to eat her lunch. She went back into her bed and kept her windows closed. Late in the afternoon, there was a knock on Miss Peggy's door and she jumped up from her sleep, almost expecting it to be her friend. She had been dreaming about him and it was around the time of afternoon that he used to visit her. Then she remembered he had died. Her heart felt heavy with grief as she came fully awake.

She went to her door to answer the persistent knocking and saw a man wearing a suit standing on her step. He asked to come in and speak with her, telling her that he was her friend's lawyer. Miss Peggy let him into her little house, wondering what he could want with her. The lawyer explained that she had been named in the man's will. She was to receive money to look after her for the rest of her life. That part of the will, he said, was very clear. He gave Miss Peggy a strange look and began to read from the paper in his hand: 'And for my beloved daughter whom I sired with Olive Barnabus, who is called: Peggy Sheila Barnabus, I bequeath the following . . .'

Miss Peggy went back in her mind to the first day she lay in a bed with the man whom she had come to call her friend. She remembered how he left her ragged inside. She remembered too, how her mother had rejoiced at the five dollars he had given Miss Peggy. She had known deep down inside that her mother had been jealous of her friendship with him and Miss Peggy had secretly enjoyed her jealousy. 'My beloved daughter whom I sired with Olive Barnabus.' Miss Peggy's mind went over the words again and again while the lawyer continued to read the terms and conditions of the will. She did not understand all that he said and could not find her voice to ask any questions she might have had.

At the funeral Miss Peggy stood on the sidelines listening to the hymns. In her hand she clutched a bouquet of ladies of the night she had begged from Mrs Sebastian on her way up the street to the cathedral. Some people in the funeral party knew her and knew of her friendship with the dead man. Others assumed her to be one of the family's servants. The few dark-skinned people at the funeral could be accounted for so Miss Peggy stood out. She noticed some questioning looks and became uncomfortable. It was not a big funeral so there was no buffering crowd Miss Peggy could melt into. When the first sod was thrown on the coffin she left quietly, hoping that no one noticed her departure.

As she left the grave she passed a handkerchief she had wet with bay rum over her forehead, then she held it to her nose and her mouth. She felt faint, but she walked with determination to another part of the cemetery where she searched the headstones until she found her mother's grave buried among weeds and grass. She bent down and pulled up the weeds crowding the lilies of the valley she had planted there after the last rainy season. She pulled one blossom from the bouquet of flowers in her hand and gently pressed it into the sod at the place she knew her mother's head rested.

'He dead, mother. He dead,' Miss Peggy said, bending to pull a weed. She sat by her mother's grave until the mourners had left the cemetery, then walked to the other grave where she sat down. Laying her bouquet of flowers at the head of the grave, she kissed her fingers and pressed them into the soft sod.

'Goodbye,' she said softly, then got up and brushed the grave-yard dirt off her dress and her shoes and set off for home. She unlocked the padlock and threw open the wooden door, letting the soft evening sun into the little house. Then drawing back the curtains and opening the windows she threw open the shutters to let in more sun. Her voice was strong and lilting as she sang, *Why should I feel discouraged/Why should the shadows fall/Why should my heart be lonely.* She paused only to change into her home clothes before continuing, *For Jesus is my potion/My constant friend is He/I sing because I'm happy/I sing because I'm free/His eyes are on the sparrow/and I know He watches me.*

She finished changing her clothes and put her tray outside next to the bench that first her mother and then her father used to sit on as she sang, *Whenever I am tempted/Whenever clouds I see* . . . Then Miss Peggy laughed a sweet joyous laugh. She sat on the little bench and took up her mother's whisk brush as a group of children walked past. One threw a little pebble at the house and shouted 'Whoring Miss Peggy!' before the group raced down the street. Miss Peggy set down her whisk brush carefully. She got up from the bench and walked into the street. Putting her arms on her hips, she bellowed, 'Whore like you mothers! It takes one to know one!'

JOHN McVICAR

Fuck Off

I always enjoyed sex. I still do. But since I tested HIV positive, not as much.

I was infected roughly a year ago. I suffer no physical effects, nor is there any outward sign of the fatal microscopic infection that lies dormant in my DNA and which will eventually break out, laying siege to my immune system until it crashes and my body becomes a sitting duck to the pneumonias and cancers that will waste and finally kill me. AIDS is cruel to the end. When you die of AIDS, your quality of death is trash.

It will probably be six to seven years before my condition begins to show. In the meantime, I remain what men call 'a looker'. I'm thirty-two years old, dark, lithe, vivacious, some might say intense-looking. There has never been a shortage of men trying to take me out, and there still isn't. But what they see then is not what they get.

I was infected by sex, and the experience, or even the thought, of sex is associated with AIDS. In my mind they are connected, linked. This doesn't put me off sex; it just spoils it a bit. I still get horny, I still want sex and sometimes I have it, but, unless you brainwash yourself, what you know you cannot unknow. Even when I come, I am in the shadow of AIDS.

If you are responsible – and I am – you must take precautions during sex to ensure you don't put anyone else at risk. And it is not as simple as insisting on a condom. I like oral sex but my vaginal secretions are infectious so if the man has a mouth ulcer or a cold sore or bleeding gums or just bit his tongue that morning he is at risk. I can hardly inspect his mouth first, so cunnilingus and *soixante-neuf* are out. Then, there are the ones who do it on their own initiative and, worse, the one who will not take no for an answer. There is always the man who is determined to be the one who will get you to like it. Frontiersmen of the bedroom. They think that opening up new territory gives them the best chance of staking out a claim.

Of course, you can always just say: 'Look, I am HIV positive, so you can't do *that*. But it's perfectly safe to have intercourse as long as you put on a condom and the condom isn't faulty and it doesn't split while we are doing it.' If you say that, the one thing you can be sure of is that you are not going to get a fuck that night. The best you can expect is a long heart-to-heart. And you might end with one of those wheelchair-pushers who want nothing more than to dedicate themselves to an attractive victim. They're really yucky. But some run a mile and the next day tell everyone they know. Others, even if they want to, can't do it because what you've just told them is about as conducive to an erection as a good kick in the balls. When you are HIV positive sex is a minefield, and as for one-night stands, forget it.

HIV puts you on death row and booby-traps your sex life, but it doesn't stop there. Take children. I hadn't really thought about it but vaguely I wanted a child or at least wanted to be able to have one if I decided to. Now, because of the high risk of transmitting HIV to the baby, that option is foreclosed. Unless you are an airhead or just don't care, being HIV positive changes your life in all sorts of unexpected ways that are as different as people are different.

One of my main differences is that I am a computer analyst, and a successful one at that. My forte is debugging programmes that cannot meet the demands placed upon them, or are crashing for the multitude of reasons – including computer viruses – that can cause software to go down. To do what I do, you have to learn to think clearly and rigorously. Now, it is not uncommon for those infected by HIV to think very carefully about their life and, given my work, it was almost certain that I would. I did it, not with a concern to identify the 'if only' clauses, nor did I have any wish to find a scapegoat, and it certainly wasn't a morbid preoccupation, or for that matter an evangelical quest for some AIDS-intensified meaning of life. It was just a search for lessons.

I grew up in Dulwich. My mother is a primary-school teacher and my father a solicitor. They had two other children – I have two brothers, both younger than me. Probably as a result of growing up in the sixties, I knew about sex long before my mother ever mentioned it. I also masturbated from an early age and I could always climax even as a child. I wasn't told by anyone or shown; I just discovered it. Orgasm, then, was never a problem for me, although there were the usual hiccups with men whom I thought I fancied, but found out in bed that I didn't. I had a couple of steamy scenes with other girls when I first went to secondary school but there was nothing particularly crushy about them. Both times we were close friends who occasionally helped each other to come. As for boys, I hardly did anything with one until I was thirteen, and then it was all quite sensible and normal. There was, however, one sexual experience when I was twelve that, while it never went beyond the petting stage, was seminal to say the least.

It involved a much older boy at the school. He was in the sixth form and quite unapproachable to a lowly squid in the second year. Somehow I kept catching his eye and while I had no idea what it was, I knew there was some secret between us. I think he must have engineered it, but one day just after hockey he called me round behind the changing rooms. I was milling around with some other girls, and he caught my eye and jerked his head at me to follow him. I did with my heart pounding, knowing something was going to happen. He had his back to me as he went between the sheds to where they once used to dump coal. When he turned he had his penis out; it was sticking up out of his open trousers.

He said, 'Have you ever done this before?'

I was just looking wide-eyed at his penis and I shook my head in wonderment. I had never seen anything like it. I had seen my brothers', glimpsed some men and dogs and things but nothing like this. It was glistening and shiny and wanting to be touched. I don't know if I put my hand on it first or he did it for me but I know that he held his hand over mine and showed me how to wank him. I remember wanting to do it on my own. I knew I could do it right. As I did it, I thought of it gliding inside me but he didn't try to do anything at all to me. He just stood there groaning slightly, his jaw clenched and his eyes half closed. I kept looking at his face and, of course, he suddenly started grunting and quivering and out shot what the girls at school used to call 'baby juice'. The first time this happened I pulled my hand away in shock and he roughly grabbed it and put it back.

All he said to me as he zipped himself up was, 'Now don't tell anyone, will you.' I said 'No,' but, of course, I couldn't wait to tell my best friends. This sort of encounter was repeated sporadically with the same boy over a period of about nine months, then he left and I never saw him again.

Soon afterwards I began going out with boys and I took to sex like a bird to the air. The experience with the sixth former, though, gave me a bead on sexual relationships that made sex the purpose of the relationship rather than the relationship being the purpose of the sex. That isn't to say the relationship was unimportant, it is just that my first sexual encounter made the raw physical aspect of male sexuality extremely erotic for me and I have always been more inclined to sleep with a man I fancy, but don't particularly like, than go out with a man whom I like but don't fancy.

I have never been sex-mad in the way that some women and some men are, although I suspect that men who are like that are doing it to feed their ego, not satisfy their sex drive. In fact, I think the way my sexuality was programmed, more towards orgasm than 'love', was rather healthy. It certainly protected me from the problems of romanticizing sex: even when it was especially intense and enjoyable, that didn't seem to me a reason to make the relationship in which it occurred the baseline of your life. People – women more than men – overload sex; however good the sex, it can't carry a happy-ever-after relationship or even necessarily provide a solid framework for bringing up children. I have always looked askance at the idea that sexual enjoyment is a man's entrance ticket to centre stage of a woman's life.

Obviously, as I look back, I am picking out that part of the picture that I now feel most reflects me. At the time there were lots more brush-marks on the canvas. As a teenager, for example, I was full of the usual dim-witted contradictions. I took on a lot of the conventions and, in my late teens and early twenties, I tried out most of what a woman is supposed to do. I fell in love, I was jealous, possessive, attached great importance to fidelity – but my heart was not in romance, and even at my most committed there were encounters with other men that were sex for its own sake and very little else. Around my twenty-first birthday, I began facing up to the double standards that were informing my behaviour with men and I started bearing down on my own hypocrisy.

By the time I left university, ideally sex for me was a means to have an orgasm with a man whom I temporarily liked and fancied; it certainly wasn't for having babies, binding you together for life, or even committing you to being faithful to whoever you were doing it with. I never formalized these ideas, but I remember bulldozing a girlfriend who was banging on about sex being sacred because it created life. I hooted at her that the average person has sex twice in a lifetime to procreate and while the other times may not all be for pleasure, they were nothing to do with babies.

My career took off in the mid-eighties and I began earning huge bonuses on top of a good basic salary. My confidence in running my sex life pretty much as it suited me was boosted by having the means to be completely independent of men. I wasn't constantly hopping from bed to bed but if the fancy took me I did and, if at the time I was involved with someone else, I didn't have any guilts about it. I wasn't married and I wasn't about to get married. I ran my sex life as I did the other parts of my life – on my terms. Those terms included not hurting or exploiting anyone and not trying to impose my standards on others. And what was sauce for the goose was sauce for the gander – any lover who thought that sexual intimacy gave him the right to impose his standards on me was shown the door.

Of course, it wasn't always easy. Most men loathe the idea of their woman having sex or merely reserving the right to have sex with another man. In my opinion their attitude is nothing to do with their needing faithfulness to feel secure about the baby being theirs, and it's fatuous to say they regard women as their property, Well, I know that some men do but I don't mix with them. It is much more about their competitive attitude towards each other. Women are one of the prizes men compete for and I think most of them would much rather be beaten up by another man than cuckolded. You see the same competitiveness in their penis fixation. They desperately want them bigger but more to impress other men than to please women.

I was a free-thinker on sex, who didn't have to do too much thinking about it, since as far as I was concerned I'd got what suited me. In the back of my mind was the vague notion that around my early thirties I'd look around for some man to have a baby with and settle down and stop having affairs or at least be a bit more discreet about them. In the meantime, my love life, while active, was still secondary to the main focus of my life – my work. As a consequence, men were nothing like the problem that, almost without exception, they were to my female friends.

About this time the first tranche of anti-sex AIDS propaganda was issued. Icebergs and tombstones and Just Say No messages and lots of stuff about staying faithful to one partner being the best protection. The big lie was to say that, as far as the risk of contracting AIDS was concerned, every time we had sex with someone we were having sex with everyone they had previously had sex with. In fact, once a person had an AIDS test, as far as that disease was concerned his or her previous sexual history was erased. The thrust of these campaigns was as sick and horrible as the disease. One suspected that the dreadful people responsible for them were rather pleased with AIDS; it was another chance for them to do what they so enjoyed doing — which was to restrict, and meddle in, the sexual lives of others.

In contrast, the message from the pro-sex camp was that, if we all used condoms, the disease would be contained. Apart from the fact that the policy could not and has not worked, my problem with it was that I could not abide condoms. That first sexual encounter had imprinted itself on to my sexuality, and a lot of what I love doing in sex is spoilt by a condom. Apart from my own aversion to them — I am not alone in this — there was also the problem of accidents and faulty ones. As I didn't like the solution being recommended, I gave quite a lot of thought to the alternatives.

Testing is the best method but it has two disadvantages. The HIV antibodies that the test screens for do not appear in the bloodstream in detectable quantities until three months after infection, although the person is still infectious to others. This means that if someone has had unprotected sex in the last three months the test can give a false and, possibly, dangerous reading. So the safest strategy would be to use condoms for the first three months. However, as many of my affairs didn't last that long, this was a counsel of perfection that unless the man insisted otherwise I chose not to follow. I merely insisted on a lover taking a test as soon as we began our affair and left the three-month risk in the lap of the gods.

Incidentally, I began by using the NHS special clinics, but they make such a palaver of it that I got driven into going private. They are reliable enough but not many of the London ones do a same-day service, and none of them will give you the result over the phone. The last straw for me was having to submit to obligatory counselling, which is done by these dreary social-worker types who just got me into a bate. After one particularly infuriating session, I found a Harley Street doctor who was quite happy to give the result of the test over the phone two hours after he'd taken a blood sample.

The other disadvantage of testing as a means to protect oneself from HIV infection is that it cannot work if people are dishonest about their sexual contacts. And most sexually active people are dishonest about sex. Unfortunately for me, my sexual path had bypassed this dishonesty, so I had no appreciation of the difficulty most people have in being honest about sex. Apart from when I was a teenager, I had not made those impossible pacts that lovers usually make with each other to remain faithful and to be honest about any infidelity. Naturally, as I saw my friends doing it, I was aware of the tortuous hypocrisies that people go through to be unfaithful without ever letting on to their partner or, in some cases, even admitting it to themselves. But this was other people, not me. I was like a non-smoker who knows that smokers find it difficult to give up the habit, but has no understanding of how difficult it is. This ignorance was also compounded by a naïve belief that people's awareness of the threat of AIDS no longer makes it tolerable to practise the kind of deceit that is as much a part of sex as the act itself.

In August of 1989, my friend Angela took me to a rehearsal of the Ballet Rambert. She was doing some PR work for Sadler's Wells and said I might find it 'interesting' – meaning I might meet some dishy men. It was all that one would expect from countless TV documentaries that I've seen over the years. A spartan barn of a gymnasium with an upright, hollow-sounding piano and lots of dancers stretching and leaping around all over the place. But the men were delicious and, transparently, as Angela said, they weren't all gay. Whether they were gay or not I did rather look at their bulges. They have cod-pieces under their tights, but what they leave to the imagination is a pleasure to imagine. Angela kept elbowing me in the ribs and giggling. Unfortunately, I didn't just look, I also fell head over heels in lust.

Gabriel could have leapt out of one of those Häagen-Dazs ads. His brown eyes smouldered, his thick, black hair glistened and he moved like a dream, all ripply and flowing and expressive. That evening a gang of us went to Joe Allen's in Covent Garden. I was bubbling over with excitement and, as I was probably earning more than all of them put together, I treated everyone to massive exotic salads and as much wine as we could drink. We were laughing and talking loudly, with lots of touching and leaning close to make asides. Friends of the dancers kept coming over to say hallo, and the table was like a ballet of conviviality. In the middle of all this exuberance I leant over to Gabriel and asked, 'You are coming back with me afterwards?' And he did. And he definitely wasn't gay. In fact, that was the one thing I asked him and he replied that despite what people believed most male dancers were not gay and he wasn't one of those who were.

He was big but it wasn't that so much as the way he domi-
nated and teased me. On the bed, he kept touching me with it
and saying, 'You want me to knob you, don't you?' He made me
say it, too. He made me say it over and over again. He would
push inside me just a little, then hold me so that I couldn't move
and whip me into a sexual fervour with his comments and
descriptions of what he was going to do to me. He would talk
me into coming and just hold and watch me as I did. After he'd
finished with me, I felt like I was wafting in and out of an erotic
coma.

In the morning, I told him that he could not catch anything
from me because I had regular AIDS tests; I also said that my
going with men was conditional upon them having the test. He
listened with his naughty-boy eyes flicking over my body and a
wry confident grin on his face, but he was perfectly amenable to
being tested. He also had the wit to point out that I'd had
unprotected sex with him without a test. I said he was an exception and that we'd soon find out if there had been a risk. It transpired that he had been having an on-off affair with one of the
dancers – female – for about a year or so and had not been with
anyone else during that time. It was all perfectly straightforward: he had a test that afternoon – negative – and we began
to see a lot of each other.

I knew it wouldn't last and didn't particularly want it to, but I
knew I'd enjoy it while it did. In getting the AIDS stuff out of
the way, I also established the ground rules by which I have
affairs with men. I told Gabriel that what I did when I wasn't
with him was my business. I said that I don't do confessions but
if I jumped in bed with someone who hadn't had the test and
had unprotected sex – like I had with him – I would tell him

and we'd have to use condoms for three months. I said I expected him to extend the same respect to me. I remember kissing him and saying, 'You gorgeous man, I can live with jealousy but not AIDS.'

Real fidelity is honouring your commitments. I was true to him and I thought he was to me.

Gabriel was two years younger than me and, while he was intelligent, he had never disciplined his mind the way he had his body. Sometimes I would become snappy, even ratty, with his half-baked and often received opinions; in turn he would often lapse into the sulks. But we kept it together. About seven months after we met, he came round to my flat without phoning first, which was unusual; he was agitated, looked haggard and was smoking intensely. One of the things I admired about him was the way he could smoke and drink, take whatever drugs were around, even binge on things, then when it suited him stop instantly. The way he was smoking this evening nagged at me but, since I had nothing to hang it on to, it had no significance.

What he had to say came out in a rush. He had been having sex with another male dancer who had told him that afternoon that he was HIV positive. I felt no shock, no anger, no panic. My whole being seemed to dedicate itself reflectively to working out the import of what he'd said. I felt icy and still. In a microsecond, long before he'd finished speaking, my mind had run through the disparate implications of what he was saying. I knew that, if he had it, the odds were that I did too, as our sex was often quite rough. If I did have it, then according to when I contracted it two other men could be at risk. I knew we would have to wait until the morning to find out. I also knew what it was in him that I had misjudged and why, but most of all I knew it was my fault. I had refused to read the writing on the screen.

Despite Gabriel's artistry and bohemian lifestyle, he did not trust himself and was cautious about what he revealed; then there was his over-sensitivity to criticism, even when he rejected the criteria on which it was based. His dancer's affectations were just that — affectations; under pressure he defaulted to the narrow-minded bigotry of his lower-class, albeit respectable, background. Lust, like love, lends enchantment to the view; I hadn't seen his limitations because I hadn't wanted to.

At that moment, however, my clarity of vision and speed of thought put far more than Gabriel's limitations in relief. As I scanned back over our time together, I could see that because he lived a lie much of what he'd been with me had been a lie. A white lie, often a charming white lie, but still a lie. Even now, he was blundering around in guilt and regret like a panicky rat in a closed-off maze, not looking for understanding but merely searching for a gap in the hedge.

There was no point in asking him why he had kept his homosexual fling a secret or even why he'd been unable to adhere to the one thing I'd asked of him, which was to tell me if he had unprotected sex. That was the agreement. Such a simple rule, which he'd understood at the time and agreed to follow. But it was in an area — sex — where the real rule was that you lived by double standards. Gabriel's kind upheld fidelity and faithfulness but accepted that as long as you didn't get found out it was OK to connive, cheat and lie to get whatever you could on the side. Of course, when he'd become a ballet dancer, Gabriel had embraced sexual openness but that was merely another convention that he paid no more than lip service to in order to be accepted by his new pack.

He sobbed and begged me to forgive him, which stirred an obligation in me to show some pity. I put my arms around him, not in affection and certainly not lust – that had been cauterized forever by his confession – but in compassion. His sexual morals were deformed. His upbringing had shackled him to an ugly and deceitful approach to sexual relations that opened the door to AIDS. As I dutifully held him, I felt disgusted with myself for letting this moral deformity into my life. The fantasy flitted into my mind of putting my hands round his neck and slowly ridding the world of his malignant character.

Of course, he misinterpreted my embrace and thought I was literally taking him back into my arms. I pulled away from him and shuddered at this obscenity of nature. I sent him home and I haven't seen him since, nor will I by choice. We have spoken twice on the phone. The first was the next morning to arrange our tests – I paid for his, of course. The second time was about a month later. He was drunk or on something and said, 'Look Sarah, we've both got it, so we are not a risk to each other. Why can't we make the best of it and enjoy each other the way we used to?'

I just said, 'Fuck off, you germ.'

That is how I think of him and that's what he is – a germ. He not only infected my body but also my mind. I now lie about sex; I now practise the exact same deceit about sex that caused me to catch AIDS. Of course, unlike the *Germ*, I take precautions to ensure I don't infect anyone else. Nevertheless, in principle, the deceit is just the same. He lied to keep his bisexuality a secret, I lie because I don't want men to know I am HIV positive. I tried being honest and it didn't work. So I am not only HIV positive, my sex life is contaminated with the sort of deceit that I despise and, if that isn't enough, I also have to use fucking condoms.

FAY WELDON
And Then Turn Out the Light

In Newcastle, New South Wales, they have the highest hysterec-
tomy rate in the entire world. There, healthy organs are
whipped out by eager surgeons in the nick of pre-cancerous
time. There is even a special laboratory, a special building,
where removed organs are stored, in a frozen state, so that students can examine them at their leisure. See, a perfect ovarian
duct! See the tiny budding eggs: each one the potential half of a
human being, that could have loved and been loved, and laughed
and wept and planned and hoped. But what use is half a human
being: the ageing female organ, everyone knows, no longer
attracts the male. So whip it out: cut, nick, clip and sew:
implant a source of oestrogen and the organ's owner is good as
new: a reliable baby-sitter for its grandchildren, not bleeding,
given to moods, hot flushes or the distressing growth-gone-wild
of cancer. It's all in the best interests of the community: the
operation prolongs life. Statistics prove it.

And here a dozen frozen wombs! Young man, young woman,
you, who have no thought of death; of such thawing flesh was
your nursery made. Perhaps here, on the slab, is the very one?
Did not Mother have her womb out, only last year? And was the

surgeon once her lover, when you were ten and she was young? You can thaw and re-freeze the organs only two or three times — after that the texture goes. Never mind: it has served its purpose. Grown a baby or two, and helped in the education of a new race of doctors. Doctors are good people. They do what they can. They have to live, of course, and the more wombs, ovaries and so forth they remove in a year, the richer they are, and the more peacefully the ponies of their little daughters graze in the escarpments that ridge the coast north of Sydney.

Loss and gain, loss and gain! Your loss, my gain.

Tandy was a doctor's daughter herself: born and bred in Newcastle. As a child she had a pony called Toddy. Doctors' daughters experience more sexual assaults at the hands of doctors than do the daughters of men in other professions. Now there's an odd statistic! What can be the look in the doctor's daughter's eye? What can the glint be, that cries out for ravishment at the hands of such normally respectable folk? Oh Daddy, Daddy, pay me some attention! No matter what, no matter how unwelcome: anything will do! Anything! Are we to believe it?

Or perhaps doctors' daughters just go to the doctor more often than other women? Surely that must be it. Doctors don't usually treat members of their own family.

When Tandy was twelve, a paediatrician laid her on her back, divided her legs, put his hand up between them, tweaked and poked and explained that the sudden, terrifying bleeding signified only a ruptured hymen.

'Good thing we live in a civilised country,' he said. 'No blood-stained wedding sheets required for our little Tandy. It's riding that does it!'

'But Toddy's such a well-mannered little horse,' said Mandy, Tandy's mother. She had wide bright eyes and a gentle manner, as did her daughter.

'Even so,' said the paediatrician, 'a sudden bump with the legs parted, and there you are. Virgin no more.'

He came to dinner sometimes. His hair was turning grey. Tandy thought he must have told his wife – a tall woman with hooded eyes – and she no doubt had told her friends. Virgin no more!

When she was fourteen and at school Tandy kept company with a fifteen-year-old boy, John Pierce. Such associations were frowned upon. It was back in the fifties, after all, and Tandy wore a gym slip and a panama hat. They loved each other, filled each other's skies with a kind of pink sunrise glow.

'Something's happened to that girl,' remarked her father, the doctor, over breakfast.

'Oh my God!' said her mother.

John Pierce's mother complained to the school that Tandy Watson was preventing her son passing his exams. Authority had already observed their affection: the way they held hands, leant into each other. The school buzzed with rumours that they'd gone the whole way. Tandy's mother's eyes widened with alarm and fear as the police were mentioned: the possibility of punitive action. Fourteen-year-old girls, in those days, were supposed to be virgins, and anyone who suggested otherwise to them went to prison.

'Good God,' said Tandy's father, 'let's find out. Open your legs, girl.'

Tandy did, up on the patients' couch. Tandy's father frowned, paled, consulted with Tandy's mother.

'But, darling,' said Tandy's mother, 'that business with the horse a couple of years back — had you forgotten?'

He had, of course.

'Goddamned horse,' he said. 'Did you or didn't you, girl?'

'I didn't,' she said. 'I didn't, I didn't and neither did he.'

'Why couldn't you say so before?' he demanded, irate, although nobody had thought to ask her before. 'I believe you, girl. Get your pants back on.'

And she did, and her mother, lying, announced her *virgo intacta* to all the world, but Tandy lost all interest in John Pierce, and had to think hard before saying anything to her father. Nothing seemed to come naturally any more, between him and her. Perhaps he knew it: he hrummed and hraaed a lot when Tandy was in the room.

Tandy wanted to be a doctor but her father said it wasn't a fit profession for a girl: there were too many terrible sights to be seen, for anyone in that line of business. Tandy went to college to do English literature.

The college gave all its students twice-yearly medical check-ups. The rather elderly doctor always had Tandy strip right off so he could palpate her breasts. He gave her internal examinations, too, putting his hand first into a thin rubber glove, then into her to pinch and peek and pry. And then a rectal examination with a light at the end of a metal tube. She'd scream and he'd say crossly, 'just relax.' Doctors always seemed to Tandy to be rather cross. After the fourth of these examinations she checked with her friend Rhoda, who had no breasts to speak of, and discovered that Rhoda was allowed to keep her clothes on and that her inside could do without checking, so after that Tandy ignored the official reminder cards and left her health to luck rather than science.

She raised the question of medical training once more at home. She thought there should be more women in the medical profession.

'Good God, girl,' said her father, 'the thing to do is to marry a doctor, not *be* one. A good doctor's wife is almost as valuable in the community as a good doctor.'

Tandy's mother had good solid-thighed legs, from running up and down stairs to answer the telephone. And indeed there was nothing she didn't know about the early symptoms of mumps, measles and chicken pox, and the management of these diseases. She had a fair, Northern skin, and died rather suddenly from a melanoma, a cancer common in Australia. A mole on her hand changed shape and size and her husband was too busy to notice it until it was too late to be operable. He had become an excellent golfer, and was playing in an interstate competition, and had a lot on his mind.

*

'Even if you had noticed,' said his doctor friends, comforting him, for he was very distressed, 'chances are she wouldn't have made it. And how old was she?'

Forty-nine, and coming up to the menopause. Better out of the way, the implication was. After the forties, from a gynaecologist's point of view, it's downhill all the way, tinker as you may with a woman's insides. Bleeding and drying and fibroids and cysts and backache – you name an unhealthy state, the woman has it. She comes to you complaining, fills the surgery with dulled voice and reproachful eyes. The age of child-bearing is past. All meaning gone, for a woman.

Tandy's father married his receptionist, who was only twenty-nine, and adored him, and raised another family.

'I want to be a doctor,' reiterated Tandy. 'No daughter of mine . . . ' reiterated her father. 'I'm not paying for that. Why don't you be a nurse?'

So she did. One year into her nursing course she became pregnant by a medical student who put his faith in coitus interruptus and could not marry her, for various reasons, and Tandy had to have an abortion; at that time a firmly and criminally illegal act. She went to see the local abortionist, a general practitioner known to feel sorry for girls in distress, when she was eight weeks pregnant. He would not accept money, saying he performed these operations from principle, rather than monetary gain: he believed in sex as the great emotional and physical cure-all, and required her to sleep with him before curettage, in order to speed the healing process. She consented, since it seemed to mean more to him than it did to her. He was very short-sighted and kept his pebble lenses on during love-making, saying that seeing was as important as touching. He reproached her for her lack of sexual response and delayed the operation until he had brought her fully to it. He showed her obscene photographs which failed to move her, though they did quite surprise her. Then he was obliged to call his cousin in to have sex with her while he watched, and she feigned the most enthusiastic response, since by now she was ten weeks pregnant and the operation getting daily more dangerous.

When he finally performed it, he did it safely, painlessly and kindly, and she healed with amazing speed. But then she was a healthy girl, and apart from the intimate relationship that doctors seemed to have with her private parts would never have had to visit one at all.

She qualified as a nurse, then as a sister, and could have become matron before she was thirty; but then, as her father remarked, who would have married her? So she stayed a nursing sister, and married an engineer, Roger, and had two children, and apart from the usual peeking and prying, enemas, shaving, cutting and sewing involved in the safe delivery of babies in Newcastle, kept her insides to herself for a considerable time. Roger was an active and pleasant lover, and did not require fellatio, or practise cunnilingus, and they never had the light on, and she managed to separate out the medical aspects of her reproductive organs from the warm, creative, sexual pleasure they now gave her, three or four times a week, during her thirties and forties.

*

Perhaps Roger was a little boring: perhaps life was rather quiet? She felt untapped, unused: as if she were the kernel of a walnut, and it was withering in the shell, instead of growing plump and interestingly formed and ripe. Roger watched television and played squash: the two boys played football and tennis. No one talked, she sometimes felt: not really talked. They exchanged information, that was all. Life was lived on the surface: some-times the flesh between her legs tingled in an expectation that infused her whole body, and made her dance and sing and then weep. The boys thought she was mad, but then everyone's mother at a certain age went mad. Everyone knew it. Women did.

Tandy took a part-time job at the local hospital, where they spe-cialised in the care of the handicapped; a place where men lived whose legs grew round their necks, or who had no arms or legs at all, and women with hands grown into claws, and children with brains that still thought better than most, and felt more than most, but could not move limbs, or mouths, or eyes.

How lucky I am to be whole, thought Tandy, even though no longer young, and fell in love with Dr Walker, the medical superintendent, who did not get on with his wife. And he fell in love with her and they managed a weekend or so together, which in a way was a pity because after that she knew what she had missed. She saw that the sunrise glow in the morning of her life, which should have grown stronger and stronger, to suffuse her whole life with a brilliant sexual light, had been deflected, and the day clouded over, and now there were just glimmers, in and out, of a muted radiance.

*

He went back to his wife and Tandy to her husband, but she told him: which was a mistake. You can trust husbands to love you so far, no more. They, too, have intimations of lost ecstasy. He paced; she brooded.

'Perhaps we would be happier apart,' he said. He was forty-seven; she was forty-four. Either life was going to go on in the suburban house, ordinary and humdrum, eventually to run down into retirement, ill-health and death: or else he would change his job, move out of Newcastle, gain some new access of health and energy, jolt himself into life again. By sleeping with another man she had broken the ties of custom: she had chosen freedom, now he would do the same.

'Go,' she said. 'Very well, go. But we'll stay friends?'
  'Of course,' he said. 'And I'll send back the money.'

She had given up the part-time job at the hospital. She found it too painful: not just the sight of so much distressed flesh but the sight of her beloved; the thought of what could have been.

Living apart from Roger was more difficult than she had imagined. She suffered from loneliness, especially in the evenings. Listening to the music she loved, instead of the TV programmes he chose, was not, in the end, sufficient compensation for the simple lack of his presence.

She asked him to come back after six months.
  'No,' he said, 'I've found someone else.'

*

Well, she was still an attractive woman. Other women's husbands sought her out. She decided to become a doctor. She enrolled at the medical school. They hummed and haaed at her age and sex, but accepted her. She loved the work: it came easily to her.

I am happy, she thought. One of her tutors asked her out to coffee, then took her to the pictures. They started sleeping together. He was forty, seven years younger than she, but he said age was irrelevant. They made love with the light on, and she learned to trust him.

One night she had a severe pain in her right side.

'You'd better see someone,' said her tutor, Peter, and she agreed that indeed she had better. All her contemporaries had gynaecologists whom they visited, on principle, once every six months, who would check over their insides and pronounce them healthy, or unhealthy, and occasionally would 'just open them up' – for they were licensed surgeons too – 'to see what's going on in there!'

But Tandy kept forgetting to go: in the end they had even stopped sending the reminder cards.

The women of Newcastle have wonderfully criss-crossed stomachs, what with the caesarians, the appendectomies and a host of openings up. And the ponies are plentiful and plump on the hillsides, and the little doctors' daughters laugh and sing, and if the grass is spotted with blood, who notices?

*

NAKED GRAFFITI

The gynaecologist was tall and fair, and well-qualified and new in Newcastle.

'He's wonderful,' her friends said. 'So kind and gentle and understanding. A conservative surgeon.' That meant though he opened you up he did not take bits away if he could possibly help it. The women of Newcastle worried a little: wondered why they had more abdomen scars per head of female population than did women anywhere else in the entire world, so conservative surgeons, these days, did better than anyone else. There were a few practising women medicos, but hardly any women surgeons. Women, custom and practice decreed, do not make good surgeons.

'You look familiar,' said Tandy to the gynaecologist, as she lay upon the couch, on her side, knees parted.

'Relax, relax! How can I examine you if you stay so stiff?

'Good God,' he said, 'it's Tandy.'

Dr John Pierce, the golden youth from long ago, from sunrise days: thin fair hair and lines of disappointment round his mouth, now that the sun was creeping down the sky.

Well, everyone gets older. He was more shocked than she: he had held an image of her in his mind, a beautiful, laughing girl, with long, thick hair. One day she'd loved him; the next she hadn't. He never knew why. Tossed her head and walked by, and wounded him for ever.

'Good God,' she said, 'it's John Pierce.'

'A long time ago,' he said. 'Do try and relax.'

148

She tried.

'I think it's just a cyst,' he said, 'causing the trouble. Probably benign, but we'd better open you up and make sure: and of course there are a lot of fibroids here. But then in a woman of your age that's to be expected. How old? Forty-seven? Good God!'

He was forty-seven too. If it's old for a woman it's old for a man but that wasn't the way he wanted to see it. Does anyone? He was married with three children and three ponies, and a receptionist he lusted after, and wouldn't have to lust after if only he had true love, and hadn't lost it long ago to Tandy Watson, who'd tossed her head one day and broken his heart. He blamed her.

He opened Tandy up: and took out everything. Womb, fallopian tubes, ovaries. Snip, snip. Forceps, nurse. (The nurse had glowing eyes above her mask, which reminded him of the past.) He sat by Tandy's bed while she came out of the anaesthetic and told her what he'd done.

'I thought we'd better be on the safe side,' he said.

'But what was wrong with them?'

'Well, nothing,' he said, 'but wombs are a great source of trouble to women your age.'

'You mean you took out three perfectly healthy organs?'

'Well, yes,' he said. 'This cyst was benign but the next one mightn't be. And I gave you an oestrogen implant so you'll be better off than you were before. Oestrogen slows the ageing process. Well, look,' he said nervously, for her eyes were enormous and witchlike, 'what use are those organs to a woman of fifty? They've served their purpose. They're no use to anyone.'

'Forty-seven,' she said. 'Those organs are *me*. I am nothing, now. You have turned off the light. No one asked you to: no one said you could: you have taken it upon yourself to turn out the light of my life.'

He thought she might sue, but she didn't. She didn't want anyone to know what had happened. She was dull and depressed for a good six months, shocked and zombie-like.

She split up with Peter, who of course had to know, and blamed it on the loss of her organs. He was only forty: what would he want with a half-woman of nearly fifty, without womb, ovaries or fallopian tubes? The few friends she told assured her that in fact no harm had been done: that Peter would have gone anyway; that many women sought out the operation: that she looked, thanks to the oestrogen, slimmer and younger and prettier than before. But Tandy was not convinced. She gave up medical school: it was too much trouble. She became a grand-mother and was glad it was a boy.

'They have a better life than girls,' she said, admiring the contained and tidy infant penis.

When she saw John Pierce in the street she would cross the road to avoid him. He seemed to her to walk in a pool of dark. But then she had, after all, turned the light of his life off, carelessly, long ago. She'd slept with him and then denied it to everyone, and failed to love him, and spoiled his life, and he couldn't forgive that. Could anyone, really, man or woman, be expected to forgive?

TIM PARKS
Keeping Distance

They were both studying to be doctors, so they had that in common. And then the ages were right, right that is for his pre-conception of how ages in a couple should be, a difference of three years in his favour, and while she would always have objected in any discussion of the issue to the notion that in the ideal couple the girl should be younger, she nevertheless enjoyed the idea of having an older man, or rather boy, he was only twenty-four, to slip under her thumb.

The same could have been said of their respective heights.

Then the place was right too, Selva di Val Gardena, he skiing with friends, spending his father's money, she working temporarily in a distant relative's hotel – every day bright and clear, the crisp exhilarating thrust of the Dolomites silenced by snow, the chattering of winter holiday-makers barely denting the mystery. You felt different here, cleaner and more passionate.

He was recovering from having been left by his first love – a girlfriend of five years' standing, Paola had walked out on him in August and married another man in November. She, on the contrary, had never had a real love, only encounters.

And then there was the excitement of each other's foreignness. He was Italian, she German. Why is it that a foreign lover is always considered a greater prize, a greater adventure? Giuseppe and Hilda made love some hours after having come across each other in a discoteque attached to a pizzeria.

She took all the initiative, for he was still sulking, and having had no other girls but that fatal first love was shy with women, despite his one-of-the-boys, heavy-drinking, loud-laughing manner with his friends. Quite simply she took him to her bed, and in doing so fell in love with him. For his part he was most impressed, with her physical prowess, with the suddenness of her devotion. He was a man who loved to be loved. Unfortunately her face was not especially attractive: the nose was too big and wide, the lips too thin, the skin unhealthy somehow. Only the bright blue eyes saved the situation, the bright honest smile displaying well-kept teeth, plus, when it came to introducing her to his friends, her slim but well-endowed and very modern body.

Giuseppe on the other hand was unbelievably handsome. In every department. She loved him and loved him. For the first time in her life she was swooning.

They spoke to each other in halting English. Which separated them from their friends. They giggled over misunderstandings. When they spoke about medical matters though, they found they had a large vocabulary in common and, being her senior, he had the pleasure of explaining things she didn't know about, at great length. In fact he was rather a bore at times, but she lapped it up: there was his face to look at, the fine intelligent forehead and Roman nose, there were his incredibly broad square shoulders. They both felt pleased to be improving their English, although there was no one to correct them when they made mistakes.

In the mountains everybody wore jeans or ski pants, thick woollen sweaters, quilted jackets. But when, having finished at the hotel, she travelled down to Verona for a week before returning for the next university term, it came as something of a disappointment for Giuseppe. He was an elegant dresser. In a very Italian way he followed fashions. In his imitation Armani sweater and generously cut autumn-coloured wool trousers he walked with an idle strut perfectly adapted for the *passeggiata*. In bright winter weather in Via Mazzini he cut a figure. But Hilda wore the same jeans, boots, sweaters and quilted jacket she had worn in Val Gardena, and her gait had a hurried a-to-b purpose about it which didn't do much for the huge attribute that was her body.

Just when he was beginning to get seriously annoyed with this, and annoyed with the way that, despite her lavish bed-time love and eager if inexpert cooking, she would argue quite belligerently against the notion that women should be sex objects and that money spent on attractive clothes was well spent, just when he was getting seriously irritated (with the fuss she made over finding an old *Playboy*, for example), it was time for her to go home. They were both sad. It had been such a passionate affair and love had been made such an impressive and unprecedented number of times. They both promised letters, phonecalls, visits. She told him very frankly she loved him. He mumbled something in his halting English into her hair, which privately he thought she would have done well to have washed more often. Perhaps permed.

She lived in Munich, five hours in the train from Verona, 400 kilometres, 60,000 lire, 88 marks. It was not an impossible distance, but expensive for young people living on student incomes, or, in his case, no real income at all. Between degree and specialisation she had six years to go. He was nearing the end of his degree, but then there was his military service to get through and the prospect of no jobs in Italian hospitals. It all made the relationship such a safe one, unlike his long affair with Paola. And at Easter Giuseppe thought of himself as travelling up to Germany for a much needed holiday and a week's solid sex.

Hilda greeted him in Italian. The progress she had made in just four months was astonishing, and likewise astonishing was the love she lavished on him. Nor did her lack of dress sense seem so important in Munich, where everybody dashed about under umbrellas between supermarket and bus stop without any regard for style. She held his arm tight and talked about the coming summer. He felt the slim suppleness of her lively body against him.

On Easter day she took him to her family home to the north of the city where he was welcomed with open arms by mother, father and brother. A young doctor and so handsome. Their kindness was doubly welcome, since Giuseppe's own parents lived and worked abroad and it was some time since he had had the chance to experience the warm bath of parental care, parental cooking. Tuned in to modern mores, the Meiers allowed Giuseppe and Hilda to share a room for the night as if already married. This gave a curious touch of respectability, permanence, general acknowledgment to something Giuseppe had so far only thought of as an affair. When he ran out of money, as he regularly would, Hilda lent him five hundred of the marks she had saved from her holiday job, though she did say a few words about not spending so much on clothes. He said if only an Italian medical degree were acceptable in Germany, he

would be able to come up permanently in a year or so, after his
military service, and do his specialisation in a German hospital.
She said, 'That's wonderful,' as if somehow this plan might be
feasible.

He did his military service in Naples and every time he had a
few days' leave they met in Verona, 700 kilometres north for
him, 400 kilometres south for her. There was a train from
Rome which left him on a cold deserted platform at 2 a.m.
where he stretched out on a bench under his combat jacket till
she got in at 3.30 and they took a taxi back to his room
together. It was very romantic kissing in the back of that taxi.
The railway people should put a plaque up for them at the station, he said, or name one of the trains after them, the amount
of money they'd spent. And it was very erotic making love just a
couple of days every couple of months. Each occasion became a
rediscovery, a first time almost. She said she loved him so much.
She said if only the Italian universities would accept the exams
she'd already done in Germany, she could come down here to
finish her degree while he did his specialisation.

'That's true,' he said.

'My Italian's good enough now,' she said.

'I know,' he said. 'It is.'

'Except I can't throw away my degree at this point, can I?'

And he agreed she couldn't.

They had no time to form a circle of friends in common.
Which made her indifferent skin and worse dress sense easier to
take. There was no one for him to lose face with. In fact he felt
a great deal of affection for her. At times he thought of himself
as being in love. Certainly the word was being used often
enough. And at the barracks, where he was assistant to the

military doctor, he spoke frequently of his German girlfriend and said she had the best pointed tits anybody could imagine.

On returning to Verona he took up residence in his room again and began his specialisation in urology. Which occupied a good sixty hours a week. He watched older people dying of cancers, young people shocked by their first serious illness. He was kind, efficient, but unmoved, in short, well suited to the job. He had no official salary or scholarship, such was the way in Italy, but after a few months they let him do the occasional night duty for a modest sum, and then there were his father's erratic cheques from Algeria. He got by and, spreading his borrowing among everybody he knew, even managed to keep a battered 127 on the road. But he was hungry for money now, for new clothes, a decent flat, a real car. What had he studied seven years for, if not for money? And when Hilda came down, or he went up there, it was so embarrassing to have to scrounge. He kept a close record of his debt to her, which, after two years now, was something over two million lire.

Hilda chided but always gave. Her evening waitressing financed two summer weeks in Yugoslavia. Two very happy weeks; the sun brought healthy colour to her face and in her bikini one could forget the dowdiness of her clothes. Roasting on the beach she thought it would be a good idea if they could both get jobs in the South Tyrol, the German-speaking part of Italy. Except that Giuseppe's German had made no progress whatsoever. And her degree still wouldn't be recognised he pointed out. Satisfied that this course of action was well and truly out of the question, they went back to the camp-site and made love quite passionately on sleeping bags in their tent using contraceptives she had paid for. In the balmy dark later they discussed the most recent advances in cancer research and a theory Giuseppe was developing about prostate problems. Who knew what progress medical science mightn't make during their lifetime? They were both more than satisfied with their chosen profession.

Back in Germany, Hilda completed her degree the following year with excellent results. Offered a paid post to specialise in Frankfurt, she agonised for a month or two, but in the end felt she would be a fool not to accept and went north. The four hundred kilometres became seven hundred.

She rented a room in a nice suburb and put her few belongings in it. She wasn't avid for special comforts or clothes as Giuseppe was. Being a Green Party supporter, she was quite content to use the bus rather than buy a car, though she could have afforded one now. Naturally gregarious, if a little bossy, she was very soon part of a new circle of friends, but took no lovers. She wore a ring on her third finger and referred to it as an engagement ring. The only decorations in her room were photographs of Giuseppe, who inevitably came up for long weekends those months when she didn't go down.

This went on for seven years. But it was curious how much of the freshness and simplicity of their first encounters they managed to retain, curious how young they still were. Distance seemed to have frozen time, so that if there was no progress (whatever that might mean), still there was very little loss either. He or she would arrive. Coffee would be made and then love. The mood was one of holiday, a well-deserved break. Saturday and Sunday they would eat in restaurants, walk in parks. There were cinemas, discoteques. The weekends, as ever, gave them no time to gather acquaintances about them. No social fabric underpinned their partnership. He hadn't seen her parents since that Easter almost a decade ago. She had never seen his. So they sat, sipping granita on sultry Verona nights in the central square, or walking arm in arm under an umbrella to stare in Frankfurt's shop windows running with October rain. Both salaried doctors now, their staple conversation was their patients, hospital organisation, Germany versus Italy, modern medicine. They never tired of it. They could talk way into the small hours, discussing difficult diagnoses. Of course her pasty skin and lack of dress sense still bothered Giuseppe occasionally, but then he was only with her for the weekend, of which a good fifty per cent was spent indoors, and a great deal of that in bed. She still chided him for his wasteful ways with money, but then their resources weren't in common, his loans had been paid back, and no mention had been made of saving jointly for a house since the geographical location of such a house was unimaginable. What they both still enjoyed very much was their lovemaking, a feeling of physical tenderness they had for each other. And if either masturbated or ever had the occasional adventure during the four or five weeks that separated one visit from the next, this was never talked about.

Until, at thirty-one, Hilda decided, or perhaps it would be more accurate to say discovered, she wanted a child. It was a disquieting discovery, the more so because entirely unexpected. She had thought of herself as a girl in love with her lover Giuseppe, that was one vision; she had thought of herself as a responsible career woman taking her rightful place in society at the hospital, that was another; but she had not thought of herself as a mother. The first two visions were remarkably easy to sustain. She divided her life into work (feminine assertion in what had once been a male preserve), and holiday (Giuseppe, restaurants, bars, summer beaches). There was no conflict here; on the contrary, all was perfect complement. But it was difficult to imagine integrating these two visions, or perhaps it would mean sacrificing them, in that third and new vision, a life that would accommodate motherhood. And yet she did want a child. It had to do somehow with a new consciousness of her life as a whole, as a human creature, of its finiteness, its inevitable span, its trajectory you might say. And this wasn't just a negative discovery, a sense of time running out, although that came into it; it was also a positive feeling of coming to fruition, of being in her prime. This, she sensed dimly – in a way that had nothing to do with politics, profession or love – this should be a moment, *the* moment, of plenitude. Now. And she wanted a child. Otherwise, and she had never really seen this before, her existence would simply go on being forever what it already was, without any shift of gear or change of rhythm or further depth or richness, without somehow being properly harnessed up to life.

Although never bringing the issue to full consciousness, for her professional mind had so much to be busy with, Hilda was aware of two choices. There was, for example, a slightly older doctor in paediatrics, shy, retiring, a little watery, but very intelligent, who had made it clear in one way or another over the last three years or so that he would like to form a relationship with her, if only he could pluck up the courage, if only she were available. A little effort, she knew, a little encouragement, and she could marry him within the year. Or some other local man. Why not? Three months' maternity leave at some point and back to work. A crêche was available for the children of hospital staff.

Or there was Giuseppe. And complete incompatibility with her professional German life.

Again without actually weighing up the pros and cons, she was aware, over a period of some months, of a decision-making process going on. Until, at short notice, just as that winter was turning into spring, Giuseppe cancelled a weekend visit in order to attend, he said, a conference in Naples, on uro-dynamics. Her acute feeling of letdown, her inkling of jealousy (why had he left it to the last moment to tell her? how was she to know there really was a conference in Naples?), her sense of desolation, cutting alone into the cake she had baked for him, brought her to a sudden decision: or so it seemed, for now she was sorting through possible ways to broach the subject, now she was definitely fearing how he would respond, as if quite suddenly he was her only hope. It would have to be him.

As it turned out only the following weekend, Giuseppe surprised and actually rather unnerved her with his ready consent, his willingness to make plans, immediately. She wondered if he wasn't being a little naive. For as it was she who would have to bear the child, so it would have to be she who left her job, who went down to live with him, became dependent on him. Did responsibility sit so lightly on his shoulders? Did he really know what he was letting himself in for? And if he was so ready to agree to the idea now, why hadn't he suggested it before himself? It wasn't a notion that required such a great deal of imagination to dream up, marrying your girlfriend of ten years' standing.

It was a curious weekend this, in that it just wouldn't live up to its apparent momentousness as the turning point of their lives. Perhaps because, with all those years of relaxing holiday breaks behind them, of cinema, restaurant, lovemaking, of fascinating case histories recounted in bed, they had never learnt the knack of declaring themselves, or even arguing. How much did they really know about each other, about living together? Sunday afternoon, after yes had been said, had a flat, dull, unreal feel to it.

In answer to her question, he explained, but unconvincingly, that he'd never felt he had the right to encourage her to leave such a good job, nor, obviously, could he ever have dreamed of leaving his and so becoming dependent on her. But now that she was actually offering to make the sacrifice, to come down and be with him, of course he was delighted. He didn't want to go on living on his own forever. It was tiresome sometimes. And then he fancied himself as a father. It was time life took a turn. Lying beside him, she was profoundly dissatisfied with this, as if somehow he'd let her down, though when you thought about it, what he'd said was perfectly reasonable. And although they had decided now, or said they had, that if a child was to be born it had better be born as soon as possible, nevertheless they used their contraceptives as usual that night, as if it might be unthinkable after all these years, or even obscene, that his naked flesh should at last penetrate hers. They used their contraceptives, all was as it always had been, apparently, yet even so, and they both sensed it, there was something deliberate, something cautious and rather self-conscious about their lovemaking tonight. The embrace had lost its old holiday feel of sheer pleasure and weekend relief between tenderly consenting adults. Their minds were elsewhere.

He found a bigger flat to rent. More decisively, she gave up her job, her world, and travelled south. After some difficulty satisfying the authorities' hunger for documents, they were married in the registry office set up romantically, if rather ominously, in the ancient *palazzo* that was believed to have housed Juliet's tomb.

After all those years of care with contraceptives, the queues in night-duty chemists, the occasional painful renunciation, it now transpired that getting pregnant was by no means automatic. As doctors of course they should have known this. Indeed for doctors they were somewhat naive. Unless perhaps a strong groundswell of naivety is a positive quality in those who daily have to exercise an imprecise profession in the face of calamity. Either way, nothing happened. Lovemaking took on a distasteful, inhibiting significance, but produced no fruit. Installed on the sixth floor of an apartment block within sight of the hospital, Hilda struggled to fill her unemployed time, cleaning, studying, improving her Italian, giving German lessons and doing the odd translation. She was a resourceful girl. But inevitably there were mornings, afternoons, evenings when time hung heavy. The more so because Giuseppe didn't always return promptly at the end of his periods of duty. For years he had been going regularly to a gym, God knows what would happen to his body if he stopped now. And then there was the paper he was writing in collaboration with someone in the pharmacy on total parenteral nutrition for post-operative kidney patients. Hours had to be spent sifting through data together, assessing case histories. For the first time in her life, Hilda caught herself staring blankly out of windows.

And more effort was required with the time they did spend together too. There was no weekend sense of occasion now. Nor did he, from one morning to the following evening, gather much in the way of news. Routine set in. When he wasn't watching television, Giuseppe liked to go out with old friends, meet in a bar, eat in a trattoria, parade up and down Via Mazzini. But gregarious and sociable as Hilda was, she found such excursions tedious. His friends were frivolous, overdressed, the women over made-up, the men interested in football if they were interested in anything at all. Back in Frankfurt the staples of her social conversation had been politics, arms reduction, the environment; she had been a serious talker; now she smiled weakly as Giuseppe retailed the endless dirty jokes he picked up on the ward, guffawing loudly as one punchline followed another. And it occurred to her that she had never really heard her handsome lover talking at any length to anybody but herself, never had the opportunity to observe him in a group; where, she now discovered, he acted rather like one of those big complacent dogs who are forever expecting a pat on the head from everybody and frequently launch into fits of barking out of sheer excitement with their own thoroughbred, beautiful, well-brushed selves.

For his part, Giuseppe was privately wondering how it had come about that he had married somebody who was so much not his ideal of what a woman should be. So unfeminine, with such poor dress sense, and never a trace of make-up on her face. Had it been just the excitement of her foreignness, of all that travelling to and fro, the train juddering to a halt at various borders (he missed it now), of saying to people, 'my German girlfriend,' and adding in certain company, 'with the best pointed tits in the world' (though what was the use if she insisted on hiding them in these baggy old sweaters)? It was not that they had stopped caring for each other, not that all tenderness had already gone, just that these two people found themselves soon bored, soon disappointed.

And when they got home, lovemaking was not as voluptuous and eager as it had been on all those weekends always so carefully arranged so as not to coincide with her menstruations. Indeed, perhaps love would not have been made at all, were it not for this child she had set her heart on having, this child whose arrival had become a matter of faith now; otherwise the move south, the marriage, the sacrifice of her job, her life, would all have been an unfortunate and expensive mistake.

But Hilda was not an unintelligent girl, and life now was giving her plenty of time to think. So she came to appreciate over the passing months that all this had probably been fairly predictable, perhaps in fact she had herself foreseen it, or at least had a pretty good inkling; it was just that she had stifled her doubts with that overwhelming determination to have a child. Yet was such determination wise? Wasn't this urgency to become a mother something she should have fought against perhaps, some mental unbalance brought about by changing hormone patterns? Should she have defended the carefree state of mind that was her younger self, the chemical equilibrium she had been so happy with? And shouldn't she have resisted that peculiar sense of fate that had invaded her, that intuition of what life was for, or rather of the subjection of her own life to the great natural cycle?

When winter set in and his paper was written and sent off, Giuseppe watched a great deal more television; adventure films and sports were his favourites it turned out. A lot of their time together passed without words, not in the silence of resolution and serenity, but against the background of a nagging tension, of something unresolved, unsettled between them, which they were becoming less rather than more capable of talking about. So that Hilda had more or less decided to call the whole thing a day before it became a lifetime, had already telephoned the hospital administration in Frankfurt about the possibility of getting her job back, when at last she skipped her period.

What great and genuine excitement! What hours spent lying in the dark in almost mystical communion with her body. What sheepish grins and thoughtfulness from Giuseppe, getting home more promptly, bringing flowers, fruit, as if she had suddenly become an invalid. When in fact she had never felt better in her life. And so elated, looking at baby clothes, calculating dates, choosing names. What festivity!

For about two weeks. Until routine began to set in again. It was, after all, the best part of nine months till the child would be born. And to set in rather worse than before. Why was this? Why, after a fortnight's intense excitement, did life suddenly seem so depressing, so unutterably dull? Why this sudden and dramatic deflation? Was it just winter beginning to make itself felt, the first fogs creeping across the Bassa Padana into the southern suburbs of the city, so that, nose pressed against the damp window pane, Hilda could barely make out the glow of lamps in the street below? Was it to do with the seething hormonal redeployment she had now unleashed on herself, her moods an insignificant by-product of this inexorable creative process that was so much bigger, she knew that, than either herself or Giuseppe? Or was it, more simply, her awareness that with pregnancy, far more than with marriage, a trap had sprung and closed; the phonecall to Frankfurt, the departure note she had already prepared in her mind, these must be things of the past; her life was here now, in this two-bedroom flat on the sixth floor, watching the fog, looking for sensible ways to fill time, battling with a sense of waste. How many years would they live here? How many hours would she spend by this window? Why, now this baby was on the way, was she experiencing such a tremendous sense of desolation? As if she had lost far more in leaving her job, her language, her homeland, than a baby could ever replace. Had lost herself perhaps.

Always businesslike in the past, equable, sensible in her work, playful in her play, well-balanced, admirably capable in every department, Hilda now began to lose her self-control. And, more particularly, she began to lose the attitude of reasonable amenability she had always imagined to be an indivisible part of herself. Why should she get in the shopping and cook for him? Why should she trail into town to eat crusty pizza and listen to him retailing jokes she had heard a thousand times. She refused. She went to the cinema on her own, sat at home and read novels, took even less care with her appearance than she had before. She had no idea why she was acting as she was, was only aware that there was an element of self-destruction involved, which at once made her feel helpless and yet afforded a grim sense of satisfaction.

Giuseppe was lost. Basically carefree himself, he simply couldn't understand what he saw as wilful unpleasantness. And in someone who had always been so friendly, so devoted. He was nonplussed. He didn't possess great powers of intuition, perhaps because it was so very long since he had lived in such close proximity to anyone else. Most of all he didn't appreciate how much his affection for Hilda had depended on her devotion to him. Naturally inclined to be generous, so long as it didn't cost him too much, he oscillated between kind attempts to cheer her up, treats, anecdotes, and angry slammings of the door when she only became more prickly than before. After all, he was tired when he got home, he deserved a little respect, deserved to be able to put his feet up in front of the TV if he wanted. She sneered at him in a German he didn't understand. He stared at her, unwashed hair lank around pale cheeks. And he saw now that she had always thought of him as less intelligent than herself. She despised him, despised his habits, despised his friends. And forgetting, as one does, the ten years of happy weekends, the lightness, the affection, the tenderness, he began to feel resentful. He began to feel he had been used. Simply to fulfil her female craving for motherhood. Because nobody else would have her. Wisely so. Except that he, like a fool, had allowed himself to be drawn in without even thinking about it. Why hadn't he thought about it?

His life before Hilda came to live with him, which he had frequently found rather dull and dissatisfying at the time, eagerly looking forward to their weekends together, now appeared to him in all the glory of its happy blend of achievement and potential. He'd had his hard-earned job at the hospital, he'd had his weekends with her for emotional and sexual fulfilment, he'd had his friends, his gym, his volleyball, and perhaps most of all he'd had the sense that anything could happen, that he could do anything, embark on any project, sleep with any woman, because his future was not a settled thing, but something he had perfect freedom to decide on day by day. And in contrast now, he thought, he might never sleep with any other woman again. This was it, permanence, the end of youth. He was to be a father. He was to be locked forever into this single embrace with this rather dowdy woman. And though in the ten preceding years Giuseppe had only rarely and very casually ended up in other women's arms, this new awareness of limitation suddenly seemed deeply disturbing and important. He would go through life hurrying home, trying to keep her happy (an apparently impossible task), missing dinners with friends, missing weekend conferences, losing out in short in every department. It had all been a terrible mistake. And just to show that he was not the kind of man to succumb to such servitude, he allowed himself to be seduced one evening by one of the girls in the lab; she was notorious. And it felt good, quite frankly, to be using contraceptives again.

Not that efforts weren't made to recapture that weekend ease and simplicity that had led Giuseppe and Hilda to believe they were so well suited to each other. For these two people were both well-intentioned. They did not want things to go wrong. So perhaps in the evening he would begin to tell her about some curious case on the ward, a child with a kidney tumour, a pensioner whose prostate had returned to normal for no reason they could imagine. Hilda would give her opinion. But without the old sense of enthusiasm, the sense of participating as an equal. The truth being that hospital talk only heightened her feeling of regret, while for his part he was only half-aware that she had lost some of her charisma for him when she had stopped working. Somehow she was less important now. So that the conversations failed to engross as they once had.

Then, the following day, ashamed that she was taking out on him what in the end had been the natural and obvious result of her own decision, Hilda might prepare a treat for his homecoming: a strudel, a plumcake with rum. After dinner she would present it, his eyes would light up and he would gobble it down on the sofa, watching television, looking up at her from time to time and smiling. It wasn't the kind of easy light-hearted communion they had experienced in the past, there was something thin and rather pathetic about it, his quick smiles between concentrating on the inevitable game of something or other on the television. But it was better than nothing. And vaguely she wondered how it would be when she was cooking for a young child too, when there would be breathless demands for second helpings. Would she feel fulfilled then? Would it all have been worthwhile? Perhaps it was just a question of waiting, of not demanding satisfaction here and now. Perhaps with time, she would find some useful part-time job in a private clinic or something, or doing research, one didn't need state authorisation to do research. Giuseppe was such a beautiful man and basically kind. And perhaps anyone would be irritating once you started living with them. So probably it was just a case of hanging on and believing in it all. She stooped to kiss his neck, bent forward over her strudel, and smelt a strange perfume. Surprised, she sniffed again. There was also an unmistakable red mark just inside the collar, the kind of thing one wouldn't imagine girls did any more.

So two days later, when he said he was on night duty, substituting for a sick colleague, Hilda phoned the hospital, something she had never done before, since she knew how irritating it could be for everybody concerned if the doctor was constantly being dragged to the phone.

She asked for no explanations. She wasn't interested. It was extraordinary how suddenly, how firmly her mind was made up, how efficiently she packed, how quickly she penned her little note. With steady ruthlessness and immense clarity she went towards a future she was still in time to turn into a copy of the past.

Some months later, seeing as he was scheduled to attend a renal disorder conference in Bonn, Giuseppe wrote to Hilda via her parents in Munich to try to arrange a meeting to discuss details of divorce. They eventually met in the foyer of a small provincial hospital some thirty kilometres outside Regensburg. It was raining heavily and being a Saturday afternoon in Germany most of the shops and bars were closed. The hospital was scruffy and depressing, so they went back to her flat in his new Alfa 90. She made him tea and offered some of the heavy black fruitcake she always kept for herself for breakfast. He began to tell her about some of the new ways of treating renal failure that had been presented at the conference, and she asked if he could let her have a copy of the conference proceedings when they were available. Her own hospital, for she'd been unable to get back her place in Frankfurt, was hopelessly provincial and out of it. She would be down in Puglia, she said, in September, with another woman, from radiology. They had booked two weeks in a Club Med, for lack of anything better to do. And of course she didn't want to forget all her Italian. Anyway, perhaps on returning she would stop by in Verona for a couple of days to sign the requisite papers and swear what in Italy inevitably had to be sworn. Giuseppe said yes, that was fine, but to phone him a couple of days beforehand just in case. Neither of them for one moment, not in the most allusive of asides, mentioned the abortion.

And then in September they made love again. She was so

suntanned, so glowing, so horny to be quite frank, and he so relaxed, laid back, self-satisfied with his various papers published and projects coming to fruition, with his clothes, his car, his expensive furnishings, that there was nothing easier than for them to make love with the same lightness, the same purely physical but tender pleasure of the years before. Even if, the following morning, they went just the same to sign the divorce papers on the grounds of complete incompatibility.

So, little by little, perhaps shamefacedly at first, but progressively less so, the weekend visits began again, the oases of holiday and eroticism in the midst of responsible, even commendable working lives. It was so much easier than taking local lovers with all their demands, their insistence on consequences. The distance, the travel, the hours in car or train (though Giuseppe travelled first class now) seemed to purify them for each other and for the brief weekend that would follow. There were no friends involved, no distractions, they asked nothing more of each other than two days' medical conversation and as much sex as a married couple would manage in a month. Only when they parted sometimes did Hilda reflect what a sad comment it was that with all the advances in medical science it had proved impossible for two healthy young people to have a baby.

PAT CALIFIA
What Girls Are Made Of

Bo (née Barbara, known as the Yeti in high school because of her fondness for snow) had just shuttled her last set of papers from one office to another. Not a moment too soon. Downtown traffic was about to change from hellish to terminal. Instead of putting thousands of people who hated their jobs and hated each other in cages and letting them race each other home, Bo thought they should just give them loaded guns and let them duel it out at twenty paces. It sure would thin out the freeway. It had been a very busy day, even for a Friday. Every piece of paper she had delivered was an emergency, although how anything that wasn't bleeding could constitute a crisis was beyond her. The clerks and receptionists she'd dealt with today weren't getting enough fiber in their diets. Cops were giving away parking tickets like they got to put the fines in their own pockets. And every taxi in the financial district seemed determined to eat a motorcycle for lunch.

Before she went home to her microwave and a freezer full of Stouffer's frozen entrées, Bo decided to detour through the Tenderloin and visit one of the porn shops. She had a hot date this weekend. Maybe she would buy a dick. The thought of putting it to somebody else made her feel a little taller, a little meaner. Yeah. That was a really good idea. Just walk into the porno shop and buy a dick, like it was something she did every day. They were just lying there behind glass, in a counter next to the cashier. A dozen of 'em, like big, pink, deformed rubber hot dogs. The clerk didn't give a shit. Who cared what he thought, anyway? Who cared what some jerk thought who worked in a dirty bookstore? It would be easy, Bo told herself, and backed her bike into the curb, between two cars that were far enough apart to leave room for her soft-tail.

'What are you looking at?' she snarled at a lanky old wino who had accidentally pointed his face in her direction. He blinked at her but couldn't quite get her in focus. He mumbled, 'Spare change?' because that was about all he said to people anymore, other than, 'Gimme a pint of Thunderbird.'

'I haven't got any,' Bo said. 'How about a cigarette?'

'Sure,' he said, putting out a hand that shook so bad, Bo didn't see how he ferried liquor from a brown-bagged bottle to his lips. She took two cigarettes out of her pack, put one in his stiff shirt pocket, lit the other one, and waited while he found it.

Now he could see her just fine. She was five-foot-six and well fed. Her light brown hair was cut like a Marine's. But Uncle Sam would never have put up with that ring in her nose. 'Did that hurt?' he asked.

'No pain, no gain,' Bo said, and backed away from the conversation and his bouquet.

'Be good,' he admonished her, and let the building prop him up again. The wall was freshly painted, which in this neighborhood meant only one thing: it housed an adult bookstore. Bo glanced up at the sign. The letters hanging on the marquee's wires spelled out XXX SUGAR AND SPICE XXX. She pushed the heavy glass door and went in, already wincing at the thought of her boots sticking to the floor.

The shop was in the front. You had to walk past racks of hard-core magazines in shrink-wrap covers and cases full of Hong Kong's finest marital aids to get into the rest of the place, which featured REAL! LIVE! SEX! ACT! GIRLS! A big guy who looked like he might have been a biker before he lost one hand was there selling tokens, one for a dollar. Sometimes groups of women came through on 'feminist tours of the red-light district'. He always told them, 'Ya can't go back there without an escort.' Sometimes one of the customers would offer (with a leer) to provide that service. Bo wondered if he would tell her that. She imagined herself saying, 'This is my escort,' and whipping out a switchblade. That would make them all step back. She stuck one hand in her jacket pocket to make sure her Swiss Army knife was still there.

She loitered by the glass case full of dildos. It reminded her of a cage at the zoo. 'See the wild, endangered, artificial phalli,' the sign by the exhibit might read. They looked like dismembered organs in the fluorescent light. The bored clerk flicked a glance at her, said, 'Back again?' in a bored tone of voice, and went back to his racing form. Bo blushed as red as the hanky in her back pocket. *Oh my God, he recognized me!* How could she possibly figure out what she wanted with this homophobic jerk cruising her? Well, he wasn't getting any money out of her today.

She turned away and walked toward the magazines. She touched some of the covers with the tips of her fingers, but what was the point in picking any of them up? You couldn't turn the pages and see what was in them. A small group of guys, including one man in a wheelchair and two men who were at least as old as her grandpa, were studying the racks anyway. One of them looked up, saw her, and edged away. *All I get from these straight assholes is constant harassment*, Bo thought bitterly, and headed for the bouncer guarding the turnstile. Just let him try to keep her out of the back. He'd find out pretty soon that he'd picked on the wrong kind of woman.

'Getcha tokens here,' he said. 'Hey, guy, how you doin'? Wanna spend some money on the foxy ladies? We got a red-hot trio today. One blonde, one brunette, and a real exotic little Asian fox. You friends with summa the dancers?'

Bo had counted on being stopped. This geek obviously thought she was a man. She didn't know what to do. If she corrected him, he might throw her out, and that would be humiliating. She glared at him, daring him to hassle her.

'Getcha tokens here,' he said, talking over her shoulder, addressing the entire room. 'If you wanna see the show or watch a movie, you gotta getcha tokens here,' he told her confidentially.

Bo felt as if everyone in the bookstore was waiting to see what she would do. She decided to just act casual, like this was something she did every day. She gave him a twenty. He wasn't impressed. 'Getcha money's worth,' he said, sliding four stacks of five tokens toward her, and motioned her through the turnstile. Looking at her back, he thought ruefully, *Why do all the cute ones have to be dykes?*

This part of the store was much darker. Bo was afraid to stop moving for fear she wouldn't be able to get herself going again. Why weren't her eyes getting used to the dark? She was going to bump into some guy, maybe some jerk who already had his dick out. Then she remembered she had her Ray Bans on and slipped them into the pocket of her overlay. The light was still dim, but she could see well enough now to know that she was in a maze of little booths with plywood walls. Most of the doors stood open. There were pictures on each door that looked like the photos on video boxes.

The temptation to cop a few minutes of privacy was too much. She went into one of the cubicles and shut the door. There was a machine on one wall of the booth. She stuck a token in it just to see what would happen. It made a sound like a coffee grinder, and then a square of color appeared on the opposite wall. A surprisingly attractive young woman was down on her knees, licking a surprisingly homely man's cock. The picture quality wasn't very good, but Bo could see enough to tell that he wasn't getting it up. Nevertheless, the sight of real people having actual sex right there in front of her was oddly arousing.

Then she noticed something moving around at the bottom of the screen that didn't seem to belong in the movie. Was that a couple of fingers, poking through a hole in the flimsy wall? 'Hey, dude, put it through! Best suck job in town!' somebody whispered.

The guy on the screen was hard now, and the woman who was blowing him had wrapped her hand around the base of his dick to keep it from going all the way into her face. Bo wanted to kill him, but she also wanted to wrap her hands around that bitch's neck and shove her head – where? Meanwhile, there were those beckoning fingers, the brave and weird offer to give a stranger pleasure. She should probably break his fucking hand, but it wasn't like he knew who was in here.

'Uh – I'm resting,' she said, pitching her voice as deep as possible.

'Maybe later,' the voice said. The fingers slid out of sight faster than a vanilla dyke who had just found poopoo in her girlfriend's anxious rosebud.

Bo thought she'd better get out of there before he saw her. As she rattled the door, she became very aware of her cunt. It was pressing into the seam of her jeans like a cat that leans on your leg to let you know it's breakfast time. *Why*, she wondered, *is there no word in English to describe this? I can't exactly say I've got a hard-on, but I bet this is sort of like what it feels like to have your dick get hard. I don't know if I want somebody to suck on my clit or fuck me, but I sure don't feel passive or receptive. It's an aggressive kind of feeling, demanding, and it's not all in my head either. It's very physical.*

This was turning into quite a trip. Maybe she should have gone to the feminist vibrator shop and purchased a leaping purple silicone dolphin. Or a pink ear of vibrating corn. Or told her trick she'd have to bring her own damn treats! Bo staggered out of the peep show section and headed for the next attraction – a round, slightly elevated, glass-enclosed stage that was surrounded by more little booths, like one of those lazy-susan Plexiglas spice racks that yuppies bought at Macy's Cellar.

The public-address system burped (a sound that momentarily returned Bo to high school), and an unctuous female voice said, 'Gentlemen, fill your pockets full of *tokens*. The performance starts in *five minutes*. Three of the hottest, *wettest*, sexiest girls on *earth* are about to *shake it* just for you. These ladies are uninhibited, they're *bad*, they're ready to cut *loose*. They also take *requests*. So *buy* those tokens *now!*'

Men started coming out of the peep shows and clustering

around the bouncer. He made change really fast for a one-handed guy. Somebody tried to sneak under his arm and pilfer a token. The bouncer lifted him with one arm and shook him until his teeth rattled. 'Don't do that. It upsets me,' the big man said mildly, and handed over tokens for the five-dollar bill he was offered in lieu of an apology.

The P.A. system crackled again, and the female voice repeated exactly the same announcement, putting identical emphasis on the words 'tokens', 'five minutes', 'wettest', 'earth', 'shake it', 'bad', 'loose', 'requests', 'buy', and 'now'. Bo shook her head. 'Sucker born every minute,' she said ruefully and headed for the nearest booth.

Backstage was a mess. Three dancers were supposed to get ready in a space that was only slightly bigger than a walk-in closet. There was only one chair and a small mirror that was losing its silver backing. The floor was cluttered with gym bags, carryalls, and discarded street clothes.

'My mascara came open in my lingerie!' Crash (née Lisa) wailed. Her blonde hair was only half teased-out, so she looked like a 'before' ad for a PMS remedy. 'Where's my hair spray?' She dug through her dancer's bag, throwing shoes, press-on nails, lace gloves, and anything else she needed over her shoulder.

'So wear black, Crash. Nobody will notice,' Killer (née Brenda) said, rubbing lip gloss into her cheeks. She was already wearing a leather miniskirt and studded leather bra, but she hadn't finished zipping up her thigh-high boots. An asymmetrical, purple-streaked, black ponytail sprouted from one side of her mostly shaved head. 'I have to make a lot of money today. The fucking manager's been harassing me about my eyebrow again. I think I'll get the other one pierced tomorrow. *And* my nipples. *And* my cheeks. *And* the spaces in between my fingers and toes!' She kicked the can of hair spray over to Crash.

'Toilet's stuffed up again,' Poison (née Candy) announced, squeezing into the room. She wore only a gold G-string. The metallic fabric nearly blended into her old-ivory skin. She was shorter than the other dancers, but her body was solid from hours of dancing lessons and soccer. Her long, black hair had one eccentric platinum-blonde stripe. 'Where is that boy, anyway? She's supposed to take care of this shit for us.'

'Literally,' Killer snickered, painting big Egyptian eyes around her own. She snapped on her favorite wristbands. Their large pyramid studs matched the ones on her bra. Then she reached for the high pit-bull collar that completed her outfit. 'Come on, Poison, get dressed. We go on in five minutes.'

'I'm really sick of Bad Dog's lame excuses,' Crash said, shimmying into a cherry red merry widow without bothering to unhook the back. She'd left the stockings attached to the garters and crammed her feet into them like they were an old pair of jeans. Miraculously, they did not run. Poison lined up her scarlet patent pumps so Crash could step into them. 'Are you trying to tell us you feel like being the victim today?' She grabbed a comb, elbowed Killer out of the way, and started flipping her hair back into a lacquered bouffant.

'Sure, I'll do it. Just don't get too rough. I wish they'd at least put a piece of carpet down on that stage. It's a hard place to fall.'

Killer stood and zipped up her boots. 'There are no easy places to fall,' she said. 'Where the fuck is your costume? I am not going to get docked again just because you like to wander around forever in your underwear.'

'I don't have to dress up. I'm a China doll, a submissive geisha, every sailor's fantasy. It drives the white boys crazy.' Poison sang, 'Such a gentle way about you, Singapore girl.' Killer shot her a nasty look. 'I'm just going to wear my kimono,' Poison said hastily, taking it off a hanger that dangled from a nail in the cracked, industrial green plaster wall. Hints of gold embroidery still glittered against the old, white silk. 'Don't worry, Killer, I have a lot of toys in my pockets to keep the customers satisfied.' She untangled her obi, printed with a green chrysanthemum pattern, from the mess on the floor, wrapped it around her waist, and then fished out her gold stiletto heels.

A knock on the dressing-room door shook the cubicle. 'Ladies,' the manager said, and came in before anybody gave her permission. Her name was Carole, but everybody just called her 'the manager'. She was a former dancer who always noticed when they were late and often failed to notify them that their time onstage was up. She was always pressuring them to do without a lunch break or work overtime on lame shifts. The dancers hated her even though she didn't demand sexual services like the men they'd worked for. 'Where's your charming assistant?' she asked snidely.

'Flaked,' Killer said briefly.

'Tell me about it later. You're on.'

She closed the door, and Crash sent her a gesture that has been getting people killed in Sicily for hundreds of years. The three dancers filed into the hallway and opened the stage door. 'We need some music!' Killer shouted, and their tape came on. Crash had made it. She called it 'my tribute to popular culture's

fascination with vicious bitches.' The first song was the Wait-
resses, singing, 'I know what boys like.' The manager hated it.

They distributed themselves around the perimeter of the
stage, dividing up the customers. If somebody started tipping,
all of them clustered there, unless the customer indicated a
preference for just one of them. The stage was about three feet
higher than the floor, which put the customers' faces at a level
with the dancers' knees. Sliding windows went up and down
between the booth and the stage, and the men had to keep feed-
ing tokens into a machine to keep the window up. There was
also a little hole in the Plexiglas, to make it possible for folding
money to get shoved through. Dancers got paid minimum wage
because tipping was allowed. They put on two twenty-minute
shows every hour, for eight hours, and on a really good night,
they might each make $500. Usually, they made just enough
money to make dancing seem a lot more attractive than being a
secretary. They were supposed to receive a percentage of the
token sales, but they all knew the manager shorted them.

The three of them had been working here for three months,
three days a week. Nobody danced full-time. Theater owners
were not about to dip into their profit margin for health insurance or other benefits. They had finally managed to get 'pro-
moted' to a weekend evening shift, when you made decent
money, so they were probably about to get fired. Managers did
that routinely to make room for new bodies and faces onstage.
But they always found nasty, personal excuses – 'You're late,
you're on drugs, you can't dance, the customers don't like you,
your tits sag, you're too fat.' Smart dancers moved on to
another theater before that happened, but nobody looked forward to working up another act or performing with strangers.

Some of the straight dancers were uptight about dykes, and transsexuals were so competitive. It was unusual for three friends to get work together. The specter of dancers cooperating with or protecting one another made managers nervous.

You could make more money as a street hooker, but that was a lot more dangerous. There was no customer contact here. A girl on one of the other shifts had been followed to her car after work and raped, but that could happen to anybody. One of the adult theaters a few blocks away featured lap dancing, and the money was supposed to be fabulous, but it sounded like a very difficult job. How many different ways could you say, 'Give me some more money or I'll go away' and make it sound flirtatious?

Killer had tried working as a dominatrix, but it was boring. 'All I did was sit on my ass all day and wait for the phone to ring,' she complained. 'The other mistresses thought I was really strange, and most of the clients hated punks. It's so bogus. All the domination ads say, 'No sex,' right? But they all gave handjobs. I made the mistake of talking about it, and after that, the tacky comments about whores just kept coming. One day I had a slave down on the floor jacking off, and he came all over my shoe. I snapped. I took off my other shoe and went after him. I got him good a couple of times, too, before the woman who owned the place threw me out.'

Today all the booths were busy. It was a Friday afternoon, and the working man was ready for some fun. Each of the girls danced, trading places onstage, for one more song. Poison had shed her kimono already, after taking some tit clamps and a small, battery-operated vibrator out of its pocket. Crash took some money from a guy who wanted to see her ass, turned around, took down her panties, and waved it in his face. He showed her a $50 bill and said, 'Give me those hot little panties, honey.' So she inched them down, bent over to take the $50 in her teeth, and pushed the scrap of red satin through the hole. *Baby gets new shoes tonight*, she thought.

Poison somehow managed to keep gyrating on her high heels while she worked the vibrator in and out of her pussy. Her other hand was busy yanking on the tit clamps. She didn't have a free hand to take tips. Crash danced over to her, started playing with her nipples, and used her free hand to collect the cash. 'Honey, don't do that,' one of the men said. 'Don't hurt yourself like that.'

'Fuck you,' Poison said, sticking her tongue out at him. 'This is the only part of this show that I like, asshole.' He let his window come down and stay down.

'You just broke that piggy bank,' Crash said, yanking on Poison's chain. 'At this rate, you're never going to finish law school.'

'Hey!' Killer said, tossing her head so her black-and-purple ponytail whipped through the air, 'you're supposed to be *my* girlfriend!'

Poison snickered. You had to hand it to Killer, she always came up with an excuse for a little girl-wrestling onstage, and the boys loved it. 'So what?' she yelled. 'I want her to fuck me, and you can't stop us!' She did a little end-zone, in-your-face dance while Crash took over manipulation of the vibrator. Then she grabbed Crash and tried to smooch her.

'Get your hands out of my beehive,' Crash said irritably, smooching her back. 'It'll look like shit if it comes down over my face.'

Killer stormed over to them, looking genuinely pissed off. The bright lights above the booth made it a hot box to work in. Crash and Poison could see the perspiration on her shoulders and breasts, above the leather bra. She pretended to slap Poison, who did a neat stage-dive onto the floor. While the customers shoved tokens into the machines like they were cops eating donuts, the blonde in her red corset and the brunette in her leather skirt struggled onstage, with Killer finally gaining the upper hand and administering a not-so-fake spanking.

'I'm sorry, I'm sorry!' Crash wailed, trying to protect her beehive. Poison floor-danced around the perimeter, running her obi back and forth between her legs and pretending to whip herself with it, picking up money, making sexy ooh-baby faces at the customers and feigning masturbation for the ones who gave her something bigger than a single. 'Don't be so mad at me, lover girl,' Crash said to Killer when she got tired of having her hair pulled. 'We can both have her!'

Poison couldn't stop giggling as her two friends picked her up and tossed her back and forth between them. Even with an audience, it was a good time. 'You don't scare me,' she told Killer. Then it was Crash's turn to collect tolls as Killer 'forced' Poison to her knees, slowly removed her studded leather bra and skirt, and 'made' Poison go down on her.

Normally Crash didn't check out the booths too much. All she saw were hands and green paper. But one member of the audience had pissed her off. The window on his booth had been open since they came onstage, and he hadn't tipped once. So she stomped over to that cubicle and glared at its occupant. 'What do you think this is, Catholic Charities?' she snapped. Then she saw the tits. 'Hey, there's a girl over here!' she yelled. The click of spike heels told her that Killer and Poison were on their way.

There was just enough room in the booth to stand up and whack off. Bo wondered why there was a machine on one wall. Who wanted to watch movies if there was a live show? Then the three space tramps came onstage, and she thought she would die. They looked like the beautiful, come-fuck-me straight girls that she didn't dare talk to in the clubs. Because the stage was higher than the floor, she could look right up their dresses. But their shoes were even more intriguing than their pussies. Bo loved high-heeled shoes. The tall, thin spikes looked like they should punch holes in the floor. How could anybody do all those turns and kicks in them? Her heart was in her mouth, for fear one of the dancers would slip or fall. But they kept their balance. It was magic.

The first time her window came down, it scared her so bad she almost peed. What was she supposed to do, leave the booth and let somebody else have it? She opened the door a crack, but nobody else was exiting. 'Are you going?' asked a hopeful onlooker who'd been too slow to get a booth.

'Well, I don't want to, but I can't see anything.'

He gave her a strange look. Bo braced herself for a homophobic comment. But all he said was, 'You gotta put a token in to make the window come up.'

Feeling like a complete idiot, Bo muttered, 'Oh. Thanks,' and closed the door. It was warped, so she yanked it into place. With the window down, it was really dark in there. She had to feel for the token slot. When the window came up, it revealed something even more wonderful than solitary dancers. They were tussling with each other! She got out another token and held it over the slot, ready to drop it in the minute her view was threatened. The leather girl with the black ponytail sure had a hard hand. But her friend in the red corset seemed to like it. A lot of girls had hinted around about kinky stuff like that with Bo – like the one who was coming over on Saturday night. It made Bo happy to know she was projecting the right kind of tough image. But when it came down to actually tying somebody up or getting rough with them, somehow the timing was never quite right. Either they wanted it too much, or she wasn't sure they really wanted it after all. Too much pressure or something. Besides, she didn't *really* want to hurt anybody. Did she?

Meanwhile, all the hair-pulling and slapping onstage was making Bo's stomach feel funny. It was awfully hot in there. She reached for her right pocket to get her bandana, realized she was keeping it in the other pocket this week, fished it out, and wiped her face. She shouldn't let herself get conned like this. It was just an act, breeder chicks faking lesbian sex, but she pulled her T-shirt up anyway and pinched her own tits. Hard.

The window began to descend, and she dropped a token. As it came up, Bo's zipper went down. She had to work her jeans down over her hips to get her fingers in between her lips. She had a moment of panic, imagining cops barging in, but even the threat of being caught here with her pants down around her ankles made her cunt wetter and plumper. If she put one finger on her clit, it would take a little longer to come, but that would leave one hand free to work her tits. If only she knew why they'd put a glory hole in the Plexiglas. What was it for, kissing the dancers? Gross!

She was so close to coming. Of course, that little Asian girl wasn't really eating out the cat lady, but Bo knew what it would feel like. She knew what it would taste like. To be that helpless

— to have all these people watching —

Her vision was blocked again, but not by the window. An angry blonde in red lingerie was plastered against the Plexiglas, looking like she might use her long red nails to claw right through it. 'There's a girl in here!' she cried. Bo's arousal was swept away by a flood of shame and fear.

'Hey, what about us?' one of the guys yelled as the other dancers converged on Bo's window. *I have to get out of here*, she thought, dragging at her clothes. She pushed on the door, but it was stuck.

'Leaving so soon?' the brunette crooned. She had taken off everything except her boots, wristbands, and collar. 'We were going to put on a special performance just for you. We don't see other dykes in here very often.'

'Don't bother, I was just leaving!' Bo panted, wrestling with the door.

'Chicken,' said the Asian girl, who was wearing only her gold spike heels.

'Enjoying the show?' the blonde jeered, rotating her hips. She had taken her breasts out of the cups of her merry widow. Bo couldn't stop staring at her bush. All this blatant female nudity and aggressive attitude were making her sweat.

'No,' Bo lied, trying to sound defiant. 'I'm not enjoying the show.'

That offended all of them. 'But we're working so hard,' the blonde pouted. 'Is there something special you'd like to see? Want me to stick that vibrator through the hole so you can lick it?'

'This is sick,' Bo blustered. 'How can you stand to do this? It's degrading, letting a bunch of men jack off while you squirm and wiggle around.'

'Ooh, Crash, degrade me some more!' the Asian girl

crooned. They started French-kissing, hands between each other's legs. The sight completely exasperated Bo.

'Cut it out! That's disgusting. You can't fool me. You're just a bunch of mercenary straight bitches. You don't know anything about making love to a woman.'

The door shrieked as Killer forced it open. 'Is that so?' she hissed, dragging Bo out by her belt. One minute, Bo was staring at the pissed-off vixen's pierced eyebrow, and the next minute she was on the floor, staring at her boot heels. Then her hands were being cuffed behind her back, and she was up on her feet again. The rapid changes in altitude made Bo dizzy. This girl ate her spinach.

The bouncer left his post by the turnstile. 'Have we got a problem here, Killer?' he asked, eyeing Bo.

'Not anymore,' Killer told him. 'We just got a new whipping boy. Maybe this one will be a good dog instead of a bad dog. Are you a good dog, honey?' She punched Bo's upper arm. 'Huh? Answer me!'

'Well, you'd better get her in back before the manager sees her,' he said. 'She just went out to get a prescription filled, and she'll be back any minute.'

A buzzer sounded, signifying the end of the act. Bo thought about putting up a fight. But where was she going to go in these damned handcuffs? Killer shoved, and Bo went. Men were coming out of the stage booths, and most of them had hurt feelings. A few of them looked like they might complain, but Killer said clearly, 'The first one of you bozos to whine at me is eighty-sixed. The show's over.'

'You could do that to me,' one of them said wistfully, ogling Bo's handcuffs.

'You'd like it too much,' Killer said scornfully. Bo couldn't believe her ears. This girl was *naked*. How could she talk to a room full of men like that when they could see everything she had? Wasn't she afraid of anything?

Killer hustled Bo into the dressing room and tumbled her onto the floor. Bo's face was buried in a pile of nylon, spandex, lace, PVC, satin, and suede unmentionables. Something – probably a pair of high heels someone had left on the floor – dug into her stomach. The tiny room smelled like perfume, makeup, hair spray, girl sweat, and pussy. Bo thought she might suffocate. She much preferred the smell of motor oil and bourbon. All these filmy, stretchy, whispery, see-through, tight, gauzy, wispy, shiny, femmy things undid her. Clothing should be durable, comfortable, sturdy, and protect you from the elements. How did they get in and out of these rags? Where did they find the moxie to walk around half-naked? How could they trust garments that were held together with itsy-bitsy hooks and eyes or skinny pieces of elastic?

Then Killer kicked her lightly in the ribs. 'Look at me, home boy.'

'I am not your fucking home boy,' Bo said hotly. But she refused to roll over.

'You're right,' somebody else said, 'but it's not very smart to argue with Killer. Hey, get off my torts textbook! Do you know how much that damn book cost me?'

The next kick was not so gentle. Bo gave up and rolled onto her side, just far enough to see all of them. God, they gave off a ferocious aura, like the three witches in *Macbeth*. 'Take off these cuffs,' she said, without much hope that they would.

Everybody laughed. Bo did not enjoy being their punch line.

'You know my name,' Killer said. 'This is Poison, and the B-52 girl is Crash.'

Bo refused to play along. She wasn't telling them anything.

'I guess we'll just have to call you shit head,' Poison said.

'Or pig boy,' Crash added.

'Or dead meat,' Killer concluded.

Such lovely options. 'Bo,' the butch on the floor muttered. 'My name is Bo.'

'That must be Bo as in "Boy, am I stupid,"' Crash said thoughtfully. 'Don't you think it's rude to call a girl a tramp when she's only trying to show you a good time, baby boy?'

Killer snorted. 'Baby boy is right. What are you, lover, all of seventeen?'

'I'm twenty-two,' Bo snarled. 'And you look old enough to be my mother.'

'That's one,' Killer said softly. 'We'll just run a tab for you, shall we? Poison, what's she got on her?'

Poison knelt and rummaged through Bo's pockets. The Swiss Army knife drew gales of hilarity. 'I'll take custody of this,' Poison said, shaking it under Bo's nose. 'This little toad-sticker won't protect you from us, sugar.'

'Give me back my knife!' Bo shouted.

'Shut the fuck up!' Crash snarled, looking nervously over her shoulder. 'The walls have ears.'

Killer leaned down and spoke to Bo. Her lips were an inch from Bo's nose. 'Don't be dumb, my little lamb. None of us happens to like your little toy, so when we're done with you, if you're a good boy, you'll get it all back. *Capeche*?'

'Look, this is getting completely out of hand,' Bo said. 'If you let me go *right now*, I won't call the cops. Okay?'

'Woojums,' Crash said tenderly. 'If you do absolutely every little thing we say, *we* won't call the cops and report you for breaking and entering. Okay?'

Bo muttered something under her breath.

'Was that an epithet?' Poison asked, her eyes wide. 'I believe it was a sexist epithet, Killer.' She took one step closer to Bo and slapped her across the face. The stinging blow brought tears to Bo's eyes. 'This is a very small place. We simply don't have room for inflammatory hate rhetoric in here.'

'I don't know about you girls, but dancing always makes me horny,' Killer said, giving Bo a very unmotherly smile.

'Oh, yes, I feel almost compelled to have an orgasm,' Crash affirmed. Poison didn't say anything, so Crash nudged her.

'Ouch! Definitely.'

'So let's just fix our little boy toy up here so she has some back support,' Killer said, and backed Bo into the corner. 'No escape attempts,' she warned her, and showed her the handcuff key. 'Crash has got a gun in her purse. Don't you, dear?'

Crash obediently stuck her hand in her purse and pointed it at Bo. 'Yeah. Don't move, sucker.'

'Oh, bullshit, she does not have a –' Suddenly Bo was looking down the muzzle of a Beretta.

'It's licensed, too,' Crash explained. 'I used to be a security guard. If I ever get off the waiting list, I'm going to be one of the city's finest. Think I'll look good in blue?'

Killer took advantage of Bo's surprise to remove one of the cuffs and lock it around a water pipe. 'Don't do any Samson imitations,' she warned Bo. 'It's a hot-water pipe. All you'll do is scald yourself. Now suck me off. And make it snappy. I have to be back onstage in five minutes.'

They stared at each other for several long seconds – the triumphant bitch goddesses and their flustered, hijacked tourist. 'Maybe she doesn't know how to eat cunt,' Poison said helpfully. 'Maybe she's one of those awful straight girls who gets a short haircut and hangs out in lesbian bars pretending she belongs there.'

'Well?' Killer said impatiently. 'What about it? Do you know what to do with a piece of cherry pie, stud, or is your tongue just for making rude comments to your betters?'

They were not going to let her go. It was no use fighting them. Whoever would have thought that girls in lipstick and pushup bras could be so mean? 'No,' Bo said finally, looking at the floor. 'I'll do it.'

It was hard to get her tongue all the way into Killer's silky inner lips. Handcuffed to the water pipe, she couldn't get her neck to bend at the right angle. But she did her best, and Killer's flexible dancer's hips and slender legs made it easier. Out of the corner of her eye, she noticed the other women changing clothes and refreshing their makeup. Geez, if Bo was going to humiliate herself this way, the least they could do was watch.

'You're good,' Killer said, tugging one of her ears. 'Do it faster. Not harder, idiot – just faster!'

Killer's inner lips were thin and long, like the two halves of a razorback clam. Her teardrop-shaped clit was very small, like a seed pearl. She seemed to like having Bo's tongue go around it without actually touching it. The thought of biting her was very tempting, but then she'd probably stay handcuffed to this pipe until she starved to death.

'Oh, yes, that's it. Do that!' Killer said, squeezing Bo's head. There was a knock on the dressing room door. One of the girls told somebody they'd be right out. Killer came silently, biting her own hand. Bo was shaken by the sexual electricity that passed through her own body when Killer peaked. She barely noticed the dancers filing out and shutting the door behind them. They had left one of her hands free. It was the wrong hand, but nothing else was in sight. Wait — there was Poison's vibrator. She'd left it on the floor. Bo had to strain to reach it with her boot toes, but she managed to nudge it within reach.

There was no way she could come sitting down with her pants on. Bo somehow managed to pry her boots off, undo the jeans with one hand, and wiggle out of them. Lucky she didn't believe in underwear. She closed her eyes and tried to remember the exact shape of Killer's clit, the way her palms fit over Bo's ears, the other girls breathing faster as Killer got more excited, how she couldn't escape, couldn't get away, and had no idea what would happen next.

The awkward fingers of her left hand kept rebelling and cramping up. Frustrated, Bo switched the vibrator on and held it against her outer lips. She was embarrassed to even touch the thing. She had seen them in porn shops often enough, in boxes that always had these dopey pictures of women running them over their faces. It felt good, but it kept getting caught in her pubic hair. She tried to point it at her clit, but she was so wet that the head of it somehow slipped down and went into her. It seemed content to stay there, purring away, while Bo stroked her clit.

It just wasn't enough. She needed more, something, anything, to push herself over the edge! She stared around the room, wild-eyed. Right by her left thigh was another love offering from Poison, the discarded pair of tit clamps. Bo could sometimes make herself come just by twisting her own nipples. It was hard to get them on one-handed. Her nipples kept wanting to slip out of the clips. But finally she got both sides to catch.

Oh, God, she was going to come. It was inevitable. Even if the building blew up or her hands fell off, so much pressure had accumulated, Bo knew she would explode. She didn't have Killer's self-control. She heard herself whining, panting, and then saying, 'Please, please.'

The door opened and Killer walked in. 'Yes, you may,' Killer said, and jammed her high-heeled shoe between Bo's legs, pinning her hand and the vibrator in place. Bo came with the sharp heel of the dancer's shoe against her perineum. 'Come again,' Killer said, and jerked on the chain that connected the clamps. She also rocked her heel into Bo's tender flesh. And Bo came again, in terror and shock. 'Still want to call the cops?' Killer asked. 'No, I didn't think so. Stick around. Pets always get smarter when you play with them.'

'Good boy,' Crash said, replacing Killer in front of Bo. 'Now it's my turn to ride the pony.'

Bo guessed it was kind of stupid, but she never really noticed before that women liked to come in so many different ways. Crash had coarse pubic hair that made her face burn. Instead of Killer's elegant Art Deco genital geometry, her cunt was built like a '50s diner. It was robust, with shorter, thicker inner lips. The head of her clit was perfectly round and the size of a pencil eraser. She didn't get wet as quickly as Killer. She wanted a lot of long, slow, light strokes with a teasing little flutter at the end. Nobody told Bo that she couldn't, so she kept masturbating while she tried to get Crash to come. For some reason, she kept thinking about the short porn clip she'd seen in the video booth. Was this exactly like that woman sucking cock, or was it completely different? Probably both, Bo decided, though she couldn't have explained why. She was too busy jamming her face into Crash's thighs, sucking her clit like it was a straw buried in a milkshake. The dancer had finally gotten really juicy, and Bo was afraid she'd have to go back onstage before she got off. Finally Crash started pulling her hair — quite a trick, since Bo's flattop was less than an inch long — and tilted her pelvis so Bo's tongue was moving in and out of her cunt. 'Yesyesyes,' she sang. 'Good dog, good dog, good dog,' and finally, 'Sweet Jesus, yes, good boy!'

Bo felt quite pleased with herself. She leaned against the wall panting. But Crash was looking at her through narrow eyelids. Had she done something wrong? 'I always have to tinkle after I come,' Crash said delicately, and placed two fingers of her right hand on either side of her clit. The V-shaped fingers lifted her lips a little, and a golden arc of piss sprang through the air.

'Hey, don't pee on my clothes!' Poison snapped.

'Don't worry, I never miss,' Crash said sweetly as the last few drops soaked into Bo's T-shirt. 'Don't forget us while we're far from home,' she smirked, and the dancers left to put on one more show.

'Here,' Poison said before she walked out, and dropped a long, thick dildo in Bo's lap. 'That teeny thing is only good for fooling around in front of the customers. A big, strong girl like you needs a substantial tool to fuck herself with. There's some lube in my dance bag — the pink one — if you need it.'

Bo covered her face with her one free hand. How had she gotten into so much trouble? And why was she having so much fun? Poison was right, she probably didn't need any lube to get that truncheon in her cunt, but it was too embarrassing to go without it. So she wrapped her toes around the straps of Poison's hot pink carryall and dragged it over.

'Who says size doesn't matter?' Bo growled, and worked the head of the dildo in. It was wide enough to make her gasp. The wet T-shirt was going to give her a chill if she didn't keep moving. It sure was funny how things didn't feel the way they looked. Getting slapped looked like the worst thing in the world, but it was actually pretty exciting. It stung a lot, but it made her heart beat faster and her PC muscle jump. The thought of getting pissed on would have made her gag this morning, but now all she could smell was Crash's cunt and her own sex. The wet shirt was like a badge or a medal. She had something that belonged to Crash now. The dancer had given Bo a part of her. You couldn't just abandon somebody you'd pissed on, could you?

She jabbed the dildo in, remembering how it felt to have Killer kick her between the legs. The spike heel was like the point of a knife. It was cruel and relentless, like . . . like a woman, Bo realized. Cruelty was a feminine quality. The dancers' wilful ways suddenly made sense. Of course they were bossy and nasty and liked to hurt people. Femmes always wanted to be in control. But you weren't supposed to notice it. No, that was one way to get yourself into shit up to your nose hairs. You were supposed to do everything they wanted, before they asked you, and make them think it was all your own idea. Nothing was ever their fault, it was always *your* fault because you were the butch and it was your job to make sure everything went smoothly.

Bo thought she preferred this up-front sexual assault to that silly game. The dildo hurt a little. The hurt made her want to come. But maybe she shouldn't come. Killer seemed to take it for granted that she would wait until she had permission. Maybe she was supposed to wait. Maybe if she waited, it would make Killer happy.

As soon as Bo thought about resisting orgasm, it became much more likely. Of course, she could just quit touching herself, but it was so boring being stuck here with nothing but a broken chair and a cracked mirror for company. She strained her ears, trying to see if the last song in the dancers' set was playing yet.

It was hard to wait. Hard to wait. Hard. Hard. So hard. So big. So –

'You *are* a pig,' Killer said, amused. 'Look at you, jacking off all covered with piss, just waiting for somebody to come and use you or hurt you or tell you what to do. Aren't you lucky that we bother to take an interest in you?' She stalked over to Bo and removed the tit clamps with one smooth jerk. Bo had forgotten they were there. Her nipples had gone numb while she was eating out Crash. She wanted to shriek, but Killer was waiting to slap her if she did. So she just whimpered a little.

'Well?' Killer said. 'Answer me!'

'Well – what?' Bo stammered.

'Aren't you lucky that we're training you?'

Is that what's happening? Bo wondered. 'Yes, I'm lucky, ma'am.'

Killer looked even more amused. 'Now I'm a ma'am. I suppose it's a step up from being your mama. Just call me mistress. I think Poison wants to check you out.'

Poison was chewing a large wad of gum. She nonchalantly

blew a bubble that was bigger than Bo's face, popped it, and sucked it back into her peony red mouth. 'You betcha,' she said, sticking the gum to one corner of the mirror. Crash peeled it off with the tips of her fingers and dropped it in the trash.

'Put some lube on your hand,' Poison told her. Bo managed, awkwardly. 'Now put your fingers up my ass,' the dancer ordered, and positioned Bo's head so her tongue was poised in just the right spot. She wanted a hard, flicking motion just above her clit, which was slightly pointed, and a lot of in-and-out work between the cheeks of her muscular behind. Bo's arm rapidly got tired, but Poison was not about to let her rest. 'Come on, you can do anything for twenty minutes,' she snapped at Bo. 'Fuck me like you mean it, put your shoulder into it, and keep that tongue busy too. I want to come all over your face, I want to suck your arm into my ass, I want to eat you alive in little bloody chunks, slave boy, boy toy, bet you never really fucked a girl in your life. You're probably used to taking it up the ass, not dishing it out. Lowlife trash, you come sneaking in here thinking you can get your rocks off and then sneak out again, serves you right getting caught. Fuck me! Fuck me! More! More! More!'

She came briefly, but very hard. Bo's shoulder hit the wall. 'Okay, stop it, I'm done now,' Poison said, and walked off to change her G-string.

And that was how it went for the rest of the night. Killer eventually took the dildo away from Bo, saying, 'We don't want our puppy to get spoiled.' Bo gathered from the high energy the dancers brought into the dressing room that they were doing very well out there. She was startled when Killer took the hand-cuffs off, made her strip, and said, 'Go in the bathroom and clean yourself up. Then come back here and we'll dress you up. Make it snappy. Poison already called the limousine.'

'My bike —,' Bo said weakly.

'I already had somebody take it home for you,' Killer said.

Bo gave her a horrified look.

'Well, your keys were right in your jacket pocket,' Killer said impatiently. 'And you do live at the same address that's on your checks, right? So what's the problem? Eddy's wife knows from Harleys. She's been taking him to runs for years. She isn't going to fuck your bike up. Look, if you don't want to go out with us, you can always walk home. Naked.'

Once again, doing as she was told seemed like much the best option. Bo tiptoed into the corridor, and hoped the only door she could see led to a bathroom. The toilet seemed to have indigestion, but a few minutes' work with the plunger fixed that. The sink wasn't very clean, and only the cold-water tap worked, but Bo doused some paper towels and sponged herself off. Shivering, she crept back into the room, and was astonished to see that all the mess that had covered the floor ankle-deep had vanished into three little bags.

Killer, Crash, and Poison looked ready to hit the streets of a sex zone on some perverted, faraway Amazon planet. Killer was wearing a strapless black leather dress with a studded bodice. The purple tips of her ponytail swept her white shoulders and back. Bo wanted to bite her, to leave a round red mark on that fair and very fragile-looking skin. The skirt was slit so high in the back, you could almost see Killer's buns. Her black stockings were decorated with a cobra on each ankle. The snakes had rhinestone eyes. And the heels of her pumps were even taller than the boots she'd worn onstage. Poison was wearing a body-harness made out of leather straps and fine silver chains. The carefully draped chains hid her nipples, and a tiny leather strap just barely concealed her sex. Her shoulders were covered with spiked leather pads, and she wore matching spiked gauntlets on each arm. She had traded in her gold pumps for a pair of knee-high engineer boots with steel toes. Bo wondered where the dancer got such butch footwear in tiny sizes. She had to wear three pairs of socks with *her* engineer boots. Crash was in a high-necked, long-sleeved PVC catsuit that had zippers in its crotch and over the nipples. She had combed out her beehive and had pulled her long, blonde hair through a hole in the back of a patent-leather helmet. Bo couldn't tell where the suit ended and Crash's boots began. Her outfit was a seamless piece of glossy midnight, except for the zippers that protected and flaunted her erogenous zones.

'You didn't have any underwear,' Killer said, 'so you'll have to wear these.'

'These' were a pair of lilac tap pants with black lace around the waist and legs. Bo's whole body went rigid. 'I will not!' she said.

Crash sighed and put her in a half nelson. Poison picked up Bo's feet, one at a time, and Killer smoothed the lingerie into place. 'We can't have you running around with a bare butt,' Killer soothed. 'You'll catch your death of cold. Nobody will know what you have on under your jeans. Now get into your Levi's and your boots.'

'You can wear my tank top,' Poison said, tossing Bo six square inches of black spandex.

'I don't think that's big enough for me,' Bo said weakly, tucking the cuffs of her jeans into her boots.

200

'Let's dress the baby,' Killer said. 'Put ooh widdle awms up, diddums. There we go.'

Bo was afraid to look at herself in the mirror. But Crash turned her bodily to face it. 'Nice delts and lats,' she said approvingly. 'How come butches have all the cleavage, Bo?'

'I hate you all,' Bo said unhappily.

'Aren't we the lucky ones?' Killer said coldly. 'Just for that, you can wear some lipstick on your way out. So everybody knows who you're with.'

Bo tried to struggle, but Poison and Crash held her in place. How could they get so many muscles just dancing? With a firm and practiced hand, Killer made a bright red Cupid's-bow mouth on Bo's trembling lips. 'They ought to be that red anyway, considering how much pussy you've chowed down today,' Crash snickered.

The dancers hustled Bo to the front of the store. Bo noticed that Crash and Killer were taller than she was. Must be the shoes. A black stretch limousine was parked in the bus zone in front of the store. 'Easy come, easy go,' a middle-aged woman told them bitterly, staring at the luxurious car.

'Oh, you're welcome, we loved making all that money for you,' Crash said, blowing her a kiss.

'She knows a hell of a lot more about going than she does about coming,' Poison muttered. The chauffeur was opening their door. 'Next time that'll be your job,' she said, jabbing Bo in the ribs. *Next time?*

The seats in the back of the limo were so wide that the three dancers sat side by side. 'Put her on the floor,' they had told the chauffeur, and he did as they asked as if there was nothing

201

unusual about their request. So Bo was lying on the carpeted floor, listening to the engine, watching Crash put a tape in the stereo while Poison uncorked a big, green bottle and Killer took three shrimp cocktails out of the little refrigerator.

'Where to first, ladies?' asked the chauffeur. He must be using an intercom. There was a pane of soundproof glass between him and the passenger compartment.

'Over the bridge and back again,' Killer said. 'We need to unwind. Then we'll visit the club.'

'Very good, madam,' he said, and did not speak again.

'Impressed?' Killer asked, nudging Bo with her toe.

'Yeah, I guess I am,' Bo had to admit.

'Sex workers make a lot of money,' Poison bragged. 'Especially if they have somebody like Killer to invest it. You should see our coop. It's a nice place, but it's too big for us to keep up with. Too bad you aren't looking for a job. We need a new houseboy. Somebody who won't put my lingerie in the washing machine because they're too lazy to get out the Woolite.'

'Somebody who can cook something besides pork chops and baked potatoes,' Crash sighed, digging into her shrimp cocktail. 'Somebody who dusts.'

'Shut up,' Killer said sharply. 'This little asshole has to make it through the night without disgracing us first.'

Bo couldn't see any higher than the ankles of the women who were taking her for this wild ride. Her eyes went back and forth between the poisonous snakes that sprang from Killer's six-inch heels; Poison's carefully polished engineer boots; and Crash's spike-heeled boots. She was mesmerized by the rhinestone eyes of the snakes, their enraged, inflated hoods; the hint of a reflection of her own face in Poison's steel toes; the spurs that Crash

cheerfully dug into the carpeted floor of the limo. Inside her
501s, the lilac-colored tap pants bunched up and slid around.
The lace scratched. What would her friends think if they could
see her now?

'Hey, good dog,' Killer said caustically, 'want a shrimp?' She
held out a piece of seafood, dripping red sauce. Bo opened her
mouth and took it carefully from her fingers. 'Don't muss your
lipstick,' Killer added. 'What would your buddies think if they
could see you now, Bo?'

Poison and Crash laughed. Bo startled like an animal that's
been hit with a BB gun. 'I think they'd laugh at me,' Bo said
slowly, 'just like y'all do.'

That shut them up. 'Yeah, they probably would,' Killer said
judiciously. 'But they'd be jealous too, honey, and don't you
ever forget it. More shrimp?'

Bo let the dancers feed her crackers smeared with brie,
pinches of caviar. Poison tilted some liquid from her glass into
Bo's mouth, and she swallowed before realizing it was champagne. 'Hey, I can't drink that,' she protested.

'What are you, allergic to sulfites?' Crash asked. 'You gonna
keel over dead if we let you eat at the salad bar? No trips to the
Sizzler for you, sissy boy.'

'No, I –'

'She doesn't drink, asshole,' Killer snapped. 'Here, Bo, this is
Calistoga. Wash your mouth out.'

It seemed only appropriate to kiss Killer's shoe to thank her.
Bo didn't think she could feel it through the finely crafted
leather. But Killer rolled her foot to the side and pressed the toe
into Bo's throat. 'You have good instincts, baby,' she said. 'But
you're supposed to ask permission.'

Bo hesitated. 'It's a great way to get the lipstick off your mouth,' Poison pointed out. That kind of spoiled it.

'I wasn't thinking about that,' Bo said. 'I'm just not used to asking for things.'

'Oh?' Crash said bitterly. 'You think butch girls like you ought to just grab whatever they want, without asking?'

'No,' Bo sighed. 'Usually I don't grab anything, I just wait and hope whatever I want will come to me. If you don't want anything, you can't get hurt when you don't get it. It's dangerous to ask for things, Crash.'

'That's Mistress Crash to you,' the blonde said loftily, and rested her boot heels on Bo's legs.

'Aren't you the deep one,' Poison said, cuddling the hard shells of her boot toes into Bo's stomach.

'Quit thinking so much,' Killer advised, and stroked Bo's cheek with her soles.

'Can I kiss them?' Bo whispered.

'Honey, it's what you were born to do,' Killer replied. 'Just don't slobber on me. I hate it when my shoes get wet.'

Once more, Bo lost track of time. She was busy creating new yoga positions to gain access to the footwear of all three women. She had never imagined doing anything like this. She had watched a leather boy set up a boot-shining stand at a benefit once, and wondered why the crowd of men who surrounded him seemed so intense, like a pack of coon hounds. The boy's daddy had made Bo get in front of the men who were waiting and ordered the kid, who was kneeling, wearing nothing but a jockstrap, his hands and face streaked with black polish, to make her cowboy boots shine. The boot boy had stoically done his job, but Bo didn't find it very exciting. She knew Daddy

Rick from meetings, and he always greeted her with a smile, but they weren't exactly friends. She couldn't tell if he was doing this to let everybody know he thought she belonged in this bar, or to subtly punish his 'son'.

This act of worship was very different. It was like taking somebody's panties off with your teeth. You had to be delicate. Not biting – not tearing anything – was what made it erotic. If you were really lucky, the girl you were with got so excited that she forgot to take her underwear home with her. Bo blushed when she thought about the secret collection she kept tucked between her mattress and the box spring. She didn't think anybody would forget their shoes that easily. And who would have guessed that the smell of perfume and leather, mingled with a little sweat, could be such an aphrodisiac? It shouldn't be as exciting as smelling somebody's wet cunt and knowing you made it juicy. But above the foot (which might kick you away), there was the ankle, and above the ankle the muscular calf (which would feel so nice draped over your shoulder), then the knees, which might part, then the thighs, round and soft with promise, and after that –

Maybe after that came even more work, more personal service, for a good dog who had a careful, soft, and respectful mouth. Bo hoped so.

'Enough,' Killer said firmly. 'Stop it, Bo. We're here. We're getting out now. Oh, don't look so upset. We're taking you with us. Poison, would you do something with our guest?'

Bo had to force herself to stop staring at the two spots of color that decorated Killer's cheekbones and look at the other dancer. The two leather bands around Poison's upper arms came off, snapped together, and went around Bo's neck. "It'll have to do until we get our real collar back from the bad dog,' Crash said, attaching a leash and extracting Bo from the limo.

Get what back from who? Bo wondered.

'We'll page you,' Killer told the driver. 'Why don't you go get dinner?'

'Certainly, madam,' he replied and the car floated away.

'Charley would kill to be in your place,' Poison snickered, tapping Bo between the shoulder blades.

'Charley can go fuck himself,' Killer said. 'The last thing I want after I get off work is one more prick hanging around looking for a freebie.'

This looked like an industrial zone. The streets were empty. But the block around the bar was crowded with motorcycles, parked so close they almost touched. The three dancers strolled into the club, which Bo recognized as one of those places that was always getting shut down by the city for violating the fire code or selling liquor to minors. What was it called, Jack's? Something like that. No, Jax! That was it. Bo's date for Saturday night had talked about coming down here for a drink, like it was some kind of big deal to walk into this joint.

The bouncer waved them through without asking for ID or a cover charge. The bartender – one of the biggest women Bo had ever seen – shouted, 'God help us all, it's the Furies incarnate.'

Bo's captors waved back, looking smug. 'We're regulars here,' Poison explained, adjusting her chain harness so her nipples showed. 'Kat likes us because we're troublemakers.'

'There's a table,' Crash said, pointing somewhere into the crowd. Somebody snatched at one of the zippers on her catsuit, and she elbowed them in the face. 'You're a bigger asshole than your asshole,' she told the unlucky and unsuccessful woman who had dared touch her without permission. That poor soul was clutching her nose. 'I'd put some ice on that if I were you,' Crash sneered.

'Go save that table for us,' Killer ordered, slapping her gloves against her palm. Crash put the end of the leash in Bo's mouth, and she went without thinking. A couple of the patrons barked at her, but she kept on going until she saw the vacant table. She stood behind one chair and put her hands on the backs of the other two.

'Perfect,' Poison said, positioning her hard little rump on the seat. Her legs were too short for her feet to touch the floor, so she propped her engineer boots up on the legs of the table. Bo thought that was pretty cute. 'I want more champagne.'

'I am not holding your head while you puke all night,' Killer said severely. She had seated herself like a grand duchess, and Bo was trying to figure out how she managed to sit down in that tight skirt without splitting it up the back.

'If you make me switch to something else, I'll get sick for sure,' Poison replied. 'Dom Perignon for me, Bo. Want to help me out, Crash?'

'Whatever,' Crash said. She had not taken a seat. She remained standing, drumming her red claws on the back of a chair and scanning the crowd. Apparently she did not find the party she was looking for, because she suddenly blew air out of her nose, picked up the chair, turned it around, and sat on it backwards. 'Champagne is as close as I'm going to get to Paris tonight, girlfriends.'

'I'm sure Bo could take a few lessons in French,' Killer said coldly. 'A Virgin Mary, with extra Tabasco,' she told Bo. 'Go on! Don't *worry* about the *money*, Bo, we run a tab here.'

Crash intercepted her before she left the table and unsnapped the leash. 'Be prompt, or this goes back on,' she warned.

More barking followed Bo to the bar. She wondered what that was all about. It didn't sound unfriendly. It was more like a cheer. The next time somebody howled at her, she howled back. This caused a moment or two of relative silence. She was still close enough to the table to hear the three dancers chortle. 'Still think she's going to embarrass us, Killer?' Poison demanded.

Bo fought her way to the bar, where a short, redheaded dyke in a leather vest and jeans was arguing with the mountainous, blonde bartender. 'You have to quit covering up for Lolly,' the redhead said. 'Look at this mess. How are you supposed to tend bar all by yourself on a Friday night?'

'Aw, Reid, ease up, I'm doing okay. You're just mad 'cause I can't take a break and sneak out to the patio and give you a blowjob. We weren't supposed to see each other tonight anyway. Why don't you go home and take a nap? I'll come over after I get off work.'

'Fuck that,' Reid said. 'This is not the way friends treat one another, Kat.'

'What do you want me to do, get her fired? In case you haven't heard, there's a recession out there. I am not going to be responsible for somebody getting laid off when there's no place else for them to go. Lolly's in love, and when she's in love, she's just not herself. She'll be back again as soon as the bitch dumps her or they run out of poppers.'

'Codependents are a pain in the ass, aren't they?' Bo said sympathetically to the redhead. Reid turned around quick, like somebody had bitten her in the ass, and snapped, 'Who asked you?' The keys on the left side of her belt jingled.

'Nobody had to,' Bo replied. 'It's a free country.'

Reid snorted. She turned her back on Kat and her talkative customer and leaned against the bar, scanning the crowd like American radar looking for Russian jets. Kat shrugged, almost stuck her tongue out at the back of Reid's head, then thought better of it.

'You need a tray, right?' Kat asked. 'Tell me what your keepers are drinking. No, I'll tell you. One bottle of champagne, two glasses, and a Virgin Mary, right?'

'Extra Tabasco,' Bo added, trying to process the idea of these two women being in a relationship and the bartender being a bottom.

'You look like a Southern Comfort girl yourself,' Kat suggested.

'Calistoga,' Bo said, smiling.

'We don't have any more that's cold,' Kat said, sounding harassed. She arranged other beverages on a tray. 'We need some ice, but it doesn't look like anybody's going out for any.'

'All right!' Reid shouted. 'I will get on my friggin' bike and somehow find a place in this godforsaken neighborhood that has ice, and try to convince myself I don't look like a complete and total dweeb running errands for you because your coworker had to pick this week of all weeks to go out on a toot!'

'Don't do me any fucking favors!' Kat snarled. But Reid kept shoving through the crowd. 'Don't let those hellcats get too riled up, now,' the bartender told Bo, pushing the tray toward her. 'I got enough on my hands tonight without them swingin' on the chandeliers and slashing people's tires.'

Bo put the tray up high on one hand, the way real waiters did it, and bayed at the women in front of her. It didn't exactly sound like a wolf pack baying at a National Geographic film crew, but Bo figured she could refine her sound effects as time went on. The patrons of Jax let her cut through like the pointer on an Etch-A-Sketch.

'What took you so long?' Poison complained. 'Don't let that cork fly – oh, you know how. Never mind.'

Bo unwrapped the little, white towel from the neck of the green bottle, put the cork on the table, and poured two flutes of champagne without releasing all of the bubbles.

'Kat and Reid are having a fight, huh?' Crash said. 'I knew it could never last. Butch-on-butch is such a joke.'

'Shut up,' Killer said. 'What about your little fling with Belinda, huh? Surely you remember her – the girl who did the snake act at the Manslaughter Brothers' Cow Palace.' She took a sip of her Virgin Mary. 'Hot!' she sputtered. 'Good,' she added, biting on the celery stick. It snapped like a little bone.

'That was hardly butch-on-butch,' Crash said, holding out her glass for some more champagne. Bo poured carefully. There was no chair for her, so she guessed she was supposed to just stand up and wait on everybody. She filched a bowl of peanuts from the closest table and offered them to Killer, who took a few but did not put them in her mouth because she was too busy hassling Crash.

'Yeah, well, how would you have responded to the suggestion that you get a crewcut if you were going to strap it on with her, huh?' she asked. 'I mean, that *is* why you broke up, isn't it? Because one of you wasn't butch enough?'

'No,' Crash snapped, putting her glass down almost hard enough to snap the stem. 'We broke up because she gave me crabs, if you must know. Did I forget to mention the torrid night we spent in your bed, darling?'

'You're awful,' Killer said, smiling happily.

'I think we're all pretty awful,' Poison said contentedly. 'Isn't it wonderful? Bo, do you smoke cigarettes?'

'No.'

'No what?'

'No, uh, mistress. I don't smoke cigarettes. I do carry a few around with me, though, for the street people. So they'll leave my bike alone.'

Poison gave Killer a significant glance.

'Stop that,' Killer said irritably. 'I know it would be nice to have a boy who doesn't smoke. I'm as sick of Donna's dirty ashtrays as you are. But for godsake, Poison, she can't even say the word "mistress" without stammering. She doesn't know a single thing about the scene. Do you really want to clutter up our lives with a novice who will probably cut and run the first time somebody teases her about giving it up for a bunch of girls?'

Crash, still smarting from Killer's sarcastic remarks about her affair with another dancer, saw her chance to get even. 'Well, I'm so glad you were born with a bullwhip in your hand,' she said lightly. 'I think Poison's right. If we ever see Bad Dog again, we ought to sic Bo on her. Winter's coming. It's time for indoor sports. And I can think of a lot worse ways to spend evenings in front of the fireplace than some training sessions with this little hunk. She knows enough to wear her red hanky on the left. That's all the etiquette I want out of my houseboy.'

Bo looked from one woman to the other as they took turns talking. Nobody looked at her. That seemed a little weird. Shouldn't somebody ask her what she thought about all of this?

Or explain it? 'Hey,' she finally interjected.

The silence was frosty. 'Yes?' Killer finally said.

'Don't you think it would be a nice idea to ask me what I want before you all go dividing me up like a pizza?'

The three dancers exchanged amused and outraged glances. 'No,' Killer said firmly. 'That would not be a nice idea. Shut up, Bo. We'll let you talk later.'

Bo shrugged and let her mind wander while the bickering resumed.

'See that stool over there?' Crash asked her, reeling Bo in by her collar. She ran her fingernails down the skin between Bo's breasts. Even through the spandex, Bo's nipples became visibly more firm. 'I want you to grab that empty bar stool and drag it over by this table. Do you understand me, butchy boy?'

Bo nodded. Her only fear was that Crash would keep hanging on to her collar so long that somebody would sit down on the bar stool. But Crash gave her a little shove, and she got to the only empty seat in the house just a split second before somebody's fanny descended upon it. The crowd hooted at her as she wrestled the awkward piece of furniture back to the table. *Why does everybody in this place seem to know somethin' I don't know?* Bo wondered. *Maybe 'cause they do. Shit.*

'Bend over it,' Crash instructed Bo, speaking over her shoulder.

'I – I – what?' Bo sputtered.

'Bend over,' Poison piped up. She pushed her chair back and walked over to Bo, who was trying to follow directions and feeling like a horse's neck. Poison stood by Bo's head and leaned forward, pinning her shoulders down. 'Remember me?' she said. Her soft belly was plastered against the top of Bo's head,

and the smell of her juicy, bossy little cunt made Bo's nose itch
with lust.

'Just what do you think you're doing?' Killer said flatly,
trying to make Crash back down.

'Come on, dearie, she already has one demerit. You said so
yourself in the dressing room. So let me give her a spanking.
That should make it pretty clear whether she's got the right
qualifications for the job.'

Bo could barely hear this conversation. Poison's thighs were
partially blocking her ears. But she heard Killer and Crash's high
heels clicking as the two friends came to stand beside her. Bo
thought it was Killer who touched her on the small of her back,
sliding her hand under Bo's spandex shirt and grazing the skin
with her long fingernails. Then Poison moved away from her,
and Bo could tell it was definitely Killer who was talking.

'You've had a very busy day,' Killer said. 'I'm sure when you
walked into Sugar and Spice, you never expected to find yourself in this position.'

'Butcha are, Blanche, ya are!' Poison crowed.

'Be quiet, please,' Killer said severely. 'Bo has some very serious thinking to do. When I gave you a demerit in the dressing
room, I really had no right to do that. You have no agreement
with us that gives us the right to discipline you or order you
around. So now you have to choose. If you want to stay with us
for the rest of the night, you have to let Crash spank you. Right
here in the bar. If you'd like to go home, I'll give you some cab
fare. No hard feelings, but if we run into you again, we probably
won't remember who you are. There are so many butch bottoms who would give their eyeteeth to be where you are right
now that I'm sure we won't have any trouble replacing the bad

dog who currently calls itself our houseboy. If you can take the spanking without trying to get up off the bar stool, we can talk about a more permanent arrangement. If you find that you can't tolerate being paddled, I'm afraid we'll have to put an ad up on the bulletin board here and start interviewing applicants. Crash and Poison mostly care about your strong right arm, darlin', but I want to make sure your hide is tough enough to deal with my strong right arm.'

Now Bo knew what the phrase 'got your tit caught in a wringer' meant. What the hell was a butch bottom? She was so wet that she wasn't sure she could stand up and walk away from the bar stool. She would probably slip across the floor like somebody who just stepped on a bar of soap. She looked at Poison. The dancer gave her a wicked smile. No wonder she had a white stripe, that little skunk. She obviously didn't care if Bo succeeded or failed. Either outcome would entertain her. Bo sighed and glanced at Crash. The blonde's attention was focused on Killer. So Bo looked that way too. Both of Killer's eyebrows were raised. 'Well?' she demanded. 'All you have to do is choose.'

'Then I choose to ask for a spanking,' Bo said defiantly. 'Please, ma'am. Uh, ladies.'

Poison applauded and scampered over to the bar stool, where she once again pinned Bo's shoulders to the padded seat. Crash threw one arm across the small of Bo's back. She let her other hand rest on Bo's denim-clad butt.

'No,' Killer said meanly, deliberately pitching her voice so that Bo and probably everybody else in the bar could hear her. 'No pants.'

Bo froze. That meant everybody would see the lingerie the dancers had forced her to wear. She was mortified. But her clammy fingers were already unbuttoning her jeans and pushing them down. 'Fine,' she said, and left it at that. If she made a longer speech, her voice would shake.

Crash ran her palm over the slippery, pastel purple cloth. God, she had big hands for a girl. 'We'll do one soft, four medium, and one hard,' she decided. 'On each side, of course.'

Bo kept her teeth together, anticipating the use of great force. She was surprised by the mildness of the blows. Was Crash going easy on her, or did she simply not hit people as hard as Killer had hit her? Could it be that she was actually disappointed that it didn't hurt more? Wasn't that a puzzle! It didn't occur to her that Crash was playing a little mistress game with Killer, making sure that the new boy didn't flunk out of class.

Bo's face was bright pink when she straightened up, but she figured that was only natural. She'd been hanging practically upside down. The three dancers were back at their table, sipping their drinks. Crash looked like a kitty with canary feathers up its nose, and Killer was obviously fuming. Bo tried not to look beyond that little table. But as she raised her britches, Bo came face-to-face with the big bartender. Kat's knowing eyes made Bo blush tomato red. To hell with those mean, if entertaining, bitches. Kat had seen the shameful undergarments. Another butch – a senior dyke – knew what she had let these femmes do to her. Bo wanted to run and hide.

'Hey, there, little dog,' Kat said softly. 'You're a good boy. Did you know that? Well, you are. You're being very good.'

Bo squared her shoulders, took a deep breath, and whispered, 'Thanks.' But Kat was already at the other end of the bar, waiting on customers, and probably never even heard her. Bo took another deep breath and then dared to look around at the other dykes in the bar. Nobody seemed to be pointing or staring at her. Was that scorn she saw in the few faces that turned toward her – or was it envy?

'Did I pass your little test?' Bo demanded.

Killer looked ready to jump on her for that. But somebody rammed her from behind, and the table slid forward. Drinks slopped out of their glasses. 'You!' Killer said angrily.

'Donna!' Kat called out warningly. 'Don't go stirring shit in my bar!'

'What do they expect, dressed up like that?' Donna jeered. 'They're a walking advertisement for sexual harassment! They just get me so excited, I can't help myself. I have to let them know how they really make me feel.' And she grabbed her crotch.

Bo thought this must be the bad dog that the dancers had been complaining about ever since she met them. Donna was as tall as Killer and outweighed her by at least forty pounds. She had short hair that curled like black sheep's wool and liquid, dark brown collie eyes. Bo had last seen that look in the eyes of a dog that belonged to an uncle of hers. Whenever it came around to lick your hand and fawn on you, you could bet that it had killed another chicken. Bo wrinkled her nose at the smell of marijuana and gin. What an uncouth combination.

'Why all the long faces? It's not like I *raped* anybody,' Donna jeered. 'I'm just sayin' hello.' She leaned into Killer's face. 'Hello!' she shouted. 'Where have you been? You're all *late*. I thought I'd have to take a doorknob home if I wanted to get laid tonight.' She took the cigarette from behind her ear and held it under Poison's nose. 'Gimme a light,' she whined. 'Who do I have to fuck to get a match around here?'

'You're fired,' Killer said firmly, pushing her away. 'So give us back our collar, Bad Dog, and get out.'

'Fired? You can't fire me! I'll sue. Besides, who's going to pay my tab?' Donna blustered.

'From now on, you'll have to pay your own fucking way,' Poison told her.

Donna took a simple leather dog collar out of her back pocket and threw it at Killer, who caught it in one hand. Then she pursed her lips and spit at her.

Kat was hustling down the bar with a sap in her hand. But Bo was faster. She reached out, grabbed the interloper by her ear-lobe, and twisted. Donna shrieked and fell to her knees.

'You're pulling out my earrings!' she yelled.

'I certainly hope so,' Bo replied, and dug her fingernails in a little deeper. She took off toward the front door of the bar, and Donna followed her, duck-walking on her knees.

'You bastard,' Donna swore. 'I hate you. What did they do, promise to let you kiss their asses? Well, they're nothing but a bunch of dirty little whores, and you know what that makes you. Let me go! Stop it, stop it!'

Apparently Donna was well-known at Jax, because there was scattered applause as the patrons became aware of what Bo was doing. The clapping grew to standing-ovation proportions as Bo reached the door, hauled Donna to her feet, and sent her out-side with a boot to her backside.

But the wretched Bad Dog wouldn't go quietly. 'I bet you lick their assholes!' she shrieked, just outside the bar. 'I hope they shit in your mouth! Whores! You run around with –'

Bo heard a roaring noise behind her head, and white light flashed at the edges of her vision. She took two steps forward, grabbed Donna by the front of her shirt, and punched her in the mouth. 'Where I come from, we don't talk that way to ladies who are paying for our drinks,' she said, letting her opponent crumple to the pavement. 'You've lost. Go home.'

Reid pulled up to the curb, three bags of ice held across the back of her seat with bungee cords. She undid the cords and threw a bag of ice at Bo. 'Help me get these inside,' she told her, stomping into the bar. She gave Donna one unpitying glance. 'Have a little trouble, did we?'

'No trouble,' said Bo. The ice felt good against the split knuckles of her right hand. She let Reid walk ahead of her, afraid Donna would rush both of them. But when the disgraced dog got up, she kept herself pointed in the opposite direction, as if Bo were a bad smell she was determined to ignore. She took some change out of her pocket and headed for a pay phone across the street.

Inside, Killer, Crash, and Poison took the bag of ice away from Bo and practically heaved it across the bar at Kat. 'You're hurt!' Crash said, cradling Bo's battered fist.

'We could have taken care of that rowdy little jerk ourselves,' Poison muttered.

'Yeah, but why should we have to?' Killer smiled. 'We have a much bigger and better dog taking care of us now. A pit bull, I think. Do you feel like a pit bull, Bo?'

From behind the bar, Kat gave Bo a thumbs-up. 'What the hell is going on here?' Reid grouched. 'I leave you alone for twenty minutes and World War III breaks out. One of these days somebody in this lunatic asylum is going to hurt you, Kat, and I'm going to have to –'.

'Page Charley,' Killer told Poison. 'Let's take our baby home.'

'We'll find out how you like your red hanky when it's on the other side,' Crash promised, pressing into Bo's side. Her perfume made Bo dizzy. She wished to hell she knew what that red hanky meant, but after finally getting this lucky, she wasn't about to ask.

TONY MUSGRAVE
Bel

'I had an ideal childhood,' she says, kneeling beside him to gently lift his penis and ease off the condom, which she holds in one hand, smoothing the air out of it with the other before expertly tying a knot in its neck. The milky liquid bobs in the teat and base as she springs off the bed and walks through the open bathroom door. 'My parents tried to show me what they knew and something of what they felt.' Out of the mirrored cupboard above the basin she takes a washer from a neat pile, slides it over the condom's knot and throws it in the toilet on which she briefly pauses to pee, looking at him through the doorway as she continues talking. 'What they had discovered for themselves was that we think things about those closest to us that we never dare to express.' She flushes the toilet, waits to be certain that the weighted condom has disappeared along with her warm yellow urine and squats over the bidet to douse her private parts. 'Feelings of hate, rage, jealousy and, oh yes, of boredom are aroused in us by our parents, our partners, our children, our lovers, our friends and we suppress these feelings or redirect them.' She dries herself with an orange bath towel. 'Oh I know it sounds banal. The man has had hell at the office — I fancy a large cup of milky coffee and perhaps a grappa, what about you – and it ends up with the kids tormenting the cat. On the other hand, bread and cheese and grapes would be rather nice and white wine is the accompaniment to that, and anyway the way to celebrate such a glorious fuck is with a chilled bottle of champagne. I keep two or three in the fridge, just in case such a thing should happen to me.'

She comes out of the bathroom with a damp purple flannel and a purple towel. She kneels on the bed again and as he understands what she intends to do, he pushes her away. 'Now, what are you thinking? Am I the mother, come to clean your willy. Am I your conscience, saying that a ritual act of cleansing will absolve you from the guilt of having slept with a woman? Or do I wish to handle you, to peel back your foreskin, to explore you in an unprotected moment? Intimacy is frightening.' He moves heavily off the bed, taking the towel and flannel from her, and goes into the bathroom, shutting, but not liking to lock the door.

She pulls on two thick woollen grey socks and her brown back straight, her bottom broad and firm, she goes into the kitchen.

When she returns, the green wooden tray she carries is heavy. He is sitting up in bed, after some internal questioning still naked, the sheet so draped that his flat stomach and the first few pubic hairs are exposed. 'I couldn't decide what we would like to eat and drink, so I've brought a wide selection.' She observes his gaze travel up from her socks to her thick dark brown pubic hair, the green tray across her middle, her breasts, her short-cropped blonde hair. 'Yes, you've noticed. I dye my pubic hair. Blonde is such an insipid colour.' She sets the tray down at an angle to his hips and sits cross-legged on its other side. 'Help yourself,' she says pouring strong coffee out of one thermos flask and hot milk out of another. There is sugar in oblong cubes and she drops two into her large coffee cup. He picks a sprig of black grapes. She catches his eye and he looks away. 'I wasn't taught as a child that it's rude to stare. A ridiculous commandment. Here, take a really good look.' And she puts down her coffee cup and sits with her legs drawn up to the knees and wide apart, her arms supporting her from behind. 'Is a profound mystery revealed? Am I less than I was before? Can you now read my innermost thoughts? Am I naked before you? Would you like to inspect my nostrils? I found some croissants in the fridge.' And she returns to her cross-legged position and chooses one. 'Flakes of pastry in the bedclothes.'

'My father left me this flat. What I remember most about him were his pauses. As a child, asking him a question, jiggling up and down, there would be this silence. He didn't affect the dead pipe and half a box of matches routine. He simply paused while I waited and he waited for the answer to come. It wasn't that he needed that length of time for his mind to focus on me. I had his full attention from the start. I could sense that. He had his own rhythm of thinking and of talking, that was all. When I was young, I found this very disconcerting, a child needs an instant response, to know immediately that she is loved, that she is accepted. His great passion as a father was to pass on to us children things he had discovered for himself. I don't mean: this evening we will discuss Einstein's General Theory of Relativity and tomorrow be prepared for the unravelling of the mystery of the DNA double helix. It wasn't facts we heard from him. He thought that these could be perfectly adequately taught at school and at university. He had this picture of a West African village, where at the age of fifteen, sixteen, the boys are gathered together and taken by their fathers to a camp in the jungle, where they all live for three months. There they are initiated into the mysteries. They are shown how to hunt and how to survive, they test the limits of their courage and their ability to withstand pain, they learn the secret rites and when they return, they are men. And what do we do, he would ask. He was a great believer in repetition, saying that when an idea fascinated you, it had depth. What do we do, he would ask and although we knew the answer, each time it came out differently, as if he was discovering more and more what he meant. What we do is, – and there would be a long pause – we acquiesce in society's demand that it and it alone should educate our children. Our responsibility is to conceive them, give birth to them, feed them, clothe them, love them and to reinforce society's great myths. Can I remember them all, can I remember what he told me then and what I have discovered for myself since? It doesn't matter. A few will give the flavour for the rest. The myth that the world functions and that we are in charge. That all illness is curable and only those die who are incapable of doing anything else. That universal sanitation means that we actually don't really piss or shit any more. That there is no tension, no contradiction between a marriage contract and the desire for adventure and eroticism. That if the non-existent tension within a marriage becomes unbearable, it is the partner who has failed and we should try again. That children should be taught that their parents are never uncertain, never overwhelmed by emotions they dare not express, never unfaithful to one another. That although young childless adults may enjoy sexual freedom, parents close their bedroom door and NOTHING

to register this. "It seems to me that one of the greatest sexual fears of a young girl must be the fear of the adult male penis. Bel, I want you to take your time, and when you feel ready I want you to stretch out your hand and touch my penis."

'My face burnt. I turned my head slowly to the side, saw his thighs, sinewy, covered in fine dark brown hairs, his hip bones, his navel with the hair growing inwards, the curve of his stomach down to his springy salt and pepper pubic hair, his fat goose-pimpled testicles on top of which rested his penis, its violet tip just emerging from the foreskin.

'There was such a short distance between my hand on the bed beside his thigh and my father's prick that I had trouble breathing. Transfer the weight to your left arm, lift your right hand up over his left thigh, stretch out your hand, I rehearsed in my mind and it seemed utterly impossible. My desire to leave was very great. I lifted my head, looked at him looking at me and tried to understand. I looked and saw only my father looking at me. I reached out and pushed gently with my finger tips against the side of his penis. I hastily withdrew my hand. It had been warm to the touch but had slid off to the right in a helpless manner. It was the movement that had frightened me, the lack of resistance. It lay there at an untidy angle against his thigh and I waited for it to right itself. It lay there and its passivity annoyed me. I picked it up, held it upright by the neck, holding it like a dead plucked chicken, looked at the whiskers on his testicles, the blue veins on his penis, squeezed its top gently and watched the slit in its tip open and close. Then, like a salamander, warmed by the warmth of my hand, it began to move. Began to move, to expand, to stiffen, the soft pulpy tissue turning to cartilage. "Stop it," I cried. "I can't," my father said with an apologetic embarrassed smile. "You must," I said in panic, unable to let go. He sat more upright, removed my hand and held it, to stop me running away. The penis remained upright, not proudly erected but lop-sided and swaying. "It's the natural reaction to your squeezing, blood pumping in and pumping it up. I can exert my will to stop it starting, but sooner or later the involuntary response to the stimulus takes over. Just wait, look, the flow of blood has stopped, the pressure is falling, the process is reversing." The swaying increased, the penis dipped, rose, dipped and settled, still at near full length, a marionette laid aside. Then it shrunk, effaced itself. We looked at one another, Carl and I, and we both laughed. "There it is," said Carl, "the great mystery revealed, the reason why there are so few women professors and why old men dream of executions."

'I sat on a hard chair and the bedside lamp shed its light on Carl, very drunk and quietly asleep. At some much later time I left and went to my childhood room to sleep.

'Carl spent the next two days in bed. A hangover, he said.'

'If you've finished with the tray, I'll clear it away. I think if you don't mind, that I'll join you in bed. Yes, jersey, socks and all. Perhaps you'd like to put your arm around me and hold me very tight. Thank you.' And she begins to cry, a measured sobbing that goes on for a long time. He waits.

'My life with Carl settled down to a careful normality. We minimised the household duties and divided them between us. We came and we went, we talked and we were silent, we ate together and we ate alone, but I felt him to be more and more like the house as I had found it when I first returned, tidy and unlived in. It was no surprise when one evening I got in late to find a note propped up against the telephone. "Gone away, Carl." At first I led my life, attended lectures, went to concerts with friends, but after two weeks, the feeling that he would arrive of an evening and that he would need me grew so strong that I began to stay in. I didn't rush to the window each time a car stopped; my enclosed life of lectures, library, shopping, books and essays was oddly satisfying.

'It was one o'clock in the morning when the taxi-driver rang the doorbell. Carl was outside in his cab and it took the two of us to help him in and to lower him, so pale, so weak, into an armchair. I shut the door on the taxi-driver and knelt by Carl's chair, holding his cold sweating hand. He burst into tears. "Bel, I'm dying."

'It was lung cancer. It killed him quickly and very painfully.'

'I'd like you to fuck me, if you wouldn't mind.'

They drift into sleep, out of sleep, drowse, shift position, sleep again.

Later she kisses his shoulder and asks him a question.

'Do you think it ethical for a psychiatrist to sleep with one of his patients?'

'Client, Bel, we prefer to use the word "client".'

EMILY PRAGER
The Alumnae Bulletin

Edda Millicent Mallory (Brearley, Class of '65) opened her
Ethiopian basket, removed from it two ounces of the finest Cali-
fornia-grown *Cannabis indica*, and, with the aid of her favourite
Bambú papers, began to roll it into joints.

'Jesus, Faye,' she said without looking up, 'I haven't seen you
since . . . Christmas Eve . . . five months.'

'I know it.' Faye O'Jones (Brearley, Class of '65) poured herself a tumbler of Glenfiddich Scotch, neat, and from a small can
which she took from her purse added to it a pinch of nutmeg. 'I
never leave the East Sixties. You never go above Fourteenth
Street. And we're both too cheap to pay for cabs.'

'Also, we hate going home alone at night, especially at our
age. It's déclassé.'

'Definitely,' said Faye and sipped her drink. 'You've gotten
better at that,' she added.

'Yes, sadly,' said Eddie and ran her tongue along the edge of the
rolling paper. 'It was one of my last hold outs against women's lib-
eration. I don't open wine bottles. I don't fill ice-cube trays. I
don't make salad dressing. And I think men should roll the joints —
which is a problem if you want to smoke when there are no men
around. I've had to learn to do it, Fay. The tenor of the times.'

'With me it's filling lighters, hailing cabs, and zippers up the back. I guess I'm a romantic.' Faye checked her watch. 'Seven forty-five. What time is Bunny coming?'

'Between seven-thirty and eight, any time now. She had to stop at the bank to pick up her phallus. It's funny, isn't it? She keeps hers in the vault at the Bank of New York. She's there now with a bunch of Park Avenue matrons who are picking up their jewels. I'd like to see that scene.'

'Good place for it. Mine lives in the freezer, at the back. I live in fear my cleaning woman will find it, my mother, or one of my nephews.'

'I, of course, as a chronicler of sexual aberrations have ample excuse, but I hide mine away with my shoes. Did I ever tell you my first word was "shoe"?'

'No. But I'm not surprised.'

Edda finished rolling the last of six joints, placed them on the coffee table, and stood up. 'There. That's done,' she said and then added, 'I think we'll want some acid, don't you, Faye? Since it's our tenth anniversary? How good's your report?'

'The best yet. You won't be disappointed. Where'd you get the acid?'

'The engineer from Rutgers who runs the Buddhist shop. You remember?'

'Ah yes, the young man with the loincloth who's into Kundalini Yoga.'

'Precisely. It's quite fresh, he promised, and pure.'

'Good. Then let's have it.' Eddie went into the kitchen to get the acid out of the icebox. 'Eddie,' called Faye, 'do you still . . . ?'

'No, no. He would only come see me when alternate-side-of-the-street parking was suspended. So he'd be assured of a parking place. I found that somewhat arbitrary, even mundane. So, in spite of his more esoteric abilities, I had to give him up. He wasn't Mr Right, Faye.'

Edda returned to the living room carrying a small Visine bottle, which she set down by the joints. Faye nodded. 'I understand,' she said and then gave a little jump. 'Oh, I almost forgot. Two things.' She rummaged through her purse and withdrew a tiny white envelope and a newspaper clipping, both of which she handed to Eddie. 'Here's the coke. From my dealer at Grey Advertising. Best in the city. Money-back guarantee. And, as you can see . . .'

'Rock Star Impersonator Jailed,' Eddie read aloud from the clipping. 'Oh, Faye. You were right about him.'

'Yes. But where did he get all those costumes?'

'We'll never know. Do you think you were in any danger?'

'Only when he reminisced about Vietnam. He got a bit intense. It was a little dicey. Otherwise he was very gentle.'

'You met him on a horse in Central Park?'

'Umhumm.'

'How odd,' said Eddie and set the envelope of cocaine down next to the acid. 'Is your report . . . ?'

'Oh, no, Eddie. Far more interesting than that, far more. A dream come true, Eddie.'

'Mine too,' said Eddie, checking the coffee table to make sure everything was organized. 'Only a bit different than usual. Quite different, when you come down to it. Do I have everything, Faye? Help me.'

'Well, let's see,' said Faye and looked slowly around the room. 'You have the uniforms, you have the candles, tape recorder, tapes. You have your phallus, I have mine. Bunny's bringing hers. Where's the Alumnae Bulletin?'

'Oh, that's it. I knew . . .', Eddie scurried into the bedroom and returned with a small stack of Brearley Alumnae Bulletins, stencilled paper pamphlets held together by staples and no bigger than the average Latin primer. 'You know there've been six of these since we last met,' she said as she piled them neatly on the table. 'Have you read any?'

'One or two,' said Faye and poured herself another Scotch. 'It's hard not to.'

'I know. The temptation is — I read one. It said I had moved to London, Faye. That I was living there happily and working.'

'Really?'

'Yes. Isn't that wonderful? I don't know why, except one night, about three years ago when Neville was in town, we went to the theatre and ran into Lucy Latham and her too-noticeably-Harvard-grad husband Willie, and I introduced them. The next thing I knew, the Bulletin reported I had moved to London. She naturally assumed . . .'

'It was Neville's proprietary air.'

'Huumm, yes.

> Beware of the Etonians,
> They're awfully, awfully nice.
> But underneath their stylish clothes,
> Their hearts are made of ice.

And yet, and yet, once, Faye, once, when I was staying with him in London, he left early one morning on a pretext. I went for a walk and saw him on the King's Road with another woman. When he phoned that afternoon, I told him I had seen him and that I thought he was a lying little cheat. We hung up and I ran a bath and got into the bathtub. Twenty-five minutes later, the bathroom door opened and there he was. He gave me a kiss, apologized, and left. Yes, he left the office, drove all the way home to give me a kiss, which he gave me, and then drove all the way back. Total time door to door: one hour for one kiss. I was impressed, Faye. Especially since he belonged to the other woman and I was the interloper. I shall never forget it.'

'Manners, Eddie, manners. English boys smell like leather and old books. They snuggle like cats on a frosty morning. Their skin is as thick and soft as clotted cream. I told you about Billy, didn't I?'

'The Rock guitarist?'

'Yes. His mother had a sheepdog. Once a week, she would go around the flat and collect all the fur it shed. Then she would have it spun into wool, with which she was knitting a blanket. He's in jail now for robbery, I think.'

'Oh, Faye, you do love those criminal musicians.'

'I do seem to, don't I,' said Faye softly and sprinkled her Scotch with nutmeg.

'Do you have the sheet music?' asked Eddie as the downstairs buzzer rang.

'Damn. No. But I do have a pitch pipe and if we can't do it *a cappella* from memory by now, what good are we?'

Eddie pushed the talk button of the intercom. 'Bunny?' she called.

'Bunny,' was the reply.

Eddie pressed the buzzer and waited. 'I wonder if Bunny's changed.' She glanced nervously at Faye. 'It's been three years.'

'Sure,' said Faye and lit a Du Maurier. 'Haven't we? But it'll all be the same when we put on the phalluses.'

The doorbell rang and Edda threw open the door. 'Bunny!' she squealed. 'Bunny!' And then more quietly and in a tone of astonishment, 'Bunny, you look gorgeous. Your eyes — what have you done to your eyes? They're like Giancarlo Giannini's.'

Bonita Warburton (Brearley, Class of '65) stood on the door-sill of Eddie's apartment, out of breath. Her thick blond hair was cropped close to her head, her skin was as tan as whole-wheat toast, and her baby-blue eyes were all iris. She was wear-ing a camel's-hair coat with big, padded 1940s shoulders, brown spike heels, and in her arms she carried her old bookbag, an eggplant-coloured sack with a white 'B' on it for Brearley.

'My eyes are the proof of my report, Eddie. You'll see. God, there must be a million charity balls going on tonight. Every dowager in town was at the bank. It took hours. And then get-ting a cab — New York City. I'm never ready for it. The cab driver was darling — a boat person, I think. He had no idea how to get here. I had to do a running monologue. We're going to meet for cocktails tomorrow, that's his day off. Six-thirty at Arirang House — it's still there on Fifty-sixth Street, I hope?'

Eddie nodded. 'Come in, Bunny,' she said, and Bunny trotted through the door.

'Thank God. Ginseng cocktails are just the thing for this man, I know it. It was his Mongoloid eyes that got to me. Have you ever had an Asian, Eddie?'

'No.'

'You, Faye?'

'No.'

'Me neither. Think they do it sideways? Gee, I've missed you both.' Bunny threw off her coat and laid her bookbag gently next to the two others that were already on the sofa. She stared at the coffee table for a moment, and then dipped her hand into the bookbag and withdrew a small brown Italian leather clutch purse. 'I brought something special,' she said, opening it. 'One for each of us.'

'Oh, Bunny,' Faye exclaimed, as the little black ball was dropped into her palm, 'you shouldn't have.'

'Opium!' cried Eddie. 'How divine!'

'Part of my divorce settlement, chicks. Arto had this cabinet full of the stuff. When I left the villa that fateful morning, I thought of you and simply couldn't resist.'

'Well, perhaps we'll do it instead of the acid, or in addition to, we'll see later. I think I have pipes, but God knows where. What would you like, Bunny?' Eddie collected the three black balls and lined them up next to the cocaine packet on the coffee table.

'Wine and a joint please, Eddie. I must calm down. It's been a harrowing year.' Bunny picked up a joint, lit it, and inhaled deeply. Eddie handed a corkscrew and a bottle of 1967 Chateau Rothschild to Faye. 'An arrogant, if lewd, foreign wine. You be sommelier, Faye. What was it like being married to an Italian and living in Italy, Bunny?'

'Like being mentally kneecapped, Eddie. Like being held prisoner in an Italian leather boutique. I took to wearing caftans day and night. And little gold sandals with thongs between the toes. I became obsessed with hair-care products and my facial sauna broke from over use.'

'And Arto?' asked Faye, pouring the wine. 'What of Arto?'

'A woman can tire of being adored, Faye. Can you understand that? My blond pubic hair seemed to surpass the Miracle of Fatima in existential importance. I thought of dyeing it, of electrolysis, of wax treatments, but I was too lethargic. In the end I ran, like a scared blond bunny, wearing the caftan and the sandals, carrying an Italian leather bag, the opium, and a recent copy of the Brearley curriculum changes which I had just received in the mail. I hopped the ferry from Brindisi and the rest is in my report. What's new with you?'

Bunny sipped her wine and passed the joint to Eddie, who took it and sat down in an armchair next to Faye. Faye O'Jones slowly crossed her long, slim legs, and toyed with her one pierced feather earring.

'Well, let's see,' she said. 'About a year and a half ago, we finished the Tyrannosaurus Rex. It was a great event. During a cocktail party held in the construction hall beneath the skeleton, I saw the man that I am going to marry.'

'Faye, you didn't tell . . .'

'No, Eddie, this is the first time I've . . .'

'Saw the man, Faye? Just saw?' Bunny, intrigued, sat forward on the couch and took the joint from Eddie.

'Yes. Like Mrs Sir Richard Burton who, seven years before she ever met him, spied the great explorer on a London street and knew that they would wed, so I . . .'

'Sir Richard Burton who explored Mecca and Medina? Who translated *The Arabian Nights*?'

'Yes. He would leave London and telegraph her, his wife. "Pay. Pack. And Follow," was the message. And she would. But seven years before they ever met, she saw him on a street and knew.'

'And this man, your man?' Eddie grabbed the joint from Bunny.

'Smoked a pipe and gave me hope. He stood by himself, his tall, lanky frame bent over, examining intently the final bone in the Rex's tail. For a long time I stared at him, unable to breathe, or speak, my limbs suddenly paralyzed by a heretofore unknown emotion. Tears ran down my cheeks, clouding my view, and when I wiped them away and looked up again, he was gone. A year and a half has passed since then. Now we are on the twenty-fifth vertebrae of a brontosaurus ordered by a museum in Minneapolis. I spend all day on a ladder contemplating a time when giant lizards roamed the earth. It's lonely and alienating work, but somebody's got to do it. Edda?'

'Congratulations, Faye,' began Eddie nervously, 'on your engagement. Bunny, you've been married. Have you any advice to give, any cautions?'

'Just remember: *Post coitum, omnis feminam est triste.* It's hormonal, not the end of the world.'

'That's rather depressive, isn't it, Bunny?'

'Well, Eddie, I'm just divorcing now. I'm not in a period of high euphoria. Or perhaps I am. It's hard to tell anymore. And you, Eddie, what's new with you?'

'I am in the middle of my eighteenth novel. This one is a departure from the rest in that it takes place in a dressing cubicle at Vidal Sassoon. This, the result of a trip Mrs Bainbridge made to America last fall. It's reminiscent of Beckett, don't you think?'

'How is Mrs Bainbridge?' asked Bunny.

'Mrs Bainbridge is in hog heaven, Bunny. She's an international star. Beloved as the writer of the Finchley pornoromance series, she has dyed her hair red and just managed to squeeze a swimming pool in the driveway of her council house.

She's doing all the right things, and the press adores her for her love of fame. She's just wonderful on the talk shows. I saw her in London — she enjoyed it so much in a way I never could. I'd want to teach them, you see. She wants to tell them stories. It's quite different.'

'How much do you pay her to be you?' asked Bunny.

'Fifteen per cent of the gross: a tidy sum. We're translated into ten languages these days. The Americans like us least. But the Spanish and the Italians keep us in hair dye and then some.'

'Eddie,' asked Faye, 'why on earth don't you want to take credit for the Finchley porno-romance series? Aren't you proud of it? I'm proud of my dinosaurs.'

'Of course I am,' Edda replied. 'But Mrs Bainbridge is prouder, and more energetic and more devoted. She was a charwoman for twenty-five years before she became me. She appreciates it so. She has humility. And she looks so lovely in designer clothes, like the richest of Third World wives. Her round little body bulges out in all the wrong places. She gives Dior a homely look, and often touches the cloth of the clothes surreptitiously as if to make sure she's actually wearing them. I love her. I often wish I was her. But if I was, I wouldn't be able to write the books. I suppose that's the irony of it.'

'Schizophrenia at its most productive — ingenious,' said Bunny. 'Can I have the joint now, Eddie? You've been Lauren Bacalling it for an hour.'

'Oh. Is that the feminine of . . .'

'Yes. Are you in love, Eddie?'

'No, Bunny. I wouldn't have set up the meeting if I were. Our reports are less mushy if we're not, I think. A hard edge coming from a pure, clean mind . . .'

'Like Nazi campfire girls?' asked Faye, taking the joint from Bunny.

'Very like Nazi campfire girls when you come right down to it. I have noticed over time that when this group falls in love, they're not good for one damn thing. Pushovers and slugs. Bruised fruit.'

'I agree with Eddie,' said Faye. 'Love turns my character to eels. Always has. Suddenly, I can't return a phone call, can't keep a date, and I certainly couldn't give an honest report. No, I couldn't be in love, Bunny, and attend a meeting. I'd be afraid the man would find out and feel betrayed, or worse that I'd betray you two by being reticent.'

'What – with all these drugs – reticent?' Bunny glanced at the coffee table.

'Calm down, Bunny, you're among friends now. Chop this up. You'll feel better.' Eddie took a single-edged razor blade from her Ethiopian basket and handed it to Bunny. From her Brearley bookbag, Bunny removed a heart-shaped mirror and set it, glass up, on the coffee table. Deftly, she poured the cocaine out of the packet and created a tiny white hill on the surface of the mirror. She began to chop.

'Bunny,' asked Edda, 'did you do any carving this year?'

'Oh yes,' said Bunny as she divided the cocaine into lines. 'The first few months I did some tortured madonnas for the villa. Really nice traditional ones. Out of olive wood. I would carve only at night because I didn't want anyone watching me – didn't want comments or any other interest. I spent more and more time alone. And pretty soon, I began to lead the life of a tortured madonna carving a tortured madonna – as if I had to experience the condition before recreating it. As if I didn't trust

248

my imagination to make its own logic. I became dangerous to myself, Eddie. I had to stop. Here, it's ready.' She passed the mirror to Faye, who sniffed a few lines and passed it on to Eddie, who did the same and gave it back to Bunny. 'Do you think it's possible to be too sensitive to be an artist?' asked Bunny.

'I think it's time to begin,' said Eddie. 'Let's take a little acid and get changed.' The others nodded. Faye finished her Scotch, Bunny her wine, and Eddie took the Visine bottle and squeezed out a droplet of LSD on each woman's wrist. 'Lick it up,' said Eddie. 'The rest will seep through your skin. Faye, you take the bathroom, Bunny the living room, I'll change in the bedroom. We'll begin in exactly ten minutes. Here's your uniform, Bunny.'

Bunny looked through the pile of clothes. 'God, I can't believe we still – it's our tenth anniversary?'

'Yes, well, it's our tenth meeting, but we began fifteen years ago. Remember, Bunny?'

Bunny smiled. 'How could I forget? Bloomers?'

'Oh, aren't they – damn! Wait.' Eddie hurried into the bedroom and hurried back clutching a pair of navy blue gym bloomers. 'Here they are. God, Bunny, I forget everything nowadays. Faye remembered the Bulletins or we'd be right in the middle of it without them. Do you think it's the marijuana? I've noticed my breasts are getting bigger too.'

'No, Eddie. Only men's breasts get bigger from dope. They never said anything about women's breasts getting any bigger.'

'No? That's odd. Naturally I just assumed . . . I wonder why not?' Eddie shook her head and left the living room for the bedroom.

For the next nine minutes, silence blew like a gust of wind through Edda Mallory's apartment. Except for the thud of an occasional shoe, the rustle of cloth, a faucet running and then not, the clink of a cosmetic brush against a water glass, refrigerator purr, and distant high-heel clicks from the carpetless hall outside, there was no sound from any of the women, as was usual.

When exactly nine minutes had elapsed, Faye O'Jones was looking at herself in the mirror on the bathroom door and marvelling at how well her Brearley uniform still fit. 'Exactly as when I was there,' she thought, 'exactly the same. Which probably means very little has happened since then to change me. What a terrifying thought.' She took one last look at her long slim frame, her tiny, loafered feet, the navy knee socks, the navy U-necked gym tunic with pleated skirt ending just above the knee, and the white blouse with circle pin on left lapel. She smiled contentedly at her perfectly oval Unicorn Tapestry face, patted her Buster Brown hairdo only recently coiffed by Raymond & Nasser of West Fifty-seventh Street, and removed the pitch pipe from her purse. She turned the knob of the bathroom door and, as it opened, blew a C.

In the bedroom, Edda Mallory picked up the note and hummed it. It was time to begin. Eddie finished fastening the heart-shaped gold studs in her pierced earlobes and then stepped back from the mirror. Her heart-shaped face was serene, her great, round eyes a bit glazed with dope and wine, and her boot-black hair flowed straight as a Moonie's from the sharply pointed widow's peak in the centre of her forehead. 'I have never looked good in knee socks,' she sighed, glancing at her childlike legs, 'and I never will. Some things do not improve with maturity, they only get worse.' Edda resumed humming, straightened her uniform, and opened the bedroom door. She joined Faye in the hall, and, humming in harmony, they entered the living room.

Bunny, also in uniform, and, by this time, also humming, rose from the couch as they entered, and joined them in a line. Faye blew the pitch again, and the three thirty-year-old women clothed in their old high school uniforms began to sing their old school song:

> 'We're Brearley born,
> We're Brearley bred.
> And when we die,
> We're Brearley dead.
> So, rah, rah, for Brearley,
> Rah, rah for Brearley,
> Rah, rah for Brearley,
> Rah, rah, rah.'

Their soprano voices melded for a moment, then broke apart as, doing descant now, they surrounded the sofa. Each woman picked up her own aged Brearley bookbag and like a possessive mother cat, carried it to a preordained corner of the living room, opened it and began to remove the contents. Eddie, as grandmistress of the evening, paused by the tape player just long enough to hit the ON button and flood the living room with the uplifting strains of 'The Theme from 2001'. And like those cinematic hominids, who in slow motion discovered tool use, so each of the former Brearley girls, in slow motion and under-scored by the music, extracted from her Brearley bookbag and held aloft a perfect eight inch replica of a male penis. Tying on by means of leather thongs, beautifully and intricately carved in light beige pearwood by Bonita 'Bunny' Warburton in 1962, the three fake phalluses hovered in the air and stayed there rather arrogantly until the music was over. The women then lowered them, tied them on like chaps, and began the meeting.

'My God, Bunny,' said Faye, stroking her phallus lovingly, 'you know you carved these when Jack Kennedy was still alive?'

'Did I?' asked Bunny plaintively. 'Did I really? So long ago?'

'Things were so different then.' Eddie lit the candles. 'No boutiques, no pantyhose . . .'

'No birth-control pills, no body language . . .' Faye picked up an Alumnae Bulletin, ruffled through the pages, and set it back down. Bunny poured her another Scotch and from her purse retrieved the nutmeg and sprinkled it on top. Then she poured herself and Eddie some wine.

'No open marriage, no high-heeled boots, no discothèques, no pantsuits. Two orgasms under God, divisible.' Once again Eddie hit the ON button and the voice of Bunny, age fifteen, filled the room.

BUNNY
(AGE 15)

And now . . . and now . . . c'mon, you guys, stop laughing or we can't do this. It's sacred, important. (Sounds and snorts from Faye and Eddie trying to calm down.) Okay. Okay. Now. We've known each other since we entered The Brearley as 'Bs' some twelve years ago. We've been through a lot together.

FAYE AND EDDIE

(AGE 15)

Like what?

BUNNY

Like the getting of periods. When it happened, you remember, you were sitting, as was usual for you, on the knees of the god as on a cuddly Santa Claus at Macy's. Looking upward with your great big eyes, you were saying wistfully, 'I'd really like a baby doll that cries real tears, or maybe one that talks if that's not too expensive,' and suddenly your blood ran, well, not cold but hot and sticky and the togas of the gods were stained forever.

FAYE

Ah, puberty.

BUNNY

Call it by whatever name you want, missy. Our foreheads are scarred with the disappointments of it.

EDDIE

In the wearing of the Phalli, what we seek is understanding of our lot and theirs.

FAYE

Boys seem happier. Are they?

BUNNY

They seem stronger. Are they?

EDDIE

Simpler, well directed. Clarity helps a lot.

BUNNY

Is it in the Phallus?

FAYE AND EDDIE

Is it? Is it?

The three women, listening to the old tape, drinking, and feeling the acid kick in under their skin, looked down at their guest genitals and murmured in unison, 'Is it? Is it?' The tape continued:

FAYE

If we don't get married and have children, is there a point to our lives, is there? I hate being a woman. I just hate it.

EDDIE

You're too intelligent to be one, Faye, that's all. Isn't it cruel that God gives intelligent women small breasts when clearly large sexy breasts would make life so much easier for them?

Eddie flipped off the tape. 'My God, nothing's changed. I still think that and it's been fifteen years. Okay. You two sit down on the sofa. Go on.'

Eddie gave Bunny and Faye a playful push in the direction of the couch. The two women, slightly unsteady, made it to the coffee table and set down their drinks. Their wooden penises bobbed up and down as they tottered to the sofa and flopped on

254

to the overstuffed cushions. Bunny, without thinking, tried to cross her legs.

'Oh, I forgot,' she said, and then, 'Ow!' as the wooden shaft bumped her thigh. 'You can't cross your legs. It's in the way. 'Course our fake ones are erect all the time. Perhaps it's different when it's flaccid.'

'No,' said Faye, 'not very. They still feel it when their legs are crossed. Especially the testes.'

'Well . . .' Bunny reached slowly for a joint and slowly lit it. 'We wouldn't know about them.'

'God, you don't trust your imagination, do you?' asked Eddie.

'Methinks the lady doth pretend too much. Let's not be hubristic, Eddie,' Bunny pouted. 'But it is true, it is true that they're always conscious of their penises. They have to be. That much' – she patted her phallus – 'we've learned.'

'Yes sir,' agreed Faye emphatically. 'From the moment I strap this on, I can't take my mind off it. What a burden it is hanging out there in the way all the time. It could get hurt, you know. I always worry about that. I once dated a guy who wore a metal athletic cup day and night, as a matter of course. I thought he was a paranoid macho asshole. Now I understand him. You know mine . . .' Faye peered down at her phallus. 'Mine has a few nicks in it just from our meetings. I'm not kidding.'

'I know exactly what you mean,' said Eddie. 'It's a real conversation stopper. It absorbs all your attention. I can't gossip when I'm wearing mine or talk about clothes. I become strong and silent. Everything seems unimportant except castration. Even rape.'

'Last week a guy tried to rape me,' said Bunny. The others

gasped. 'I told him I gave at the office. He believed me.'

'Men don't perform sex acts with girls who wear contacts,' countered Faye.

'I don't know why they say women aren't funny. Every time a man dresses up like one he gets a laugh,' said Eddie, and the three women fell silent for a while, contemplating their phalluses.

'I think I have crotch rut,' said Bunny finally. 'Anyone have any gentian violet?'

'I'd like a Bud myself,' said Faye. 'Want a brew, Eddie?'

'No, but I would like some ballpark figures on a few things, if you guys don't mind. Bunny: At last count in your life you had had sex with forty guys?' Edda picked up a checklist and pen from the coffee table.

'Fifty now,' said Bunny. Edda made a note.

'Faye, it was twenty-five?'

'Thirty.'

'Me was thirty-five, now forty. You know I can't remember all their names any more?'

'Last month I met one I had actually forgotten about.' Faye clutched at her phallus. 'Can you imagine? Surprised myself. Couldn't remember his name or where I'd met him even. We're getting old . . .'

'Hey, we're thirty. We're in our bloody prime and don't forget it!' Bunny spoke in a northern English accent. 'If I were a man, I'd like to be Albert Finney.'

'Why?' asked Faye. 'I mean, I'd like to sleep with him, of course, but . . .'

'I don't know. He seems happy, doesn't he? Uncluttered. Bearlike.'

'Yeah, but I'd like to be Alain Delon,' said Eddie, pursing her lips to imitate his pouty mouth.

'Wanting to be Alain Delon,' said Faye snippily, 'is like wanting to be Frank Sinatra only French.'

'Of course you read that in a fan magazine,' Eddie sneered. 'You don't know shit about Alain Delon's real life.'

'It's common knowledge he's a gangster, Eddie, for Christ . . .'

'Well, who do you want to be?' asked Bunny.

'And living, Faye, living,' said Eddie archly, 'no dead Irishmen, okay?'

'For your information, the best Irishmen are dead Irishmen, but be that as it may, I'd like to be . . . Jerzy Kosinski.'

'How odd,' murmured Eddie to herself and blushed. She would have said more, but at that moment the acid kicked in fast and close and there was no more reason to speak.

Bunny, however, was floored. 'Jerzy Kosinski?' She couldn't believe it. '*The Painted Bird* Kosinski? *Cockpit* Kosinski?' Faye nodded solemnly. 'What does that mean, Faye? What does it mean to want to be Kosinski?'

'I don't know. I guess it means I want to be mysterious, literary, and kinkily macho. What's wrong? Did you want me to choose a fairy?'

'Of course not, but Kosinski's so esoteric, perhaps even domineering.'

'If I want to be Kosinski, I can be Kosinski. Finis.'

'Course you can, Faye. Sorry. Are you going under?'

'Not yet. Are you?'

'No, and I can tell it won't be fierce this time. Shall I give my report first?'

Eddie nodded. 'Yes,' said Faye, 'go ahead.'

Bunny rose from the sofa and made her way to the middle of the room. Edda, still silent and bubbling, sat down next to Faye and focused on Bunny.

Bonita 'Bunny' Warburton, age thirty, stood before her two girlfriends from childhood wearing her old faded Brearley uniform and over it an erect eight inch wooden phallus. She sighed deeply. Then she trotted to the coffee table, picked up a joint, and after lighting it said,

'This acid's cut with speed. I know it. I can always tell.'

'It's the coke,' said Faye.

'Oh . . . maybe . . . it's possible.' Bunny looked down at her phallus, grabbed it and, standing like a man who is peeing by the side of the road, began.

'Billy Dusenberg is, even as we speak, bald.' Faye and Eddie gasped.

'Yes, the man on whose penis our own were modelled and carved some fifteen years ago is now forty-eight years old. I saw him on the street in Rome and nearly died. This was not the same young god we watched through the air vent of my parents' bathroom on East Eighty-fourth Street. I remember very clearly how beautiful he was, showering and soaping himself until he came.'

Faye and Edda murmured in assent. Bunny, staring into memory as she talked, dreamily pulled at her wooden pud.

'I wish I hadn't seen him. I don't like reality much, as you know. For example, it's curious, but typical of me, that when I carved the phalluses, I looked through the air vent night after night, sometimes with you both, sometimes alone, noted every detail of the male shaft, every cord and vein . . . perfect. I was into Leonardo da Vinci at the time, but in the end, when I carved them, I forgot completely about the testicles. Or blocked them. At any rate, left them out. It's fitting that we've had no balls, that we've had to imagine them, invent them for ourselves. That's what it's all been about, I think, anyway.'

'Bald,' muttered Edda and Faye sadly and shook their heads.

'Yes. I'm sorry, but I had to tell you.' Bunny bent over and touched her toes. On the way up she did a long isometric stretch to remove the tension from her neck. Over the years, she reminded her childhood friends alternately of Peter Pan and Wendy, depending on her mood, and often of Tinker Bell. She was unearthly in her kindness but not cloying, and except for the meetings, at which she felt safe, she never got angry. When circumstances overwhelmed her, which they frequently did, she either blocked them out or fled. She made up charming stories to explain her disappearances, but they were all just trapped-rat fantasies. The meetings were the only times she ever told the truth.

'In accordance with the rules,' she began, 'I have told no one else of this adventure, nor will I ever tell. I have changed no names, for there are no innocents, except, of course, for me.

'Having escaped the villa, as I told you, I determined to seek out the tiniest, most inaccessible island I could find, a place where Arto could not find me, and where I could hide out until I was back in one piece. I found Antiparos. Deep in the Cyclades, a pimple of land a quarter of an hour by boat from Paros, it housed an ancient island community, population three hundred in winter, six hundred and fifty in summer.

'There was one main street along which all the houses were built, and sandwiched in between them, the shops: the wine shop – Parian wine, the kind Lawrence Durrell so dearly loves, and with good reason – the bakery, the meat shop, and the sweet shop. At one end of the street was the harbour, at the other, a minute main square, stark white and shaded by a huge plane tree. In one corner of the square sat a round, white church with a cross on top and a cross-eyed Byzantine saint in mosaic on the floor inside, in another, the bar where the old men bought and drank their ouzo.

'In the summer there, the sun was like a golden gift. It spilled over on the squat, white houses with their aqua deco doors, and in the shadows it created, there was peace. The glare from this sun was so white that it burned away my memory and it melted all my fear. I was like a child again, but like no child I had ever been.'

'Uh oh,' said Eddie.

'Uh oh,' chorused Faye.

Bunny twirled around, her phallus bobbing, and struck an adventurous pose, her arms open wide for emphasis.

'It was in this state that I deflowered the baker,' she said gravely. Faye and Edda gasped. 'Go on,' they said. 'Go on.'

'I rented a room in the side of a house, a simple room with a bed, a chair, a table, and a picture of a Byzantine madonna on the wall. Over the lintel of my door was a grapevine which promised fruit, and on the earth outside, chickens chatted or fought among themselves – it's hard to tell the difference.

'I kept to myself at first, doing the odd woodcarving, contemplating my future, eating one meal at the harbour *taverna* and going to bed at seven. Anything to avoid contact with men. Anything to avoid trouble.

'And then one evening I stopped in at the bakery and I saw him.'

Eddie pushed the button of the tape player:

FAYE, EDDA, AND BUNNY

(AGE 15)

WAS HE DARK OR WAS HE LIGHT?

WAS HE BIG OR WAS HE LEAN?

WAS HE DUMB OR WAS HE BRIGHT?

WAS HE NICE OR WAS HE MEAN?

Eddie pushed PAUSE. Bunny spoke in a wistful tone.

'He was covered in flour, hunched over a wooden table near a huge medieval-looking mixer. He was rhythmically kneading phyllo pastry. He was making *spanakopites*.'

'Jesus,' murmured Faye and Eddie.

'He was young,' Bunny continued, 'and tall and lean and blond and so filled with kinetic energy that he moved with the staccato excitement of an animal at play. As I entered the shop, he whipped around and stared at me from beneath white, floury eyelashes. He was naked to the waist, but wearing an apron and covered with this fine white powder like a tribesman in some fragile culture that will soon be wiped out.

'His first expression was one of surprise, and then he smiled and his features were filled with such complete and utter joy that my reserve fell round my ankles like a loose pair of panties. I moved toward him and he extended his pastry-covered hand and spoke the only English words he knew. "Hello," he said. "Me: Apollo. You?" "Bunny," I replied.'

'Apollo,' said Eddie. 'He was a god.'

'With feet of dough,' said Bunny, and her eyes filled up with tears.

'What is it, Bunny?' asked Faye gently.

'I don't know. I don't feel secure unless I'm married,' she answered.

'I don't feel secure unless I'm not married,' offered Eddie.

'I don't feel secure unless they're married,' ended Faye. The three women laughed.

Bunny hiked up her imaginary nuts and continued.

'For three days we flirted like teenagers. The bakery became my malt shop. Invisible bobby socks adorned my feet. And then one night, he invited me to the open-air disco at the end of the island to eat a rabbit he had killed with a giant slingshot. And to watch him dance.

'There were long tables under the stars and a jukebox playing island songs. The bunny, barbecued and charred, lay stiff on the plates in juiceless rigor mortis. As I watched, four heavenly young men rose from their chairs, led by my Apollo, and glided to the dance floor. Slowly, very slowly, as if winding from the earth, they grasped each other's shoulders and began a dance as old as art. With long, unbending legs, Apollo held his brother's hand and flipped over and over like a wheel of a donkey cart on an island hill. He leapt and knelt and juggled chairs and tables and all the life his culture trapped within him crackled forth like lightning.

'That night, he walked me to my little room and we made love beneath the Byzantine madonna.'

'And was he good?' the women asked.

'I was as filled with desire as I have ever been before or since,' she answered.

'But was he good?' they asked again.

'He killed a bunny and he came like one. But he was so large

that I forgave him for it. I chalked it up to Third World techni-
cal ignorance.'

The women nodded in understanding.

'For two more days we were in love, and then he changed.
Overnight, like a weather kitty from pink to blue, and I didn't
have the language to ask him why.' Bunny paused a moment to
watch a tear drip off her cheek and on to her circle pin. Then
she went on.

'Durrell was right. Things are never what they seem in
Greece. The average person could have written *Rashomon*.
Where there should have been smiles, there was icy detachment. Where there should have been pleasure was a vacuum of
pain.

'I determined to learn Greek so I could find out what had happened. I sat beneath my grapevine and studied and studied. I
memorized my paradigms till I had them down and then some.
One evening I saw some young German men, drunken tourists,
goose-stepping down the main street in the moonlight. The
omen-like quality of the event filled me with foreboding. I shrank
into the shadows and bumped into Ianni, a young college student
who was learning English and had come to practise it on me.

' "Bunny," he said, wringing his hands with much disgust, "I
don't know words to say this, but I try. Apollo tells everything
you do at night. He laughs about you with the pals. He is bad,
Bunny. He is . . ." He used the word for "crude".

'I was so embarrassed, girlfriends, and so shocked, that for a
moment, my soul actually left my body and hovered above it —
as in situations where people have almost died, same thing. I
suffered in that instant a kind of emotional death and then — I
laughed.'

'Bravo,' yelled Eddie.

'Bravo,' yelled Faye.

'Give 'em humour, Bunny, give it to 'em!' they yelled together.

'In the cheeriest of moods I denied it all: love, sex, flirtation, everything. And, having no experience of women, Ianni believed me. I sent him on his way to plead my case, and off he went.

'Apollo still came to me at night and I still made love with him, I'm not sure why. In some strange way I was biding my time, spinning a web of words with which I could finally have my say. A say I could never have with Arto, or my father, or my mother. The release of my body meant little in return for the release of mind I would finally effect.

'Old Theodoros came to warn me too. This toothless fisherman, age ninety-five, laughing and dancing in senility, part weathered grandpapa, part *commedia dell'arte* clown, brought me fruit and, pressing his gnarled hands in prayer, rolled his eyes heavenward and moaned, "Bad boys. You watch." Then he tried to kiss me and scampered out the door.

'My resolve was set. The episode was drawing to a close. As was the summer weather. Arto's yacht had been sighted in Paros and the island was no longer safe for me. Ianni was returning to Athens by the next boat, and I would go with him. The night before our departure, Apollo came to my room one last time. The moment had arrived.

'I had a speech prepared. A good one too. Phrases from Cavafy and Homer, epithets of outrage from the street, but I never got to give it. Because when I asked why, why were you so mean, the opening salvo, he hung his head and cried.

264

"Because I was a virgin, Bunny. Because I was afraid." "You've never had a woman before?" I had to make sure. "No," he answered simply. I crumpled up my speech and threw it to the chickens. My only regret is that I left before the grapes had ripened.'

'Isn't that always the way?' said Eddie.

'Bunny, what a coup!' said Faye.

'And how bizarre,' mused Bunny. 'I deflowered him and he treated me badly. Can you believe it? No woman would do that. Would she?'

'*No!*' the women had no doubts.

'So I won,' Bunny went on, 'without knowing it. I expect he'll never forget me. You always remember the first one.'

'Don't remind me,' said Faye.

'It was sad, actually. He said he was afraid he'd fall in love and then I'd leave and he'd be heartbroken. So instead he ruined my reputation in the village and almost got my head shaved. What a jerk. But my revenge was in the fact of having sex with him. I mean, I'm an experienced American woman. A repressed Greek girl's going to have to go some to top me.'

'Definitely,' agreed Faye.

Edda took up the checklist. 'Anal sex?' she asked, pencil poised.

'No, no,' said Bunny, 'I save that for my husbands. But everything else. I was in love. I told you.'

'You really couldn't tell he was a virgin?' asked Faye.

'No. I guided him in as I always do, *et voilà*, he plunged like all the rest.'

'Did you feel powerful when you found out?' asked Eddie.

'Very powerful, Eddie. Magical almost. And dumb, really dumb.'

'Wait a minute,' said Eddie, 'something's wrong here. I can't believe that this guy was locker-rooming all over the island and you didn't do something.'

Bunny smiled. 'I never should have shared my frog with you in Biology X.'

'Well?' the women asked.

'Well,' Bunny admitted, 'there was one olive-skinned, black-eyed, perfectly formed, young sailor with whom I dallied on the sly. He wore a silver bullet from Cyprus around his neck. I couldn't resist.'

'Bravo, Bunny,' Faye and Edda applauded. 'Great report.'

Bunny did a low curtsy and pretended to almost poke her eye out with her phallus. The women howled and Bunny collapsed on the floor.

'All right, ladies.' Faye imitated their sixth-grade homeroom teacher: 'Quieten down.'

'Do you have an imitation for us?' asked Eddie.

'Okay, yes, but I need some coke first.' Bunny went to the coffee table and snorted two lines. She loitered for a moment, feeling it kick against the acid, and then when she felt it lift her up out of the ooze, she returned to the centre of the room and faced her friends.

Like a cat interested in something funky, Bunny stretched out her neck and sniffed exaggeratedly at the head of her wooden pecker. Her girlfriends roared. Then with a perplexed expression, she gave it a few short licks and then looked even more perplexed. They laughed more.

'Okay,' she began, 'I am going to do my husband, Arto Veneziano, Italian financier, age thirty-seven. The speech that made me flee the villa. *Buono*. He's a big man, Arto, heavyset, stands up real straight like Benito Mussolini.' Bunny drew herself up until her back was ramrod-straight, her nose up in the air, and an arrogant holier-than-thou mask claimed her face. Her big, stiff penis protruded from her groin as if it owned the airspace around it. In profile she looked like an obscene pouter pigeon.

'Ah, you laugh.' Bunny spoke in a deep voice with a heavy Italian accent. 'American women are so hard, so demanding. They do not have the gentleness, the wish to comfort a man, to soothe him.' She gestured with cupped fingers, a pained expression shadowing her face and passing into condescension, grabbing occasionally at her phallus for emphasis. 'I do not ask the earth of you, Bunny, just that you open your mind a little. You are no longer an innocent little child. You are a thirty-year-old woman, though in certain lights you hardly look it, *cara*.

'Can you not do this one tiny thing for your Arto? Such a little thing to make an old man happy? The costume is stupendous, worth a fortune, the gleaming feathers of a thousand tropical birds – all illegal to import and kill, but done so at my request, for you, because it is my whim. Costumed thus, as a new and glorious phoenix, I will place you in a giant birdcage made of golden filigree fashioned by Arab friends in Agadir, and there you'll stay chirping and fluttering aboard a golden trapeze until our anniversary party is over. If we don't make Italian *Vogue* with this, we cancel our subscription, *pronto*.'

Bunny strutted about and then continued. 'It's magnificent, Bunny, the whole fantasy, and I really don't see how you raise objections of this vulgar women's lib when I am talking of surrealism. Not only is it beneath you intellectually but it hurts me. You are my little bird, Bunny, and the golden cage is symbolic of our love and how I want you. Please do not throw away all we have had together for some women's group's principle of life. Ah, by the way, *cara*, within the cage, you will find a new caftan. Woven of golden thread and beaded with semi-precious stones, it is yours for doing me this one wifely . . . duty.'

Bunny adjusted the crotch of her imaginary trousers and, miming Arto's goosestep, left the room.

'Jesus Christ,' said Eddie.

'For really and truly?' asked Faye.

'Umhumm,' answered Bunny as she strolled back into the living room. 'I need more acid. I didn't get off.' She picked up the Visine bottle and dabbed two drops of liquid behind her ears.

'Hey, be careful, now that I'm not screwing Kundalini Ken it's a lot harder to get that stuff out of him. Limited supply, definitely not for use when bitter.' Eddie took the bottle from Bunny.

'I'm sorry,' murmured Bunny weakly and headed for the couch.

'Psychedelic, though, Bunny,' said Faye, getting up. 'Very psychedelic guy, Arto. You have had a year. Sit down, kiddo. These men are exhausting. It's my turn, I think. Let me fix myself a Scotch and I'll proceed.'

Faye poured herself a drink and sprinkled it with nutmeg. She took a few sips and then carried the glass to the centre of the room, faced Eddie and Bunny, and began.

'I'd like to propose a toast.' Faye raised her glass. 'To our tenth anniversary. I wonder if we'll still be doing this when we get married – if we get married. Don't get me wrong, I'm very glad to be wearing my phallus again. Frankly, I've missed the old dick.' Faye looked fondly at her imitation manhood and patted the tip. 'Excuse my *crudité*. There are times when I'm alone when I'm simply dying to strap it on, to calm myself down and get another perspective. Does anyone else feel like that? It kind of worries me.'

Eddie and Bunny nodded. 'I'd like to wear it while I write,' confessed Eddie. 'I have this feeling that if I wore it while writing, I'd have more confidence and use less adjectives. It's okay, Faye O. It's just fantasy. Don't worry about it.'

'Okay,' Faye sighed and drank her Scotch. 'It's just we never talk about stopping, you know, or maybe graduating's a better word, and I have this picture of us at eighty, stooped over and doddering, still wearing these by-then-petrified dildoes, and it's weird.'

'Of course it's weird, Faye.' Bunny was getting off on the acid and this was her last verbal assay. 'It was weird when we were fifteen, it's weird now and it'll be really weird if at eighty we still have incidents to report.'

'We'll stop when it's time, Faye. I think we'll all know when, and that will be it. But, of course,' Eddie glanced down at her phallus, 'any girl who wants to stop now can do so.'

'No, no.' Faye put down her drink. 'I'm sorry. It's been a while. I'm between boyfriends and a little cranky. Momentary drug paranoia. I went with it. I apologize. Okay. Big treat. My report is entitled "The Massage Parlour", and yes, I bought a man for sex.'

Edda pushed the ON button of the tape player.

FAYE, EDDA, AND BUNNY

(AGE 15)

WAS HE DARK OR WAS HE LIGHT?
WAS HE BIG OR WAS HE LEAN?
WAS HE DUMB OR WAS HE BRIGHT?
WAS HE NICE OR WAS HE MEAN?

Edda pushed PAUSE. Faye spoke in a sarcastic tone.

'He was very hard to find. Most hustlers in this town are either women or gay.'

'But he was straight?' asked Eddie.

'He was straight, all right.' Faye seemed upset at the memory. Her friends braced themselves. It happened. All the stories weren't pretty. That was part of the pact: they didn't have to be. And if they weren't, nobody blamed the woman who told them. Rule No. 4 said it clearly: 'Just because you have a weird experience doesn't make you weird.' It was because of this rule and others like it that the women kept on meeting. It was the only place on earth they didn't have to mind their P's and Q's.

Faye O'Jones was very beautiful with her slim, model's body and her deep-red Buster Brown hair. She was a classicist and a physical anthropologist with a Ph.D. from the University of Chicago. She was as well educated as a woman could get, and as socially prominent, and yet there was a hardness in her that seemed misplaced in one so perfect. She attributed it to a trace of white trash she once found in her family tree. 'Irish scum,' she joked. But her close friends knew it was a terror of sex, not because she told them, but because they were women too and they just knew. They were at a loss how to help her.

270

'What a great idea, Faye O',' said Edda.

'Yes,' said Faye, stroking her phallus and staring into space as she spoke, 'I just wanted to have some sex, you know. Get off.' She pushed her pelvis forward obscenely. 'Get my end wet. Pop the big cork. I wanted to buy a hooker and get serviced. A guy who wouldn't judge me. The freedom to release the tension in my body without a big production. Do you understand?'

'Do we understand?' the women shouted. 'Do we understand!'

'Okay,' Faye continued. 'I heard about this massage parlour in the Commodore Hotel that had guys who serviced women. I called up and made an appointment. Fifty dollars for hot-oil massage, champagne bubble bath, fingertip powder rub. Anything else – extra. I would have to ask. How do you ask? Do you come right out with it? Are there code words? Are men born knowing these things? Or what?'

'Or what?' Eddie and Bunny chorused. 'Or what?'

'It was a place that catered to men and women. The entrance way was round, which I liked. I paid my money and was escorted by a bubbly young woman in a red leotard and black net stockings, into a room with some black leather couches and a bar at one end. Several other young women, also clad in leotards, offered me a drink, and when I accepted, scurried off to get it.'

'Excuse me,' said Eddie and leaned forward. 'What did you wear to this event?'

'Good question. It wasn't easy choosing an outfit, I can tell you. Black tee shirt, black trousers, black suede jacket, black boots, dark glasses – the mirrored aviator kind. I looked like a hitter girl from Vassar. I was nervous, I admit it. The women were all very pretty, young, under twenty-five, and filled with bouncy good humour. They seemed to enjoy their job at the massage parlour and after they brought me my drink, they perched all together on one of the couches, smiling lazily, a profusion of full lips, big eyes and slender arms, like a pile of lizards on a Galápagos island. A businessman entered the room now, as I had, glanced around nervously, saw me and asked if he could buy me a drink. The mound of women laughed and a mouth said, "She's here for the same purpose as you." More giggled. The businessman blushed.

'At the other end of the room, a gaunt, wimpy young man with acne, glasses, and a breast-pocket pencil case murmured through painful shyness, "New Jersey and I just don't get along," to the girl in the red leotard who nodded sympathetically and encouraged him in his story. I turned away to look at my watch and the girl in red suddenly screamed. The mound of women froze, heads and eyes snapping towards the danger like a tableau of frightened antelopes when a lion is near. The wimpy young man was writhing on the floor. He was having an epileptic fit. Through the contortions on his face, the full scope of his vulnerability was laid bare. Of all the places, of all the times . . . The manager appeared swiftly and carried the young man off to a back room. "I was going to put my bag in his mouth," said the girl in red. The mound of women, all wide eyes and open mouths, sighed in relief.

'I got up to leave. All I needed was to be arrested in a midtown massage parlour. Can you see me ringing Mummy for bail? The manager stopped me. "Come this way," he said. It was he I had purchased for the afternoon.

'The man was tall and well-built, in his early thirties, curly hair and a moustache, good-looking in the way of guys who frequent discos or singles bars. Not my usual type. Not a criminal musician, not a preppie with a good brain and a screwed-up sexuality. Not at all.

'He led me through the same door through which he had carried the epileptic, into a dimly lit corridor. I followed him along this silent and airless passageway, fearing, curiously, not for my life, but for my youth, as if what I was about to do would somehow take it from me. It was guilt, of course, and old morality. Nothing changes you unless you let it. Even bad sexual experiences. Even good ones.

'We hurried into a black room, with a black leather massage table and pink neon lighting. The manager, Mr Singles Bar I'll call him, smiled and said in a soft, deep voice, "We'll be in here." He bade me get undressed and then disappeared through a side door down another corridor.

'As I removed my clothes, which wasn't easy, let me tell you, I was shaking with anxiety, telling myself to relax and enjoy it – a man would, for God's sake. Get your money's worth. The manager returned.' Faye ran to her Brearley bag and removed from it a small towel, which she secured around her waist like a miniskirt. The wood pecker bulged against the terry cloth. Faye went on.

'He was wearing' – she modelled it – 'a small towel. Which, frankly, I found undignified, if not presumptuous. But I guess there's only so much time. You can't dawdle. I was nude, lying on the table, desperately trying to fantasize something. He began to massage me and as he did so, he asked me questions: Where was I from? What did I do? Why did I do it? Everything but why was I there, which was what he really wanted to know.

'Of course I told him nothing. I was wondering how to ask

for "extras". Do you offer money first? Do you not mention money 'cause that's weird? Are men born knowing these things or is it always all right to be rude to a hooker?'

'The latter,' the women interjected. 'A man can treat a prostitute like dirt under his feet. It's the law.'

'Well . . .' Faye scratched her phallus through the towel. 'It doesn't work the other way. I was afraid he'd yell at me if I asked him wrong. Or hit me, you know?'

'We know. We know.' The women smiled ruefully. Eddie pushed the ON button of the tape player.

FAYE, EDDA, AND BUNNY
(AGE 15)

ON MY POWER, I WILL TRY
TO DO MY DUTY TO DAD AND MY COUNTRY,
TO HELP OTHER PEOPLE MOST TIMES OF THE
   MONTH
AND TO OBEY THE GIRL SPROUT LAWS.

Edda pushed PAUSE. Faye continued.

'Finally I got my courage up. So far, the massage was terrible, too soft. There's a German lady at the Health Club for Women in the Ritz Tower who is far superior. Anyway. Mr Singles Bar was fingertipping around my nipple. I looked up at him and in my most girlish voice I asked, "Do you do any extras?"

'"What extras?" he asked coquettishly. I blushed.

'"Foreplay," I muttered.

'"Cunnilingus?" he asked, smiling.

'I breathed a sigh of relief. I wouldn't have to say it.

'"Yes," I replied, eyes tightly closed.

'"No," he said simply. "No. I never do cunnilingus with clients. I have to draw the line somewhere. I save that for the women I love."'

'*Oh no!*' Bunny and Eddie wailed. '*Oh no!*'

'I sat up. "What?" I said. I couldn't believe it. "No cunnilingus? Just my luck."

'"No," he said again, "never with clients. I'm no weirdo, I have my pride."

'"But do you really do it with the women you love?" I asked.

'He turned away. "I will when I find Miss Right," he said wistfully. "I'm not sure I'm capable of love."

'"I see," I said and thanked him for the massage.

'"Is that all you want?" he seemed surprised.

'"Yes, that's all, thanks." I got off the table and began to dress. "Yes, thanks. That's all." He nodded and made for the side door.

'"I'm going through some changes right now. You understand?" he asked.

'"Sure." I waved to him as he left. "I understand."'

'Faye O', that's hilarious!' Eddie was preparing the opium for smoking. She got out a piece of tinfoil, a candle, and three straws and placed them on the coffee table. She lit the candle and dropped one of the opium balls on to the tinfoil. She handed Faye and Bunny the straws and held the foil over the candle so the flame was just beneath the opium. When it began to run, she cried, 'Okay, Brearley girls, chase the dragon! Chase it. Chase it.'

The women inhaled and held their breaths and then Eddie said, 'Jesus. You can't even buy oral sex. You can't even buy it.'

'If I ever have a son' – Faye exhaled and her voice was incredibly deep – 'cunnilingus will be his first word, bet on it.'

'It's true' – Bunny exhaled – 'women bring up their goddam sons to hate oral sex. What a travesty.'

'Do you have your imitation, Faye?' asked Eddie.

'I do. Ladies, please welcome: Johnny Carson's proctologist.' Faye whipped off the towel, and her phallus popped up cheerily. 'No, just kidding. I'm doing the impostor. And frankly, the impostor will never let you down.'

Faye adjusted some imaginary testicles and attempted to push down her phallus. It sprang up and she began.

'I met Ben on a horse in Central Park. He claimed to be the lead-singer of the mediocre rock group Puss. He lived at the Navarro, and indeed his room was filled with costume trunks and musician's equipment. The picture on the album, which I checked out at Sam Goody's, was blurry but resembled him. I suspected he was an impostor, but until I read of his arrest in the *Daily News*, I wasn't sure. Here is an excerpt from our last night together.'

Faye rounded her skinny shoulders, flexed her puny muscles, and tried to look like a bear of a man. She ran to her Brearley bookbag and took from it a miniature football, which she then began tossing from hand to hand. She bent over like a player in a huddle and grunted, as her wooden penis bobbed against her chest. Clutching the football under her arm, she raised her head and addressed Eddie and Bunny.

'I had this with me in 'Nam,' she said and shook her head. 'Oh, not this' – she patted the phallus – 'the football. Used to throw it around at Khe Sanh during the lulls. Kept it with me to the end, you know, Faye, through everything, even when the guy next to me –' She gasped for breath, large noisy gulps that consumed her body and made her phallus wiggle in rhythm.

'Excuse me, Faye.' Gasp. Gulp. 'Throw the football with me before bed, Faye, it's good for you. C'mon, girl, get that skinny body moving. Het hup. Het hup. Okay, you're defence and I'm coming through – first and ten at the ten, eight seconds left. I'm coming through. Run, girl, stop me, stop me, Faye.'

Faye, impersonating the impersonator, ran forward hunched over, wildly dodging the imaginary defence that included herself. She was out of control, bobbing and stumbling, and finally fell to the floor screaming, 'Touchdown! Touchdown!' She lay there wide-eyed and gasping for a moment and then said softly, 'You know, Faye, you look Asian. Did anyone ever tell you that? 'Cause you do, Faye, you know, you really look Asian. So skinny and everything. They don't get enough to eat either, girl. You got some smack, Mamasan?'

'Jesus, Faye, you all right?' Eddie helped her up.

'Before sex,' Faye said as she dusted herself off, 'we always played football. Someone had to get a touchdown before we could go to bed. No field goals allowed – I tried once.' Faye put the football back in her bookbag.

'I slept with a Vietnam vet once,' said Bunny. 'Got my period and bled all over the sheets. Didn't faze him.'

'Well, they're not all nuts, Bunny,' said Faye, 'only the ones I pick. Well, Eddie, I think it's your turn now. Where's that Scotch?'

'Why do you put nutmeg in your Scotch, Faye?' Eddie was chopping up the last of the cocaine and dividing it into lines. Bunny, who was now tripping heavily, watched the movements of the razor blade silently and with complete absorption.

'For effect and because it keeps people from noticing how much booze I drink. It gives it an air of cuteness it wouldn't ordinarily have.'

With this, Faye lost her balance, careened on to the couch, and fell violently against Eddie, causing the razor blade in her hand to skidder off the heart-shaped mirror and into Bunny's lap, lodging finally at a punkish angle in Bunny's wooden phallus.

'Oh my God,' screamed Eddie.

'I've castrated her,' screamed Faye.

Bunny stared at her wounded phallus and began to cry. The downstairs buzzer rang insistently, and Eddie, in total confusion, ran to answer it.

'Oh my God, let me remove it, Bunny.' Faye leaned over drunkenly and tried to pull out the razor blade. She was too drunk and stoned to dislodge it. Bunny just cried.

'Leave it, Faye, you'll cut yourself.' Eddie hung up the intercom.

'Who was it?' asked Faye.

'I'm not sure.' Eddie looked blank.

'What do you mean?'

'I'm really blitzed, Faye. I could be hallucinating.'

'Well, who do you think it was?'

Eddie looked sheepish. 'Jerzy Kosinski. I told him to come up.' The doorbell rang, and the three women looked in the direction of the door.

'Do you know Jerzy Kosinski or is this some kind of Zen miracle?' Faye had sobered up in about three seconds and was talking fast and furiously.

'Yes. My report's about him. It was a surprise.'

The doorbell rang again, three short rings and a long, three short rings and a long.

'That's a code we have. He likes spy stuff.'

'Are you saying that Jerzy Kosinski's at the door and we're

here like this?' Faye was on her feet now, albeit weaving.

'You said you wanted to meet him.' Eddie was staggering toward the door.

'I had hoped for more dignified circumstances, Edda — a literary cocktail party, the National Book Award luncheon, anything but this. Am I right, Bunny?'

Bunny nodded and continued weeping. Eddie turned the doorknob and Faye shouted in desperation, her hands shielding her phallus, 'No men allowed, Eddie, never for fifteen years — what the hell are you doing — I said I wanted to *be* him, not meet him.'

'I didn't ask him over, for God's sake, Faye, he just dropped by, like manna from heaven if you ask me, since everyone was talking about him all evening. He'll understand, Faye. This is child's play compared to war-torn Poland, you know what I mean?'

Eddie opened the door. Faye froze and Bunny stopped crying. Kosinski was startled.

'I thought you said you were alone, Eddie,' he said with a heavy Eastern European accent. 'I lied, Jerzy,' Eddie replied matter-of-factly. 'I'm here with two girlfriends. We're wearing our old private-school uniforms with wooden phalluses tied over them and chattering about men.'

'Ah, well, in that case.' Kosinski strode quickly into the apartment and surveyed the scene. Eddie closed the door behind him. He made sure it was locked.

Faye looked up at the tall, skinny author with his hooked nose and his piercing pupilless black eyes and stammered, 'I'm terribly embarrassed, Mr Kosinski. These, uh . . .' She pointed to her phallus. 'We — well, Bunny actually carved them and we certainly never thought anyone else would see.'

'No, please, I love it,' said Kosinski, took off his coat and sat down next to Bunny.

'Oh, Jerzy, that's Bunny Warburton next to you and F —'

'No names, Eddie,' Faye interrupted desperately. 'I had thought I might meet you under more/less vulnerable circumstances, but fate was very unkind and I . . .'

'You look beautiful, if that's what you mean. May I?' Kosinski took Faye's phallus in his hands and examined it intently.

'You carved this, Bonny?'

'Bunny to you,' said Bunny with hostility. She was verbal again but wildly drugged and resented his intrusion. 'You really write *The Painted Bird*?'

'Yes.'

'That stuff really happen to you?'

'Well, Bonny, there are always questions. Is there such a thing as fact? Is there such a thing as fiction?'

'Yeah. Yeah. You see this?' Bunny grabbed her phallus. 'This is definitely fiction.'

'On you a penis is fiction. On me it is fact. You see?'

'He keeps a comet in the back of his car. I've seen it,' offered Eddie.

'Listen.' Bunny grabbed Kosinski's coat by the neck and with her face close to his, spoke to him through clenched teeth. 'Did you really see those peasants break a bottle inside that retarded woman? 'Cause if you didn't I'm going to kill you. I hate that scene. I hate it so much and it's frightening and painful and ugly. And ever since I unsuspectingly read that, it haunts me and comes back to me when I least suspect it. And if you made that up, then you're a sick guy and I'm going to kill you.'

'No!' screamed Faye and pushed Bunny away. 'Do you know who this is? Do you know whom you're talking to? Eddie, Bunny, it's the man with the pipe, the man I told you about at the party for the Rex in the museum.'

'Your fiancé, Faye?' Eddie and Bunny looked at each other conspiratorially. Kosinski's eyes darted wildly.

'This jerk?' shouted the crazed Bunny. 'This torturer of women? This avowed rapist is the man you love?'

'I see you've read all my books.'

'Really, Bunny.' Faye's voice was icy. 'Mr Kosinski is a distinguished author. I cannot allow you —'

'No, please, I love it.' Kosinski smiled. 'I have touched her. Readers often become angry with me. I am used to it.'

'That's very gracious of you, Mr Kosinski.' Faye spoke haltingly and with great emotion. 'I think you deserve an explanation.'

'Yes, please. Tell me about the phalluses — when did you start wearing them? Why? Eddie, why didn't you let me know?' He scrutinized the coffee table and added, 'My God, so many drugs. How does it work?'

'Oh, that,' said Faye, disappointed. 'I'm going to get that Scotch now. Like something, Mr Kosinski?'

'No. No thank you.'

'He doesn't do drugs. And he rarely drinks,' said Eddie.

'Never,' advised Bunny, 'trust a man who doesn't get high. But don't necessarily trust one who does.'

'Thank you, Bunny.' Eddie was standing before Kosinski and Bunny, who were seated side by side on the sofa. Faye bustled in from the kitchen and took the seat on the other side of Kosinski.

'Okay, Bunny, relax.'

Eddie smiled at Kosinski.

281

'Let's see, Jerzy: this is our tenth anniversary of meeting together and wearing the phalluses, but actually we started doing this about fifteen years ago in high school, which is when Bunny carved them.'

'But why? Why do you put on phalluses? What is the real reason?' Kosinski was captivated. He was almost taking notes. Faye ran her fingers through his thick black hair.

'Penis envy,' said Bunny, and with a violent wrench, she pulled the razor blade out of her phallus. She keened for a moment over the thing between her legs and then continued, 'Simple classic penis envy. Could there be another reason?' She examined the wounded wood pecker to see what recarving she would have to do.

'Eddie, what do you say?' he asked.

'Sympathetic magic. Make a sound like lightning and it might rain.'

'But how does it work?' he pressed. 'Why do you put on your private-school uniforms? Why the drugs?'

Eddie considered this. 'The uniform – we used to wear the uniforms in high school of course, and after that . . .' She turned to Bunny, who took up the explanation in annoyance.

'They remind us of a virginal state. I saw a movie once where Sophia Loren puts on a white dress and walks into the sea to commit suicide. After she's been promiscuous, of course. Sort of like that. Understand, Mr K.? As The Brearley wisely pointed out, you have no status, past, or future in the uniform. No image. It's a levelling, egalitarian factor, dig? Like a crew-cut.'

'Ah.' Kosinski smiled mischievously. 'Sincerity. I see.'

'You better believe it, buster!' Bunny saluted him. 'As for the drugs, well, this is a sixties trio. We like drugs. They relax us after a hard year of dealing with guys.' Bunny sat back and started whittling her phallus with the razor blade.

Eddie resumed speaking. 'Anyway, Jerzy, we meet every three years or so and give reports about experiences we've had that have, uh, widened our horizons. Given us a glimpse of who we are and what we can endure. My report this year was on you. I'm not quite sure what to do now.' Edda looked to Bunny, who shrugged uncaringly. Faye was snuggled up to Kosinski's neck with her eyes closed, possibly asleep.

'Please.' Kosinski grinned in gleeful anticipation. 'Give your report. I'd love to hear it.'

'I bet,' Bunny snapped. 'Do it, Eddie. But if you do, don't soften it.'

Faye sat bolt upright. 'Don't do anything of the kind,' she gasped. 'You can't rip someone to shreds in front of him, Eddie, especially a man. They can't take it. It's bitchy and cruel and not necessary.'

'I am dying to hear it, really,' said Kosinski, and he was.

'We'll see about that,' Bunny chuckled and sat back waiting for Eddie to begin. Faye took another swig of Scotch, dropped her head onto her chest and massaged the temples beneath her bangs.

Edda Millicent Mallory stood before the couch in her gym tunic and her phallus, her heart-shaped face flushed with some embarrassment and many drugs. Her great blue eyes twinkled with fear and lust, and the sharpness of her widow's peak made her look, she knew, like a depraved little angel. She stared at Kosinski and began.

'My report is entitled "The Master Beater".'

'Great title, Eddie,' Kosinski said.

Eddie nodded.

'One night, at a fancy dinner party, I was seated next to a beautiful young socialite whose name often appears in the columns. About halfway through the meal, she suddenly turned to me and asked, "Would you like to meet my friend Jerzy Kosinski?" I knew better than to ask for explanations so I simply said, "Of course I would," and gave her my card.

'I was afraid it wouldn't happen. It was a wish come true. Of course I'd read *The Painted Bird* — what sensitive, intellectual, inwardly submissive woman hasn't? And, of course, it had changed my life.'

'It sure did,' Bunny hissed at Kosinski. 'What about the retarded woman? What about her?' She brandished the razor blade near his face. 'Let's cut him.' She grinned evilly. 'Let's get some winos in here to sodomize him — what d'ya say?'

'Bunny!' Faye was horrified. She leaned over and extracted the razor blade from Bunny's fist and put it in her purse.

'Quiet, Bunny,' said Edda and continued her tale.

'He called the next morning and arranged a lunch for the following Wednesday at one o'clock. I could hardly wait. I was thrilled. A date with Jerzy Kosinski — it's a Brearley girl's wet dream, let's face it. For you, Bunny, it'd be the equivalent of having a date with Edvard Munch, okay?'

Bunny nodded.

'Okay. The Wednesday of the lunch, I was so excited I could hardly stand it. The doorbell rang at noon — one hour early. It was Kosinski. He apologized but told me he had come an hour early to catch me unaware to see what I was really like. Little did he know, I'd been dressed and ready since nine a.m. But anyway, I was captivated.

'He was very mysterious. He checked my doors and windows to make sure they were locked and questioned me about the neighbours in the building across the way. He paced the floor like a caged panther and hissed so violently at a kitten I had just gotten that it didn't come out for the next three days. He was a sexy Scrooge, a gamin Raskolnikov. I was putty in his hands.'

'Yes, yes you were, Eddie,' Kosinski nodded happily.

'He took me out to lunch that day and dinner many times after, but at no time did he ever order anything himself. He told me he ate only enough to stay alive, and that at home. His favourite food is Mrs Paul's frozen fish sticks.'

'Mrs Paul's fish sticks.' Bunny turned to Kosinski. 'Really and truly?'

'Yes,' he replied, 'I quite like them.'

'God.' She rolled her eyes in disgust.

'Shut up, Bunny, will you?' barked Faye. 'Nobody cares what you think of Jerzy's favourite food.' Faye was very angry.

'Oh, it's Jerzy now. Fast work, Faye. Not two minutes ago it was a thoroughly demure Mr Ko —'

'Stop!' commanded Edda, her hands on her hips, her phallus trembling. 'No fighting during my report. I continue.

'After our first meeting, he sent me everything he had written — a big package of books, pamphlets and magazine tearsheets which I read avidly. I was terribly impressed by the clarity of his mind and the energy that emanated from it. I am not ashamed to say that I wanted some of that clarity to rub off on me. I wanted some of that energy for my own. I wanted to sleep with him. But he refused.'

'He *refused*?' Faye and Bunny couldn't believe it.

'Yes' — Edda blushed at the memory — 'he refused. But he

called me constantly and demanded my opinion of things. He praised my writing to the rafters and showered me with literary oddities he thought I should be exposed to. I demanded to have sex with him. But he refused.'

'*Oh no!*' Faye and Bunny chorused.

'Yes.' Edda stared menacingly at the gaunt author sandwiched between her high school chums. 'Yes. He refused again. I was wild. Finally a man of such angst and savvy that he truly understood me! Finally a man who could match my intelligence and then some! A perverse child-adult just like me. Brutalized and abused at puberty, mute for seven years, what woman could resist such an obvious need for love? I pleaded to have sex with him.'

'And did he refuse?' Faye and Bunny leaned forward with rapt attention. Edda let a few beats go by and tapped her phallus with her fingernail.

'No, this time he did not refuse.' All three women looked at Kosinski. 'This time he agreed.

'One night, about two months after we met, he brought me to a weird little apartment near Brearley. It was not his home, no, but something of a storage room for his toys. In the closet was a collection of nondescript military-type uniforms which he told me he used to assume false identities in situations where false identities were needed. He did not elaborate.

'In the main room was a sofa, which he unfolded and made up. I would have thrown over everything for him, even the Finchley porno-romance series, even Mrs Bainbridge, everything. He removed from a drawer a black doctor's bag which he set carefully by the bed. I have never been so turned on in my life. He bade me get undressed and lie down with my arms and legs spread, which I did. He vanished momentarily and then reappeared clutching a handful of old club neckties: the Harvard Club, Yale, Princeton. And with these slim proclamations of status, he bound my wrists and ankles to the bedframe.'

'Eddie' — Faye was chewing a nail anxiously — 'I don't think you should go on with this. It's one thing if the man is not here, but under the circumstances . . .'

'Go on, Eddie.' Kosinski was clearly delighted with the proceedings.

'Yeah,' agreed Bunny. 'Get to the good part!'

'All right.' Edda shifted uneasily. 'He removed from the doctor's bag a hand vibrator and a little black whip. And he —' Edda stopped. She thought for a moment and then ran to the bookcase and removed from it a copy of *Blind Date*, Kosinski's latest work. She flipped through the pages impatiently until she found page 230, the one she sought. 'And then he . . .' She handed the open book to Bunny and pointed to a specific line midpage. Bunny took the book, leaned over Kosinski's lap and, with Faye, read the paragraph Edda had pointed out.

'He did that?' Bunny was shocked. So was Faye.

'Yes.' Edda leaned over the sofa. 'Only here, where the girl says "Yes," I said "No" and broke the ties. Ripped them from the bedframe!'

'Good for you,' said Bunny, outraged. 'But what about the whip? There's no mention of the whip here.'

'I know. But that's the whole thing, don't you see? He wrote about it but he told it differently. He left out the most important part.'

'The vibrator,' said Faye, 'what did he do with the vibrator? Point it out.' She held out the book and Edda pointed to a line.

Kosinski shook his head. 'I never saw anything like it. She is a puritan, a direct descendant of the Mathers. I have told her so.'

'You did this?' Faye asked Kosinski directly.

'I had to. She is terrified of orgasms. She had never had a real orgasm. I had to do something.'

'That isn't true!' Eddie stamped her foot and her phallus quivered.

'Well . . .' Kosinski threw up his hands.

'Why didn't you write about the vibrator and the whip?' demanded Eddie.

Faye took hold of Kosinski's hand and stood up, pulling him with her. 'Really, Eddie, this is too much. C'mon, Jerzy, we're getting out of here.' She went to get her coat.

'What about the whip?' asked Bunny again.

'Eddie, you are always picking over details like an unsatisfied spinster. I'm not writing true confessions, are you?' Kosinski put on his coat. 'Why do you fixate on the vibrator and the whip? As symbols perhaps of some unfinished business?' He smiled warmly and patted her shoulder.

'Perhaps,' said Eddie, smiling back, 'I had the courage to endure it but you didn't have the courage to write about it.'

'Why,' ended Kosinski, 'are you so sure page 230 refers to you?'

Eddie threw up her hands and imitated Kosinski's accent.

'Woman's intuition,' she replied.

Faye returned carrying her coat. 'Untie me, Eddie, will you?' She turned her back and presented the thong bow of the phallus.

'You ain't never gonna be no nineteen inches again, Miss Scarlett, you done had a baby,' screamed Bunny in falsetto.

Eddie untied the bow and the phallus clattered to the floor. Faye gathered it up, stuffed it in her Brearley bookbag, and, taking Kosinski by the hand, made for the door.

'Don't you want to see my imitation of Kosinski?' shouted Eddie after her. 'I worked on it for months.'

'No,' said Faye and exited.

'I'd love to see it, Eddie. I'll come by another time.' Kosinski followed Faye out of the door, shutting it behind him.

Eddie and Bunny laughed. 'God, that was heavy,' said Bunny.

'Can you beat it?' said Eddie. 'Faye made off with the prize.'

'If I wasn't so wrecked, I would have done the same.' Bunny smiled lewdly. 'What about the whip, Eddie?'

Edda shielded her phallus with her hands and struck a mock pose of innocence. 'What about it?' she asked.

'What's it like to be tied down and whipped?'

Edda thought for a moment and then spoke matter-of-factly.

'It's curious,' she began. 'In bondage, you are forced to make a mental choice. You can either feel the sensation as pain, which is simple and immediate, or you can relax completely and investigate it further. If you make enough effort, you can even turn it into pleasure. It is a parody of the female experience in concrete physical terms. Going through it was simply extraordinary. Not sexual. Far more important than that. I almost cracked. I don't think I could go through it again.'

'Hmm,' said Bunny. 'Interesting. Well, Eddie, what do we do now? All dressed up and no place to go.' She tapped her phallus. 'What time is it — five a.m. — good. I know. We'll gather up our things and go back to my room at the Stanhope. We'll bathe in the marble tub, breakfast in the lovely, wood-panelled dining room, and then go see the latest thing at the Costume Institute at the Met. We'll do a little shopping at Bendel's, a new hairdo, perhaps a leg waxing. And in between, box lunches in Arto's limousine, which I happen to have at my disposal. Don't ask why.'

'Oh, how wonderful.' Eddie rushed off to change but returned and presented her back to Bunny. 'I forgot,' she said and Bunny untied the thong bow.

'Bunny,' she asked, 'why did we put on the phalluses in the first place? Do you remember?'

' 'Cause we thought it was funny.'

'Was that all?'

'Yes, no great earth-shattering reason, just that.' Edda grabbed her phallus as it fell.

'Oh, Eddie,' Bunny exclaimed, 'we never read the Alumnae Bulletins. Can I?'

'Of course. Let me go change.' Eddie put her phallus into its Brearley bag and took it with her into the bedroom to hide it. Through the door she could hear Bunny laughing as she read of the doings of their former classmates.

PETE TOWNSHEND
Tonight's the Night

'I was young once,' said the Baron.

'Yeah?' said Pete, 'But you're still you. Every day you wake up and you are still you. It must be a great daily disappointment.'

The Baron smiled. Any outsider could see that Pete was the star but the Baron was the boss. Between them at the bar sat a pretty, spicey girl.

'He's gorgeous,' she said, nuzzling the older man, 'I love you.' The Baron grinned at this and kept his attention on Pete:

'I still wake up feeling sexy. I feel as sexy as I did when I was three years old.' Pete and the pretty girl looked at him along the bar. 'We were in some holiday camp in England, not long after the war. We stayed in a chalet. The mums and dads could go dancing while baby-sitters ran up and down checking the kids. I poured all my mother's perfume down the sink one night. I called to the nurse (she was kissing her boyfriend on a bench outside). She came in and I could feel her heat.'

'At three years old?' sneered Pete.

'Yeah. I was super-bright even then. She picked me up and told me off. The place stank of gardenias. Then she put me to bed and kissed me. I fell in love with her. I had no idea who she was, or even what she was, but I remember feeling something erotic. She was there; my mother was out dancing.'

'Poor thing,' cooed the strawberry blonde.

'It explains a lot,' said Pete, sinking his Guinness.

Back at the Baron's apartment they drank vodka. Pete sat next to the girl.

'You like music?' he asked her.

'Surely,' she replied, sounding like a telephone operator.

'What kind of music?'

'Rod Stewart,' she said, 'My favourite is "Tonight's the Night".'

'I've got some Irish folk music,' said the Baron. 'The Moving Hearts. I'll educate you.' He moved quickly to the pile of cassette tapes.

'I've got my Rod Stewart right here,' said the girl. 'Put it on for me.'

Crestfallen, the Baron acquiesced. The song wafted round the room. It was about a virgin girl getting her first lay. She was really lucky: her first lay was Rod. Pete sat there looking like he wasn't going to be able to stand it, but the song improved. He was checking her profile as she nodded wistfully to the rhythm; she was a very nice catch and he wasn't sure he would be able to achieve what Rod could achieve.

'Do you believe in reincarnation, Pete?'

'Yes. It makes some sense of life.'

'Here's where she gets it!' she cut in, 'he sings about her spreading her wings – you know what that means?'

'I think I get the picture.'

The Baron was gazing into his vodka. Suddenly he got up. 'I'm gonna turn in and read some Chandler.'

'Don't go,' cried the girl, 'we want to hear your tape.'

'Goodnight,' said Pete. His manager turned around and went into the bedroom at the back shouting: 'Stay if you like, spare bedroom's made up. 'Night.'

The door closed. The girl looked at Pete and grinned. He placed her drink on the table and kissed her, feeling her body. After a few minutes' smooching around he stopped, lit cigarettes for each of them and gazed at her. They talked long and hard and Pete began to have difficulty keeping up with her flow of thought. She was sharp; uneducated but demanding and perceptive, quick to follow his stumbling reasoning. When he became exhausted she talked to him. He started to feel very unsettled. She was pretty. Every time he looked at her in the rosy light in the little sitting room he felt an old-time swoon.

Pete was a singer with a band. He hadn't had to fight to lay his hands on the girl. Some guy had made the mistake of bringing her into his dressing room after a show and he had impressed her. Six months later she appeared again, alone. Pete was an attractive guy, and he was talented, but he didn't really know that much about reincarnation. He bullshitted along, though, and the girl seemed eager to hear everything he had to say.

'Being a successful singer is like being a guru,' he said. 'Everyone wants to talk to you, be near you, love you.'

'That's nice for you,' she said, 'really nice.'

'It can be really hard too. Responsible. You know?'

'I need someone, Pete.'

'Tonight's the night.'

'No, Pete, I mean I need someone who can help me.'

'I'm your man.' Pete was being clumsy and he suddenly

sensed it. 'Listen, let me tell you about my boss, my chief. I've got a guru . . . this is him.' Pete pulled out a picture of a man riding a little white donkey. The girl gazed at the picture and seemed transfixed.

'Take it,' said Pete, 'keep it, I've got another one with me.'

Next morning the Baron was up first and his clattering woke them both. Pete looked at her and felt that swoon again. Her skin was so white, and she seemed so young.

'Ham and eggs. Okay?' shouted the Baron from the kitchen.

'Great,' replied Pete, 'and coffee?'

'Comin' up.'

The girl jumped out of bed. Her body was delicate in the daylight. Pete looked as she brushed her hair. A few minutes later they were eating their breakfast. Pete was rehearsing, so he and his manager had to leave straight afterwards. They dropped the girl at her hotel.

'She's great, Pete. You in trouble?'

'Yes, I am.' He was not smiling. He didn't crow like he usually did when he'd made a cheap conquest. 'She's really great.'

The car bounced over the San Francisco crossroads and then wheeled into a little yard near the Chinese district. They got out and went in to the small rehearsal room. They were a little early, so they poured coffee from the beaker and sat on the tired, picked-at sofas.

'She told me her story; it's really weird.'

'Yeah?'

'Her father was a very successful dentist. Really big man physically too. Her mother was a stunning English girl. She was a very pretty baby. At eleven years old she had a promising bosom and early periods. Her father ran off with his assistant nurse. Her mother moved her own lover in, a crazy stud of twenty-five who worked as an occasional logger in the hills. He lived off her.'

'Asshole,' said the Baron.

'You've heard nothing,' said Pete, sipping from his plastic cup with shaking hands. 'She fell in love with this guy.'

'She was eleven?'

'What does that prove? You were saying yesterday you got the hots for a nurse when you were three.'

'Not the hots exactly . . .'

'Listen, will you?' Pete spread his hands. 'One night he crept into her room.'

'What happened?'

'Nothing much at first. Then he started to go to her room a lot and finally brought her off one night without actually penetrating. She said that he was very big and they were both afraid, but he was careful with her.'

'That was nice of him.'

'She said he felt like a horse. She learned how to get him off. She would be completely drenched.'

'I don't believe it. You're making it up.'

'It's what she told me. She didn't cry. She didn't make any sort of big deal out of it. I don't know why, but I believed her. She said that eventually it had happened properly.'

'Tonight's the night,' sang the Baron tunelessly.

'Yeah. But the next night was another night.'

'What happened the next night?'

'The woodcutter kidnapped her.'

'What?'

'He took her up to his cabin in the Sierras.'

'How old was she then?'

'She was just twelve years old. They had been building up to her first time for a few months and did it on her birthday.'

'What about her mother?'

'Her mother did nothing.'

'Nothing?' The Baron screeched in a whisper. 'Didn't she call the police?'

'Nope.'

'Shit.'

'They lived there for three years in total isolation,' continued Pete. His manager sat open-mouthed, not knowing what to believe. 'He brought her books and food, and the rest of the time they just kept at it. She hated her mother for not coming to find her, but she hated her more for having loved the logger before she did and for losing her father too.'

The Baron thought about the girl as Pete lit a cigarette. He couldn't believe the story. She was an innocent, fragrant girl. It couldn't be true.

'What was it like with her?' he asked.

'She was good, very good, she has a wonderful body but . . .'

'What?'

'She was really big, you know, down there. Enormous. It embarrassed me.'

'Why? Did you feel small?'

'Of course I felt small, you toe-rag. But it was the noise we made, she was big and wet. I can't spell it out, she's a sweet lady but . . .'

'Okay, so she was big. Go on.'

'When she was fifteen he took her back.'

'To the mother?'

'Yeah.'

'Jeez. I bet the old lady went crazy.'

'She did nothing. She took the logger back and her daughter went up to her room and resumed listening to them making love at night. The police had listed her missing, but when they heard from her father, who told them she'd been found again, everyone was happy. She couldn't work out why no one was making any kind of fuss. Neither her mother nor father mentioned anything. She was grown up, seasoned and mature. Last time either of her parents had seen her she'd been a little girl.'

'What did she do, Pete? Go crazy?'

'No, she went to work for the father as a dental assistant. His girl had left him. She kept living with her mother and the logger. The logger never touched her again and none of them ever mentioned it.'

'Three years in a cabin. With a logger,' said Baron.

'Three years in a cabin with her,' corrected Pete.

Pete had nearly wept when he and the girl were parted the next night. He was off to Reno and she went back to Southern California where her father had his practice and her 'family' were. She wore a rose in her hair. She said she would prefer to see him with a beard when they met again. 'And an axe?' he thought.

Five years had passed and Pete grew older. His luck stayed in for a long time. He never met the girl again, or anyone like her, but he and his manager did the circuit and made a good living. One Christmastime Pete's liver finally gave out. He was trying to give up the booze, taking all kinds of pills and vomiting a lot, seeing little stars and using sleepers to keep himself from being bored. With a bottle he was alone, without it he was catatonically fucked up. The Baron kept an eye on him. He telephoned as usual one night: he had a special message.

'That crazy bint from Southern Cal just called the office, Pete. She wanted to talk to you. She wanted your number. She sounded very weird. She didn't really remember me. I told her that I couldn't give her your number.'

'It's okay,' Pete was trying not to retch, 'give me the number. I'll call her from here.' The Baron gave him the number and left him to make his call.

Pete sat down and thought about the girl. She was pretty. It was all he could remember really. He dialled and she came on the phone.

'Pete! Oh, Pete, thank God!'

'What's up? How are you?'

'Pete, I'm in trouble.' She sounded so familiar. 'You still got your guru?'

'I still have a picture or two, yeah.' Pete was mystified.

'I got a guru, Pete. Not like yours exactly, but a bit like him. When you left me in Frisco I was really sad.'

He laughed bitterly: 'I'm married to my work.'

The girl carried on, ignoring him: 'I met this guy in LA. He had a kind of ashram. I joined it. I wanted to be a part of something good. A family. We were all friends. We helped one another. It was great, Pete. It was all thanks to you.'

'Well, that's wonderful . . .'

'Mmmm, wonderful,' she agreed.

'Where do you meet?'

'We don't meet any more. The guru went to Houston. He got into Jesus. He has a TV show, pay as you pray, y'know?'

'Yeah,' said Pete. 'What happened to his followers?'

'He keeps in touch with us by a kind of telepathic contact.'

'Oh yeah?'

'With me, he keeps very close. I am in this house and he visits me here. I can't leave.'

'He keeps you there against your will?'

'Well, not exactly, but I can't leave. He would miss me when he visited me.'

'How can he visit you, if he lives in Houston?'

'He comes in the guise of a little boy, from down the street.'

'A what? I feel like I should come and see you straight away. You're in trouble.'

'Would you?' she asked, with a great sigh of relief, 'That would be incredible. You know about all these things, don't you? When could you come?'

'Well, I would have to work out some flights . . .'

The girl interrupted him suddenly: 'He's back, he's here. I'll have to go.'

'Who's back?' shouted Pete. Down the other end of the line she was babbling at someone in the background.

'My guru. Sorry, have to go . . .' The line went dead and Pete shoved the receiver down.

He wasn't going to Southern Cal; he could hardly get out of bed. He was weak and he was sick. But the girl had worried him; he wanted to help. He called a friend of his near her. The guy was a psychotherapy student. He would be able to help her. Pete went to bed, forgot all about it and slept well for the first time for a month.

Next day he woke up blearily. The Baron stood over him.

'What are you doing here?'

'Get up, Pete, I got some news.' The manager was cool. Pete

got up, took a trip to the bathroom and joined the Baron in the
kitchen of the large apartment on Nob Hill.

'What's up?'

'I got a call from your friend in South Cal.'

'The girl?'

'No, the guy you sent to her. He tried to call you direct.
Those pills make you dead, Pete. Be careful.'

'Yeah. What happened?'

'She's in a home, man.'

'What?' Pete leaped up.

'She's accused of kidnapping some twelve-year-old boy. She's
been doing bad things to the kid.'

Pete finally got himself straight about a year later. He quit the
booze, quit the casinos, and the Baron went home to England.
Pete decided to close the Nob Hill apartment and put it up for
sale. Clearing it up he came across a magazine full of naked
people. He was about to throw it into the trash when he recognized her face. She was with a very big man. She was holding
him in one hand, and her little Cindy doll in the other. The photograph had been taken in a dentist's chair.

TAMA JANOWITZ
The Great White Wedding Cake

Once upon a time there was a very young talented Film Director and a very sincere and petulant Actress who were living
together in a Penthouse on 57th Street. More than anything
they wanted to have a baby together, and for a long time this
seemed as if it would be impossible, but finally after three
weeks they got pregnant and decided to have a fabulous combination Wedding/Christening party when the baby was born.

Now the artistic Film Director and the Actress already had
every material possession it was possible to own, so on the invi-
tations they suggested the guests — who were to be the godparents — bring presents for the baby. And they asked everyone
in the business to come. The one person they forgot to invite,
however, was an ex-boyfriend of the Film Director's, a Poet,
because the Film Director had put those days behind him.

The ex-boyfriend lived in the Penthouse above theirs — it was
one of those new apartment buildings where every apartment
was a Penthouse, with one-bedrooms starting at $375,000.
Normally a poet would not be able to afford such a place, but
this poet had won the Cenius Award and also knocked off a
movie-script in his youth on which his agent had gotten him
excellent points and which was a surprise smash hit.

After the Christening/Wedding everyone went back to the Penthouse, where there was a lot of food such as Gravlax, fresh figs, Iranian caviar, and Cuban cigars of the finest quality. All the godparents stood around making a fuss of the new baby. She was named Princess, because she was in fact a real Princess, or would have been had the Russian Revolution never taken place and her father the Film Director not been one-eighth Chippewa Indian and one-sixteenth Jewish.

Just as everyone was sitting down to eat, the Poet from Upstairs appeared carrying a fabulous cake. It was a giant cake topped with icing that looked as if it was made out of sugar but was actually a combination of whipped tofu, and decorated with all kinds of incredible activity. When the Movie Actress saw the famous Poet/Film Director's ex-boyfriend at the door carrying the cake, she ran up to him and said nervously, 'Oh, I'm so glad you could make it! We thought you were in Europe! And this cake! How fabulous!'

'It's macrobiotic,' the Poet said, sourly.

In the meantime all the godparents began to give their gifts to Princess. One wished her the good fortune to appear on the cover of *People* magazine; another, that she would go to Episcopal, Brearley, and then Harvard; the third, that she might write a best-selling novel; the fourth, that she would never need root canal or dental surgery of any kind; and the last, that she might win the Academy Award and her acceptance speech be mercifully short.

The ex-boyfriend's turn came next, and he stood up and said, 'Princess should have her hand pierced with a Spindle, and die of the wound.' This terrible gift made the whole company tremble, and wonder what the hell he was talking about.

At this very instant a young Tennis Pro came out from behind the antique Japanese screen (it had once belonged to a Zen monastery and dated from the thirteenth century) and spoke these words aloud: 'Don't worry about it, the guy is off his rocker. Maybe I can't undo what's been done, but I will say this — Princess might get into trouble, but in the long run I think it will turn out that she has fabulous talent for Public Relations and Marketing. Maybe she'll run an art gallery.'

About fifteen or fourteen years later, one winter afternoon Princess — who had been raised by a Spanish maid named Dulcinea — was riding her bicycle in Central Park when she stopped for a few minutes to rest on a rock next to a group of gaily decorated Youths. 'What are you doing here?' said Princess.

'We smoking a magic potion, pretty Child,' said one of the Youths.

'Might I try some?' Princess said. 'My father is a famous film director, and my mother an award-winning actress.'

'So what?' said one of the Youths. They were the first people Princess had ever met who did not seem impressed by her background, and while Princess had often been warned and also forewarned about the dangers of a Spindle, she had no idea what was going on and she smoked some of the magic elixir with the Youths.

Immediately thereupon became addicted and went out into the streets and sold her body in order to obtain more of the stuff.

So everybody turned up to try to help: they sent her to the best Psychiatrists; to a 'Tough-Love' center; and to horse-back riding camp. By now, sadly, the Film Director was on location in Tunisia, filming a major horror film called *Septicemia*, and the

Actress was re-married to a cowboy-musician and living in Aspen with four step-children, two more of her own, and three adopted Laotian refugees. Neither parent wanted anything to do with her.

But they agreed to let Princess stay in the high tower of the Penthouse, because they both felt so guilty that they had no time for her. Pretty soon the place was a disaster — Princess sold everything in it to buy more drugs, including the thirteenth-century Japanese screen, the American art pottery collection and the exercise equipment. Sometimes to make some fast cash she and her friends would take a piece of Wonderbread and scrunch it up and put it into a vial and make twenty bucks off an unsuspecting buyer. And so in this fashion she was able to survive.

Still her teeth remained strong and white, despite the fact that she never went to the dentist, and this story might have turned out unhappily had not one day the Tennis Pro (by now he was too old to play Tennis and instead was teaching Semiotics at Princeton) stopped by for a visit and insisted on getting Princess signed up for an Art History class over at the New School.

To her surprise, Princess found she was interested in Art History, in particular from 1963 on, and she convinced her father she had gone straight and got him to invest some money in a gallery space in the East Village.

It was quite obvious she had a real talent for this, for after six months she had discovered four new young artists, and their paintings began to sell for upwards of fifteen thousand dollars, even though most of the sales were to friends of her parents who were anxious to help out.

Pretty soon, on a trip to an art fair in Basel, Switzerland,

Princess met a young Italian painter named Domenico, who came from Naples, where his family still lived in a decrepit Palazzo, and they fell in love and he moved to New York to be with her and she forgot about drugs entirely.

They always spent the month of August in Martha's Vineyard, and from time to time they would bump into her father's old boyfriend on the beach. He had given up being a poet and had opened a catering service where the world's most fabulous cakes were Federal Expressed around the world.

ADAM MARS-JONES
Baby Clutch

The half-dozen Walkmans that used to live on this ward, bought
by a charity for the use of the patients, were walked off with in
a matter of days. The next batch, if the charity decides to
replace them, will have to be chained down, I expect, like
books in a medieval library.

At least the television in my lover's room has a remote control; that's something. There used to be a remote for every
room on the ward, but one or two have also gone walkies.
Replacing them isn't a high medical priority, though perhaps it
should be. Life on this ward can seem like one big game of
musical chairs, as if death, being spoiled for choice, will come
by preference to the person with no flowers by the bed, with no
yoghurts stashed away in the communal fridge, the person
whose TV has no remote control.

A television looms larger in a hospital room than it could
ever do in someone's home. There are so few excuses not to
watch it: visitors, coma. Once I came in and was shocked to see
a nurse comforting my lover. She was bending over him with a
tenderness that displaced me. My lover was sobbing and saying,
'Poor Damon.' It was a while before he could make himself
understood. The nurse wasn't amused when she found out

Damon was a young man on *Brookside* who'd just been killed.

She'd have been even less amused if she'd known it was the first episode of *Brookside* my lover had ever watched. He hadn't seen poor Damon alive. But I suppose it was the mother's grief having no actual content for him that let him share it so fully.

There's another television in the day-room, which even has a video recorder and a little shelf of tapes. The day-room also contains an eccentric library, *Ring of Bright Water* rubbing spines with a guide to non-nuclear defence and a fair selection of periodicals. My lover and I find ourselves listing the self-descriptions we find least beguiling in the small ads of the gay press.

'Antibody-negative,' is his first contribution. He resents the assumption that good health is as intrinsic to some people as blue eyes are to others, or the condition, so common on these pages, of being 'considered attractive'.

It's my turn. 'Straight-appearing.'

'Healthy,' is second on my lover's list.

'Discreet.' What kind of boast is that, after all?

'Healthy.' My lover can't seem to get over this little preoccupation of his, so I shut myself up, without even mentioning *non-camp*, *looks younger*, *genuine* or *first-time advertiser*.

Deep down I'm pleased by the silliness of the small ads, pleased to find any evidence that there are still trivial sides to gay life. More than anything, I want there to be disco bunnies out there somewhere, still. But I expect even the disco bunnies are stoic philosophers these days, if only in their free time. What used to be the verdict on men who loved men — something about being locked in the nursery, wasn't it? There's nothing like being locked in a hospice to make the nursery look good.

We are having a respite between waves of my lover's visitors. Less than half-joking, I suggest that one of the nurses on the ward should function as a secretary, to make appointments and space the visitors out, to avoid these log-jams of well-wishers. I resent the brutal etiquette of hospital visiting, which means that a new visitor tapping hesitantly at the door instantly shuts down our intimacy. I try to be tactful, do some shopping in the area or talk to one of the other patients, but I doubt if I manage to be nice about it. Making myself scarce only encourages the other visitors to stay, to cling like leeches. I find the whole business of dealing with the visitors exhausting, and I'm not even ill.

Gently, taking care not to scare off his good fortune, my lover tells me that he is the only patient now on the ward who would benefit from a secretarial service like the one I am proposing. The other inmates have, at the most, two guests at a time. The difference may be one of character (my lover is agreed to be lovable); it may also turn out that the other patients have come back here so many times they have lost the ability to reassure their visitors, after which point the visits tend to dry up.

This is my lover's first major stay in hospital. Transfusions for anaemia don't count, even when he is there overnight. Everybody I come across refers to transfusions in the cheeriest possible terms ('just in for a top-up, are you?' is the standard phrase) though everybody also knows that transfusions can't go on for ever. That's an example of something I've been noticing recently, of how easy it is for people to rise above the fates of third parties.

I'm generally impatient with the visitors, but I make exceptions. I'm always glad to see Armchair, for instance. My lover

knows so many Davids and so many Peters he gives them nick-
names to tell them apart. Armchair is a Peter; other Peters are
Poodle and Ragamuffin.

Armchair is, as advertised, reassuring and cosy, all the more
comfortable for having one or two springs broken. Armchair is
a fine piece of supportive furniture. When he phones the hospital to leave a message, he doesn't bother any more with his
proper name; he just says Armchair. A nurse will come into the
room and say, 'Someone called Armchair asks if it's all right to
visit,' or, 'Armchair sends his love,' with a faint gathering of the
eyebrows, until she's used to these messages.

Armchair is actually, in his way, my lover's deputy lover, or I
suppose I mean my deputy. They met a month or two ago,
while I was away, and they've slept together once or twice, but
it's clear enough that Armchair would like More. It isn't a physical thing between them, exactly – my lover isn't awash with
libido at the moment – but Armchair would like my lover to
spend nights with him on a more permanent basis. Armchair
would like to be a regular fixture at bedtime.

I wouldn't mind. It's my lover who's withdrawn a bit. But
Armchair assumes I'm the problem and seems to think he's
taking a huge risk by putting his hand on my lover's leg. My
lover's arms are sore from the VenFlow, the little porthole the
doctors keep open there, and his legs have taken over from
them as the major pattable and squeezable parts. My lover's
blood beneath the porthole, as we know, is full of intercepted
messages of healing and distress.

Armchair looks at me with a colossal reproach. But can he
really want to sit where I sit? Where I sit is sometimes behind
my lover on the bed, wedging him as best I can during a

retching fit, so that he is cushioned against the pain of his pleurisy. I hold on to his shoulders, which offer a reasonable guarantee of not hurting him. My medical encyclopaedia tells me that the pleura are 'richly supplied with pain fibres'. My lover has worked this out all by himself.

My lover threatens to give Armchair the yo-heave-ho. I tell him to be gentle, not to dismiss these comforting needs, and not only because Armchair too is richly supplied with pain fibres. I have my own stake in Armchair and Armchair's devotion. If Armchair stops being a fixture, I'll have to think long and hard about my own arrangements and my tender habit of spending as much time away from my lover as I possibly can. I do everything possible to look after him, short of being reliably there.

Whatever it is that ties us to each other, my lover and I, he is much too sensible to tug on it and see, once and for all, how much strain it will take. Much better to stay in doubt.

When I told my lover -- he wasn't in hospital at the time -- that I was thinking of spending half the week in Cambridge for a few months, he didn't say anything. It took him a while even to ask exactly how far away Cambridge is by train, and he seemed perfectly content when I said an hour and a bit – as if it counted as normal variation, in a relationship, for one party to keep himself an hour and a bit away from the other. He didn't ask if I had some grand plan, like writing a textbook, which I think I mentioned once a while back as one of my ambitions. There's something very stubborn about his refusal to call my bluff.

He knows, of course, that part-timers don't have a lot of say in their timetables (part-timers least of all), so if I've managed to fit all my teaching this term into Monday, Tuesday and

Wednesday, then I've been setting it up for months.

In Cambridge I stay in the flat of an actress friend who has a short-term contract with the RSC. She's staying with friends in London herself, and all she wants is for the place to be looked after. She warned me that she might come back for the odd weekend, but she hasn't shown up yet and I've stopped expecting her, stopped cleaning madly on a Friday and filling the fridge with fine things. So all I have to do is keep the place reasonably clean, water the plants and listen from time to time to her accounts on the phone of Barbican Depression and of understudy runs that the RSC potentates never stir themselves from the Seventh Floor to see. Her flat is very near the station, which keeps my guilt to a minimum. It's not as if I was holed up in Arbury or somewhere. I'm only an hour and a bit away.

What I do here, mainly, is take driving lessons. In anyone else, learning to drive – especially after thirty – would be a move so sensible no one would notice it. With me it's different. It's a sign of a secret disorder, a malady in its own right, but only I know that.

I've always set my face against learning to drive. I've used public transport as if I'd taken a pledge to do nothing else and have always been careful not to accept lifts unless I have to. You get superstitious about favours when you can't pay them back, not in kind. If someone who has offered me a lift stays on soft drinks, I find myself refusing alcohol as if that was a helpful contribution to the evening. It's probably just irritating. I dare say people think, if he likes his drink so little he'd make a handy chauffeur, why doesn't he get his bloody licence?

I seem to have based a fair bit of my character around not

being a driver. Perhaps that's why I was so disorientated when I walked through the door of the driving school that first time. It felt like learning to swim, and this the deep end. But in all fairness, the air in there would give anyone's lungs pause. All the instructors smoke away at their desks when they're on phone-duty or doing paperwork, and there's a back room that's even smokier, with a sink and a dartboard and a little fridge, not to mention a tiny microwave and a miniature snooker table.

I must say I admire the way the driving school draws a new pupil smoothly into apprenticeship. I was given a time for a two-hour consultation with an instructor, who would suggest a test date. I was certainly impressed, and mainly with myself, the competent me they were hypothesizing so suavely. It'll take more than suavity to convince me that I'm viable as a driver, but I signed up for my session of consultation just the same, rabbit paralysed by the headlights, unable to disobey the order to climb into the driving seat.

Now that I'm familiar with the place, I can't help thinking that BSM stands for British School of Macho. There's only one woman in the place, who does paperwork the whole time and smiles at me with a forlorn sweetness. The rest of the staff, I imagine, conduct their job interviews in the pub, brusquely screening out non-drinkers, non-smokers, non-eaters of meat, non-players of pool, non-tellers of jokes. I imagine them rolling back with the candidate to the driving school after closing time for some cans of Special Brew, and I imagine them huddled outside the lavatory with their fingers to their lips, when he goes to relieve himself, listening for the clinching chuckle when he sees the HIGH FIRST TIME PASS RATE sign stuck up inside the lid. I imagine them giving each other the thumbs-up sign when they hear it. And only then, after the candidate emerges from the lavatory, do I imagine them asking, 'By the way . . . can you drive?'

But somehow Keith, my instructor, slipped through their net. He does all the manly things, but he isn't a man in their sense, not at all. He's not a bachelor, but he's not by a long way a family man either, and he moved out of a perfectly nice house to live in a field.

He's a pleasantly runty fellow, brought up in a Barnado's Home, and he still has a boyish spryness although he's in his late forties. To get from the driving school to the car, or back again at the end of the lesson, he bolts across Bridge Street, whatever the traffic's like, nipping through the smallest gaps between vehicles.

We set off in the driving school's sturdy Metro. It's white but very dirty, so someone has been able to trace the words ALSO AVAILABLE IN WHITE in dust on the coachwork. The side mirrors are both cracked, and one is even crazed. I promise myself that I'll reward the car, if and when I finally pass, and not the examiner as is customary. I'll splash out on some replacement fixtures.

Towards Keith I have absurdly mixed feelings. I trust him blindly, and have for him the sort of disproportionately solid affection that goes with the analyst's couch more often than the steering-wheel. I admire his self-control. It's not that he doesn't get irritated – when I don't lose enough speed, for instance, approaching a roundabout – but he calms down right away. It's as if he was offering me an example, in terms of temperament, of the use of the gearbox, and how to lose momentum as efficiently as possible. When I stall, he says, 'Never mind, re-start,' without any hint that he's disappointed in me. As with any indulgent parental figure, I have an urge to test his patience to the limit, to make sure that he cares underneath it all.

Once the car ran out of petrol on Queens Road, but all I could think of when I lost power was that Keith had withdrawn his faith in me, and was overruling my accelerator with the brake on the passenger side. 'Are you braking?' I cried, and he said, 'No, I'm scratching my arse as a matter of fact,' before he realized I wasn't messing him about. We weren't far from the driving school, but he's so little of a walker that he insisted on staying put. We sat there, while his eyes flickered between the windscreen and his multiple mirrors, waiting for one of the other school cars to come by and give him a lift to the petrol station. No one came, and at last, with the light dying, we had to walk after all. But I was so pleased not to have made the mistake myself that I let slip a precious opportunity for mockery – which is pretty much Keith's natural language – and I didn't tease him at all. It was nice to be the one doing the forgiving.

Alongside the exaggerated trust I feel a sharp submerged resentment towards Keith and a desire to do something atrocious, like run someone over on a crossing, while he's taking responsibility for me. In reality, he would put the brake on in a second, but I imagine myself unfastening my seat-belt after the impact and walking away, never traced for some reason though the driving school has my details, and leaving Keith to deal with the consequences.

Sometimes he sets out to provoke me, as if he wanted to bring the crisis on. He murmurs, 'Closer, son, just a little closer, and you're mine,' when a child is playing too close to the road, and remarks on the economic advantage to parents of having a child wiped out sooner rather than later, before too much money has been spent on it. But I know this is just his style of cussedness, the same style that makes him answer 'no' in the back room of the driving school to the question, 'Got a light, Keith?' even when he's busy smoking away. It seems to be his solution, as a member of the artificial tribe of driving instructors, to the problem of how to be popular, without being despised for wanting to be liked.

Keith doesn't ask why I want to learn to drive. He takes it for granted, like everybody else, that I should, though in that case he should at least be curious about why it's taken me so long to get round to it. Even if he asked, I don't think I'd tell him my own theory on the subject: that it's to do with control, and also with risk. Anything that gives me the feeling of control is obviously going to come in handy at the moment, whether or not it's a sort of control that I have historically had any use for, but I think I'm also giving myself an education in risk. Being a pedestrian, being a passenger, isn't so very safe – and rattling around on a bicycle, as I do, isn't safe at all – but behind the wheel of a car you have a different relationship with the risks that you take.

I try not to keep secrets from my lover, but I don't talk a lot about what I do in Cambridge. I'm superstitious about that. I seem to think that if I talk to him more than vaguely about Cambridge, the seal will be broken and I'll start talking about him to the people I meet in Cambridge. For the whole cock-eyed arrangement to work, I need to think of the railway line from London to Cambridge as an elaborate valve, which allows me to pass from one place to another but strips me each time of my mental luggage and preoccupations.

The ward is full of its own life, and I don't think my silence shows. The patients tend to keep their doors open, so as to make the most of whatever passes along the corridors. The staff don't tell you when someone has died, but at least if your door is open someone comes along and says, with an apologetic smile, 'Let's just close this for a moment.' I expect that other people do what I do and peek out of the window in the door, which has horizontal bars of frosting so that I can't be seen, with any luck. I try to work out, from how long it takes for the trolley to make its collection, who it is that's inside it.

I'm sure I'm not the only one making calculations, though it's not a subject that comes up a great deal in conversation at the regular Tuesday tea parties. Then the focus of attention tends to be the chocolate cake brought in every week by an ex-patient, the offering that is richest in symbolism as well as in calories, which somehow always gets finished. Even my lover puts in his few bites' worth.

There's just one man on the ward who's in a different category, a private patient who's recovering from a heart attack in a room that is costing his firm, or BUPA, £210 a day, not including the phone. He takes only short walks as yet, but sooner or later he'll come to the tea party or twig in some other way to what the problem is with everyone else in the ward. Once he asked my lover why he thought he had come down with this particularly nasty pneumonia. My lover just scratched his head, as if it had never occurred to him to wonder. But it's only a matter of time before the cardiac patient or his wife see two men holding hands. They'll be on that expensive telephone to BUPA right away, demanding to know why someone with a bad heart but otherwise good character has been sent to spend his convalescence in Sodom.

The day-room plays host to other events, as well as the tea

parties. There are the art classes and the Wednesday morning discussion groups. Often there's someone over by the window on these occasions, making faces and emitting harsh sighs, but if so it's just a patient strapped into the emetic aqualung of pentamidine, grimacing with controlled disgust as he inhales through a mask filled with bitter gas. Sometimes it's even a discharged patient, coming back for a few lungfuls of fly-killer to keep the bugs at bay.

Through the open doors, at various times of the week, come the visitors who aren't quite friends. There's a manicurist, for one, who asks her clients, when she's finished, if they'd like a dab of nail polish. She quietens any protest by saying brightly, 'Some does and some doesn't so I always ask.' The first time she offered her services to my lover, she'd broken her wrist and had her arm in a sling. She couldn't work, obviously, so what she was really offering was manicure counselling, rather than manicure as such. My lover said, to comfort her, 'I bite my nails anyway,' and she said, to comfort him, 'Well, you do it very well.'

An aromatherapist comes round from time to time to rub essential oils into people. She doesn't rub very hard, and my lover longs for a real massage, but it isn't easy telling her to be merciless. His pentamidine drip has brought his blood pressure right down, and it's easy to see how she might get the idea he should be handled with care – seeing he needs to be helped if he wants to go as far as the lavatory, which is three steps away. The aromatherapist takes away the pillows and blankets, and gets my lover to lie face down, with his feet where his head usually goes.

I get a shock every time I visit my lover after she has laid her too-gentle hands on him. It's as if there was some new symptom that could spin him bodily round, from end to end and top to bottom, casting him down passive and aromatic, his eyes half-closed, on the crumpled sheets.

In the evenings, there are volunteers manning the hot-drinks trolley. They're noticeably more generous with the tea and the coffee than the domestics who push the trolley during the day, who can make visitors feel about as welcome as bedsores. With the evening trolley-pushers, I don't have to pretend that it's my lover who wants the drink if it's me who does really, and we don't scruple to ask for two if we're in the mood. The evening staff don't look right through me if I sit up on the bed next to my lover in my usual slightly infantile posture, facing the other way down the bed and hugging his big feet. This is the arrangement we've evolved now that so much of him is sore that a hug calls for as much careful docking as a refuelling in deep space. For him to see my face has become proportionally more important, as our bodies have had their expressiveness so much restricted.

My lover's soreness is dying down; I can tell because the fidgeting has gone out of his feet. I ask, in an interviewer's tenderly wheedling voice, 'What strikes you most about the whole terrible situation?'

Obligingly he answers, 'It brings out the best in people. And the worst.'

'What, you mean the best *and* the worst?'

'Both. The two.'

He's getting drowsy from the drugs he's on, as the chemical invasions of his body get the better of the surgical ones.

There's a hesitant knock on the door, and when I say to come in, this evening's volunteer stands in the doorway and asks what

we want in the way of tea and coffee. I see him flinch when he
spots the bag of blood on its wheeled stand, and the tube going
into my lover's arm. But I notice too a quickening of interest in
my lover, in the few seconds before our volunteer leaves the
room to get the drinks from the trolley. Even before my lover
murmurs, 'Isn't he gorgeous?' I have realized that the volunteer
is very much my lover's type. He bears a passing resemblance to
Joy Adamson's husband in the film of *Born Free*, a furry-faced
scoutmaster on safari.

But now the volunteer returns with the teas and keeps his
eyes turned down from the blood-drip. My lover has noticed his
aversion and asks kindly, 'Does the blood bother you?'

'A bit.'

'Just a bit?'

'A lot.' Finally he admits that he sometimes feels faint. My
lover looks affectionately at the sump of blood suspended above
his arm and drawls, from the drastic languor of his medication,
'Just think of it as a big plastic kidney.' The volunteer resists the
cue to look at the blood-bag, with the result that he continues
to look deeply into my lover's eyes.

My lover pats the side of the bed. 'Do you have a moment to
sit down?' I move over so that my lover can move his legs out of
the volunteer's way, but my lover leaves his legs where they are,
so the volunteer must make contact or else perch on the very
edge of the bed.

The volunteer sits quiet for a moment, then clears his throat.
'Do you mind if I ask you a question?' he asks.

'Feel free,' my lover says. 'You're the guest.'

'Well, you're having a transfusion, and what I can never work
out is, what happens to the blood you have extra, when you get

someone else's on top of your own?'

'Yes, I used to wonder about that,' admits my lover. 'What happens is, they put another tube in your big toe, and drain the old blood out of there.' He gives the sheet a tug to loosen it from the bottom of the bed. 'Do you want a look?'

For the moment, the volunteer wants to go on looking at my lover's face.

'Don't you think you should?' my lover goes on. 'Shouldn't you try to overcome this silly fear of yours, if you're going to do the sort of work you're doing? Wouldn't that be the responsible thing?'

Mesmerized, the volunteer looks down at my lover's foot under the sheet. My lover pulls the sheet away from his foot. The big toe is pink and normal-looking. My lover looks startled and says, 'Oh, *Christ*, it must have come out, *now* we're in trouble, can you see it anywhere?' The volunteer casts his eyes desperately this way and that.

For some time I have been sending my lover signals of mild reproach about the wind-up job that is giving him so much pleasure; finally he gives in to them. He drapes the sheet over his feet again and says, 'Actually, since you ask, I pee away the surplus.' He smiles at the volunteer, who smiles back, at first incredulously and then with wonder at my lover's healthy sense of mischief.

My lover asks him please to tuck in the sheet around his feet, since it seems to have come adrift.

When the volunteer has gone at last, my lover says again, 'Isn't he gorgeous?' He looks thoughtful. 'But he can't be gay. That's never a gay beard. It's too overgrown.'

'I'm afraid you're right.'

'And you saw those corduroys.'

'Cords are a bad sign. Still . . .'

My lover sighs. 'At least he's not mutton dressed as lamb. He's mutton all right. But he has definite mutton appeal.' It sounds like an advert for stock cubes. 'He just can't be gay, that's all.'

My lover has a fantasy about living in the country with a vet who drives a half-timbered Morris Traveller, and this stranger comes close enough to set it off. A half-timbered Morris Traveller is apparently a car which even animals recognize as the appropriate vehicle for a person who will take care of them, so that they quieten down, even if their injuries are severe – or so my lover says – when they hear its engine note, some time before the car comes into view.

There is something I recognize as authentic in this fantasy of my lover's. It has about it the whiff of self-oppression, which we are as quick to recognize in each other as other couples, I imagine, are at spotting egg-stains on ties or lipstick on collars. The imaginary vet is classified by fantasy as virile and caring, in a way no man could be who loved other men, while my lover enters the picture as a damaged animal, a creature who can't hope to be treated as an equal but who accepts subordinate status, the price of tenderness.

All the same, the volunteer pays a number of return visits. He goes on holiday to Malta for a week and phones the hospital twice, so that the cordless phone – a treat that testifies to the volunteer's special status – is delivered to my lover's room, its aerial extended and gleaming. My lover has exercised once again his knack for being loved. The volunteer out of *Born Free*, meanwhile, is awarded a mark of privilege, a nickname: the

Vet. Now my conversations with my lover have an extra layer of mysteriousness to nurses who hear me asking him if he's seen the Vet today. The Vet turns out to be older than he looks, in his mid-forties, so that he could almost be my lover's father. There's certainly something fatherly about the Vet when he sits on the bed and plays absent-mindedly with the hairs on my lover's leg. Sitting there, he might indeed be a father, trying to put off explaining the facts of life to an adolescent son, or a public-school housemaster explaining the meaning of confirmation.

One day I give my lover a bath; feeling clean, after all, is the nearest that people on this ward can come to feeling well. My lover is dizzy and unsteady on his feet, so I use a wheelchair to carry him back along the corridor to his room. I return the wheelchair to the bathroom right away, like a good boy, and the Vet must have arrived just while I was down the corridor, because when I come back I see that the door is closed. I look through the window and see the Vet perched on the bed, conducting his usual earnest conversation with my lover's leg. So I kill time doing a tour of the ward.

I offer to buy the patient in the room next to my lover's some of the ice-lollies he sucks when his mouth flares up, but he's well supplied at the moment, and his thrush doesn't even seem too bad. In fact he's unusually perky altogether. It was his birthday last week, and his ex-lover continued the custom they'd had by bringing him one practical present (a toasted-sandwich-maker) and one pampering present: a big bottle of essence of violets from Jermyn Street. I'm mean enough, by the way, to think that ex-lovers can afford to be generous when they visit; I look on them the way lifers in a prison must look on youngsters who are in for a short sharp shock.

The sandwich-maker was taken home, and the essence bottle was wrapped in a flannel and put by the basin, where a cleaner smashed it two days later. She burst into tears, and he told her not to worry about it, but in fact he wants to be reimbursed, and if the hospital doesn't have the relevant insurance he wants it taken out of the cleaner's wages. So now he's unpopular with the staff, but he's sticking to his guns. If dirty looks were radio-therapy he'd have lost a lot of hair by now, but the sense of defending a principle has given his health a definite boost.

When I return to my lover's room and peep through the window, the conversation shows no sign of stopping, so I leave them to it and go back to his neighbour's room, where the basin still smells like a florist's. There was something I glimpsed on the window sill a minute ago that puzzled me, and I summon up the nerve to ask about it.

It's a soft toy in the shape of a fat scheming cat, but a cat that seems to have two tiny hoops of wire fixed high on its stomach.

'That's my hospital Garfield,' explains the neighbour with a little embarrassment. 'I only use it in hospital.'

'No, I don't mean that,' I say, 'I mean, what are those?' I point at the little hoops.

He blushes outright and shyly opens his pyjama jacket. 'What you really mean is, what are these?'

His nipples have little inserted hoops of their own, and the hospital Garfield is indeed, as I thought incredulously at first glance, a soft toy with an erotic piercing.

My lover's neighbour nods at his customized toy. 'The nurses have this great sense of humour,' he says. 'They did that while I was out.'

I am slow to take in the information he is giving me. It is a few moments before I realize that by 'out' he means not just *socially unavailable* but *profoundly unconscious*.

I keep away from my lover as long as I plausibly can. Purely from a medical point of view, flirtation is likely to have a beneficial effect on his low blood pressure. A little teasing romance may actually make him stronger at the knees.

From my own point of view I feel not jealousy, but a definite tremor of worry. My lover's instinct for help is profound and I trust it. If he thinks I'm capable, then I am. But if he enlists the Vet, I lose confidence. It's not that I don't want to share the load. I'd love to. But if my lover is hedging his bets, then I suddenly fear that he has good reason. Perhaps he now realizes I will crack up or get ill myself. My equilibrium falters, and the glands of selfish worry, that I have been suppressing for the duration, flare up at once and all together.

On subsequent visits, the Vet consolidates his burly charisma in my lover's eyes by turning out to own the right cars. He doesn't drive a Morris Traveller as such – that would be a little bit spooky. But he does buy glamorous or gloriously dowdy cars cheap in auctions, and garages them with friends or in fields when they need a little more work than he can do, handy though he is. He drives an Alfa that costs him more in insurance every year than he paid in the first place. One of these days he knows that the police will pull him over and ask him ever so nicely not to wear it in public again. Waiting in various locations for a little more cash or an elusive spare part are a Bentley, an Aston Martin and a Wolseley.

My lover has a passion for fast and/or classic cars. Before I knew him he owned an MG – he put an old phone in it, in fact, the kind you crank, and used to mime conversations at traffic-lights in summer, with the top down. This was before the days of car phones, let alone the days of commercially made imita-tion car phones – which I think makes it all right.

I don't follow my lover's car conversations with the Vet. I don't begin to understand what makes one car boxy but lovable, and another one nippy but a little Japanese about the hips.

There must be something about cars that makes people use a different register, almost a different language. Keith, my instructor, uses a whole mysterious vocabulary of phrases, so that I had to learn to understand his language, if not actually to speak Instructor, before I could really begin learning to drive. He mutters, 'Baby clutch . . . *baby* clutch,' when he wants me to be subtle with my left foot, and, 'Double gas . . . TREBLE gas,' when he wants me to be brash with my right. When I'm fumbling between gears he prompts me ('then three . . . then two'), and when I've finally got it right and married speed to ratio, he says with mild put-on surprise, 'It works!' or else he gives a sort of jeer of approval ('Yeeeeah!'). If I don't need prompting for a minute or so, he'll murmur, 'Looking good' or, 'I'm almost impressed.' More often he gets me to slow down, with a warning 'Cool it,' or to speed up – for which he mutters, 'It's not happening' and makes gestures with his hands, sweep-ing them forwards.

I used to interpret the phrase and the gesture the wrong way, as if what Keith wanted was for the road to be taken away from in front of him, but I suppose that was just my old reluctance surfacing again in the lightest of disguises. I've got it worked out now and give the accelerator a squeeze. If I've been slow to understand him and to deliver the speed he requires, Keith gets more direct. The phrases for this are 'Let's piss off out of here' or 'Give it a bit of poke.'

If I take my time before changing up, he goes 'mmmm', with a sharp intonation that says what-are-you-waiting-for? If I'm not properly positioned in my lane, he makes a flick of the hand to guide me in the right direction. Often, when I've misjudged a manoeuvre or underestimated a hazard, he says, with a quiet satisfaction, '*Not* a good gear.' To remind me of the mirror he sometimes taps it with his forefinger or mutters – there seems no obvious reason for his choice of language – '*Spiegel*'.

I start to relax in the lesson at the point where Keith lights up his first cigarette. I'm sure he's got enough of a craving that he'd light up sooner or later, whatever sort of idiot I was being, but I become more competent knowing he's felt able to focus his attention on the cigarette packet and the matches for a few seconds. Unless of course it's my terrible driving that makes the comfort of a cigarette so hugely attractive.

Keith opens the window a crack and leans forward to adjust the heating. I take every move he makes as a looming comment on my driving, so I'm absurdly relieved when he's only making adjustments to the car's interior climate. Then Keith talks. It's as if he's trying to simulate the distractions of traffic, when we're on a clear road. There's nothing I find harder than giving talking a low priority; left to my instincts, I'd rather be attentive in the conversation than safe on the road. It's not that I get flustered when he's really trying to put me off my stride – like the time he asked, 'When you going to get married, then?' after he had warned me he was about to request an emergency stop, and before he actually smacked the dashboard to give me my cue. That question doesn't faze me, though I gather it's pretty much guaranteed to make the young men botch their manoeuvre. But I'm interested in Keith and what he has to say, and when he stops talking because there's tricky work ahead I can't wait to get the hazards behind me, whatever they are, and go back to what he's saying.

Sometimes Keith talks about nothing, anything, the daily papers, and how he's going to give up the *Sun* when they stop running their Bingo game – unless of course they announce another. He wrote a letter to the *Sun*'s Grouse of the Week column just recently, which they didn't print, complaining about a doctor in the news who'd overturned the car giving his daughter a driving lesson in the grounds of his house. It was taking a living away from driving instructors, that was Keith's Grouse, and served the doctor right, and what would *he* think if people started doing operations on each other in their kitchens?

Sometimes he talks about his history, about Barnardo's and the army and home-ownership.

'I had a lovely house in an acre, lovely car, two-car garage, garden with a rockery and floodlights – spent a grand on land-scaping – fruit trees, currant bushes, but it wasn't what I wanted, none of it. I think I worked that out before I finished laying the rockery, but I still installed those bloody floodlights.'

He moved out from the house he shared with Sue and took up with Olga. Olga is the battered mobile home where he lives, parked in a muddy field a few miles out of town. She's a hulk, but he seems well set up there, in his way. We went out there once, on a lesson; I needed practice, apparently, manoeuvring in muddy conditions, and Keith certainly needed a Calor Gas container picked up and taken for refilling. We had a cup of tea in Olga while we were at it, though his eyes narrowed with distrust at the idea that anyone could drink it without sugar. He takes four spoonfuls and gives the tea-bag a good drubbing with the spoon, as if the point of the procedure was not to infuse a drink but actually to wash the tea-bag free of stains.

Laundry is one of the few services that he's not found a way of doing for himself. He does any telephoning he needs at the driving school, and even brings his electric razor in to work for recharging with BSM current. He leaves the right change for milk and newspapers in Olga's mighty glove compartment and has them delivered right into her cab. But laundry is one thing that's beyond him and so he pops over to Sue's every week or so (and takes a bath while he's at it). He has a 'leg-over' while he's there, but to hear him talk about it, that leg-over isn't the linch-pin of the arrangement. I imagine Sue in front of her mirror on one of the evenings Keith is expected – he doesn't always turn up, but he knows how to keep just enough on the right side of her that she doesn't come to find him, her horn sounding furi-ously all the way from the main road as her car crawls into the treacherous field where Olga sits. I imagine her powdering her face and wondering whether she should try some new perfume. She doesn't know it's Ariel that arouses Keith's senses, not Chanel.

I need a pee after my cup of tea. Keith shows me the lavatory, which is chemical and tucked away in a low cupboard. Keith can stand up in most parts of Olga, but there's nowhere that the roof's high enough to give my head clearance. To use the lava-tory, I have to kneel and face forward. Keith gives me a little privacy by going to the cab, where he hasn't bothered to put up cork tiling. He presses a hand to the roof and says, 'Some mornings the condensation's unbelievable in here. It's like Niagara bastard Falls.'

Only when I'm finished with my rather awkward pee does he mention that personally, *personally*, speaking for himself, he finds it more convenient to piss in a bottle and then pour it away, though of course everybody's different, aren't they? There's a coffee jar, scrupulously clean and free of labels, tucked away at the side of the lavatory, which I suspect is his chosen bottle. I wish I'd spotted it earlier, though I doubt if I'd have had the nerve to use it.

Before we leave, Keith shows me his photo album. It's like anybody's photo album – anybody who wasn't thought worthy of a photograph before he joined the army, who built a raft in Malaya based on what people built in films when they were marooned, who had four children by two wives before there was ever a Sue, who kept sheep and chickens for a while in Devon – except that nothing's in order. It's the sort of album where each thick page has a thick sheet of Cellophane to hold the pictures down, no need of photo corners, and Keith seems to like keeping even the past provisional. Perhaps on non-bath evenings he amuses himself by rearranging the photographs, shuffling the blurred sheep and the precise soldiers, the blurred children. In every picture that shows Keith, he is pointing out of the frame, insisting that the real subject is out there somewhere, refusing to be the focus of the composition.

On the way back to town, he gets me to do some emergency stops. If it's at all possible, he synchronizes them with young women walking alone. He smacks the dashboard just before we pass. The woman usually glares at us as we stop dead right next to her and then she relaxes into a pitying half-smile when she sees it's only a learner driver. No real threat. Then her face goes halfway back to its original expression, when she sees that Keith is staring at her with a defiant hunger. At times like this, I am able to look at Keith outside the terms of our sealed-in little relationship, outside its flux of resentment and dependence, and he seems, I must admit, like a pretty ordinary little shit.

Even when I have passed my test and put Keith behind me, I can't imagine that I'll do a lot of driving. Public transport is enough to get me to the hospital, though I sometimes use my bicycle on a Sunday, partly for the exercise and partly to dramatize my errand, if I'm bringing something for my lover. On the bicycle I can feel like a courier whose package will make a difference to the person waiting for it.

My lover keeps the television on all the time, just turning up the sound when there's something he actually wants to watch. At the moment, a weatherman is standing in front of two maps of the country. I expect they represent the weather tonight and tomorrow. But the weatherman, if he wanted, could also show us the weather of our two healths. His vocabulary of symbols is meagre but it will stretch. My map will be full of smiling suns and light refreshing breezes, a fantasy of summer; my lover's map a nightmare winter, chock-a-block with gales and freezing showers. My lover looks without interest at the screen as it changes. Some of his calm is really exhaustion, but some of his calm is really calm. It helps that he's still in touch socially with the few people he exposed to risk. With a bravery that to me seems insane, they've all taken the test, and they all tested negative.

He keeps a list of his sexual partners, does my lover, though it's not so detailed he could use it to track people down if he'd lost touch. I only found out about it recently. It's at the back of his diary, but then I only found out about the diary recently. Suddenly there was this battered book on the bed, and my lover was saying, oh yes, he always used to keep a diary, he'd just got out of the habit. He'd just now come across it and was taking a look.

Even my lover had to admit, after a little reading, that his diary-keeping had never been regular; he wrote in his diary only when a relationship was on the rocks. It took tears to get the words flowing and then he would write what were in effect letters to his lovers, full of sombre accusations and depressive spite. He even read me a detailed account of my own selfishness. This was his version of a crisis of which I have no version, since I survived it by not noticing.

I asked if I could look at the diary, and he passed it across. At the back of the book there was a list of numbers and names, starting with '1. John in Toyota Corolla.' Number two was Mark, and number three was Mark and Ben. The list went into the low forties before it met a scrawl, twice underlined: '*Enough of this rubbish.*' The list-making impulse had started to falter even before then. Two numbers in the thirties were entered as 'What was the name?' and 'Macho Letdown'.

My lover gave me a beady look as I read his diary and asked, 'Are you the sort of person who reads people's diaries?'

I didn't know there was any other sort of person, but I avoided the question by holding the book up and waving it. 'The evidence against me is strong.'

'I mean, when the owner's not around?'

'Only if I can find it.' I've only made a couple of searches since then – as much to see if he was bothered enough to hide it as because I'm curious – and I haven't found it, so I suppose the answer to the question is, Yes, he was bothered enough.

The limitations on my lover's future make his past the more precious, and I find that I'm a bit bothered, after all, that I don't know where his diary is.

I bring my lover hot thick soups, in a big old-fashioned vacuum flask with a wide neck. Conventional soups bear the same relationship to my soup as the sun bears to those collapsed stars whose every speck outweighs it. An oxtail is a wispy thing compared to what I make of it with the strong rendering of my pressure cooker. My soups are concentrated expressions of the will to nourish.

But tonight my lover is not to be nourished. 'You know I hate innards,' he says, pushing the plate of soup away almost as soon as I've poured it.

I'm ashamed that I don't know my lover's preferences as well as I should, but I'm also offended and I protest. 'Oxtail isn't innards!'

'It's as good as.'

'Oxtail couldn't be further from innards. Be reasonable. If cows kept their tails on the inside how could they deal with flies?'

Even as I say this, I realize that talk of flies is among the poorer triggers of appetite. The ward is full of tiny insects, as it happens, sustained out of season by the warmth and the abundance of fruit.

Even unmolested, the fruit would look incongruous beside the stack of moulded cardboard vomit-bowls on my lover's bed-side table. They look, with their broad rims turned down at one side, like jaunty little hats, as if they were there for use in a big dance production number. We've tried to bring them into our private world by referring to them as 'Berkeleys' or 'Astaires', but the name that has stuck, *vomit-hats*, leaves them uncomfortably real. These homely objects resist the final push into euphemism.

Our little tussle over the soup reminds me of how poorly matched we are in habits and appetites. We don't even have the same taste in bread. I like wholemeal, but his stomach can deal most easily with inflated plastic white, and naturally I give way to him. All the same, I'd have thought somebody could make a killing out of couples like us, by producing a hybrid loaf that combined the two, all the goodness and bran sucked out of each alternate slice and shunted into the next one.

In this way among others, we don't present a united front. Our teamwork seems ragged, while the illness we're fighting is ruthlessly co-ordinated. But then it's only recently, since he came into hospital in fact, that I have thought of him, truly, as my lover.

Before then I compared him in my mind – often very flatteringly, it's true – with other men past or possible. But now I compare him only with the world as it will be when he is subtracted from it, not with rival beds but with his bed, empty. That is what locks the phrase in place: my lover.

My lover and I never used pet names or endearments before his first visit to hospital, but how stupid it sounds when I say so. It's like saying *I never had much use for pot plants and cushions before I came to live in this condemned cell*. Except that the unstoppable progress of medical science has taken our condemned cell and turned it into a whole suite of condemned cells.

Our endearment system is based round the core-word *pie*,

derived from the phrase *sweetie-pie* but given its independence in a whole series of verbal caresses. The turning-point in its history was my buying an Easter egg with the message piped on it, 'WITH LOVE TO MY SWEETIE PIE.' This was at a time when a raised patch on the roof of my lover's mouth had been diagnosed as a cancer, a separate sentence on his mouth that his tongue must read and remember every time it makes contact, and I wanted to go to meet him armed with more than a hug. It comforted me to watch the woman at Thorntons in Cambridge – where a free message in icing was a seasonal offer – at work on the egg with her expert nozzle of fondant and her smile of romantic voyeurism. The smile would have hardened on her lips like painted sugar if she knew she was decorating a sweet to take the bitterness out of a malignancy.

Pie was the word that stuck, the last part of the inscribed egg that my lover would have eaten, I'm sure, if he hadn't kept the whole thing intact, as a totem of chocolate. *Pie* stuck to a number of phrases, private ones at first and then sentences of ordinary conversation, by slip of tongue to start with and afterwards defiantly, mixing embarrassment and the refusal to be embarrassed. *Pie* functions as pet name (*dear one*), as interrogative (*are you awake?*), as exclamation (*how could you say such a thing!*).

So near have I approached to that which I vowed I would never use, the edged endearment of the grown-up, the *darling* of protest if not yet the *darling* of bitter reproach.

Pie is allied by assonance with *my* (*my Pie*), by alliteration with expressive adjectives: *poor Pie*, *precious Pie*, *pretty Pie*.

Occasionally it appears in phrases of estrangement, though its use acts as a guarantee that estrangement is reversible: *crusty Pie*, *poison Pie*, *piranha Pie*.

Written down and rationalized as an irrational number – π – it loses a little of its sugar. Transposed into fake Italian *mio Pio* – it acquires a register almost operatic. As a double diminutive – as *pielet* or *pilot* – it brings into play a fresh set of overtones.

Perhaps endearment, verbal sweetness so concentrated nothing else can survive, will prevent infection, the way honey does. Honey yanks the moisture out of bacteria with the violence of its osmosis. Honey has been found uncorrupt in the tombs of the Pharaohs, though it had been left there to be used, after all, to sweeten the darkness of the dead.

Who could have thought when the treasures were laid out in the vault that the bees' modest embalming would last so well, that their glandular syrup of flowers would turn out so nearly eternal?

My lover raises the remote control panel and turns the television off. Late at night, the nurses stop being so demanding, and even Armchair and the Vet can be relied on to stay away. My lover and I don't have to be so guarded in our behaviour.

This is the time we draft our imaginary letters to newspapers and public figures, our radical complaints and proposals. My lover wants to live long enough to be the only survivor of an air crash, so that he can say at the press conference, where he will have an arm in plaster – perhaps only a finger – 'You see? God doesn't hate me after all. Whatever *you* think.' In the meantime he will settle for composing imaginary letters to the papers, setting the record straight day by day.

Sometimes one or the other of us will shed some tears, but we haven't properly settled the agenda of our crying. We're both New Men, I suppose that's what it comes down to, so we have a lot of respect for tears and what they represent. Crying is a piece of expressive behaviour that needs no apology and isn't, absolutely isn't, a demand for attention. We pride ourselves on being able to ask for affection straight out, without needing to break down to do it. There's something a little crass about a hug as a response to tears. A hug can be an act of denial, even, and neither of us is going to make that mistake. We claim the right to cry uncomforted, letting the discharge do its work uninterrupted.

But in practice, I get so distressed by his tears, and he by mine, that we regress just as fast as we possibly can, and smother the expressiveness that we have so much respect for under a ton of hugs.

Endlessly we reformulate our feelings for each other. This is the same superstition that makes people put up bumper stickers – *Keep Your Distance, Baby on Board, I ♥ my π* – to make the roads safe and life go on for ever.

Fate is a dual-control Metro, that much I know, but I'm not clear about who's in which seat. It may be me, or it may be my lover, that squeezes the brake when we approach a bend too fast, or who pops the clutch in to prevent a stall. 'Baby clutch,' I can hear a familiar voice saying in my ear, '*baby*-baby clutch,' as we move off up the hill to where we must go.

EVELYN LAU
Pleasure

The blindfold hugged her cheekbones. The window was open, the night air blew across her body. She licked her lips, tasting scotch and her own lipstick, the flavor of raspberries. She couldn't tell if it was raining or not; it sounded like rain outside, but sometimes traffic could sound like rain. She wasn't sure. She felt confused, cold without her clothes, and the skin itched where her hair brushed against her shoulderblades. She flexed the muscles in her face, trying to shift the blindfold, to let in some thin horizon of light.

But everything was dark.

A breeze blew over her breasts, her stomach. She shivered when his fingers closed on her wrist, tracing lightly the veins in her forearm. She started breathing hard when he took her arm and did that, running his thumb along the artery like it was a blade he was testing. For a wild moment she thought of bolting while she still could, but forced herself to lie still as he caressed her. She had made her decision by coming tonight, understanding fully what would happen to her if she did. Not like the first time, when she could not have known, when she had woken up the next morning in her own bed, drawn back the duvet, and seen what he had done to her body — this man who had touched the back of her hand so gently the night before when they met in the hotel lounge high above the city. 'How sad you look,' he had said. 'Do you feel like talking?' She would have brushed him off if he had not said that he had once worked as a counsellor; although she had not been in therapy since the break-up of her marriage years ago, she automatically trusted people in the helping professions, saw them as full of wisdom and good intention. Green candles had flickered on the tables and he had let her drink and talk and even cry about the pressures of her job and the hopelessness of her ongoing affair with a married man. 'What's that?' he had said then, grinning at her as she sniffed and wiped her eyes, 'Is that a smile? Oh, I think so – right there, look, almost a smile, a little more, perfect!' And as they left for his apartment she had smiled dazzlingly through her tears.

The next morning she had spent wrapped in her sweater, slumped on her living-room floor in front of the fireplace, in shock. But underneath there had even then pulsed a vein of excitement, remembering the flames reflected in the stranger's green irises across the table, his oddly full, sensuous mouth. Remembering how at the instant she knew she was incapable of movement in his restraints, she had been stunned by how safe she felt in the absolute darkness of her life given over to another.

Now he pulled her left arm back past her head, buckling a strap of leather around her wrist. She wrapped her fingers around the bedpost, felt the leather clamping on her other wrist. A momentary silence. Where was he? Standing above her? Was he waiting by the far wall with lamplight on his face, studying her? She tried to turn her wrists but they would not turn inside the restraints.

Hands gripped her ankles, pulled them down. The slap of leather cuffs against bone, her legs stretched wide. Someone was breathing evenly in the room. She tried to move her limbs and couldn't. When she turned her head towards her right wrist, pulling at the shoulder, she could feel the tension all the way down her left leg to where her ankle was strapped to the railing. She was spread like a star on the bed, the cool comforter under her and the wind flying across her body.

Even as the fear increased, she felt a strange relief creeping in, that he was now in control of what would happen to her. She could not be held responsible for anything that happened next.

She thrust her hips towards the ceiling, pressing her fingers together and trying to slide them back through the cuffs. She knew he liked to see her struggle. He was standing over her, breathing into her hair; she could feel his breath quicken with excitement, warmer than the air from the window. He tugged gently at her chin and then shoved a ball gag into her mouth, like a fist. She choked, panicked, forced herself to relax the muscles of her face. Leather straps ran down her chin and up her forehead; he lifted her head and started to buckle the straps underneath her hair. Pain clenched the base of her jaw as she held the ball between her teeth.

Someone crying, salt in her mouth and the fabric of the blindfold moist and hot. Something rising from her chest and her shoulders like an ache, something being massaged out of her until gradually a part of her mind grew dark and sleepy, cradled like a baby inside the restraints. A chain was dragged across her stomach, and then she felt the clamps bite into both nipples. He tugged at the chain, it lifted from her body in a silver arc, and her nipples rose to meet his invisible hands. Someone was still crying. Shut up, shut up, she wanted to say, but the sobs kept coming and wouldn't stop, like the first night in the lounge, when she wept in front of this stranger and felt the tremendous release. Then she heard the short, sudden whistling high in the air. It seemed to swoop down from the ceiling, and it split across the surface of her body.

Afterwards he sat by the bay window in his armchair, crossing his legs, adjusting the belt of his bathrobe. Light from the street lamps draped thin shadows over the floor, long and blue. He watched her across the room – she was bent over the bed, running her hands through her hair and then through the ropes and chains on the rumpled sheets. Her navy blazer lay crooked across her shoulders and her face was a blur of wet color, the smudged mouth, the pastel eyelids, and the wavy mascara lines down her cheeks. He didn't think she even knew that she was crying.

The air from the open window was crisp against his bare legs. He flicked the belt of the bathrobe off his thigh and reached for his cigarettes. Watched her lean down to pick up her dress, a designer affair from an expensive boutique; his eyes traced the buttons of her spine, her thin back. Women like her always did amaze him. Often they were as trusting as the underage girls he sometimes picked up in east-end bars with pool tables and staggering men in stained jeans and baseball caps. The only difference was that the girls grabbed their purses and ran from his apartment counting their blessings that they were still alive. The women with the careers and the condominiums were the ones who came back.

Now her hands were trembling, breasts bobbing inside the

jacket like bruised fruit. He eyed her marks keenly: the welts, the drying blood zigzagging down her thigh, the abused nipples misshapen from the clamps that had remained on her throughout the session. Her breath was ragged in the air, halting like she'd forgotten how to breathe, then starting up again too fast, her throat chiseling up and down in her neck. He surveyed her body, then swiveled around to face the window.

It had begun to rain, lightly at first, and then coming down hard. Rain so thick it looked white in the night, smacking the pavement and the grass like bullets. Behind his own reflection in the windowpane he saw her straighten up, hiccupping, pushing hair out of her eyes and trying to fasten it in a clip at the base of her neck. The window reflected the lights of the chandelier blazing above the bed, the pink cloud of the comforter, the dull antique bed frame. The ropes lay uncoiled around her and the riding crop was propped against the wall, stiff and slender. He thought with pleasure that he could see its leather tongue still vibrating.

The rain poured down. He waited, and a moment of lightning filled the sky, bleaching everything silver – cars parked along the street, trees, other buildings. His own face loomed in the window, the smooth cheeks flushed boyishly from exertion, his lips curved and generous and undistorted by cruelty.

He rubbed his palm absent-mindedly. It was reddened from the friction of the whip handles. He glanced again at her reflection; she was sucking in her breath, trying to stop a sob. They both waited for the sound of thunder, but it came from so far away it could have been the sound of someone coughing in the next room of the west-end building.

He sighed, crushing out his cigarette and rising from the

chair. Tonight he would let her go, and another night she would return. He knew. Already in the window he could see her starting towards him, tugging her skirt over her lashed thighs, as though he had done nothing.

ETIENNE VAN HEERDEN
Bull Factory

The fastest gun in town, you're up front. Leading the field.

The crowd follows. You set the pace.

But success has a price tag. Peak performance takes its toll.

In love you've got to be number one.

Naturally: you're a top dog.

We understand.

That's why we've taken an old recipe, proved by lovers down the ages. And in our laboratories we have developed it into NEW Don Juan ointment.

I drew a deep breath and read on.

Don Juan ointment will put the bang back in your love-life! Shoot you through to total pleasure!

The creative director pressed a button and the bottom of an ointment tin flashed onto the projection screen: *Don Juan: tested in San Francisco, sex-mecca of the world. The secret of movie stars who stay on top in spite of great pressure and tension. Heroes of the silver screen who go for the bull's-eye every time!*

Guaranteed safe and free from side-effects for you or your lover! Order now from Venus Products, PO Box 3386, Bellville Industria. And receive a FREE surprise gift from Loveland with your first tin of success ointment!

The MD's cigar tapped against the gold-plated ashtray. He watched Big Bill van Niekerk out of the corner of his eye, keeping the other eye critically fixed on my presentation, from market analysis to concept and media plan. I pushed my seat back, signalled to the creative director and the logo which we'd created flashed onto the screen. I read the slogan once, twice, three times; first quietly, then louder, then emphatically: *Venus – won't let you down*.

Big Bill started to laugh. He chuckled and chortled and guffawed. Unsure, we sat in the gloom. The MD shifted uncomfortably. The creative director mopped his brow. Just the week before he'd blown a big pitch. He was living on borrowed time: the Afro, the Pierre Cardin shirt, the jeans and the silver neckchain didn't quite disguise the fact that he was pushing 40. In this game, over the hill.

While Big Bill laughed, the MD gestured to the secretary. She laid the written proposal, elegantly bound in gold, before Big Bill, accidentally brushing against his shoulder as she did so.

I flashed back to my first meeting with him, the day he'd come to brief us about yet another new product.

'So, you're the new account executive,' he'd said, and as he thrust a warm paw in my direction he was already looking over my shoulder at what we'd laid on for him in the MD's office: a wooden box of his favourite cigars (standard equipment for every advertising agency pitching for Big Bill's accounts), a brace of chic little female media assistants draped around the table and a bottle of the KWV's finest brandy.

'We must get together for a drink tomorrow,' he'd said, pushing past me. 'You can pay. Where the fuck is that secretary of mine? She's all tits and no brains. Come on, Hilary baby, let's get going. I've only got seven minutes.'

We sat. I couldn't help assessing Big Bill's monumental paunch which rose and fell heavily as he breathed. His coarse fingers were heavily weighted with rings. Big Bill's Hilary noted down every word he uttered.

'Right, it's bloody straightforward,' he'd bellowed, 'but it's dynamite. I believe in it and I'm ready to fight for it. I'm giving it to you because this is a young agency, you run with a campaign, and you're randy buggers. You've got the account, but I'm only giving you one chance at a media splash and if it doesn't take first shot, you're on your arses on the street.'

We'd nodded. We all knew Big Bill's war-cry: 'I carry a helluva lot of weight in this city.'

'Fair enough,' said the MD, tapping his cigar on the gold-plated ashtray.

There'd been a moment's silence. Then, 'Here it is,' said Big Bill, and Hilary produced a small bottle from her briefcase. We'd waited in anticipation as Hilary solemnly unscrewed the lid and handed the bottle to Big Bill.

He stuck a fat pinkie into the ointment and held it out to the MD.

'Careful, girls,' he'd teased.

We'd all sniffed the pink ointment and nodded approvingly.

'This is IT,' pronounced Big Bill, tossing back the rest of his brandy. The MD flicked his lighter as Big Bill's hand moved towards the cigar box.

'Hell, boys,' said Big Bill through clouds of smoke. 'You've got to give this thing one helluva name, because it's a knockout product. Supermarkets, cafés – these are the distribution points. Cafés, man. That's where you must push it. Along with bread, Blitz, *Scope* and the Sunday paper. This is a Sunday game:

they've got air-conditioning, they've got slim-fasters, they've got aerobouncy mattresses, they've got vibrators. What they need now is the performance. And there you have it. There it is.' Big Bill had tapped the bottle. We nodded: no one in this town argued with Big Bill's marketing savvy.

'We're gonna take the suburbs by storm with this product,' bellowed Big Bill.

Filthy rich, with a liver beyond the rescue of any health farm, this was a man who'd gone into liquidation four times, and every time bounced back with a new Alfa Spider, driving from agency to agency with a new wonder product.

'Media?' The MD raised an enquiring eyebrow.

'TV,' said Big Bill. 'We go big.'

'The SABC will never approve it,' cautioned the MD.

'You're the agency,' said Big Bill. 'What does it say out there in reception? "We sell ice to Eskimos." Come on, man.' He'd stubbed out his cigar. 'This is your game. Chuck it at your best studio and see what they come up with. And have a look at the competition. I want a market analysis. And you present within a week. Agreed?'

He stood up while Hilary scribbled down his last words. Their car, a company BMW, was already idling at the door. It sank down on its axles as Big Bill climbed into the back.

Back inside, the MD had drawn a deep breath and pushed the blond forelock back off his forehead.

'Bastard,' he'd said, and then, to the receptionist: 'Set up a meeting, seven tonight in my office. This is a biggie.'

Now, four days later, we sat limply in the presentation room waiting for Big Bill's stomach convulsions to subside. What was the verdict?

Finally, he looked up and announced: 'I know a campaign

when I see one!' The MD's cigar flew to his mouth, the creative
director whistled softly.

'For fucksakes,' I heard him mutter.

'Talk about market penetration!' gloated Big Bill. The MD
made a small movement with his head and a fresh brandy
appeared before Big Bill.

I sighed too. Three hard days had followed that first brain-
storming session at the round table from 7 p.m. on the Monday.
We'd started tired and tense after a long and exhausting day and
broken up the meeting half drunk and irritable. For one whole
day a researcher had called every gynaecologist, quack, muti
shop, pharmacist and analyst. The next day she explored every
nook and cranny of the city, and finally, with the campaign that
gradually crystallised from the chaos of sketches and photos and
words, she produced a neatly typed list of aphrodisiacs and sex
aids. They were all there, from countless mixtures of Spanish fly
to indigenous rhino-horn powders, passion fruit cordials from
the French Riviera, witchdoctors' mutis and potions from the
Bo-Kaap. And a row of pink pills from Woodstock's drug belt.
The minute we had the list we were up and running.

It was already 1 a.m. by the time we started the nightclub
round, tired but enthusiastic. I got stuck in a joint with a saxo-
phone player and a blind clown; the others went off somewhere
to gamble with the cast of Marthinus Basson's new production.
Next morning I heard that the MD, exhausted and drained to
the dregs by cars, perfume, brandy, Bible courses, short-term
insurance and chewing-gum, had started folding R50-notes into
little pink aeroplanes which he sent flying round the club. The
chronically broke actors scurried like fowls after the little
planes, fawned on him, applauded him and hated him with his

paunch and his heavy gold signet ring.

And now, with Big Bill lyrical, it was an evening of relaxation.

'I know a campaign when I see one,' chortled Big Bill again. Then he leaned over to say something to the MD. I caught the creative director's eye. Behind his relief, I could see the exhaustion of twenty years in the bull factory. Later he excused himself; he was off to the Big Wheel, where the men sat for hours drinking beer, eating German sausages and giving the come-on to each other's reflections in the mirrors.

As he left, he cried over our jollity the cry that always signalled he was fucked-out: 'I'm bisexual: I love men *and* boys!'

'Goodbye, Arthur Murray,' said the MD. The man in jeans had earned his spurs again. We had Big Bill in the bag.

The MD glanced at his watch. Seven o'clock. 'What about an early night?' The PAs and secretaries made a happy and chattering bee-line for the door. Shortly afterwards a couple of AEs followed them, each with a file under one arm, briefcase in the other hand. Silence fell in the palace. So there we were: the MD, Big Bill, Hilary, the copywriter, the media director and I.

We sat in the blue haze of cigar smoke, waiting until the last door banged. We charged our glasses. Big Bill fidgeted restlessly: he wanted his pound of flesh. Earlier, a messenger had deposited an *Argus* on the MD's desk. Now the MD drew it nearer, running a finger down the smalls. He dialled. The gold ring gleamed in the low light.

While we waited, I had to move Big Bill's Spider from the kerb in front of the office to our parking garage. He'd refused to allow a messenger to do it.

'If you want to handle my account,' he growled at me, 'you'd better learn to handle my Spider. Some days I have a gut full of driving.'

In the luxury car, I recalled what the tired art director had said to me the evening before: 'It pays to cut your ear off.'

At the same time, the English copywriter had pushed his typewriter back and leaned over to me. I could smell stale brandy on his breath.

'When the pupil is ready,' he murmured, 'the master will arrive . . .'

'Zola shits,' was how I'd shut him up and left. Behind me jazz blared from the loudspeakers. They were under a lot of pressure. I'd brought a bottle of Nederburg Baronne up to the studio for them; there was the crazy aroma of dagga and the copywriter's head was slouched forward on his arms.

With Big Bill's Spider safe beside the MD's BMW, I made my way up the stairs from the basement garage. I stopped at the toilet on one floor. Above the urinal, someone had written in koki pen: *Enjoy the last great white erection*. And alongside: *Aids rules OK*. Someone had crossed out the *Aids* and replaced it with *PW*. On the floor below ours, I greeted the security guard and his fierce Alsatian with its shifty eyes.

At our office, I rang the doorbell.

The intercom crackled. 'Yes?' It was the MD.

'Yup.'

The electronic Yale sprang open. I entered. A bunch of red poppies on a chrome and glass table. Fallen petals lay on the glass. Aha, I thought: the Sanlam ad.

The girls hadn't arrived yet. Big Bill was telling his favourite story: about the Ciskeian mama who'd been bribed into having a minute microphone implanted behind one nipple so she . . . Big

Bill was in paroxysms of laughter. So that at night she could milk the Minister of Development for information on new transactions. 'Via that big mama's left tit,' said Big Bill, 'I made my first million.'

I sat down and poured more wine. For Big Bill's entertainment, the media director went to the Big Bill file drawer, took out a video and slipped it into the VCR. Bored, we watched a girl with a briefcase enter an office block, ride up in the lift, walk down a corridor, knock on a door and enter. With a nod, she acknowledged the man behind the large desk, put her briefcase down, and began to strip. The man bent over his intercom and, when she was naked, three young men came into the office. They stripped too and the man at the desk relaxed back in his chair and watched the panting performance.

'And Hilary?' I whispered to the media director. He frowned and shook his head.

'She stays,' he mouthed. Sitting next to Big Bill, Hilary watched the video with interest. She giggled at one point and asked me to pour her another drink.

We all prayed that it wasn't to be a night for Big Bill's most enduring passion: kerb crawling: the long convoy led by Big Bill's Spider and the MD's BMW, creeping along Sea Point's main road, Woodstock's main road, down Loop Street . . . for hours on end: Big Bill in the leading car, filthy rich, *almost* a member of the President's Council, red-faced, blustering.

At last the doorbell rang. The MD looked at me. As I went out, the girl on the video shrieked something ecstatically in Italian.

'Mamma mia!' groaned Big Bill.

It was late night, in fact early morning – one could tell by the subtle change in the drone of the city – when I cautiously opened the door. In an elderly Ford Cortina slung low on its axles, I saw white female elbows, a wrist smothered in bangles. The man before me sported a droopy cowboy moustache. His pants hung low on his pelvis. In a comic replication of a Hollywood movie, a revolver occupied the holster on his hip.

'You phoned Thrill Girls?' he asked.

I nodded. 'Let's go in.'

I made sure the door was latched. I could hear the girls tittering in the Cortina. We moved through the dimly-lit entrance foyer, on deep-pile carpets, past the glossy wall-posters, manicured indoor plants; past framed Loerie Awards, logos, glossy pictures of models, a cheetah posing on a locomotive, a spacecraft splashing down in a blue sea, a giant hot-air balloon with an entire city in its belly. The ape following me slid his eyes over glass and chrome, gleaming desks behind transparent partitions, designer vases with fresh roses, the blank gaze of computer monitors, and past the studios: the colourful roosts of the visualisers, copywriters and artists.

'Go for the gold,' he read in a murmur and a sceptical laugh stirred the moustache.

'Capitalism gives everyone a chance,' I told him sarcastically.

'Plenty bucks here,' he said and whistled softly. We turned a corner in the corridor. Before us, through the open door, lay the arresting elegance of the MD's suite.

I heard Big Bill's snigger. He was telling yet another well-known story: about the milk culture chaps from the North, already driving a flashy car seven years ago, who had come to him for backing.

'And now,' Big Bill threw out an arm, 'look at the buggers

queueing up there in Loop Street in front of TeKaibos. Look at the big Mercs from the platteland. There are fat cats in that queue, pal. And now I hear even the fucking English are starting to buy.'

We entered the room. The MD tapped his cigar against his cheek.

'What have you got for me?' he asked the cowboy.

'My agency fee is only fifty a head. Beyond that you must negotiate.' He fingered his holster.

'Why so cheap?' asked the MD. He had a few under the belt and I could tell he was spoiling for an argument.

The cowboy-pimp stepped forward and extended a hand to the MD. 'Alcock,' he introduced himself.

'What cock?' quipped Big Bill and Hilary's giggle tinkled round the room. On the video – the sound had been turned down – the girl with the briefcase once more walked down the corridor and knocked at the door. Without a word, she nodded to the man at the desk and he bent over his intercom. She unhooked her bra and her breasts fell out. Three men came into the room. The man at the desk relaxed into his chair.

The MD raised an eyebrow at the creative director, who speedily topped up Big Bill's glass – three fingers of brandy this time. The sooner we had him paralytic, the sooner we could get him out. Hilary crossed her legs and I imagined I heard the sound of silky stockings rubbing against each other.

'Fuck the protocol,' said the MD, ignoring Alcock's out-stretched hand. 'What have you got?'

'Two blondes, a redhead and three brunettes. The brunettes are all Spanish. And clean. All checked this evening. Safe like mommy.'

The MD looked sideways at Alcock. The ash at the end of his

cigar was longer than usual. 'And the piece?' he asked without allowing his eyes to move to the revolver.

'The city's getting rough,' Alcock shrugged.

'The Cape isn't Dutch any more,' smirked Big Bill; then, with an expansive gesture: 'Bring in the follies!'

Alcock turned to Big Bill.

The MD looked at Alcock. 'That fellow,' he said, 'is one of the heaviest of the Cape's heavies.'

Big Bill giggled. 'Wild Bill,' he bragged, redder in the face than ever.

'Fine. My girls are experienced.'

'If I touch something,' began Big Bill, rising out of his chair. Alcock looked slightly nervous as Bill drew himself up to his full height. 'If I get hold of something, it turns to gold. Even if I get hold of a girl's tits.' He winked at Hilary who got a fresh cigar out of the case for him.

'As long as your cheques are healthy,' said Alcock.

'I own the fucking bank. The whole fucking bank.' Big Bill was a bit unsteady on his feet.

'How much?' asked the MD, signing a cheque with a flourish. He looked at Hilary; the first time he'd looked directly at her or spoken to her. 'Are you sticking around or fading?'

She simpered, 'My job is my job.'

'Deliver,' the MD told Alcock, waving his hand like an orchestra conductor. He threw himself back in his chair. We waited in silence. Even Big Bill said nothing as he fixed his eyes on the video screen.

Outside we heard a car. The MD glanced at his watch.

We could hear them coming down the corridor, their high heels whispering on the wool matting. I could imagine their eyes darting about for booty to filch later when the men were docile and drunk.

Even before they came through the door we could smell the sharp sweet stench of the spermicide which they'd sprayed into their slippery orifices.

'If there's one thing I hate,' said the MD as they entered, 'it's that smell.'

Even when the girls were standing before us, Big Bill kept his eyes on the video screen. The MD lit another cigar and scrutinised each of the girls in turn.

Ill at ease, I poured more wine into my glass. The media director was gazing fixedly at the blonde third from the left. He smiled at her. She winked back but then returned her gaze to the MD who was gesturing to Alcock. 'Delivery accepted,' said the MD looking at me. I escorted Alcock to the front door.

'Grab the little blonde for yourself,' he told me. 'She's double-jointed.'

When I got back to the office, a redhead had taken the seat beside mine. She smiled at me.

I poured her a glass of wine and topped mine up.

Big Bill, Hilary and their three girls were ushered to the presentation studio with its soundproof walls and deep-pile carpet. The MD went along to show them how to open the stinkwood bar cabinet and where the small video screen was concealed – behind a framed Loerie that swung aside at the touch of a button. In one hand Big Bill held the video cassette of the Italian girl, with the other he waved at us.

I followed the redhead to the promotion studio. She wore a shiny black blouse and tight jeans and she swayed her hips as she went up the stairs in front of me. I heard the MD's door shut

with a bang, and jazz was already spinning from the wine studio
— Brubeck's *Give it all ya got*, the copywriter's favourite.

I closed the door to the promotion studio. A big chrome
robot under construction for an oil company's careers exhibi-
tion gleamed electronically in the corner. They'd forgotten to
switch it off. I pulled out the wall plug, the eyes flickered, the
robot sighed, shuddered and went dead.

I sat down.

She was not unattractive: gingery hair, rather heavy mascara,
freckles on her nose. She paced coquettishly about the studio,
leaning over half-finished sketches, smiling at the posters. Outside, far away, a siren wailed. Then it fell silent again. Slowly
the city subsided into its late-night sleep.

She came to sit opposite me so that our shoes touched. In the
curve of her neck, where the blouse fell open, there was a blue-
green bruise. She leant forward towards me, her elbows on her
thighs.

'The night is still young, hmm?'

I nodded and poured us each a drink. She read the label on
the bottle and pursed her lips. 'Nothing but the best, hey?' I
shrugged. We heard a door slam somewhere. Heels tapping on
the marble floor of the toilet. Another slam, voices. A telephone began to ring deep in the belly of the firm. We heard it
ring ten, twenty times.

'Hard day?' she asked.

'I can't remember,' I said, taking another mouthful of wine.

'When did you start this morning?'

'Clock-watching is a cardinal sin.'

'Oh.' She shrugged as if to say sorry-I-asked and looked
around the room again. Would she get up and walk about, run-

ning her finger over the sleeping icons of the bull factory?

But she remained seated, and I did too, with tie awry and waistcoat unbuttoned. Then she remembered her strategy. She pouted, pulled her shoulders back and aimed her nipples provocatively at me.

'Cigarette?' she asked. I nodded. She snapped her small handbag open, holding it pressed intimately against herself as she delved about in it. What did she keep in there? Condoms? Tissues? Vaseline?

I took a cigarette from the red-nailed fingers. Dagga? A sanitary pad?

We lit up and drew on the cigarettes. A set of red underwear, should the client require it? A little apron, should the client desire that?

She watched me awhile through the smoke. Then, 'You don't like me,' she complained with a pout.

I shifted on my stool.

'What are your rates?' I asked.

She looked at me for a long moment. 'I've had my tits done recently,' she said. Fixing her eyes on mine, she slowly unbuttoned her blouse. One breast appeared: full and curved, perfect. Then the other nipple slipped out. She had large breasts, round as melons, and the nipples pointed pertly upwards from rosy stains the size of your palm.

She pushed one breast sideways. 'See the marks?' The flesh swelled out from her hand, thrusting through between the fingers. She left the full breast; it swayed dizzyingly back.

We sat; smoked.

Behind her on the wall, the copywriter who normally worked here had pinned up a passage from Ogilvy:

'I always use my clients' products. This is not toadyism, but elementary good manners. Almost everything I consume is manufactured by one of my clients. My shirts are by Hathaway, my candlesticks by Steuben. My car is a Rolls-Royce and its tank is always full of Shell. I have my suits made by Sears, Roebuck. At breakfast I drink Maxwell House coffee or Tetley Tea, and eat two slices of Pepperidge Farm toast. I wash with Dove, deodorize with Ban, and light my pipe with a Zippo lighter . . . and why not, pray tell? Are these not the finest goods and services on earth?'

She stood up and started to peal off her jeans. They were very tight, and she had to wriggle her hips. She folded the jeans neatly over the artist's drawing table. Then she took off her panties, tossing them onto the jeans.

I poured more wine. There was a smudge of red lipstick on her glass. She sat before me again. Her pubic hair was rusty red, growing lustily in a single tuft from just below the sunburn mark, halfway to the navel. She'd shaved the inside of her thighs and new growth was showing from under the skin. I lit two more cigarettes and gave her one. She ran red fingernails across her lips. Then she began to rub herself, and I could hear the sound of her hand against the wiry hairs. Moaning softly, she put her cigarette in the ashtray and massaged her left nipple. I drew on my cigarette, taking a mouthful of wine now and then. I could smell her now.

When she came, I heard the swishing of the big yellow machine that moves along the city's kerbstones, sucking up refuse from four o'clock each morning. In the little death she sat before me, her body jerking, her mournful eyes on me, her mouth a crushed, sorrowing flower of the night.

BRIAN McCABE
Table d'Hôte

Maria sits opposite Eric, not drinking her wine.

She has raised her glass and now she holds it there, just a little below her chin. Soon she'll drink, or put the glass back down on the table, but not yet. For the moment she'll go on looking across the table at Eric, watch him as he fidgets with his glass, his knife, his serviette.

How did it happen? Be honest, Eric.

Now the hand can resume its mission, tilting the glass as it carries it to the mouth. Maria's lips take the rim of the glass at last, the more eagerly for having been made to wait. She drinks.

Eric sits opposite Maria, not drinking his wine.

He is looking down into his glass. He tilts the glass from side to side, making his reflected face change shape. In the red wine his features distort. Drunk again – was that how it happened? He looks up at Maria, for a moment confronts that trusting, candid stare. Be honest.

I met her. I kept meeting her, bumping into her.

Eric's hands begin a restless, evasive gesture above the flowers, the little vase of flowers on the restaurant table. When Maria looks at the hands, the hands begin to feel foolish. They catch hold of one another, retreat behind the flowers, but no –

they can't hide there. At length Eric knits his two hands together and places them on his place-mat, where he'll endeavour to make them stay. His head is bowed, and all in all it looks very much as if Eric might be about to say grace. *For what we are about to receive . . .* that's how it happened, those restless hands.

One night I met her at a party, a party at Frank's.

Cleverly Eric pauses to let the name resonate. If he were to think aloud now he would say: *Frank — remember him, Maria? The one you said had hairy shoulders.* Instead he pauses, sniffs at the bouquet of the wine despite the fact that it has none, takes a civilised sip, winces, then throws his head back and drains the upturned glass.

Maria, meanwhile, watches his Adam's apple pulsate. It reminds her oddly, of a fish — the opening and closing of gills. When Eric puts down the glass she sees the mouth: it pouts, smacks its lips, smiles. She finds herself addressing his teeth:

How long ago was this?

Eric's smile becomes less than a smile, then vanishes. The lips form an O-shape, and the initial vowel disintegrates into words:

Only a few weeks ago. When you were in London, and.

And so Eric, wearily, recounts the events by which he and Lillian became lovers. How they met that night at Frank's party, danced for a time together, drank far too much wine, retired to the room being used for coats in order to smoke a little joint and talk about . . . but what had they talked about — *relationships?* Occasionally he glances at Maria, and from the sceptical look in her eyes it is clear that none of this explains how anything happened. But how is Eric to convey it? The atmosphere of lust and romance, the excitement of the banal music, the drunkenness and the drugs, the tacit intimacy behind the sordid procedure? Especially in a restaurant and besides . . . how the memory dissembles! Because that night wasn't the night, not the night that he and Lillian.

Eric interrupts his narrative to pick at his teeth with a tooth-pick, though the starters haven't come yet. He extricates a morsel of breakfast, examines it closely then discards it. To avoid Maria's eyes (be honest, Eric) he stares into the alcove beyond her shoulder, where the ornamental mirrors on the wall slice his image into two. By moving his head a little this way and that, he plays at making his face fragment and then reform. Best keep it simple.

Then I went back to her place for coffee, and.

And Eric's hands come to life again: one tugs a cigarette from the packet, while the other swoops for the bottle and, catching it, offers it to Maria. Maria's hand holds out her glass, while Eric's hand tilts the bottle and pours. Maria's other hand lights the lighter and offers the flame to Eric's other hand, the hand with the cigarette. His hand steadies hers as he takes the light. Both watch with distrust the hands which go on serving one another regardless, parting and coming together, regardless of how it happened.

Maria, exhaling two jets of blue smoke from her nostrils, begins to examine her fingernails impatiently. Realising that the story – this tale of the unexpected: How Eric And Lillian Happened – is lacking still its denouement, she decides to prompt the teller:

Is she good in bed?

Eric spills a little wine as he puts down his glass. He studies his hands, the cigarette, the red stain growing on the white tablecloth. He smiles sorrowfully at his drink, unwilling to lie to Maria. Reluctant, also, to be honest. His one-eyed reflection stares up at him from the wine, a gloomy fish. Eric shrugs his shoulders.

Yes.

Maria begins to suffer.

Sooner or later someone will have to say something. The starters, inedible as they were, have been eagerly consumed. The wine too has come in useful and Eric has already ordered a second bottle of the same. And everything is going smoothly but for the fact that silence has joined the two at the table. On the one hand Maria ought to say something since it is, strictly speaking, her turn. On the other hand Eric ought to qualify that fateful *yes* of his. A little smalltalk is all that is required, but neither is able to provide it.

At the next table, quite the contrary situation has come about: a young, well-dressed couple, having opted immediately for the *a la carte* menu, now discuss animatedly which dishes to select. But then there are so many to choose from, and clearly they have so many other things to talk about, that the young man calls to the waiter and orders a bottle of champagne to be going on with. The young lady expresses her delight by blowing the young man a little kiss over the table. The young man responds by taking her hand and squeezing it gently.

Maria, turning her eyes from the kiss-blowing and hand-squeezing, begins to brood on the fact that she and Frank, during their brief but exhilarating affair, dined out only once, decides to ask Eric how often he and Lillian have eaten out. It is a way of estimating how far things have gone.

Eric, how often have you and Lillian . . .?

But Eric averts his eyes to see the waiter at his side, presenting the second bottle of the same bad wine for inspection. Eric nods, smiles. Carefully then the waiter unpeels the seal, places the bottle on the table, begins the slow ritual of uncorking the wine.

Everything all right, sir?

Eric affects nonchalance as he utters his *uh huh*.

Easing the cork soundlessly from the bottle, with neither Eric nor Maria caring to disturb the silence, the waiter proceeds to refill each of the glasses. At length he lays the bottle down between them and, before he departs, makes a few small alterations to the arrangement of the objects on the table – the little vase of flowers a little more to the side, the pepper and the salt a little closer together, the ashtray out of sight behind the flowers. He makes a slight bow before he turns to depart. Eric nods, smiles.

Alone together again, Eric and Maria pick up their glasses and drink in unison. It tastes better than the first, and Eric looks at his glass appreciatively as he resumes the conversation:

Slept together? A few times, quite a few.

He picks up his knife and tries to balance it on his finger, but it tilts this way and that precariously. He looks forgetfully at Maria, pities her: sipping her wine, frowning slightly, twisting and untwisting a lock of her hair between her fingers. She appears so forlorn, suddenly, that Eric feels within himself an irresistible rush of affectionate regret. Regrettably, his knife rebounds off the sideplate and falls to the floor. The couple at the next table look over briefly, then away. Eric dives, begins to grope around Maria's shoes. Retrieving the knife and on the way back up, he is stunned momentarily by the apparition, between skirt and stockingtop, of her soft, coral! aceous thigh.

362

Maria looks with pity at the bald spot on the crown of Eric's head as he climbs back on board the table. His face is flushed, his breathing harsh, and for a moment he looks simply old and exhausted. Maria finds herself offering him a cigarette, and though the question she asks is a difficult one, the tone of her voice is warm and consolatory:

Are you in love with her, Eric?

Eric does not know, or is unwilling to state the answer. He looks over his shoulder to the kitchen – surely the main course must be on its way by now. He scratches his chin impatiently, rubs one of his eyes, makes the most of blowing his nose, but no – it still hasn't come. He picks up his knife, puts it down again, then hazards a kind of guess:

I'm fond of her. I don't know . . .

His hand goes for the bottle, picks it up and waves it around a little – a gay gesture, but done with sorrow. Maria offers her empty glass, and as Eric refills it her wrist begins to sag with the weight of the wine.

You make it sound like a misfortune.

Eric manages to smile and frown simultaneously at this acute observation, but when the smile goes the frown remains, and it is with a bitter curl of the lips that he replies:

Isn't it?

As if to reassure herself that love need not be a misfortune, Maria glances at the couple at the next table. Their conversation has paused, but somehow they give the impression that even silence is a kind of sharing. She turns to Eric, watches him smoke his cigarette. How he prevaricates even with that: worrying at the ashtray with it, rolling it around in his fingers, tapping his lips with the tip . . .

363

So what are you going to do, Eric?

Eric's lips droop to the rim of the glass. As he gulps the wine a thin trickle escapes from the corner of his mouth and meanders down his chin. He dabs his face with the paper serviette, shrugs.

I'm not sure . . . what to do.

Eric takes the paper serviette and begins to do some origami. He makes a triangular fold. Perhaps a little boat? His fingers fidget with the sail, tugging and pressing. When it is finished, he places it in the little harbour between his knife and his fork. Maria watches Eric's thoughtless finger push the little boat out of the harbour, around the salt-cellar light-house, out into the open table. Looking away, she sees that the waiter is approaching and yes, the main course has arrived at last.

Sooner or later, Eric, you'll have to decide.

And as the waiter lays out the clean plates he suppresses a yawn and once again enquires:

Everything all right, sir?

This time, what is it but despair in Eric's voice as he utters his *uh huh?*

Eric begins to suffer.

Maria is very disappointed.

She has moved back from the table and now she sits almost sideways in her chair: her legs crossed away from Eric, her body averted. She sips her wine, then holds the glass in her lap. When she looks down her hair swings over her face, hiding her profile. She looks down now, frowning at her wine.

Eric is very disappointed.

The '*Boeuf Bordelaise*' lacked garlic, among other things –

notably *boeuf* — and was really a kind of non-committal stew. Placing his knife and fork in the position that means it's finished, he now sets aside the plate and turns to the waiting trifle. He dips his spoon into the cream, moves it around a little, then leans towards Maria and pleads with the hair:

At least I've been honest with you.

Maria looks up, but not at Eric. Her glance goes to the Ideal Couple, who are now beginning their steaks. Their conversation, less punctuated now by laughter, has obviously moved on to deeper, more serious topics. The young lady listens intently to what her escort is saying; the young man appears both elegant and sincere as he talks, and from his gestures alone it is possible to assume that he is well beyond all petty considerations and is already drawing analogies, guiding the discourse to its proper and highly interesting conclusion.

Maria drains her glass and puts it down in her lap. She looks down, hides behind her hair.

Maria, this is ridiculous.

This time she does glance at Eric, but it is over her shoulder virtually, and her eyes lack interest. She raises her eyebrows slightly:

Mmm?

When Eric throws his hands out to either side of his pudding, expressing his exasperation, his left wrist collides with the bottle. He watches in wonder as the wine blooms huge in the white linen, a beautiful blood-flower. His hand, acting on its own initiative, rights the bottle before it rolls off the edge of the table.

Christ I'll order another.

He pours the remaining inch of wine into his glass, then leans over the chair-back and waves the empty bottle at the waiter, the waiter who isn't there. He turns back to confront Maria, missing the table with his elbow.

I mean the way you're sitting, Maria. How can I talk to your profile?

Reluctantly then Maria turns to face him, moves the chair forward a little, puts her glass on the table and begins too unwrap the frigid little triangle of camembert which turned out to be the fromage.

Eric, we can't afford another bottle.

Dejectedly she collects the dirty plates and cutlery, then lays them on top of the wide red stain on the tablecloth. It covers some of it, at least. She puts her elbows on the table, hiccups, presses her fingers into the roots of her hair, whispers:

Eric, don't you love me any more?

Eric brings his glass down on top of the little glass ashtray. The glass against the glass makes an unfortunate noise, and the Ideal Couple turn to stare in unison. Eric tries an apologetic smile. They look away pointedly, resuming their togetherness. Eric plays with his trifle and frowns as he considers this new riddle.

I think so . . . yes.

A barely perceptible quiver passes over Maria's lips and chin. Then a deeper tremor makes her cheeks shudder and her eyes close tightly. She raises her glass, holds it there, just a little below her chin. Evidently the glass is empty.

Maria, of course I . . .

But of course it is far too late: already she has bowed her head as the tears come, darting quickly from her eyes, racing one another down the cheeks, dripping from the curve of the chin. Grey spots occur here and there on the tablecloth as Maria, discreetly, weeps.

Eric offers her — oddly enough, still intact — his little paper boat.

Of course I do.

He looks around to see who's looking. No one seems to have noticed, and it is with a feeling of gratitude for this that Eric sends his hand over the table to pat Maria's bare arm. Of course he does, if the question should arise, love her.

Maria sniffs, hiccups, dabs her cheek with the crumpled boat, then sits up and bravely pushes the hair back from her face. Seeing the waiter approach, she excuses herself from the table.

Coffee, sir?

Eric nods but does not smile. As the waiter collects the dirty plates, Eric stutters an apology for the Red Sea underneath. The waiter makes a polite comment to the effect that it is nothing, then departs. Unwilling to face his schizoid twin in the alcove, Eric goes to the gents.

Maria has lost her self-respect.

Standing before the wash-hand basin, she searches for it in her bag. She finds a hairbrush, her mascara and the rectangular little mirror which, though too small for the job, presents her with a less literal self-portrait than the one she sees behind the taps. Even so she can see quite clearly that her eyelids are red-rimmed and swollen and that the mascara has trailed down her cheeks. Wondering if she is still attractive, Maria stoops to the running water and cups it in her hands. After splashing her face in it, she starts work on the disguise.

Eric has lost his self-respect.

Washing his hands, he searches for it in the mirror. He tries on various expressions, eyes his image from a number of angles.

He attempts a broad, confident grin and his image leers back at him quickly. Sincerity comes next, and this time Eric has to avert his eyes. He tries on a few ugly faces: grotesque, gargoyle-like pouts; cross-eyed consternations; a doleful Frankenstein mask; demonic, wicked grins. Drying his fingers on a paper towel, he wonders if he is still an upright citizen. He zips up his flies.

Out in the restaurant, meanwhile, everything has been going on smoothly until now. The waiter has taken the opportunity, during Eric-and-Maria's absence, to clear up the debris they have strewn all over the table. Already he has delivered the coffee and the bill. But now, suddenly, something dreadful is happening at the next table. The young man, his fork on the way to his mouth, can hardly believe that it is really happening . . . but yes, it really is: she has stood up so abruptly that the chair has overturned. From her accent and appearance it is clear to everyone in the restaurant that she is a well brought-up, well educated girl but . . . all that has gone, suddenly, and she is banging her fist hard on the table, making the dishes and the plates jump, and she is shouting, really shouting at the young man:

Bastard! You fucking . . . swine!

A unanimous silence. Then, perhaps because the swearwords were so well pronounced, a snigger. Then a gasp from another table, and a low-toned comment from another. The young lady, having burst loudly into tears, refuses to be pacified by either the waiter or the bastard-fucking-swine. Another waiter appears with the coats, and it is clear that the young man is being requested to leave – after settling his bill, of course. The young man says something quiet and earnest to the young lady as he takes out his wallet, but she won't wait another moment: breaking free of the many hands which seek to hold her and subdue her, she grabs her coat and her bag and marches adamantly out. The bastard-fucking-swine pays the bill, leaving a generous tip, and follows her – feeling the eyes on his back, sensing the theories being put forward at the tables around him.

It all happens so quickly that Eric and Maria, returning to their table from the toilets, are unaware that anything has happened. Indeed, they are mystified by the waiter's apology. But gradually, noticing that the next table has been hastily cleared, and sensing the scandalised chatter going on all around, they are able to surmise that something out of the ordinary has taken place at the next table in their absence. What it was, exactly, they can't imagine.

Eric takes out his cheque-book, turns the bill over and looks for the name of the restaurant. Underneath the name he notices a brief italicised message: *We hope you have enjoyed your meal. If you have, please come again soon, and tell all your friends about it!* And as he writes out the cheque Eric yawns repeatedly, and between the yawns there are fragments of a question:

Want to . . . go to . . . my place . . . or yours?

Maria's lips turn down at the corners with sincere disgust. She stirs the skin into her coffee, rattling the spoon in the cup.

Or how about both, Eric?

Eric looks up from his half-made signature, puzzled for a moment. Then, realising what Maria means, he proceeds with the surname. As the waiter collects the bill, Maria adds:

Or maybe you should call on Lillian?

Eric shakes his head, shrugs his shoulders and attempts a smile, uneasy that such a suggestion should have been made and impatient to leave the restaurant. And now that the meal is finished, and now that the bill has been paid, though Eric and Maria may yet have much to discuss, there is really nothing left to do but leave. And clearly they will have to go somewhere.

WILL SELF

The End of the Relationship

'Why the hell don't you leave him if he's such a monster?' said Grace. We were sitting in the Café Delancey in Camden Town, eating *croques m'sieurs* and slurping down *cappuccino*. I was dabbing the sore skin under my eyes with a scratchy piece of toilet paper – trying to stop the persistent leaking. When I'd finished dabbing I deposited the wad of salty stuff in my bag, took another slurp and looked across at Grace.

'I don't know,' I said. 'I don't know why I don't leave him.'

'You can't go back there – not after this morning. I don't know why you didn't leave him immediately after it happened . . .'

That morning I'd woken to find him already up. He was standing at the window, naked. One hand held the struts of the venetian blind apart, while he squinted down on to the Pentonville Road. Lying in bed I could feel the judder and hear the squeal of the traffic as it built up to the rush hour.

In the half-light of dawn his body seemed monolithic: his limbs columnar and white, his head and shoulders solid capitals. I stirred in the bed and he sensed that I was awake. He came back to the side of the bed and stood looking down at me.

'You're like a little animal in there. A little rabbit, snuggled down in its burrow.'

I squirmed down further into the duvet and looked up at him, puckering my lip so that I had goofy, rabbity teeth. He got back into bed and curled himself around me. He tucked his legs under mine. He lay on his side – I on my back. The front of his thighs pressed against my haunch and buttock. I felt his penis stiffen against me as his fingers made slight, brushing passes over my breasts, up to my throat and face and then slowly down. His mouth nuzzled against my neck, his tongue licked my flesh, his fingers poised over my nipples, twirling them into erection. My body teetered, a heavy rock on the edge of a precipice.

The rasp of his cheek against mine; the too peremptory prod-ding of his cock against my mons; the sense of something casual and offhand about the way he was caressing me. Whatever – it was all wrong. There was no true feeling in the way he was touching me; he was manipulating me like some giant dolly. I tensed up – which he sensed; he persisted for a short while, for two more rotations of palm on breast, and then he rolled over on his back with a heavy sigh.

'I'm sorry – '

'It's OK.'

'It's just that sometimes I feel that – '

'It's OK, really, please don't.'

'Don't what?'

'Don't talk about it.'

'But if we don't talk about it we're never going to deal with it. We're never going to sort it all out.'

'Look, I've got feelings too. Right now I feel like shit. If you don't want to, don't start. That's what I can't stand, starting and then stopping – it makes me sick to the stomach.'

'Well, if that's what you want.' I reached down to touch his penis; the chill from his voice hadn't reached it yet. I gripped it as tightly as I could and began to pull up and down, feeling the skin un- and re-peel over the shaft. Suddenly he recoiled.

'Not like that, ferchrissakes!' He slapped my hand away. 'Anyway I don't want that. I don't want . . . I don't want . . . I don't want some bloody hand relief!'

I could feel the tears pricking at my eyes. 'I thought you said –'

'What does it matter what I said? What does it matter what I do . . . I can't convince you, now can I?'

'I want to, I really do. It's just that I don't feel I can trust you any more . . . not at the moment. You have to give me more time.'

'Trust! Trust! I'm not a fucking building society, you know. You're not setting an account up with me. Oh fuck it! Fuck the whole fucking thing!'

He rolled away from me and pivoted himself upright. Pulling a pair of trousers from the chair where he'd chucked them the night before, he dragged his legs into them. I dug deeper into the bed and looked out at him through eyes fringed by hair and tears.

'Coffee?' His voice was icily polite.

'Yes please.' He left the room. I could hear him moving around downstairs. Pained love made me picture his actions: unscrewing the percolator, sluicing it out with cold water, tamping the coffee grains down in the metal basket, screwing it back together again and setting it on the lighted stove.

When he reappeared ten minutes later, with two cups of

coffee, I was still dug into the bed. He sat down sideways and waited while I struggled upwards and crammed a pillow behind my head. I pulled a limp corner of the duvet cover over my breasts. I took the cup from him and sipped. He'd gone to the trouble of heating milk for my coffee. He always took his black.

'I'm going out now. I've got to get down to Kensington and see Steve about those castings.' He'd mooched a cigarette from somewhere and the smoking of it, and the cocking of his elbow, went with his tone: officer speaking to other ranks. I hated him for it.

But hated myself more for asking, 'When will you be back?'

'Later . . . not for quite a while.' The studied ambiguity was another put-down. 'What're you doing today?'

'N-nothing . . . meeting Grace, I s'pose.'

'Well, that's good, the two of you can have a really trusting talk – that's obviously what you need.' His chocolate drop of sarcasm was thinly candy-coated with sincerity.

'Maybe it is . . . look . . .'

'Don't say anything, don't get started again. We've talked and talked about this. There's nothing I can do, is there? There's no way I can convince you – and I think I'm about ready to give up trying.'

'You shouldn't have done it.'

'Don't you think I know that? Don't you think I fucking know that?! Look, do you think I enjoyed it? Do you think that? 'Cause if you do, you are fucking mad. More mad than I thought you were.'

'You can't love me . . .' A wail was starting up in me; the saucer chattered against the base of my cup. 'You can't, what-ever you say.'

'I don't know about that. All I do know is that this is tor-
turing me. I hate myself – that's true enough. Look at this. Look
at how much I hate myself!'

He set his coffee cup down on the varnished floorboards and
began to give himself enormous open-handed clouts around the
head. 'You think I love myself? Look at this!' (clout) 'All you
think about is your-own-fucking-self, your own fucking feelings.' (clout) 'Don't come back here tonight!' (clout) 'Just
don't come back, because I don't think I can take much more.'

As he was saying the last of this he was pirouetting around the
room, scooping up small change and keys from the table,
pulling on his shirt and shoes. It wasn't until he got to the door
that I became convinced that he actually was going to walk out
on me. Sometimes these scenes could run to several entrances
and exits. I leapt from the bed, snatched up a towel, and caught
him at the head of the stairs.

'Don't walk out on me! Don't walk out, don't do that, not
that.' I was hiccupping, mucus and tears were mixing on my lips
and chin. He twisted away from me and clattered down a few
stairs, then he paused and turning said, 'You talk to me about
trust, but I think the reality of it is that you don't really care
about me at all, or else none of this would have happened in the
first place.' He was doing his best to sound furious, but I could
tell that the real anger was dying down. I sniffed up my tears
and snot and descended towards him.

'Don't run off, I do care, come back to bed – it's still early.' I
touched his forearm with my hand. He looked so anguished, his
face all twisted and reddened with anger and pain.

'Oh, fuck it. Fuck it. Just fuck it.' He swore flatly. The flap of
towel that I was holding against my breast fell away, and I

375

pushed the nipple, which dumbly re-erected itself, against his hand. He didn't seem to notice, and instead stared fixedly over my shoulder, up the stairs and into the bedroom. I pushed against him a little more firmly. Then he took my nipple between the knuckles of his index and forefinger and pinched it, quite hard, muttering, 'Fuck it, just fucking fuck it.'

He turned on his heels and left. I doubled over on the stairs. The sobs that racked me had a sickening component. I staggered to the bathroom and as I clutched the toilet bowl the mixture of coffee and mucus streamed from my mouth and nose. Then I heard the front door slam.

'I don't know why.'

'Then leave. You can stay at your own place —'

'You know I hate it there. I can't stand the people I have to share with —'

'Be that as it may, the point is that you don't need him, you just think you do. It's like you're caught in some trap. You think you love him, but it's just your insecurity talking. Remember,' and here Grace's voice took on an extra depth, a special sonority of caring, 'your insecurity is like a clever actor, it can mimic any emotion it chooses to and still be utterly convincing. But whether it pretends to be love or hate, the truth is that at bottom it's just the fear of being alone.'

'Well why should I be alone? You're not alone, are you?'

'No, that's true, but it's not easy for me either. Any relationship is an enormous sacrifice . . . I don't know . . . Anyway, you know that I was alone for two years before I met John, perhaps you should give it a try?'

'I spend most of my time alone anyway. I'm perfectly capable of being by myself. But I also need to see him . . .'

As my voice died away I became conscious of the voice of another woman two tables away. I couldn't hear what she was saying to her set-faced male companion, but the tone was the same as my own, the exact same plangent composite of need and recrimination. I stared at them. Their faces said it all: his awful detachment, her hideous yearning. And as I looked around the café at couple after couple, each confronting one another over the marble table tops, I had the beginnings of an intimation.

Perhaps all this awful mismatching, this emotional grating, these Mexican stand-offs of trust and commitment, were some-how in the air. It wasn't down to individuals: me and him, Grace and John, those two over there . . . It was a contagion that was getting to all of us; a germ of insecurity that had lodged in all our breasts and was now fissioning frantically, creating a domino effect as relationship after relationship collapsed in a rubble of mistrust and acrimony.

After he had left that morning I went back to his bed and lay there, gagged and bound by the smell of him in the duvet. I didn't get up until eleven. I listened to Radio Four, imagining that the deep-timbred, wholesome voices of each successive presenter were those of ideal parents. There was a discussion programme, a gardening panel discussion, a discussion about books, a short story about an elderly woman and her relation-ship with her son, followed by a discussion about it. It all sounded so cultured, so eminently reasonable. I tried to con-struct a new view of myself on the basis of being the kind of young woman who would consume such hearty radiophonic fare, but it didn't work. Instead I felt quite weightless and blown out, a husk of a person.

The light quality in the attic bedroom didn't change all morning. The only way I could measure the passage of time was by the radio, and the position of the watery shadows that his metal sculptures made on the magnolia paint.

Eventually I managed to rouse myself. I dressed and washed my face. I pulled my hair back tightly and fixed it in place with a loop of elastic. I sat down at his work table. It was blanketed with loose sheets of paper, all of which were covered with the meticulous plans he did for his sculptures. Elevations and perspectives, all neatly shaded and the dimensions written in using the lightest of pencils. There was a mess of other stuff on the table as well: sticks of flux, a broken soldering iron, bits of acrylic and angled steel brackets. I cleared a space amidst the evidence of his industry and taking out my notebook and biro, added my own patch of emotion to the collage:

I do understand how you feel. I know the pressure that you're under at the moment, but you must realise that it's pressure that *you* put on *yourself*. It's not me that's doing it to you. I do love you and I want to be with you, but it takes time to forgive. And what you did to me was almost unforgivable. I've been hurt before and I don't want to be hurt again. If you can't understand that, if you can't understand how I feel about it, then it's probably best if we don't see one another again. I'll be at the flat this evening, perhaps you'll call?

Out in the street the sky was spitting at the pavement. There was no wind to speak of, but despite that each gob seemed to have an added impetus. With every corner that I rounded on my way to King's Cross I encountered another little cyclone of rain and grit. I walked past shops full of mouldering stock that were boarded up, and empty, derelict ones that were still open.

On the corner of the Caledonian Road I almost collided with a dosser wearing a long, dirty overcoat. He was clutching a bottle of VP in a hand that was blue with impacted filth, filth that seemed to have been worked deliberately into the open sores on his knuckles. He turned his face to me and I recoiled instinctively. It was the face of a myxomatosic rabbit ('You're like a little animal in there. A little rabbit, snuggled down in its burrow'), the eyes swollen up and exploding in a series of burst ramparts and lesions of diseased flesh. His nose was no longer nose-shaped.

But on the tube the people were comforting and workaday enough. I paid at the barrier when I reached Camden Town and walked off quickly down the High Street. Perhaps it was the encounter with the dying drunk that had cleansed me, jerked me out of my self-pity, because for a short while I felt more lucid, better able to look honestly at my relationship. While it was true that he did have problems, emotional problems, and was prepared to admit to them, it was still the case that nothing could forgive his conduct while I was away visiting my parents.

I knew that the woman he had slept with lived here in Camden Town. As I walked down the High Street I began – at first almost unconsciously, then with growing intensity – to examine the faces of any youngish women that passed me. They came in all shapes and sizes, these suspect lovers. There were tall women in floor-length linen coats; plump women in stretchy slacks; petite women in neat, two-piece suits; raddled women in unravelling pullovers; and painfully smart women, Sindy dolls: press a pleasure-button in the small of their backs and their hair would grow.

The trouble was that they all looked perfectly plausible candidates for the job as the metal worker's anvil. Outside Woolworth's I was gripped by a sharp attack of nausea. An old swallow of milky coffee reentered my mouth as I thought of him, on top of this woman, on top of that woman, hammering himself into them, bash after bash after bash, flattening their bodies, making them ductile with pleasure.

I went into Marks & Sparks to buy some clean underwear and paused to look at myself in a full-length mirror. My skirt was bunched up around my hips, my hair was lank and flecked with dandruff, my tights bagged at the knees, my sleeve-ends bulged with snot-clogged Kleenex. I looked like shit. It was no wonder that he didn't fancy me any more, that he'd gone looking for some retouched vision.

'Come on,' said Grace, 'let's go. The longer we stay here, the more weight we put on.' On our way out of the café I took a mint from the cut-glass bowl by the cash register and recklessly crunched it between my molars. The sweet pain of sugar-in-cavity spread through my mouth as I fumbled in my bag for my purse. 'Well, what are you going to do now?' It was only three-thirty in the afternoon but already the sky over London was turning the shocking bilious colour it only ever aspires to when winter is fast encroaching.

'Can I come back with you, Grace?'

'Of course you can, silly, why do you think I asked the question?' She put her arm about my shoulder and twirled me round

until we were facing in the direction of the tube. Then she
marched me off, like the young emotional offender that I was.
Feeling her warm body against mine I almost choked, about to
cry again at this display of caring from Grace. But I needed her
too much, so I restrained myself.

'You come back with me, love,' she clucked. 'We can watch
telly, or eat, or you can do some work. I've got some pattern
cutting I've got to finish by tomorrow. John won't be back for
ages yet . . . or I tell you what, if you like we can go and meet
him in Soho after he's finished work and have something to eat
there – would you like that?' She turned to me, flicking back
the ledge of her thick blonde fringe with her index finger – a
characteristic gesture.

'Well, yes,' I murmured, 'whatever.'

'OK.' Her eyes, turned towards mine, were blue, frank. 'I
can see you want to take it easy.'

When we left the tube at Chalk Farm and started up the hill
towards where Grace lived, she started up again, wittering on
about her and John and me; about what we might do and what
fun it would be to have me stay for a couple of nights; and about
what a pity it was that I couldn't live with them for a while,
because what I really needed was a good sense of security.
There was something edgy and brittle about her enthusiasm. I
began to feel that she was overstating her case.

I stopped listening to the words she was saying and began to
hear them merely as sounds, as some ambient tape of reassur-
ance. Her arm was linked in mine, but from this slight contact I
could gain a whole sense of her small body. The precise slope
and jut of her full breasts, the soft brush of her round stomach
against the drape of her dress, the infinitesimal gratings of knee

against nylon, against nylon against knee.

And as I built up this sense of Grace-as-body, I began also to consider how her bush would look as you went down on her. Would the lips gape wetly, or would they tidily recede? Would the cellulite on her hips crinkle as she parted her legs? How would she smell to you, of sex or cinnamon? But, of course, it wasn't any impersonal 'you' I was thinking of – it was a highly personal *him*. I joined their bodies together in my mind and tormented myself with the hideous tableau of betrayal. After all, if he was prepared to screw some nameless bitch, what would have prevented him from shitting where I ate? I shuddered. Grace sensed this, and disengaging her arm from mine returned it to my shoulders, which she gave a squeeze.

John and Grace lived in a thirties council block halfway up Haverstock Hill. Their flat was just like all the others. You stepped through the front door and directly into a long corridor, off which were a number of small rooms. They may have been small, but Grace had done everything possible to make them seem spacious. Furniture and pictures were kept to an artful minimum, and the wooden blocks on the floor had been sanded and polished until they shone.

Grace snapped on floor lamps and put a Mozart concerto on the CD. I tried to write my neglected journal, timing my flourishes of supposed insight to the ascending and descending scales. Grace set up the ironing board and began to do something complicated, involving sheets of paper, pins, and round, worn fragments of chalk.

When the music finished, neither of us made any move to put something else on, or to draw the curtains. Instead we sat in the off-white noise of the speakers, under the opaque stare of the dark windows. To me there was something intensely evocative about the scene: two young women sitting in a pool of yellow light on a winter's afternoon. Images of my childhood came to me; for the first time in days I felt secure.

When John got back from work, Grace put food-in-a-foil-tray in the oven, and tossed some varieties of leaves. John plonked himself down on one of the low chairs in the sitting room and propped the *Standard* on his knees. Occasionally he would give a snide laugh and read out an item, his intent being always to emphasise the utter consistency of its editorial stupidity.

We ate with our plates balanced on our knees, and when we had finished, turned on the television to watch a play. I noticed that John didn't move over to the sofa to sit with Grace. Instead, he remained slumped in his chair. As the drama unfolded I began to find these seating positions quite wrong and disquieting. John really should have sat with Grace.

The play was about a family riven by domestic violence. It was well acted and the jerky camerawork made it grittily real, almost like documentary. But still I felt that the basic premise was overstated. It wasn't that I didn't believe a family with such horrors boiling within it could maintain a closed face to the out-side world, it was just that these horrors were so relentless.

The husband beat up the wife, beat up the kids, got drunk, sexually abused the kids, raped the wife, assaulted social work-ers, assaulted police, assaulted probation officers, and all within the space of a week or so. It should have been laughable – this chronically dysfunctional family – but it wasn't. How could it be remotely entertaining while we all sat in our separate padded places? Each fresh on-screen outrage increased the distance between the three of us, pushing us still further apart. I hunched down in my chair and felt the waistband of my skirt burn across my bloated stomach. I shouldn't have eaten all that salad – and the underdone garlic bread smelt flat and sour on my own tongue. So flat and sour that the idea even of kissing myself was repulsive, let alone allowing him to taste me.

The on-screen husband, his shirt open, the knot of his tie dragged halfway down his chest, was beating his adolescent daughter with short, powerful clouts around the head. They were standing in her bedroom doorway, and the camera stared fixedly over her shoulder, up the stairs and into the bedroom, where it picked up the corner of a pop poster, pinned to the flowered wallpaper. Each clout was audible as a loud 'crack!' in the room where we sat. I felt so remote, from Grace, from John, from the play . . . from him.

I stood up and walked unsteadily to the toilet at the end of the corridor. Inside I slid the flimsy bolt into its loop and pushed the loosely stacked pile of magazines away from the toilet bowl. My stomach felt as if it were swelling by the second. My fingers when I put them in my mouth were large and alien. My nails scraped against the sides of my throat. As I leant forward I was aware of myself as a vessel, my curdled contents ready to pour. I looked down into the toilet world and there – as my oatmeal stream splashed down – saw that someone had already done the same. Cut out the nutritional middlewoman, that is.

After I'd finished I wiped around the rim of the toilet with hard scraps of paper. I flushed and then splashed my cheeks with cold water. Walking back down the corridor towards the sitting room, I was conscious only of the ultra-sonic whine of the television; until, that is, I reached the door:

'Don't bother.' (A sob.)

'Mr Evans . . . are you in there?'

'You don't want me to touch you?'

'Go away. Just go away . . .'

'It's just that I feel a bit wound up. I get all stressed out during the day – you know that. I need a long time to wind down.'

'Mr Evans, we have a court order that empowers us to take these children away.'

'It's not that – I know it's not just that. You don't fancy me any more, you don't want to have sex any more. You've been like this for weeks.'

'I don't care if you've got the bloody Home Secretary out there. If you come in that door, I swear she gets it!'

'How do you expect me to feel like sex? Everything around here is so bloody claustrophobic. I can't stand these little fireside evenings. You sit there all hunched up and fidgety. You bite your nails and smoke away with little puffs. Puff, puff, puff. It's a total turn-off.'

(Smash!) 'Oh my God. For Christ's sake! Oh Jesus . . .'

'I bite my nails and smoke because I don't feel loved, because I feel all alone. I can't trust you, John, not when you're like this – you don't seem to have any feeling for me.'

'Yeah, maybe you're right. Maybe I don't. I'm certainly fed up with all of this shit . . .'

I left my bag in the room. I could come back for it tomorrow when John had gone to work. I couldn't stand to listen – and I didn't want to go back into the room and sit down with them again, crouch with them, like another vulture in the mouldering carcass of their relationship. I couldn't bear to see them reassemble the uncommunicative blocks of that static silence. And I didn't want to sleep in the narrow spare bed, under the child-sized duvet.

I wanted to be back with him. Wanted it the way a junky wants a hit. I yearned to be in that tippy, creaky boat of a bed, full of crumbs and sex and fag ash. I wanted to be framed by the basketry of angular shadows the naked bulb threw on the walls, and contained by the soft basketry of his limbs. At least we felt something for each other. He got right inside me – he really did. All my other relationships were as superficial as a salutation – this evening proved it. It was only with him that I became a real person.

Outside in the street the proportions were all wrong. The block of flats should have been taller than it was long – but it wasn't. Damp leaves blew against, and clung to my ankles. I'd been sitting in front of the gas fire in the flat and my right-hand side had become numb with the heat. Now this wore off – like a pain – leaving my clammy clothes sticking to my clammy flesh.

I walked for a couple of hundred yards down the hill, then a stitch stabbed into me and I felt little pockets of gas beading my stomach. I was level with a tiny parade of shops which included a cab company. Suddenly I couldn't face the walk to the tube, the tube itself, the walk back from the tube to his house. If I was going to go back to him I had to be there right away. If I went by tube it would take too long and this marvellous reconciliatory feeling might have soured by the time I arrived. And more to the point there might not be a relationship there for me to go back to. He was a feckless and promiscuous man, insecure and given to the grossest and most evil abuses of trust.

The jealous agony came over me again, covering my flesh like some awful hive. I leant up against a shopfront. The sick image of him entering some other. I could feel it so vividly that it was as if I was him: my penis snagging frustratingly against something . . . my blood beating in my temples . . . my sweat dripping on to her upturned face . . . and then the release of entry . . .

I pushed open the door of the minicab office and lurched in. Two squat men stood like bookends on either side of the counter. They were both reading the racing form. The man nearest to me was encased in a tube of caramel leather. He twisted his neckless head as far round as he could. Was it my imagination, or did his eyes probe and pluck at me, run up my thighs and attempt an imaginative penetration, rapid, rigid and metallic. The creak of his leather and the cold fug of damp, dead filter tips, assaulted me together.

'D'jew want a cab, love?' The other bookend, the one behind the counter, looked at me with dim-sum eyes, morsels of pupil packaged in fat.

'Err . . . yes, I want to go up to Islington, Barnsbury.'

'George'll take yer — woncha, George?' George was still eyeing me around the midriff. I noticed — quite inconsequentially — that he was wearing very clean, blue trousers, with razor-sharp creases. Also that he had no buttocks — the legs of the trousers zoomed straight up into his jacket.

'Yerallright. C'mon, love.' George rattled shut his paper and scooped a packet of Dunhill International and a big bunch of keys off the counter. He opened the door for me and as I passed through I could sense his fat black heart, encased in leather, beating behind me.

He was at the back door of the car before me and ushered me

inside. I squidged halfway across the seat before collapsing in a nerveless torpor. But I knew that I wouldn't make it back to him unless I held myself in a state of no expectancy, no hope. If I dared to picture the two of us together again, then when I arrived at the house he would be out. Out fucking.

We woozed away from the kerb and jounced around the corner. An air freshener shaped like a fir tree dingled and dangled as we took the bends down to Chalk Farm Road. The car was, I noticed, scrupulously clean and poisonous with smoke. George lit another Dunhill and offered me one, which I accepted. In the moulded divider between the two front seats there sat a tin of travel sweets. I could hear them schussing round on their caster-sugar slope as we cornered and cornered and cornered again.

I sucked on the fag and thought determinedly of other things: figure skating; Christmas sales; the way small children have their mittens threaded through the arms of their winter coats on lengths of elastic; Grace . . . which was a mistake, because this train of thought was bad magic. Grace's relationship with John was clearly at an end. It was perverse to realise this, particularly after her display in the café, when she was so secure and self-possessed in the face of my tears and distress. But I could imagine the truth: that the huge crevices in their understanding of each other had been only temporarily papered over by the thrill of having someone in the flat who was in more emotional distress than they. No, there was no doubt about it now, Grace belonged to the league of the self-deceived.

George had put on a tape. The Crusaders — or at any rate some kind of jazz funk, music for glove compartments. I looked at the tightly bunched flesh at the back of his neck. It was malevolent flesh. I was alone in the world really. People tried to understand me, but they completely missed the mark. It was as if they were always looking at me from entirely the wrong angle and mistaking a knee for a bald pate, or an elbow for a breast.

And then I knew that I'd been a fool to get into the cab, the rapistmobile. I looked at George's hands, where they had pounced on the steering wheel. They were flexing more than they should have been, flexing in anticipation. When he looked at me in the office he had taken me for jailbait, thought I was younger than I am. He just looked at my skirt – not at my sweater; and anyway, my sweater hides my breasts, which are small. He could do it, right enough, because he knew exactly where to go and the other man, the man in the office, would laughingly concoct an alibi for him. And who would believe me anyway? He'd be careful not to leave anything inside me . . . and no marks.

We were driving down a long street with warehouses on either side. I didn't recognise it. The distances between the street lamps were increasing. The car thwacked over some shallow depressions in the road, depressions that offered no resistance. I felt everything sliding towards the inevitable. He used to cuddle me and call me 'little animal', 'little rabbit'. It should happen again, not end like this, in terror, in violation.

Then the sequence of events went awry. I subsided sideways, sobbing, choking. The seat was wide enough for me to curl up on it, which is what I did. The car slid to a halt. 'Whassermatter, love?' Oh Jesus, I thought, don't let him touch me, please don't let him touch me, he can't be human. But I knew that he was. 'C'mon, love, whassermatter?' My back in its suede jacket was like a carapace. When he penetrated me I'd rather he did it from behind, anything not to have him touch and pry at the soft parts of my front.

The car pulls away once more. Perhaps this place isn't right for his purposes, he needs somewhere more remote. I'm already under the earth, under the soft earth . . . The wet earth will cling to my putrid face when the police find me . . . when they put up loops of yellow tape around my uncovered grave . . . and the WPC used to play me when they reconstruct the crime will look nothing like me . . . She'll have coarser features, but bigger breasts and hips . . . something not lost on the grieving boyfriend . . . Later he'll take her back to the flat, and fuck her standing up, pushing her ample, smooth bum into the third shelf of books in his main room (some Penguin classics, a couple of old economics text books, my copy of *The House of Mirth*), with each turgid stroke . . .

I hear the door catch through these layers of soft earth. I lunge up, painfully slow, he has me . . . and come face to face with a woman. A handsome woman, heavily built, in her late thirties. I relapse back into the car and regard her at crotch level. It's clear immediately – from the creases in her jeans – that she's George's wife.

'C'mon, love, whassermatter?' I crawl from the car and stagger against her, still choking. I can't speak, but gesture vaguely towards George, who's kicking the front wheel of the car, with a steady 'chok-chok-chok'. 'What'd'e do then? Eh? Did he frighten you or something? You're a bloody fool, George!' She slaps him, a roundhouse slap – her arm, travelling ninety degrees level with her shoulder. George still stands, even glummer now, rubbing his cheek.

In terrorist-siege-survivor-mode (me clutching her round the waist with wasted arms) we turn and head across the parking area to the exterior staircase of a block of flats exactly the same as the one I recently left. Behind us comes a Dunhill International, and behind that comes George. On the third floor we pass a woman fumbling for her key in her handbag – she's small enough to eyeball the lock. My saviour pushes open the door of the next flat along and pulls me in. Still holding me by the shoulder she escorts me along the corridor and into an over-heated room.

'Park yourself there, love.' She turns, exposing the high, prominent hips of a steer and disappears into another room, from where I hear the clang of aluminium kettle on iron prong. I'm left behind on a great scoop of upholstery – an armchair wide enough for three of me – facing a similarly outsize television screen. The armchair still has on the thick plastic dress of its first commercial communion.

George comes in, dangling his keys, and without looking at me crosses the room purposively. He picks up a doll in Dutch national costume and begins to fiddle under its skirt. 'Git out of there!' This from the kitchen. He puts the doll down and exits without looking at me.

'C'mon, love, stick that in your laugh hole.' She sets the tea cup and saucer down on a side table. She sits alongside me in a similar elephantine armchair. We might be a couple testing out a new suite in some furniture warehouse. She settles herself, yanking hard at the exposed pink webbing of her bra, where it cuts into her. 'It's not the first time this has happened, you know,' she slurps. 'Not that George would do anything, mind, leastways not in his cab. But he does have this way of . . . well, frightening people, I s'pose. He sits there twirling his bloody

391

wheel, not saying anything and somehow girls like you get terrified. Are you feeling better now?'

'Yes, thanks, really it wasn't his fault. I've been rather upset all day. I had a row with my boyfriend this morning and I had been going to stay at a friend's, but suddenly I wanted to get home. And I was in the car when it all sort of came down on top of me . . .'

'Where do you live, love?'

'I've got a room in a flat in Kensal Rise, but my boyfriend lives in Barnsbury.'

'That's just around the corner from here. When you've 'ad your tea I'll walk you back.'

'But what about George — I haven't even paid him.'

'Don't worry about that. He's gone off now, anyway he could see that you aren't exactly loaded . . . He thinks a lot about money, does George. Wants us to have our own place an' that. It's an obsession with him. And he has to get back on call as quickly as he can or he'll miss a job, and if he misses a job he's in for a bad night. And if he has a bad night, then it's me that's on the receiving end the next day. Not that I hardly ever see him, mind. He works two shifts at the moment. Gets in at three-thirty in the afternoon, has a kip, and goes back out again at eight. On his day off he sleeps. He never sees the kids, doesn't seem to care about 'em . . .'

She trails off. In the next room I hear the high aspiration of a child turning in its sleep.

'D'jew think 'e's got some bint somewhere? D'jew think that's what these double shifts are really about?'

'Really, I don't know — '

''E's a dark one. Now, I am a bit too fat to frolic, but I make sure he gets milked every so often. YerknowhatImean? Men are like bulls really, aren't they? They need to have some of that spunk taken out of them. But I dunno . . . Perhaps it's not enough. He's out and about, seeing all these skinny little bints, picking them up . . . I dunno, what's the use?' She lights a cigarette and deposits the match in a free-standing ashtray. Then she starts yanking at the webbing again, where it encases her beneath her pullover. 'I'd swear there are bloody fleas in this flat. I keep powdering the mutt, but it doesn't make no difference, does it, yer great ball of dough.'

She pushes a slippered foot against the heaving stomach of a mouldering Alsatian. I haven't even noticed the dog before now – its fur merges so seamlessly with the shaggy carpet. 'They say dog fleas can't live on a human, yer know, but these ones are making a real effort. P'raps they aren't fleas at all . . . P'raps that bastard has given me a dose of the crabs. Got them off some fucking brass, I expect, whad'jew think?'

'I've no idea really – '

'I know it's the crabs. I've even seen one of the fuckers crawling up me pubes. Oh gawd, dunnit make you sick. I'm going to leave the bastard – I am. I'll go to Berkhamsted to my Mum's. I'll go tonight. I'll wake the kids and go tonight . . .'

I need to reach out to her, I suppose, I need to make some sort of contact. After all she has helped me – so really I ought to reciprocate. But I'm all inhibited. There's no point in offering help to anyone if you don't follow through. There's no point in implying to anyone the possibility of some fount of unconditional love if you aren't prepared to follow through . . . To do so would be worse than to do nothing. And anyway . . . I'm on my way back to sort out *my* relationship. That has to take priority.

These justifications are running through my mind, each one accompanied by a counter argument, like a sub-title at the opera, or a stock market quotation running along the base of a television screen. Again there's the soft aspiration from the next room, this time matched, shudderingly, by the vast shelf of tit alongside me. She subsides. Twisted face, foundation cracking, folded into cracking hands. For some reason I think of Atrixo.

She didn't hear me set down my cup and saucer. She didn't hear my footfalls. She didn't hear the door. She just sobbed. And now I'm clear, I'm in the street and I'm walking with confident strides towards his flat. Nothing can touch me now. I've survived the cab ride with George – that's good karma, good magic. It means that I'll make it back to him and his heartfelt, contrite embrace.

Sometimes – I remember as a child remembers Christmas – we used to drink a bottle of champagne together. Drink half the bottle and then make love, then drink the other half and make love again. It was one of the rituals I remember from the beginning of our relationship, from the springtime of our love. And as I pace on up the hill, more recollections hustle alongside. Funny how when a relationship is starting up you always praise the qualities of your lover to any third party there is to hand, saying, 'Oh yes, he's absolutely brilliant at X, Y and Z . . .' and sad how that tendency dies so quickly. Dies at about the same time that disrobing in front of one another ceases to be embarrassing . . . and perhaps for that reason ceases to be quite so sexy.

Surely it doesn't have to be this way? Stretching up the hill ahead of me, I begin to see all my future relationships, bearing me on and up like some escalator of the fleshly. Each step is a man, a man who will penetrate me with his penis and his language, a man who will make a little private place with me, secure from the world, for a month, or a week, or a couple of years.

How much more lonely and driven is the serial monogamist than the serial killer? I won't be the same person when I come to lie with that man there, the one with the ginger fuzz on his white stomach; or that one further up there — almost level with the junction of Barnsbury Road — the one with the round head and skull cap of thick, black hair. I'll be his 'little rabbit', or his 'baby-doll', or his 'sex goddess', but I won't be me. I can only be me . . . with him.

Maybe it isn't too late? Maybe we can recapture some of what we once had.

I'm passing an off-licence. It's on the point of closing — I can see a man in a cardigan doing something with some crates towards the back of the shop. I'll get some champagne. I'll turn up at his flat with the bottle of champagne, and we'll do it like we did it before.

I push open the door and venture inside. The atmosphere of the place is acridly reminiscent of George's minicab office. I cast an eye along the shelves — they are pitifully stocked, just a few cans of lager and some bottles of cheap wine. There's a cooler in the corner, but all I can see behind the misted glass are a couple of isolated bottles of Asti spumante. It doesn't look like they'll have any champagne in this place. It doesn't look like my magic is going to hold up. I feel the tears welling up in me again, welling up as the offie proprietor treads wearily back along the lino.

'Yes, can I help you?'

'I . . . oh, well, I . . . oh, really . . . it doesn't matter . . .'

'Ay-up, love, are you all right?'

He's a kindly, round ball of a little man, with an implausibly straight toothbrush moustache. Impossible to imagine him as a threat. I'm crying as much with relief – that the offie proprietor is not some cro-magnon – as I am from knowing that I can't get the champagne now, and that things will be over between me and him.

The offie proprietor has pulled a handkerchief out of his cardigan pocket, but it's obviously not suitable, so he shoves it back in and picking up a handi-pack of tissues from the rack on the counter, he tears it open and hands one to me, saying, 'Now there you go, love, give your nose a good blow like, and you'll feel better.'

'Thanks.' I mop myself up for what seems like the nth time today. Who would have thought the old girl had so much salt in her?

'Now, how can I help you?'

'Oh, well . . . I don't suppose you have a bottle of champagne?' It sounds stupid, saying that rich word in this zone of poor business opportunity.

'Champagne? I don't get much of a call for that round here.' His voice is still kindly, he isn't offended. 'My customers tend to prefer their wine fortified – if you know what I mean. Still, I remember I did have a bottle out in the store room a while back. I'll go and see if it's still there.'

He turns and heads off down the lino again. I stand and look out at the dark street and the swishing cars and the shuddering lorries. He's gone for quite a while. He must trust me – I think to myself. He's left me here in the shop with the till and all the booze on the shelves. How ironic that I should find trust here, in this slightest of contexts, and find so little of it in my intimate relationships.

Then I hear footsteps coming from up above, and I am conscious of earnest voices:

'Haven't you shut up the shop yet?'

'I'm just doing it, my love. There's a young woman down there wanting a bottle of champagne, I just came up to get it.'

'Champagne! Pshaw! What the bloody hell does she want it for at this time of night?'

'I dunno. Probably to drink with her boyfriend.'

'Well, you take her bottle of champagne down to her and then get yourself back up here. I'm not finished talking to you yet.'

'Yes, my love.'

When he comes back in I do my best to look as if I haven't overheard anything. He puts the bi-focals that hang from the cord round his neck on to his nose and scrutinises the label on the bottle: 'Chambertin demi-sec. Looks all right to me – good stuff as I recall.'

'It looks fine to me.'

'Good,' he smiles – a nice smile. 'I'll wrap it up for you . . . Oh, hang on a minute, there's no price on it, I'll have to go and check the stock list.'

'Brian!' This comes from upstairs, a great bellow full of imperiousness.

'Just a minute, my love.' He tilts his head back and calls up to the ceiling, as if addressing some vengeful goddess, hidden behind the fire-resistant tiles.

'Now, Brian!' He gives me a pained smile, takes off his bi-focals and rubs his eyes redder.

'It's my wife,' he says in a stage whisper. 'She's a bit poorly. I'll check on her quickly and get that price for you. I shan't be a moment.'

He's gone again. More footsteps, and then Brian's wife says, 'I'm not going to wait all night to tell you this, Brian, I'm going to bloody well tell you now –'

'But I've a customer –'

'I couldn't give a monkey's. I couldn't care less about your bloody customer. I've had it with you, Brian – you make me sick with your stupid little cardigan and your glasses. You're like some fucking relic –'

'Can't this wait a minute –'

'No, it bloody can't. I want you out of here, Brian. It's my lease and my fucking business. You can sleep in the spare room tonight, but I want you out of here in the morning.'

'We've discussed this before – '

'I know we have. But now I've made my decision.'

I take the crumpled bills from my purse. Twenty quid has to be enough for the bottle of Chambertin. I wrap it in a piece of paper and write on it 'Thanks for the champagne'. Then I pick up the bottle and leave the shop as quietly as I can. They're still at it upstairs: her voice big and angry; his, small and placatory.

I can see the light in the bedroom when I'm still two hundred yards away from the house. It's the Anglepoise on the window-sill. He's put it on so that it will appear like a beacon, drawing me back into his arms.

I let myself in with my key, and go on up the stairs. He's standing at the top, wearing a black sweater that I gave him and blue jeans. There's a cigarette trailing from one hand, and a smear of cigarette ash by his nose, which I want to kiss away the minute I see it. He says, 'What are you doing here, I thought you were going to stay at your place tonight?'

I don't say anything, but pull the bottle of champagne out from under my jacket, because I know that'll explain everything and make it all all right.

He advances towards me, down a couple of stairs, and I half-close my eyes, waiting for him to take me in his arms, but instead he holds me by my elbows and looking me in the face says, 'I think it really would be best if you stayed at your place tonight, I need some time to think things over – '

'But I want to stay with you. I want to be with you. Look, I brought this for us to drink . . . for us to drink while we make love.'

'That's really sweet of you, but I think after this morning it would be best if we didn't see one another for a while.'

'You don't want me any more – do you? This is the end of our relationship, isn't it? Isn't that what you're saying?'

'No, I'm not saying that, I just think it would be a good idea if we cooled things down for a while.'

I can't stand the tone of his voice. He's talking to me as if I were a child or a crazy person. And he's looking at me like that as well – as if I might do something mad, like bash his fucking brains out with my bottle of Chambertin demi-sec. 'I don't want to cool things down, I want to be with you. I need to be with you. We're meant to be together – you said that. You said it yourself!'

'Look, I really feel it would be better if you went now. I'll call you a cab – '

'I don't want a cab!'

'I'll call you a cab and we can talk about it in the morning – '

'I don't want to talk about it in the morning, I want to talk about it now. Why won't you let me stay, why are you trying to get rid of me?'

And then he sort of cracks. He cracks and out of the gaps in his face comes these horrible words, these sick, slanderous, revolting words, he isn't him anymore, because he could never have said such things. He must be possessed.

'I don't want you here!' He begins to shout and pound the wall. 'Because you're like some fucking emotional Typhoid Mary. That's why I don't want you here. Don't you understand, it's not just me and you, it's everywhere you go, everyone you come into contact with. You've got some kind of bacillus inside you, a contagion – everything you touch you turn to neurotic ashes with your pick-pick-picking away at the fabric of people's relationships. That's why I don't want you here. Tonight – or any other night!'

Out in the street again – I don't know how. I don't know if he said more of these things, or if we fought, or if we fucked. I must have blacked out, blacked out with sheer anguish of it. You think you know someone, you imagine that you are close to them, and then they reveal this slimy pit at their core . . . this pit they've kept concreted over. Sex is a profound language, all right, and so easy to lie in.

I don't need him – that's what I have to tell myself: I don't need him. But I'm bucking with the sobs and the needing of him is all I can think of. I'm standing in the dark street, rain starting to fall, and every little thing: every gleam of chromium, serration of brick edge, mush of waste paper, thrusts its material integrity in the face of my lost soul.

I'll go to my therapist. It occurs to me – and tagged behind it is the admonition: why didn't you think of this earlier, much earlier, it could have saved you a whole day of distress?

Yes, I'll go to Jill's house. She always says I should come to her place if I'm in real trouble. She knows how sensitive I am. She knows how much love I need. She's not like a conventional therapist — all dispassionate and uncaring. She believes in getting involved in her clients' lives. I'll go to her now. I need her now more than I ever have.

When I go to see her she doesn't put me in some garage of a consulting room, some annex of feeling. She lets me into her warm house, the domicile lined with caring. It isn't so much therapy that Jill gives me, as acceptance. I need to be there now, with all the evidence of her three small children spread about me: the red plastic crates full of soft toys, the finger paintings sellotaped to the fridge, the diminutive coats and jackets hanging from hip-height hooks.

I need to be close to her and also to her husband, Paul. I've never met him — of course, but I'm always aware of his after-presence in the house when I attend my sessions. I know that he's an architect, that he and Jill have been together for fourteen years, and that they too have had their vicissitudes, their comings-together and fallings-apart. How else could Jill have such total sympathy when it comes to the wreckage of my own emotions? Now I need to be within the precincts of their happy cathedral of a relationship again. Jill and Paul's probity, their mutual relinquishment, their acceptance of one another's foibles — all of this towers above my desolate plain of abandonment.

It's OK, I'm going to Jill's now. I'm going to Jill's and we're going to drink hot chocolate and sit up late, talking it all over. And then she'll let me stay the night at her place — I know she will. And in the morning I'll start to sort myself out.

Another cab ride, but I'm not concentrating on anything, not noticing anything. I'm intent on the vision I have of Jill opening the front door to her cosy house. Intent on the homely vision of sports equipment loosely stacked in the hall, and the expression of heartfelt concern that suffuses Jill's face when she sees the state I'm in.

The cab stops and I pay off the driver. I open the front gate and walk up to the house. The door opens and there's Jill: 'Oh . . . hi . . . it's you.'

'I'm sorry . . . perhaps I should have called?' This isn't at all as I imagined it would be — there's something lurking in her face, something I haven't seen there before.

'It's rather late — '

'I know, it's just, just that . . .' My voice dies away. I don't know what to say to her, I expect her to do the talking to lead me in and then lead me on, tease out the awful narrative of my day. But she's still standing in the doorway, not moving, not asking me in.

'It's not altogether convenient . . .' And I start to cry — I can't help it, I know I shouldn't, I know she'll think I'm being manipulative (and where does this thought come from, I've never imagined such a thing before), but I can't stop myself.

And then there is the comforting arm around my shoulder and she does invite me in, saying, 'Oh, all right, come into the kitchen and have a cup of chocolate, but you can't stay for long. I'll have to order you another mini cab in ten minutes or so.'

'What's the matter then? Why are you in such a state?'

The kitchen has a proper grown-up kitchen smell, of whole-some ingredients, well-stocked larders and fully employed wine racks. The lighting is good as well: a bell-bottomed shade pulled well down on to the wooden table, creating an island in the hundred-watt sun.

'He's ending our relationship – he didn't say as much, but I know that that's what he meant. He called me "an emotional Typhoid Mary", and all sorts of other stuff. Vile things.'

'Was this this evening?'

'Yeah, half an hour ago. I came straight here afterwards, but it's been going on all day, we had a dreadful fight this morning.'

'Well,' she snorts, 'isn't that a nice coincidence?' Her tone isn't nice at all. There's a hardness in it, a flat bitterness I've never heard before.

'I'm sorry?' Her fingers are white against the dark brown of the drinking-chocolate tin, her face is all drawn out of shape. She looks her age – and I've never even thought what this might be before now. For me she's either been a sister or a mother or a friend. Free-floatingly female, not buckled into a strait-jacket of biology.

'My husband saw fit to inform me that our marriage was over this evening . . . oh, about fifteen minutes before you arrived, approximately . . .' Her voice dies away. It doesn't sound malicious – her tone, that is, but what she's said is clearly directed at me. But before I can reply she goes on. 'I suppose there are all sorts of reasons for it. Above and beyond all the normal shit that happens in relationships: the arguments, the Death of Sex, the conflicting priorities, there are other supervening factors.' She's regaining her stride now, beginning to talk to me the way she normally does.

'It seems impossible for men and women to work out their fundamental differences nowadays. Perhaps it's because of the uncertainty about gender roles, or the sheer stress of modern living, or maybe there's some still deeper malaise of which we're not aware.'

'What do you think it is? I mean – between you and Paul.' I've adopted her tone – and perhaps even her posture. I imagine that if I can coax some of this out of her then things will get back to the way they should be, roles will re-reverse.

'I'll tell you what I think it is' – she looks directly at me for the first time since I arrived – 'since you ask. I think he could handle the kids, the lack of sleep, the constant money problems, my moods, his moods, the dog shit in the streets and the beggars on the tube. Oh yes, he was mature enough to cope with all of that. But in the final analysis what he couldn't bear was the constant stream of neurotics flowing through this house. I think he called it "a babbling brook of self-pity". Yes, that's right, that's what he said. Always good with a turn of phrase is Paul.'

'And what do you think?' I asked – not wanting an answer, but not wanting her to stop speaking, for the silence to interpose.

'I'll tell you what I think, young lady.' She gets up and, placing the empty mugs on the draining board, turns to the telephone. She lifts the receiver and says as she dials, 'I think that the so-called "talking cure" has turned into a talking disease, that's what I think. Furthermore, I think that given the way things stand this is a fortuitous moment for us to end our relationship too. After all, we may as well make a clean sweep of it . . . Oh, hello. I'd like a cab, please. From 27 Argyll Road . . . Going to . . . Hold on a sec – ' She turns to me and asks with peculiar emphasis, 'Do you know where you're going to?'

Notes on the Authors

KATHY ACKER was born in New York and began writing for mostly underground presses in the early 1970s. *Blood and Guts in High School* (1982) attracted wider attention, and since then she has gained recognition as one of the leading voices of the counter-culture with novels like *Don Quixote*, *Empire of the Senseless* and, most recently, *My Mother: Demonology*. After spending several years in England she now lives in San Francisco, and has recently been touring with a female rock band.

MARTIN AMIS is one of Britain's best known writers, whose high media profile has not detracted from his literary achievements, in evidence from his first novel, *The Rachel Papers* (1973), through his key novels of the 1970s and 80s — *Success*, *Other People* and *Money* — to his most recent work, *The Information*. He has also worked as a journalist and literary editor for several national magazines and journals.

PAT CALIFIA has been described as 'the Dr Ruth of the alternative sexuality set', exploring and advising on dominant/submissive and other unorthodox sexual practices in books like *The Advocate Adviser* and *Sensuous Magic*. She is based in San Francisco and her taboo-breaking stories, collected in *Macho Sluts* and *Melting Point*, are exhilarating and (to outsiders) often eye-opening.

LINDA JAIVIN is an Australian writer and translator specializing in contemporary Chinese culture, whose articles have appeared in a wide range of publications, from *Rolling Stone* to *The Asian Wall Street Journal*. She has also written on and contributed to debates on sexuality (e.g. 'Why Sex Makes Me Laugh' at the Sydney Writers' Festival), and her first novel, *Eat Me*, was published in 1995. A second novel, *Rock'n'Roll Babes From Outer Space*, is on the way.

TAMA JANOWITZ is the author of the bestselling novels *Slaves of New York* and *A Cannibal in Manhattan*. Her stories have appeared in a variety of magazines, including *The New Yorker*, *Paris Review*, *Interview*, *Mississippi Review* and *Spin*. She lives in New York City, the setting for most of her sophisticated stories, and is an Alfred Hodder Fellow in Humanities at Princetown University.

JAMES KELMAN's novel, *How Late It Was, How Late*, was the controversial winner of the Booker Prize in 1994. Like most of his fiction, it deals in uncompromising terms with life at the lower end of the social scale – often in his native Glasgow. His stories have been collected in *Not Not While the Giro* (1983), *Greyhound for Breakfast* (1987) and *The Burn* (1991).

EVELYN LAU ran away from her home in Vancouver when she was fourteen after a row with her Chinese immigrant parents. They wanted her to train as a doctor; she wanted to write. The story of her subsequent life on the streets as a prostitute and drug addict is told in *Runaway*, which became a bestseller. Her first collection of short fiction, *Fresh Girls*, was published to great acclaim in 1993.

ADAM MARS-JONES was educated at Westminster and Cambridge, and his first book, *Lantern Lecture* (1981), won a Somerset Maugham Award. In the last ten years much of his fiction has been concerned with the AIDS epidemic in the gay community. *The Darker Proof: Stories From a Crisis* (1987) was written in collaboration with Edmund White, and *Monopolies of Loss* followed in 1992.

BRIAN MCCABE's poetry and short stories have appeared in numerous magazines and anthologies. After being awarded a writer's bursary by the Scottish Arts Council he took up writing full time, and some of his short stories have been collected in *The Lipstick Circus*. He lives in Edinburgh with his family.

JOHN MCVICAR was Britain's most wanted criminal in 1968, following his escape from the maximum security wing of Durham jail. After his recapture, he took an Open University degree in Sociology, and wrote movingly of his experiences in and out of prison. His story was filmed as *McVicar*, with Roger Daltrey in the title role. He now works as a freelance writer and broadcaster in London.

SUSAN MINOT was born in Boston and grew up in Manchester-by-the-Sea. She has written one novel, *Monkeys* (1986), and some of her stories – which have appeared in numerous literary magazines – are collected in *Lust* (1989), and have earned her a reputation as one of the most talented writers of her generation. She lives in New York.

TONY MUSGRAVE grew up on Merseyside, and has lived in Berlin since 1973, where he worked as a computer consultant until deciding to write full time in 1990. 'Bel' (in this collection) was selected as one of the best short stories of 1993 (in *Best Short Stories 1993*, edited by Giles Gordon and David Hughes). He is currently at work on a novel, *Black Milk*, set in Berlin and Cracow.

TIM PARKS, brought up in Blackpool and London, now lives in Italy where he works as a writer, translator and teacher. His first novel, *Tongues of Flame*, won both the Somerset Maugham and Betty Trask Awards, and subsequent novels have confirmed his reputation as one of Britain's finest writers. He has translated several works by Alberto Moravia into English.

EMILY PRAGER has worked as a contributing editor to *The National Lampoon* and *Viva*, as a satirical columnist for *Penthouse*, and works currently as TV critic and humorist for *The Village Voice*. Raised in Texas, the Far East and Greenwich Village, she now lives in New York and has published three collections of her blackly humorous short stories.

ALTHEA PRINCE was born in Antigua, educated at Johns Hopkins University and at York University, where she gained a doctorate in Sociology, and since 1965 has lived in Toronto. Her stories, essays and poetry have appeared in many magazines, and she has written two books for young people as well as a short-story collection, *Ladies of the Night*.

WILL SELF, educated in Finchley and at Oxford, worked as a road-sweeper and as a cartoonist for *The New Statesman* before publishing *The Quantity Theory of Insanity*, one of the most highly acclaimed debuts of recent times. Since then his reputation for innovative and often macabre fiction has grown, with books like *My Idea of Fun*, *Cock and Bull* and *Grey Area*. A recent collection of non-fiction, much of it concerned with drugs, is entitled *Junk Mail*.

PETE TOWNSHEND is of course best known for his work with the seminal rock band, The Who. In recent years he has combined a solo musical career (plus occasional re-formations of The Who) with work as a commissioning editor for Faber & Faber, encouraging new writing. His own collection of stories, *Horse's Neck*, was published in 1985, and was hailed as 'a brilliant, troubling work' by *Melody Maker*.

ETIENNE VAN HEERDEN, the son of a Merino sheep farmer, qualified in law and worked as an attorney in the Supreme Court of South Africa before turning to literature. He is a prolific writer of short stories; his first novel, *Toorberg* (translated as *Ancestral Voices* in 1994), won several awards, and his work is now published in many languages. He is currently Associate Professor in Afrikaans and Dutch Literature at the University of Rhodes.

MARCO VASSI is one of the most interesting figures in contemporary erotic literature. His work has been praised by writers as diverse as Norman Mailer and Gore Vidal, while *The Village Voice* called him 'our champion sexual energist . . . His plan is to shock us through our prurience and out the other side into enlightenment'. His ideas are expounded in *A Divine Passion*, *The Stoned Apocalypse* (an erotic autobiography) and the stories collected in *The Erotic Comedies*. He died in 1990.

FAY WELDON, born in England and raised in New Zealand, is one of Britain's best known writers whose work, in several media, often delights in raunchy female sexuality. Her novels include *The Fat Woman's Joke*, *Puffball*, *The Life and Loves of a She-Devil* (memorably televised in 1986; less memorably filmed as *She-Devil* in 1989) and *The Cloning of Joanna May*. She lives in London, and her most recent story collection is *Wicked Women*.

Acknowledgements

'Girls Who Like to Fuck' by Kathy Acker, from *In Memoriam to Identity* (London: Pandora, 1990), copyright © 1990 by Kathy Acker, reprinted by permission of Peters Fraser & Dunlop Group Ltd.

'Let Me Count the Times' by Martin Amis, first published in *Granta 4*, copyright © 1981 by Martin Amis, reprinted by permission of Peters Fraser & Dunlop Group Ltd.

'What Girls Are Made Of' by Pat Califia, from *Melting Point* (Boston: Alyson Publications, Inc., 1993), copyright © 1993 by Pat Califia, reprinted by permission of Alyson Publications, Inc.

'Fireworks' by Linda Jaivin, from *Eat Me* (London: Chatto & Windus Ltd, 1996), copyright © 1995 by Linda Jaivin, reprinted by permission of Random House UK Ltd.

'The Great White Wedding Cake' by Tama Janowitz, first published in *Interview*, copyright © 1988 by Tama Janowitz, reprinted by permission of International Creative Management, Inc.

'Jim Dandy' by James Kelman, from *Not Not While the Giro* (Edinburgh: Polygon, 1983), copyright © 1983 by James Kelman, reprinted by permission of Polygon.

ACKNOWLEDGEMENTS

'The Alumnae Bulletin' by Emily Prager, from *A Visit From the Footbinder and Other Stories* (London: Chatto & Windus/The Hogarth Press, 1983), copyright © 1983 by Emily Prager, reprinted by permission of Random House UK Ltd.

'Ladies of the Night' by Althea Prince, from *Ladies of the Night and Other Stories* (Toronto: Sister Vision Press, 1993), copyright © 1993 by Althea Prince, reprinted by permission of Sister Vision Press/Black Women and Women of Colour Press.

'The End of the Relationship' by Will Self, from *Grey Area and Other Stories* (London: Bloomsbury, 1994), copyright © 1994 by Will Self, reprinted by permission of Bloomsbury Publishing Plc and the author's agent, Ed Victor Ltd.

'Tonight's the Night' by Pete Townshend, from *Horse's Neck* (London: Faber & Faber Ltd, 1985), copyright © 1985 by Pete Townshend, reprinted by permission of Faber & Faber Ltd.

'Bull Factory' by Etienne van Heerden, from *Mad Dog and Other Stories* (London: Allison & Busby, 1995), copyright © 1992 by Etienne van Heerden, reprinted by permission of Blake Friedmann Literary Agency Ltd.

'Subway Dick' by Marco Vassi, from *The Erotic Comedies* (London: Black Spring Press, 1988), copyright © 1981 by the Estate of Marco Vassi, reprinted by permission of Serafina Clarke.

'And Then Turn Out the Light' by Fay Weldon, first published in *Cosmopolitan*, collected in *Polaris and Other Stories* (London: Hodder & Stoughton, 1985), copyright © 1985 by Fay Weldon, reprinted by permission of the author's agent, Giles Gordon/Curtis Brown Group Ltd.